"THE STORY'S NOT PANNING OUT...."

"What do you mean? Your sources were no good?"

"It's tough to tie all together," Burton said, fumbling for words that would sound plausible to Malachek. "I had a woman in Vegas I thought could make the whole piece for me, but she isn't working out."

"Keep working on it. Don't throw it away yet," Malachek said, and he hung up.

Burton stared at the phone as if somewhere inside the receiver he could find the answer to his dilemma.

Painfully, he confronted again the fact that he could have blown open a big scandal that any correspondent on any network would have loved to have.

He already had the shards of the story. All he had to do was keep digging until he could put the various pieces together, until they were assembled into a story he could deliver to Malachek.

But breaking the story would violate the network's cardinal rule—don't hang out our own dirty laundry. . . .

SHATTERED IMAGES

Ed Planer

BANTAM BOOKS
TORONTO · NEW YORK · LONDON · SYDNEY · AUCKLAND

In memory of my father

SHATTERED IMAGES

A Bantam Book / January 1989

ISBN 0-553-27634-4

Published simultaneously in the United States and Canada

Bantam Books are published by Bantam Books, a division of
Bantam Doubleday Dell Publishing Group, Inc. Its trademark,
consisting of the words "Bantam Books" and the portrayal of a
rooster, is Registered in U.S. Patent and Trademark Office and
in other countries. Marca Registrada. Bantam Books, 666 Fifth
Avenue, New York, New York 10103.

PRINTED IN THE UNITED STATES OF AMERICA

O   0 9 8 7 6 5 4 3 2 1

Author's Note

I am indebted to Stephen Rubin of Bantam Books for his willingness to take a chance way back when and to Barbara Alpert, my editor at Bantam, for her guidance and patience.

This is a work of fiction. The people, the network, the events are solely the products of the author's imagination. Any conjecture or wonder are solely the products of a reader's imagination. Any resemblance to persons living or dead is purely coincidental and unintended.

PART
ONE

Chapter 1

Somewhere over the Mississippi Gulf Coast, Art Burton heard the wheels of the 727 jet start to lower and then lock into place. He waited for the inevitable announcement.

"Ladies and gentlemen, we have begun our initial descent. Please extinguish all cigarettes. Place seats and tray tables in the upright position."

How many times in how many places had he heard the recital? He smiled as the flight attendant finished her announcement and walked quickly through the first-class section on a perfunctory check of the passengers. She had recognized him when he boarded in New York and now she nodded pleasantly as she passed his seat. I wonder, he thought, if she fucks in the upright position.

He looked out of the window and saw in the distance the blue-green waters of the Gulf of Mexico washing up on the shoreline of the Mississippi Gulf Coast. He tried to pick out, by looking at the land quilt below, the plane's location and its distance from New Orleans.

Then he saw a gleaming white bridge, spanning a body of water, and he knew that they were over Pass Christian and Bay St. Louis. If you drove east from New Orleans, Bay St. Louis would be the first city you would come to on Highway 90 on the Mississippi Coast. It was joined to Pass Christian and the other Gulf Coast cities by the bridges they were flying over now.

The plane's flight pattern meant that they would be coming in to New Orleans from the south, over the mouth of the Mississippi, up over the marshlands and the bayous and the two-lane highway that led through the oil refineries and the sulphur domes and the sugar refineries from the Gulf to New Orleans.

Even now the plane was making a slow turn to the right over the Gulf toward New Orleans, making a wide, graceful arc in the sky. In the distance, he could see a string of barges being pushed slowly up the Mississippi from the Gulf.

Every time he flew back to New Orleans there was a sense of anticipation. A hunching forward in the seat. A straining to look out of the window and pick out familiar sights. It was no different this time.

The plane was following the serpentine curve of the river, its shadow gliding over the tops of oil tanks in a refinery below and then, at last, he saw the beginnings of the city shimmering in the reflected sunlight.

He could see the homes on the lakefront, the occasional glistening of crystal blue water from a backyard swimming pool, the campus of the University of New Orleans, the housing projects in the black wards and then, up ahead, the twin ribbons of the Causeway stretching across Lake Pontchartrain.

The plane was banking now. The flight attendant was announcing the "final approach" and he could pick out cars moving along the old Airline Highway and the new Interstate that bordered the airport.

The plane was passing over swamp, watery and foreboding. Then, with a quick thump-thump, the big jet landed. I'm back, Burton thought.

Walking through the passenger gate, he was aware that some of the passengers waiting to board the flight, which was continuing to Houston, had recognized him.

He had learned, in the past few years, to casually look for the recognition and, at the same time, pretend not to notice it. It was better that way—no one could accuse him of being conceited.

Like many of those who appeared on television, Art Burton was better looking in person than he was when seen within the confines of a television screen. Because he was always seated behind a desk, and the camera shot him at a level just below his chest, people who saw him in person were surprised by his height.

He was, in fact, three inches over six feet and even though he was forty-one years old, his face was not lined with any marks of age. He had a smooth face, handsome enough to be attractive to women but, had he not been on television, there would have been nothing memorable about him.

Brown eyes, coal black hair carefully combed to look casual, a narrow mouth, whose lips seemed to part only wide enough to let words slip through, these were the features that, in ordinary circumstances, would have made him forgettable.

It was television that made the difference, television that made his face appear familiar, television that transcended the ordinary features and made him recognizable to the flight attendant on the plane and, now, to the clump of passengers standing in the waiting area.

Television had made his face familiar because it was there, once a week, in prime time, anchoring the network's magazine program, *Focus on America*. And if you see someone often enough—a postman, a bank teller, a supermarket clerk—you feel a familiarity even if you know nothing about the person other than the name.

It was that way with Art Burton. He was known because he was known.

A man with a familiar face was coming toward him now, hand stretched in greeting. Burton saw that it was Bill Andrews, the general manager of WBID-TV, the network's affiliate in New Orleans. It was the station where Burton had started his career in television news. WBID. We're Best In Dixie.

"Art," Andrews said warmly. "It's good to see you. How was the flight? Okay?"

"It was fine," Burton replied, shaking Andrews's hand and noticing the traces of red veins on Andrews's cheeks. Too many Rotary Club luncheons. Too many cocktail receptions. "I didn't expect an official welcome," he added.

"Why not?" Andrews responded. "It gives us a chance to talk and besides, there's no reason for you to take a cab."

"I've done it a lot of times," Burton said. "But it's nice of you to come. How are things at the station?"

"The news is doing all right but prime time is turning to shit," Andrews replied with annoyance. "What's the matter with Rossman and those geniuses at the network?" he asked in an aggravated voice. "Can't they find a program that will do more than a 20 share?"

Burton shrugged. "It's not my line of work." Then: "How is *Focus* doing?"

"Not bad," Andrews said.

"Meaning?"

"Meaning it had a 19 share in our last book. But it's up against movies on the other channels," he added, sounding apologetic. "That's not bad, considering the lousy lead-in you've got."

Burton admired Andrews's mastery of the local ratings picture. Mention any hour of the day or night to him, Burton thought, and he'd give you the numbers for his station and his competitors. Open his veins, and ratings and share percentages would be coursing through them like red and white corpuscles. They were in his bloodstream.

"What about the network news?" Burton asked.

"Network news will always be a three-horse race," Andrews said. "Unless you put some clown on there, it will always get its rating.

"And Jack Cornwall," he added, "is always going to do well. He's a pro."

They walked out of the air-conditioned comfort of the main terminal and Burton could feel the heat beginning to climb all over him. A sudden summer rain had come up from the Gulf an hour before his flight had landed and had washed over the city, leaving it soaked and dripping.

Now the warm tropical sun was shining brightly and wisps of steam were rising from the puddles in the airport parking lot. Little rivulets of sweat dripped from Burton's face and he could feel the shirt underneath his suit jacket starting to get moist and clinging to his skin. By the time they got to Andrews's car, he had removed his coat and necktie.

"Damn heat always gets worse after a rain," Andrews said as they got into his car and he maneuvered it out of the parking lot.

Burton nodded. "I had forgotten how bad it can get."

"You should be used to it, having grown up here," Andrews said.

"It was different then," Burton pointed out. "I didn't know about air-conditioning until I was eight or nine years old so I didn't know the difference. All I remember is those big wooden ceiling fans. It was miserable all the time."

"I bet it was," Andrews agreed. He drove the car up the

entrance ramp of the expressway leading to New Orleans. He lit a cigarette and asked, "How's Malachek?"

"Grumpy as ever," Burton replied noncommittally. He could picture Malachek, the president of the News Division, prowling the main newsroom, intimidating everyone just by his presence.

"He was down here a few weeks ago speaking to some journalism group," Andrews said. "I had breakfast with him before he left."

"I didn't know he had been here," Burton said. He wanted to know more about Andrews's breakfast with Malachek but without appearing too inquisitive.

Like every other correspondent and anchor at the network, he devoured every dropping, no matter how meager, from Malachek's mouth if it was delivered *ex cathedra*—outside the network's offices. That was where the future could be gleaned, from some informal remark by Malachek at a cocktail party, luncheon or in a chance conversation on the New York-Washington shuttle.

The standings of the correspondents, the transfer of assignments, the potential anchor slots, the appointment of executives; all these never seemed to be formally discussed in the cool atmosphere of Malachek's office with all those pictures of Jimmy Carter and other former Presidents staring down from the walls. Somehow they just seemed to happen and the only harbinger was if somebody, somewhere, heard something.

"Do you know Malachek well?" Andrews asked.

"Well enough, I suppose," Burton answered. He was surprised by Andrews's question and wondered why he was asking. The answer came next.

"I have a nephew," Andrews said. "Bright kid. Just finished LSU. That's where you went, isn't it?"

"Yes."

"I was thinking of asking Malachek if he could meet with him if he came to New York. You know, give him some career advice. What do you think?"

Bullshit, Burton thought. You want a job for the kid and you are going to throw your weight around. When general managers need to take a shit, Burton had learned, the network reaches for the toilet paper.

"Of course he'll see him," Burton said. "What does he want to be?"

Andrews laughed. "An instant success." He accelerated the car in order to pass a slow-moving van with a Jesuit High School sticker on the rear window and a Confederate flag decal on the bumper.

It wasn't until they were in the French Quarter, driving down Chartres Street on the way to the Royal Orleans Hotel, that Andrews mentioned the speech that Burton would be giving to a luncheon for United Way campaign workers.

Andrews was chairman of the local campaign and had asked the network's affiliate relations department if they could provide a speaker for the luncheon. He had suggested Burton as the best choice. The network had been happy to oblige. So had Burton.

"You're going to draw a big crowd," Andrews said, "being a local celebrity and all that. But you don't have to speak for more than thirty minutes. Thirty-five at the most. And leave some time for questions."

"I think the speech runs about twenty-five minutes," Burton replied, neglecting to mention that it had been written by the network's corporate relations department and had been used, by other network people, in Columbus, Ohio; Nashville, Tennessee; and Salem, Oregon. After all, who was to know?

"I won't run too long," Burton added. "I have somebody else to see while I'm here."

"Relatives?"

"No," Burton answered, staring out the car window at a sign in a restaurant window advertising red beans and rice and po'boy sandwiches. "I don't have any relatives left here. My parents died ten years ago. It's a story I'm working on."

"Anything our newsroom should be doing?"

"No, it's just some information I need from a guy I grew up with who's with the Police Department. I called him from New York when I knew I was coming.

"We're doing a story on the mob and big-time illegal gambling," he confided after a short pause. There was no harm in telling Andrews, he figured. Who was Andrews going to tell? "There was a big raid here last week on a bookie operation. I want to find out some more about it."

"I guess that's the advantage in coming back," Andrews said. "There's always somebody you know."

"You lose touch with a lot of people though. It's never the same."

"This was your home," Andrews reminded him. "You were born and raised here. You don't come back as a stranger."

No, not as a stranger, Burton thought. But as somebody who doesn't live here any more. Somebody who went away and can see the changes, and doesn't know if he can ever come back.

The changes had been evident to him ever since they had left the expressway and turned into the old residential streets of the uptown university section. These were the streets with the French-sounding names that had been the boundaries of his childhood. Napoleon Avenue, Fountainbleau Drive, Claiborne Avenue. He remembered what it had been like growing up here; playing kick-the-can in the soft summer twilight, seeing the azaleas and dogwood burst into pink and white and red in the parks and neutral grounds, standing in the crowds waiting for the Carnival parades, grasping for the beads and trinkets, at the end of winter.

But now there was a Burger King where once there had been a drugstore. The snowball stand where he had savored the chocolate- and cherry-flavored syrups over crushed ice had been replaced by a QUIK CARWASH, and Mistellas— the tiny grocery where his parents had shopped for years for creole tomatoes and gumbo filet and small loaves of French bread—had become a videocassette rental franchise.

He was like a blind man tap-tapping his way through a familiar house where all the tables and chairs and lamps had been rearranged. Everything changed.

Only the afternoon heat stayed the same, leaving people hanging like a dripping sheet on a backyard clothesline.

Even in the air-conditioned comfort of Andrews's car, he was aware of the heat outside. He could see it flushing the faces of the tourists on Chartres Street. Some of them were wiping the sweat with handkerchiefs, not knowing enough to stay in the shade of the storefront awnings. Big-spending gawkers from New York or Houston or Chicago.

In the Quarter, too, there had been obvious changes. The unique, historic flavor of the old Vieux Carre had slowly succumbed to the blandishments of rampant tourism. The symptoms were everywhere—souvenir shops, card stores and miniboutiques, their windows framed by dozens of coffee mugs, glazed with cheap scenes of horse-drawn carriages or paddle wheel steamboats, their shelves crammed with mammy dolls, boxes of praline candy in the shape of cotton bales, or T-shirts with I LOVE NEW ORLEANS stenciled on them.

Despite the increasing tawdriness, Burton loved the French Quarter.

He knew all of its tiny, hidden delights in a way that only years of loving intimacy could bring; the way the sun hit the latticed Spanish grillwork on the balconies of the low-lying buildings, sending shadows of lacework patterns to the sidewalk below; the sudden swooping of pigeons over Jackson Square, foraging for food in the early morning hours; the waiters in frayed tuxedos standing outside Antoines in the late afternoon, taking a break before the first surge of customers lined up at the entrance on St. Louis Street; the little Italian grocery on Decatur Street that sold the best muffelatas and the coldest beer in the city; and the old black men sitting on the front steps of their shotgun cottages along Dumaine Street.

Someday, maybe, he might come back. Back to a simpler life.

Art Burton came back to the French Quarter once before, in 1969, soon after returning home from Vietnam and all that had happened there.

At first he stayed at the home where he had grown up, the old, gray, stucco house on Fern and Willow streets in the uptown section near Tulane University.

But he was twenty-five years old and he wanted the freedom of living alone. Within a month, he rented an apartment in the French Quarter.

He also needed a job and, with the help of one of his former LSU professors who knew Bill Andrews, he got a job as a news writer at WBID-TV.

He had no formal training in journalism but he had been on the staff of the college paper and, in his last three years at LSU, he had worked one afternoon a week at a television station in Baton Rouge.

He got that job by answering a "Help Wanted" ad the

station had placed in the college paper: "Part-time wrk for student intrstd in tv, Eng major prefrred."

Every Friday afternoon he came to the station's newsroom and answered the phones, stripped the wire service machines of AP and UPI copy, monitored the state and city police radios, picked up the news film after it had been processed in a laboratory downtown, and occasionally wrote a story for the six o'clock news.

There was an excitement to all of it and even from his low-man vantage point, he was caught up in it. Years later, Art Burton could still recall standing by the AP wire machine on a Friday afternoon and watching the Teletype spit out the first words of the JFK assassination.

BULLETIN—Dallas—Three shots were fired at the Presidential motorcade in downtown Dallas today.

He tore the piece of paper from the machine and raced into the tiny control room where the noon news was being put on the air.

"They shot at Kennedy!" he shouted to the news director. The news director ran out of the control room and, out of camera range, placed the bulletin on the anchorman's desk. Burton always would remember the news director frantically pointing to the jagged piece of paper, silently urging the anchorman to pick it up. I'm one of the first people who knew about this, he thought.

His fascination with the news business went back to when he was fifteen years old.

It was 1960, and the civil rights battle, which had been spreading throughout the South, finally reached New Orleans. Federal courts had ordered the first grades of two public schools in New Orleans to be integrated.

The schools were in the downtown section of New Orleans, in low-income neighborhoods far removed from the leafy, languid uptown section where Art Burton lived. But even in the insular all-white world where he was growing up, where blacks always had been part of the background landscape, like trees or mailboxes, he felt the impact of what was happening.

Night after night, he watched the scenes on television as

large crowds of whites, held back by police, jeered and cursed at a few frightened eight-year-old black children.

A cross was burned on the lawn of the federal judge who issued the integration orders and there was talk that all the schools, even his high school, would be closed.

He was fifteen years old and never had thought much about the blacks. He liked their music, particularly Dixieland jazz, and he admired their athletes, although he didn't know of any at the southern colleges.

But he always had accepted, as a matter of natural, daily life, that whites and blacks didn't mix. The blacks went to separate schools, drank from separate water fountains, ate at separate lunch counters, and sat in the back of buses and streetcars.

His parents had rarely talked about it, but now they were saying that a few agitators were behind the school integration.

"Most of the nigras want to be with their own," his father said. "Get a few radicals stirring them up and this is what happens. Maybe Ike will send in the troops and then you'll see them keep to their own schools. Most of them are too stupid to know what's good for them."

Art Burton said nothing but he was old enough to realize that everything was not what he'd assumed it to be. Even his father, who'd never said anything derogatory about Negroes before was showing him a side he'd never seen before—and didn't like.

The deep divisions in the city, the venom and hatred he saw expressed on his television set every night, were a revelation to him. Like an underground spring feeding a stream, the sudden exposure to the racial struggle formed the wellspring of his interest in the world beyond the boundaries of his neighborhood.

Art wrote for the high-school paper and joined the Debate Club. John F. Kennedy had been elected and he admired the youthful President who seemed to symbolize new ideas. In the all-city Debate Club finals in his senior year, he won top honors by taking the affirmative on, Resolved: The Peace Corps Should Be Permanently Funded.

He'd wanted to study journalism in college, but LSU was the only school his parents could afford to send him to and the university offered only one course in the subject.

Instead, he majored in English, and, buoyed by his internship at the television station, tried to get a job in television news when he graduated.

He wrote to news directors at stations around the country but did not receive any offers. He thought about going into the Peace Corps, but the only countries where volunteers were needed were in Central America and that part of the world really didn't interest him. Instead, he decided to enlist in the Army and go to Officer Candidate School in Georgia. Even if he were sent to Vietnam, he reasoned, he would be out in three years and it would be easier to find a job at twenty-five with college and the Army behind him.

When he got the job at WBID-TV, he knew, despite what had happened in Vietnam, he had been right.

"I can give you a lift up to Police Headquarters after the lunch," Andrews was saying.

Burton turned his attention from the outside, from the heat, the signs for bayou tours, carriage rides, and palm readings; the store windows filled with Cajun foods, the hole-in-the-wall restaurants with Creole Gumbo signs painted on old boards, and he told Andrews, no, he would not need a ride.

He would take the streetcar, he decided. It would be fun and, besides, he was meeting his friend at a barroom uptown, near the St. Charles Avenue streetcar line, away from Police Headquarters.

He could picture Baglio now, hunched over a Dixie beer, his fat ass hanging over the edge of a bar stool, his eyes glued to a television set watching some shitty soap opera. Frank Baglio. The only man he knew who actually watched the soaps. And a cop at that.

"Let me know if you change your mind about the ride," Andrews said as he steered the car into the parking garage of the Royal Orleans Hotel.

"Don't worry about it. I can find my way," Burton said.

Burton climbed out of the car and took his garment bag from the rear seat of the car. "We got you a room here," Andrews explained, "in case you wanted to change. Gives you a chance to freshen up."

"Thanks," Burton said. "What time do you want me at the lunch?"

Andrews glanced at his watch. "In about forty-five minutes. It's the big banquet hall to the left of the elevators in the lobby. Past the reception desk."

Burton handed his garment bag to a bellboy who had materialized out of the cavernous darkness of the garage. "I'll be there in a minute," he said to the bellboy, who already was moving toward a door marked To Lobby.

The bellboy stopped and turned. "No hurry, Mr. Burton."

Burton smiled. "It's nice to be remembered in your hometown," he said to Andrews.

"Local boy makes good," Andrews concurred.

"I'll see you later," Burton told Andrews.

He followed the bellboy to his room, tipped him two dollars and, as soon as the bellboy left, he drew open the curtains covering the windows on the far side of the room.

The hotel was only seven stories high and his room was on the top floor. Because the room faced away from the main business district and toward the remainder of the French Quarter, there were no tall buildings obstructing his view.

The perfect grid of the Quarter was spread out before him. He quickly found Esplanade Avenue, the broad, tree-shaded avenue that formed the furthermost boundary of the Quarter. Using that as a reference point, he tried to pick out the apartment on Royal Street where he had lived when he first moved into the Quarter all those years ago.

But it was too many blocks away and he could not find it, although he could recall it perfectly and with a fondness that the apartment itself did not deserve.

The apartment was on the second floor of a three-story building on Royal Street near Esplanade. The first floor was a combination art gallery and coffee shop, and the third-floor apartment was occupied by a Bourbon Street stripteaser who, he recalled, liked to make love to Elvis Presley records. The floorboards above him always seemed to creak late at night just when "Heartbreak Hotel" was wailing through his window.

The apartment had a small kitchen, a small bathroom, a small bedroom, a small living room, and a lot of big cockroaches. But it had a balcony overlooking Royal Street and on late summer nights, when it was too humid and sticky to fall asleep, and the Elvis Presley records were throbbing above him, he would take a wicker chair out on the balcony and sit and watch the stream of cars and people in the street until two or three in the morning.

Bourbon Street, with its strip joints and nightclubs, was only a block away but, for him, the real advantage of the apartment's location was that it was only a few minutes' walk from Preservation Hall, the huge room on St. Peter Street where black musicians, some of them in their seventies, played authentic Dixieland jazz every night.

He had liked Dixieland jazz since his early teens, ever since he had first heard it on a Sunday afternoon radio program from a jam session in the Quarter. He had started a record collection while in high school and had added to it while in college, carefully storing his records at the house on Fern Street when he went into the Army.

For an admission fee of one dollar a night, he could go to the Hall on any night of the week and listen to musicians such as Jim Robinson, Sweet Emma Barrett, Percy Humphrey, and others, all rescued from obscurity, playing live the music he had heard only on scratchy 78 rpm records from years ago.

The musicians were recording again, on LPs; numbers such as "Milenburg Joys" and "Back O' Town Blues" and "Didn't He Ramble". Soon, one corner of the living room of the Royal Street apartment was filled with a record collection of over four hundred albums.

When he moved away eight years later, the record collection was the only possession he took with him.

He sold almost everything else; the wicker chair, the secondhand couch, the Andrew Wyeth print of *Christina's World*, the Formica table, even his Oldsmobile Cutlass.

The only thing he left in New Orleans was a three-speed fan he had purchased at Maison Blanche in 1969. He left it in the middle of the living room floor, an artifact from another time, as a reminder to those who followed him of the hot summer nights when he couldn't sleep and the stripper was fucking to the Elvis Presley records.

He often wondered what happened to her and who had the fan now.

From his hotel room window, he could see the huge bend in the Mississippi River and a ferryboat gliding across the water. It moved slowly, as if it had been pushed from one bank of the river in an attempt to float it across to the other side. He thought back to all the times he had taken the ferry when he was a child, and he had a sudden urge to run out of the hotel and race over to the water's edge, to the ferry landing, and get on the boat for the next ride. He wondered if it still cost a nickel.

Beneath him, a small traffic jam was beginning to develop on Chartres Street as a horse and carriage, filled with tourists with cameras draped around their necks, blocked a string of cars trying to pass in the narrow street. Even with the window tightly closed, he could hear the car horns being pounded in frustration.

Decatur Street unfolded a block away and he could see the riverfront wharves, shaded by the long sheds whose corrugated roofs seemed wrinkled from the sun. Several freighters were docked at the wharves, basking like animals sleeping on the riverbanks in the hot sun.

Burton wanted to open the windows, let in the air, the sunlight, even the heat, and smell the coffee beans wafting up from the long wharves, the tangy aroma of the red and green bell peppers and the yellow squash rising from the open stands in the farmer's market near Esplanade, the sweet smell of the beignets, showered with powdered sugar, freshly baked in the ovens near the French Market coffee stands.

But the windows were an unbroken pane of thick glass, seemingly stitched into the walls. Outside, there was a whole world of smells and sounds—a world he could plunge into like a swimmer diving into a pool. But inside, there was just another hotel room. You can't go home again.

He switched on the television set and turned the dial to WBID. Almost time for the local news.

He thought: eight years ago and I would have been getting ready to do this show. It was crazy how far and how fast he'd come.

Art Burton was promoted to reporter after a year as a news writer at WBID-TV. The first story he covered was a meeting of the City Council to discuss an increase in the garbage collection fees. At the conclusion of the meeting, he interviewed one of the Councilmen but, when he prepared the story for the six o'clock news, there was no room to include any of the interview.

"You didn't use any of our interview," the Councilman, a

florid-faced Irishman from one of the riverfront wards, complained to him on the phone the next day.

Burton was surprised that the Councilman had even bothered to call him. It was his first direct indication of the impact of television news. One minute-and-a-half story in a half-hour newscast and here was a City Councilman calling to complain about it. Calling him.

"There wasn't any room for the interview," he answered. "Anyhow, we did show both sides of the debate."

"Listen," the Councilman said angrily, "I stayed after that meeting because you asked me to. You want to jerk me off like that, you won't get any more favors out of me. Go to somebody else. I was trying to give you a break because you're new around the Hall."

Fuck you, Burton thought, but he was pleased. The complaint was a sign of his acceptance into the cloistered society where politicians and reporters spoke to each other in a language unheard by the public, a society where leaks, complaints, tips, animosities, and favors were the daily litany and both sides took a vow of silence regarding what was said between them.

Over the next eight years, as he reported on an ever-widening range of stories, he learned to keep the faith and maintain the vow of silence even when, occasionally, he wanted to scream and shout and kick someone in the balls.

It was, he realized, a test of his own integrity. He could not afford to let his own feelings about individuals, or issues, sway his editorial judgment about how—or if—a story should be reported.

He was tempted only once.

In 1975, two years before he went to the network, he covered a campaign rally by a sheriff running for reelection in one of the parishes upriver from New Orleans.

In the late 1950s and early 1960s, the Sheriff had been one of the state's leading segregationists, vowing that the For Colored Only signs at lunch counters, restrooms, drinking fountains, and waiting rooms would never come down.

But the Civil Rights Act of 1964 and massive voter registration by blacks since then changed the political landscape in Louisiana and other southern states forever.

Now, eleven years after the Civil Rights Act, the Sheriff

was openly courting the black vote and promising to name black deputy sheriffs when the next vacancies occurred.

In his story on the campaign rally, Burton referred to the Sheriff's previous record on segregation and how he was adjusting to the political realities of the 1970s.

When he got back to the Royal Street apartment that night, the Sheriff called him.

"You trying to fuck me? That what you're trying to do?" the Sheriff said. Burton could tell that the man was drunk.

"C'mon," Burton answered, annoyed. "You know me better than that."

"You New Orleans TV people, all big liberals down there. Trying to stir up the niggers on me, aren't you? Trying to make them remember me from back then, that what you're trying to do?"

"I'm not trying to do anything," Burton said patiently. "It was a legitimate part of the story. You're a changed person, politically."

"You wanna know something?" the Sheriff asked, the words beginning to slur together. "I never changed. I've been fucking the niggers all my life. I got some black pussy next to me right now. What do you think of that? You want a little piece too?"

Burton slammed the phone down and then took it off the hook so the Sheriff could not call him back.

I could finish him, Burton thought. I could do a story tomorrow night about how a sheriff running for reelection got drunk and called up a reporter to boast about having sex with black women.

But the unwritten code, the veil of silence he had taken as part of a reporter's way of life, restrained him from saying anything.

When he was executive vice president of the News Division, Carl Malachek had come to New Orleans to make a speech, and had seen a report by Art Burton on WBID's six o'clock news.

There had been a tornado in a small town in southwest Louisiana and Burton and a cameraman had flown there as soon as the story appeared on the AP wires. They had been the first newsmen from any of the television stations in New Orleans to get to the area before the cleanup began.

Burton still could recall the scenes as if the videotape were unwinding in front of him: houses blown apart and lying like broken sticks in the streets, uprooted trees flattening the roofs of cars, dead household pets—dogs, cats, a rabbit, a raccoon—lying in backyards with flies buzzing around them and maggots starting to crawl over their bodies, children's toys scattered in the grass.

And his first thought, his very first thought, had been: it looks like mortar rounds were fired in.

He had taped enough material for a three-minute report, ending his report with a close-up of himself standing in the wreckage of what once had been a small grocery store. There was no roof on the building, just open sky, and he was framed by irregular rows of smashed cans of vegetables and fruits.

It had been an effective closing shot, with the camera pulling back to show the impact of the tornado on just one store, and he let the picture carry the story with no closing narration.

A week later, he got a letter from Malachek complimenting him on the story and inviting him to New York to discuss working for the network as a correspondent.

"How long have you been at WBID?" Malachek asked him as they sat in his office in the executive wing of the network's News Division offices.

"Eight years," Burton replied. He never had thought it would happen like this, if at all—sitting across the desk from the executive vice president of the News Division, being interviewed for a job with the network.

He had wondered about it, of course, many times, particularly in the last year or two when he had begun to feel that local news had nothing else to offer him. He had done it all. But you didn't apply to the networks for a job. You had to be asked.

So he sat in the WBID newsroom, watching the network news, and wondered whether he would ever move up to the network, just as John Cornwall and other correspondents had moved up from the affiliates.

The networks were the major leagues, where the men were separated from the boys, and being offered a job was like being selected for an elite fraternity that carried a cachet all its own. Now it was happening to him.

"Your tape reel was very good," Malachek said, referring to a cassette Burton had compiled of several of his stories.

"So was your résumé," he added. Malachek was impressed by the way Burton had started in the business, working one day a week at a television station while he was in college.

It reminded him of his own beginnings. Burton had paid his dues and he liked that.

"Network is different than local," Malachek cautioned him. "You don't get on the program every night, even every week. There are a lot of reporters competing for those twenty-two minutes."

"I'd like the chance," Burton said, trying to keep his eyes off an old baseball that Malachek had taken from his desk and was rolling around in his hand. It reminded him of Captain Queeg from *The Caine Mutiny* but Malachek didn't seem the type. Whatever the reason for the affectation, he didn't want to ask.

"Maybe you'll get the chance," Malachek said affably.

"I hope so," Burton answered, not embarrassed by his eagerness.

When Malachek called him a week later and offered him a job with the network, Burton was elated.

After eight years in local television, he was ready to move on. The news had taken on a cyclical nature. He was seeing it all over again.

One more City Council meeting, one more hurricane, one more local election campaign, one more Mardi Gras, and he would lose interest in all of it.

The network was a challenge, and he needed it.

Besides, there was no compelling reason for him to stay in New Orleans. His parents had died a year earlier. And, despite an assortment of airline stewardesses, young instructors at Tulane, and nurses at Charity and Baptist hospitals, he hadn't developed a lasting relationship with any woman.

It was time to go.

The job was in the network's Atlanta bureau although, it seemed to him now, he spent all of his three years there just going to and from the Atlanta airport.

He covered stories all over the southeast and, on occasion, in Central America. He was grist for the network's mill, dropping in and out of cities and countries just long enough to do a story or two and then go back to Atlanta and wait for the next assignment.

He started out at $50,000 a year—$15,000 more than he had been making at WBID—and at the end of three years he was making $62,500 a year. The work was exhilarating and exhausting and, when he was transferred to the New York bureau in 1980, he was disappointed even though it was considered a promotion and he got a $7,500 raise.

You didn't get the variety of stories in the New York bureau's territory that you did in Atlanta—nothing much ever seemed to happen in Buffalo or Pittsburgh except a snow-storm or a steel mill closing—but you did get to see the News Division's executives and top producers every day. Visibility—that was the name of the game.

And, when the network decided to launch a prime-time magazine show, he was chosen as one of the correspondents. That had been the turning point for him. Just two years ago. And then, with the assignment of Michael Swanson, the program's anchorman, to the morning show last year, he had been picked as anchorman. Six-figure salary. Weekly visibility. Just like that. A hell of a long way since that tornado.

The program on the screen now was one of the network's game shows. An Air Force Sergeant and a woman who looked like a cocktail waitress were trying to unscramble some letters on a big board. He watched it absentmindedly for a minute, then decided he wouldn't have time to watch the newscast, and switched the set off.

For the first time, he noticed a cellophane-wrapped bowl of fruit on the dresser. There was a note pinned to the wrapping. He opened it and read, "Welcome back to New Orleans. The Management." The note made him feel good.

He showered and shaved and then took out of his garment bag the dark blue suit that was his favorite. The cut of the jacket made him look thinner and taller. It was important that a live audience see him at his best, even if the audience was only a few hundred people.

There were always two audiences for television anchor-people—the huge, amorphous one "out there" that you never saw and the infinitely smaller one that you saw in person every day: the people in the street, in the high rise where you lived, in the restaurants where you ate.

Somehow, there was a symbiotic relationship between the two audiences. It was as if, by some mysterious quirk, the relatively few people who saw you in person could communicate to the large group the knowledge that you were a nice guy, or a prick, or a dummy, or one of the boys. It was very important that the smaller group get the correct impression. Word of mouth could kill you.

He looked at his watch. It was time to go down to the lobby and meet Andrews. He wondered who would be in the audience, how many people would really know him or just recognize him from television.

It was an ego trip, he knew. All speeches were. Of course, there usually was money involved, some sort of honorarium, although he was doing this one for free. But last week Jack Cornwall had picked up $10,000 just for flying to Boston one night after the evening news to speak to a group of insurance executives after dinner.

He left the room and took the elevator to the lobby. A group of men were standing just inside the entrance to the room where the luncheon was to be held, drinking Bloody Marys and Ramos gin fizzes. Moving toward them, and looking past them into the room itself, he figured the crowd would number over two hundred people. Maybe two fifty.

He walked into the room and shook hands with the men who greeted him. They recognized him immediately and he quickly joined their talk about the chances for the LSU and Tulane football teams in the fall.

Football. He almost had forgotten. It was a religion down here. *The '58 LSU team with Billy Cannon.* He wrapped his hand around the gin fizz glass somebody had brought him. *That was a hell of a team, eh, buddy?* Watched the room fill with seersucker suits and linen dresses. *Beat Ole Miss on Halloween night, remember?* Saw the waiters set out the shrimp rémoulade. *Played in the Sugar Bowl and whomped 'Bama.* Looked at Andrews glad-handing the Archbishop. *Oh Hold that Tiger! Hold that Tiger!*

He was back.

Chapter 2

The headquarters building of one of the major television networks filled most of a square block bounded by Fifth and Sixth avenues in midtown Manhattan. There was a small plaque, with the network's initials engraved on it, by the building's entrance but—other than that—there was little to distinguish the building from the other skyscrapers surrounding it.

The ground-floor lobby was starkly barren. The only furnishings were some towering rubber-plant trees and a huge glass-topped stainless steel reception desk behind which sat two women, dressed in brown skirts and red jackets. The jackets were embroidered above the breast pocket with the initials of the network.

A roped-off area, guarded by two men, wearing uniforms in the same brown and red colors, led to a single bank of elevators. The tiny lettering on the jackets was the only evidence confirming that this building was in fact, the radial point for one of America's great television networks. It was as if the severe effect had been achieved at the instruction of the network's lawyers who, afraid of creating some adverse impression with government agencies, had told the building's decorators, "Don't make us look too powerful."

It was only when a visitor looked at the building's directory, discreetly placed by the elevator banks, that one realized that this seemingly sterile arrangement housed a major power of the entertainment industry in the United States.

Floor after floor listed the various arms of the network: news, sports, entertainment, radio, sales, affiliate relations, network-owned stations, legal, business affairs, worldwide enterprises, press, and publicity. The machine that powered the network's invasion of millions upon millions of homes every day and night could be seen in a single glance—spelled out in tiny white letters set in grooved insets of black.

News occupied six of the network's twenty-eight floors. Three of the floors contained the studios, control rooms, and necessary appendages, such as makeup and set storage, for the News Division's major news programs—the morning show, *American Sunrise*, the evening newscast, and the once-a-week magazine show, *Focus on America*. The other floors of the News Division were occupied by the production units of the various programs, the business offices, the technical operations units and, in a small wing of the seventh floor, the executive offices.

These offices, known throughout the company as "Seven West" for the floor and section of the building they were located in, were actually a collection of warrens, each office guarded by a secretary. There were eight offices, one for each vice president and the executive vice president. Another, much larger, office belonged to Carl Malachek, the division's president.

For organizational reasons, the network labeled its various components as divisions and the News Division, albeit subconsciously, sometimes took on the aura of its military counterpart. The walls of Seven West were lined with pictures of News Division heroes from past and present—correspondents who had died in World War II, Korea, Vietnam, the Mideast, and Central America; anchormen who had been legendary figures a generation ago; and the newer, younger stars whose pictures, in living color, looked down on all visitors to remind them of the continuity of the division's glory.

The executive offices were approached through a reception area and here, instead of regimental banners and battle commendations, were the framed certificates commemorating the various awards the division had won over the years—the Emmys, Peabodys, Sigma Delta Chis, Headline Clubs, Overseas Press Clubs, every major and minor award given out by the industry. All that was lacking were the battle streamers: Civil Rights, Assassinations, Space Shots, Iran Hostages, Presidential Campaigns, all the major events spanning previous decades.

For Carl Malachek, however, none of this history and tradition mattered at the moment. What did matter was the phone call he had received early in the day from Jack Cornwall, the anchorman of the evening news.

"Are you free for lunch today?" Cornwall had asked.

"Let me look," Malachek answered. He gave a perfunctory glance at the appointment calendar on his desk. It showed a luncheon date with Mike Castelli, one of the network's documentary producers. Castelli, he knew, wanted to pitch him on doing a show about Afghanistan. The lunch could easily be postponed. Forever.

"I'm free," he told Cornwall, "and I'll even pick up the check. How's one o'clock?" he suggested.

"That's fine," Cornwall said agreeably. "I'll come by your office."

Malachek hung up the phone and reached for a cigar in a humidor on his desk. The cigars had been brought back, at his instruction, by a correspondent who'd recently done a story in Cuba. It was one of the minor perks of being a network news president.

He chewed on the cigar for a moment and wondered why Cornwall wanted to have lunch with him. It was unlike Cornwall who, while not remote, was a remarkably private person. Although he was Cornwall's boss, and they had known each other professionally for years, they never had been particularly close.

Their paths had taken them to the top of their individual careers, and they remained pleasant to each other, but they were not bound by their years of experience in the business. They were in the same world but traveled in different orbits.

There was, in fact, very little to bind them together.

Cornwall was the only child of wealthy parents. His father was managing director of one of the biggest brokerage houses on Wall Street and, had he wanted to, John Cornwall could have started at the firm the day after he graduated from Yale in June 1950.

But John Cornwall never had been interested in Wall Street. He wanted a career in journalism—he had been editor of the *Daily Record* while at Yale—and, after touring Europe for a month as a graduation present from his parents, he began to look for a job on a newspaper or magazine in New York City.

He was helped in his search by letters of introduction from friends of his family to editors on *The New York Times*, New York *Herald Tribune*, and *Time* and *Look* magazines. His search ended two months later when he received his draft notice from the United States Army.

In October 1952, John Cornwall was honorably discharged from the Army at Camp Atterbury, Indiana. He planned to pick up his civilian life where he had left off: looking for a job in New York City.

But a family friend who lived in Chicago had told his father about an opening for a beginning reporter on the City News Bureau—a news cooperative serving the newspapers and radio and television stations in Chicago.

Cornwall took a bus to Chicago and, still in his Army uniform, applied for the job and got it.

When he flew back home, he learned that his father's friend had been the college roommate of one of the top editors at the City News Bureau. The knowledge that family connections had helped him get the job did not bother him. It was, in a way, just like being tapped for Skull and Bones at Yale.

It was just the way things worked.

Things had never worked that way for Carl Malachek.

He had taken his first job, as a one-man newsman for a small radio station in Mt. Vernon, Illinois, not because of a great desire to be a reporter but for the one reason that had driven him since childhood—a need for money.

He had grown up in Chicago in a poor, working-class family that had barely survived the Depression. By the time he got to college at the University of Illinois in 1944, he had not thought about a career—only about finishing his education.

His main concern was to keep up his grades so he could stay on the academic and financial scholarships he had been awarded. Once he graduated, he would worry about what kind of a job he could find.

The problem was that a degree in American History really didn't help much in finding a job. And, even in the postwar boom of 1948, jobs were not all that easy to find for a twenty-two-year-old who was competing with thousands of World War II vets who were graduating under the GI Bill.

His only work experience in college—other than waiting on tables at the student union—had been on the campus radio station. The station had needed someone to do a sportscast and, because he had been an avid sports fan for years, Malachek took a chance and applied for the job. He had a good voice, a thorough knowledge of Big Ten sports, and he was hired.

Sports with Carl Malachek became a weekly feature on the radio station and he was paid fifteen dollars a week.

On the day before he graduated, Malachek saw a notice on the bulletin board of the campus job placement office. It was for a newsman's job at a 250-watt radio station in Mt. Vernon, Illinois. It would pay fifty-five dollars a week.

Two days later, he borrowed a friend's Nash and drove down through the farmlands of southern Illinois to Mt. Vernon. One block from the radio station, the car ran out of gas and Carl Malachek pushed the car the rest of the way to the station. Years later, in speeches to journalism students, Malachek would tell how, in 1948, he rolled into journalism. The hard way.

Malachek had chosen a small French restaurant west of Eighth Avenue, a fifteen-minute walk from the network building. He and Cornwall walked up Sixth Avenue together, Malachek noting with satisfaction that Cornwall was recognized by many people on the street.

It was one of those summer days in New York when the ugliness of the city did not seem to matter. Thousands of persons swarmed along the avenue, oblivious to the sidewalk peddlers hawking T-shirts, belts, costume jewelry, or imitation designer label shirts arrayed on makeshift tray table stands. Ice cream, frozen yogurt, hot pretzel, and Italian ice vendors competed for space on the curbs with carts selling hot dogs, egg rolls, souvlaki, and falafel.

The avenue resembled a giant, noisy, open bazaar, alive and throbbing with excitement.

"Are you going away this summer, Jack?" Malachek asked as they came to Fifty-eighth Street and turned west.

"Maybe to Israel," Cornwall answered. "I've got a chance to do a piece for the *Times* and it might be fun."

"We've got a good bureau there," Malachek said, as if he were ticking off a report card on the division's strengths. "Laporde's a good man," he added, referring to the network's correspondent in Tel Aviv.

"I thought his piece last week on the West Bank problem was first-rate," Cornwall said. "We need more of that kind of journalism. Good insight."

Get off it, Malachek thought. Let me run the fucking News Division. You read the news.

They jaywalked across the street, dodging several taxicabs and delivery trucks, and a few minutes later they were at the restaurant. Malachek had selected it because he liked

French food and because the restaurant's location was just far enough from the headquarters of all three networks to be a bit out of the way. If Cornwall wanted to have lunch with him alone, Malachek thought, then he didn't want to be in a place where there would be a lot of other network people. There were enough restaurants like that; places where, every day of the week, you could see the vice presidents of network sales, news producers, and correspondents from all networks lined up at the bar or seated at favored tables.

Chez Cinc Ami, the restaurant he had chosen, was too small to accommodate a big crowd. Quickly glancing around the room as he and Cornwall were being seated, Malachek felt reassured. He didn't recognize anyone, although he could tell that several couples seated at the tables recognized Cornwall.

The waiter, addressing Cornwall by name, took their drink orders—a white wine spritzer for Cornwall and a Bloody Mary for Malachek.

"Do you come here often, Carl?" Cornwall asked.

"Once in a while," Malachek answered, flipping the restaurant's matchbook over in his fingers. "They do a nice job with poultry. Chicken, duck."

"Have you been to 21 recently?" Cornwall asked. "Since the new owners?"

"Not recently."

"They have a chicken dish that's really superb. They do something with rice and spices."

"Indian?"

"Not really. More Mediterranean. Reminds me of something I had in the south of France last summer."

"I'll have to try it," Malachek said blandly. "Did you see the O and O overnights from last night?" he asked, switching the conversation to the ratings report that came in every morning from the five cities where the network owned television stations.

"I don't recall seeing them," Cornwall replied. "I really don't give a shit about them," he added, surprised at his own bluntness.

Malachek ignored the remark and continued. "We did a big number in New York last night with the local news lead-in. Those clowns are really helping us even if they wouldn't know a news story from a bag of shit."

"I never get to watch any of their shows," Cornwall said and he arranged the water glass and ashtray in front of him to make room for the drinks the waiter was placing on the table. "Are they really bad?"

"They don't do news. They interview every movie star who's in New York plugging a movie and every writer who's plugging a book. It's a fuckin' promotion show. And they have the balls to thank the guests for coming."

"I guess it works," Cornwall said, and raised his glass in a mock toast to the unseen program.

"The business is changing," Malachek said. "Local news is different in the big cities. It's all celebrities. *People Magazine* changed the whole business. All glitz and glitter. That's what most of it is these days."

For Carl Malachek, "these days" always were seen in the perspective of the old days and, when he compared the two, the old days always were better.

It was not just the difference between the huge, worldwide operations of the network News Division and the tiny AM radio station where he had started his career.

The difference was deeper and more fundamental. In the old days, there had been a feeling of excitement in the news business, a sense of being part of a select group who were devoted to the pursuit of news. He had felt it even in that first fifty-five-dollar-a-week job, driving the radio station's car—with its dial numbers painted on both sides—over every road and highway in downstate Illinois, looking for stories he could report.

There had been others like him: young kids just starting out, willing to work for low salaries, eager to break a big story, unrelenting in their desire to make a career for themselves. But television had changed the news business and, over the years, television news itself had changed.

Now, the news was just part of a larger spectacle of entertainment. The newscasts were promoted like movies, the anchormen were celebrities, reporters had agents—reporters, for God's sake!—and, if a big story broke, the final measure was whether it had helped to boost the ratings of the newscast.

Once, Malachek had walked through the production offices of *The Evening News with John Cornwall* and had overheard a producer asking the assignment desk, "Who's the talent going to be on that story?"

Malachek had slammed a phone book on the desk and shouted, "Our people are reporters, goddamit! The talent is on the fucking soap operas." Nobody in the News Division ever called reporters "talent" again.

Cornwall admired the intensity Malachek brought to any discussion of news although he knew that Malachek was consumed by the news business twenty-four hours a day.

He also admired Malachek's toughness and even though his short, lumpy stature had long ago earned Malachek the nickname The Toad, Cornwall knew that Malachek's mind worked with the speed and agility of a panther.

"Fuck 'em," Malachek once had growled to Cornwall about nobody in particular. "I only know how to play hardball."

I'll find out today, Cornwall thought, how much hardball he can play.

Malachek pulled a cigar from the inside pocket of his suit coat and moved it around his mouth as if he were tasting a lollipop. He finally lit it.

"You want one?" he asked Cornwall through a cloud of smoke.

"Before lunch?" Cornwall replied, unable to hide the hint of admonition in his voice. "How do you do it?"

"It's easy, Jack," Malachek responded with a sly grin. "You just light it and inhale."

"It's bad for your health, Carl," Cornwall said. "Shit, it's bad for my health."

Malachek put the cigar in an ashtray and looked at it as if it were a household pet, waiting to be stroked. "I like to get one started before the meal. I finish it off afterward. Ready to order?"

Cornwall nodded and Malachek signaled to the waiter. They each ordered coq au vin, coffee, and a strawberry tart for dessert.

By the time the waiter brought dessert, Malachek had decided that Cornwall had asked to have lunch with him for no reason other than a social one. It had been a pleasant hour and a half, the conversation ranging from mutual friends at other networks to the network's problems in prime time. Cornwall had delighted Malachek with a sprinkling of anecdotes about his early days as a correspondent and then as co-anchor of *American Sunrise*.

Malachek had drifted easily into the flow of conversation and had responded to Cornwall's anecdotes with stories of his own: the first scandal he had uncovered—the use of county prisoners to work on a state senator's farm—and how proud he had been to put it on the air even for his relatively small audience; the two years writing radio news in the early morning hours at WGN in Chicago; and his introduction to television as the assignment editor at a Chicago station in 1952.

"The news director told me we needed nat sof for a story. I thought he was talking about a person, you know, Nat Sof. I didn't know he was using the abbreviation for natural sound on film. Christ, was I embarrassed!"

Cornwall smiled to himself at the thought of how far Malachek had come from that early initiation into the street language of television. He knew that there were social strata in television news. He had entered the highest levels when he was named anchorman of the evening news. But even within that rarified atmosphere, Malachek was a head of state and was treated accordingly.

When Malachek visited the network's London bureau, Cornwall knew, there was always a car and driver to meet him at Heathrow and stay with him the duration of his visit. He was booked at the Dorchester or Connaught and dined in the best restaurants of Mayfair and Belgravia.

In France, arrangements would be made by the Paris bureau for a trip to the Monet gardens and there was always a bottle of fine wine in his room at the George V.

Cornwall did not know that the treatment he received amused Malachek. It was not something he ever had aspired to.

Raised in a Polish neighborhood on the northwest side of Chicago during the Depression, Carl Malachek had seen his father, one generation removed from the potato fields near Czestochowa, slowly die as he was laid off every three months from his job at the meat-packing plant on the South Side.

His mother kept her job as a saleswoman at Carson Pirie Scott on the Loop but his parents never had enough money to give him even a small weekly allowance.

In the summer of 1939, when he was thirteen years old,
Carl Malachek dreamed of going to the New York World's
Fair and looking at all the exhibitions and pavilions he had
seen in a newsreel once. In the dream, Grover Whelan and
Mayor Fiorello La Guardia would meet him and drive him
around in a open car just like FDR and the King of England.
The day would end with a trip through the General Motors
Futurama, which would take him right back to Chicago.

The dream was so vivid that he came to think of it as a
preview of something that actually was going to happen, like
a coming attraction in the movies.

But it did not happen—his parents never could afford a
vacation—and Carl Malachek spent the summer working as a
stock boy in a grocery store on Lincoln Avenue.

He used his spare money to buy a bleacher seat on
Saturday afternoons at Wrigley Field when the Cubs were
playing. That summer, he caught a home run ball hit by Stan
Hack and the ball became a personal good luck charm.

At night, lying in his bed, he would rub it as if he were
pitching on the mound and then, just before striking out Mel
Ott of the hated New York Giants, he would put it under his
pillow and fall asleep.

Years later, the ball rested on a small tray on his desk in
New York.

In the fall of 1939, when the Nazis invaded Poland, and
his father talked about how the world would never be the
same again, Carl Malachek became interested in history. He
hung a map, which he had cut out from the *Chicago Tribune*,
on his bedroom wall and placed colored thumbtacks on the
map to indicate where the fighting was taking place.

Because he had little spending money, Carl Malachek
took up reading as a hobby. Once a week, he would go to the
main public library on Michigan Avenue and take out books
on history or biographies of famous people.

"An educated man, Carl. That's what counts," his father
always had told him. It was as if he had been given a piece of
generational wisdom, first proclaimed by his father's father;
the man in the peasant's shirt standing in front of the small
church in Poland; now a fading figure staring out from a
picture in a silver frame on top of the chest of drawers in his
parents' bedroom.

Carl Malachek knew that if he followed the advice it

might, someday, get him a college education but he also knew that even if he read every book in the Chicago Public Library, it still wouldn't get him to the New York World's Fair.

Years later, staring out the window of his hotel room at the Dorchester in London, looking out across Park Lane to the burgeoning fields of tulips and daffodils in the springtime greenness of Hyde Park, Malachek suddenly recalled that summer long ago and his vivid dream.

"You know," he said, turning to his wife, Mary Lou. "This isn't bad for a kid who never made it to the '39 World's Fair."

The waiter had refilled their coffee cups now and Malachek wiped the last smattering of strawberry tart from his mouth.

"We ought to get together more often, Jack," he said pleasantly.

"Well, I hope to have lots of time," Cornwall responded. It was time to start playing hardball.

Malachek absentmindedly began to toy with the cigar that had been lying unsmoked in the ashtray. A fingernail's length of gray ash had accumulated on the end of the cigar and he tapped it off quickly. He felt his jaw beginning to tighten ever so slightly.

"What does that mean?" he asked.

This is where it all starts to end, Cornwall told himself. Right now.

"That's why I wanted to have lunch with you," he said, trying to avoid looking directly at Malachek. "To tell you in person."

"To tell me . . ." Malachek repeated. His voice trailed off but his eyes remained fixed firmly on Cornwall.

Cornwall saw, almost felt, Malachek's stare. Malachek was looking at him with eyes that seemed to be narrowing into slits. Their color was no longer soft gray but seemed hardened, as if they suddenly were encased in marble.

He knows, Cornwall thought. The son of a bitch knows.

But Malachek did not know what Cornwall was going to tell him. Only that, whatever it was, he wasn't going to like it.

"I've been doing a lot of thinking," Cornwall said slowly. "I think I've had it. I don't want to do this anymore."

He needs stroking, Malachek thought. That's all. Just a couple of pats on the shoulder and some high-class stroking. That's why he wanted to have lunch. Care and feeding. It comes with the territory.

"You sound tired, Jack," he said quickly. "If you're telling me you need some time off—a couple of weeks to go off to Israel or wherever, don't worry about it. You deserve it."

"No, it's more than that," Cornwall responded. "I'm going to quit." He was surprised at how easy it had come out. Just like that. I'm going to quit.

"We all quit someday," Malachek retorted, unable to tell if Cornwall was serious.

"Not for me, Carl. Someday is now." Cornwall paused to sip from his wineglass. It was going easier than he had suspected it would. Maybe Malachek wasn't such a hardball player after all.

"I want to do some writing," Cornwall continued, "some lecturing, some traveling and if I don't do it now, I never will."

"You're fifty-four years old. What's the rush?" Malachek was beginning to worry.

"It's very simple," Cornwall said, eager to take advantage of the opportunity Malachek was giving him to explain his reasons. "I'm tired of coming in every night and writing twenty-second lead-ins to a script some other correspondent has done. I'm tired of wondering whether the story is going to make it in time from Beirut or Managua or Houston or Walla Walla, or wherever it is, to lead the show.

"I'm tired of having to answer a letter from some thirty-year-old news director at one of our affiliates who's pissed off because we didn't cover a story in his city. You reach a point where all of this doesn't matter anymore. I don't need it."

Carl Malachek had been in TV news for over thirty years and he could not believe what he was hearing. He had known temperamental anchormen and prima donna correspondents and executive producers who had to be treated like lap dogs. But Cornwall was none of these.

He didn't even look like an anchorman, someone who, by simply reading no more than a few hundred words a night, was paid close to a million dollars a year by the network. Tall and angular, with a hawklike face that, at times, made him look gaunt, Cornwall could have been plucked out of the television screen and dropped back into the middle of Yale University, dressed in a tweed jacket and corduroy pants.

Cornwall was one of the few people on the staff who could write a magazine article, even a book, who could converse with State Department experts, economists, ambassadors. He was a thinker. That was the goddamn trouble. He was a thinker. Not only that, but he was walking away from a pile of money. Malachek couldn't believe it.

"I suppose you've given this a lot of thought," Malachek said as he relit his cigar.

"A lot," Cornwall answered, waving the smoke away from his face.

Malachek thought. You're not going to do this on my shift. I'm not going to be the one who goes down in flames as the one who let Jack Cornwall walk out on the network. Not when we're first in the ratings at night. No way.

Malachek did not even want to think about how Jerry Rossman, the president of the network, would react. The whole fucking thing was too much.

"You've got a lot of years with the network, Jack," Malachek pointed out to him.

"Look, Carl," Cornwall said, "that's the problem. I've got a lot of years. I got into television in the late 1950s because it was new and it intrigued me and I figured I could make more than the eighty-five bucks a week I was making with the City News Bureau in Chicago. And I was right.

"But I've done it all. London, Moscow, the JFK assassination, the LBJ years, *Sunrise,* the evening show, everything. I'm tired of the whole damn business. Can't you understand that?"

"I gather this has been building up for quite a while," Malachek observed quietly. Despite his distress over what Cornwall was telling him, he admired the man's sincerity.

"For a long time," Cornwall concurred. "You know when it started? Back during the Vietnam War when I was covering the White House. I never could show it, certainly not when I was standing there on the West Wing Lawn every night doing my one minute and forty-five second reports, but that's when I realized how shallow this whole business is.

"I'd stand there every night and I'd want to report

'Those kids in the streets are right, folks. We're being jerked off, folks, right here at 1600 Pennsylvania Avenue and across the river at the Pentagon. We're going right down the tubes in Vietnam but I'm going to give you the official word from our President that we're winning.' Hell, Carl, I was frozen with network neutrality. I couldn't raise an eyebrow without getting a couple of hundred letters."

"Okay," Malachek said. "So a lot of us realized that maybe we didn't do enough strong reporting during the war. We bought the line. But in our business that was a lifetime ago, Jack. You move on, you get better. Look how we're reporting on Central America, Iran, Korea, these days. Don't you think we're showing the whole picture this time around?"

"Maybe so," Cornwall agreed. "But I don't want to be the messenger anymore. I don't want the monkey on my back anymore."

"What monkey, for Chrisake?" Malachek said, trying to contain his rising anger. He almost had been feeling sorry for Cornwall but now Cornwall was talking in circles.

Cornwall wrapped his hands around his wineglass as if it were a warming mitten. There was no way, he felt, he could make Malachek—or anyone, other than his wife—understand.

"Do you ever think about the power you have?" he suddenly asked Malachek.

"Not often," Malachek responded.

"Well, it's considerable, as we both know. But it's nothing compared to what I carry around. Let me tell you something. A few years ago, my wife and I were driving through the Rockies and in the most remote areas I'd see these cabins with television antennas. They were on a cable system, I found out later. Our news was on the cable, along with baseball from Chicago, wrestling from Atlanta, and every old movie you ever saw. But I was it for them. Twenty-three minutes a night."

"So?" Malachek said.

"So there are three network anchormen in this country who are giving a thimbleful of news every night to some poor bastard on the western slopes of the Rockies or a housewife in Queens or a mailman in Tucson, all of whom need a hell of a lot more than we're giving them. I just don't want to be the town crier in the electronic village anymore, that's all."

For an instant, Malachek thought: Maybe he's cracking

up. But he knew that Cornwall was serious and there was no way of dissuading him. At least not now.

He took another puff on his cigar. "Have you spoken to Roger Blumberg?" referring to Cornwall's agent.

Cornwall smiled. "There's a window in the contract, if that's what you're asking."

"A window!" Malachek exclaimed incredulously. He had not been president when Cornwall's last contract had been negotiated but the circumstances surrounding the negotiations were familiar to him. Cornwall had been wooed with huge salaries by the other networks but finally had decided to stay with the network with a long-term contract.

The negotiations had been reported in the trade press and big city newspapers. New York, Chicago, LA. All over. Anchor talents, and their salaries, were big news. When Cornwall re-signed, the network threw a big party for him at Tavern on the Green and flew in television columnists from all over the country.

When Malachek was promoted from executive vice president to president, he discussed Cornwall's contract with Jerry Rossman but Rossman did not mention a window in the contract. Malachek remembered only that it was for seven years at a beginning salary of $750,000 and rising to over a million and a half dollars at the end. That had been five years ago. There still were two years to run.

Malachek rubbed his hands with his chin. "If there's a window, there's a window. What does it give you?"

"It gives me the right to leave at the end of five years as long as I don't work for another network for five years." Cornwall said it matter-of-factly, as if he were reciting his home address and telephone number.

How the hell did that slip by, Malachek wondered. Why didn't somebody flag it? And why didn't Rossman tell me?

"And that's what you want to do?" he asked Cornwall.

"Yes. We've got a house in Bucks County and we'll probably move there. Maybe we'll get up to New York once a month or so."

He's talking as if it's done, Malachek thought. There's no sense in fighting it now. I'll have to do it later when there's more time. If there is any time.

"When's all this going to happen?" he asked.

"Next month. I'm not going to hold the network to the

absolute letter of it. We can work it out as far as the timing and the announcement."

"The fall season," Malachek reminded him. "It doesn't give us much time to decide on your replacement."

"There's never going to be a good time, Carl," Cornwall answered. He wasn't going to let Malachek get a wedge in. Not when he had come this far.

"Who else knows about this?" Malachek asked warily.

"Just my wife. And Blumberg."

"I need to tell Rossman," Malachek said. He was surprised that he was beginning to feel a bit ill. Maybe it was the chicken.

"Well, it's been an interesting lunch, Jack," Malachek said wearily. There was no sense in continuing it and he signaled to the waiter to bring the check. He wanted the lunch to end now.

Cornwall did not know whether Malachek was being graceful or sarcastic with his remark about "an interesting lunch" but he didn't care. He had taken the leap and from now on it would be easy. Cutting the cord was the hard part. He had just gone snip-snip and Malachek had not flinched.

It's over, he thought. All those years of running around the country, the world; election nights, space shots, state funerals, summits. It's all coming to an end. Just like that. All those years of deciding what stories I wanted on the program, which correspondents should do them. All that power. It's all ending.

His mind flashed back to the time, five years ago, when he had been named anchorman of the evening news. He had been doing the morning show, *American Sunrise,* cohosting with a succession of pretty blonds, all of whom seemed to come from California. Then the word flashed through the building that Robert Miniver had been killed in a mountain climbing accident in Alaska.

Miniver, the great anchorman who had taken the network news to the top of the ratings in the early 1960s and kept it there for fifteen years. Miniver was gone, and he was chosen to replace him.

From that moment on, he was in a new half-world of news, entertainment, and, driven by the ratings, the business of television news. He looked at himself in succeeding years and could not recognize what he saw.

Today was the first time in a long time that he felt in control of his life again.

Malachek signed with his credit card for the check and the two of them left the restaurant and walked back to the network building.

It was not yet two-thirty but Malachek felt as if the day had ended. He was drained. He had been completely unprepared for Cornwall's announcement and now, as he and Cornwall slipped through the afternoon crowds on Fifth Avenue, Malachek tried to cope with the onslaught of problems that kept coming at him.

The important thing was to keep it quiet, keep it out of the goddamn *New York Times* and *Washington Post* until everything was settled. Maybe there still was a way to dissuade Cornwall. But how? And what was Rossman going to say? The whole damn thing was falling in on him.

He knew that he had to have a fall-back position with Rossman, a recommendation for a replacement for Cornwall. Cornwall's walkout could kill the evening news unless he made the right choice to replace him. Time to think, to work this out, was the problem. Time was always the problem.

As soon as he got back to his office, Malachek went to his phone and dialed the number of Tom Hixson, the News Division's contract administrator.

"Hixson," was the cheerful response on the other end of the phone.

"Tom, could you come down to my office?" Malachek asked. "And bring Jack Cornwall's contract with you."

"Is there a problem?"

"No. I'd just like to see it," Malachek answered dourly.

Malachek hung up the phone and stared at the display of framed photographs on the wall across from his desk. There were pictures of him and all the former Presidents starting with Eisenhower on the farm at Gettysburg.

Pictures of Malachek on the floor at several Republican and Democratic conventions. Malachek in a huge fur hat at the Great Wall of China. Malachek in a sport shirt at the very first space shot at the Cape.

They were some of the souvenirs of a long career in television, a career that had started, after four years in radio, on the assignment desk of a television station in Chicago in 1952.

Two years later, he had taken a job as news director of a television station in Rochester, New York, and then had returned to Chicago in 1957, newly married, as head of the network's Midwest bureau. Each move had been another step up the ladder.

He had come to New York in 1960, with his wife and their two-year-old son, to a job on the national assignment desk and had started his climb through the network ranks.

They lived in a small apartment in Queens, an apartment so small that the bedroom for their son, Francis, had room enough only for a bed. The boy's clothes were kept in a plastic chest of drawers in the bathroom. But there was a crucifix over Francis's bed and when, at the age of twenty, the boy chose to go into the priesthood, Malachek jokingly told everyone, "It was the crucifix over the bed that did it. It wasn't his father's influence."

They had moved to the two-story house in Rye by then but the crucifix was still on a wall, even though Malachek went to church only when Francis came home to visit.

Malachek's career had culminated with the presidency of the network's News Division and, with Cornwall as anchor, he had kept the network on top of the evening news ratings.

But now, for the first time, that position was threatened.

What was it his father had told him years ago?

"An educated man. That's what counts."

He wondered what his father, dead all these years, would say now if he knew that his son's biggest weapon, the anchorman, was going away to be a thinker.

Well, dammit, he wasn't going to lose everything he had worked for.

He knew, though, that he would have to go to Rossman soon with the grim news. And, when he did, he would have to be prepared with an alternative.

He thought for a moment about Francis, ministering to a flock in a small community in Wisconsin. If Francis was faced with a problem, all he had to do was turn to the Bible and find a quotation. There was one for everything: sorrow, happiness, life, death, everything. It was easy for Francis. There always was an answer.

Malachek reviewed in his mind the immediate possibilities as replacements for Cornwall. Swanson from *American Sunrise* in the morning and McVea from the weekend news

shows. They both were good but they both lacked that extra
ingredient that would make them permanent fixtures in the
hearts and minds and living rooms of millions of viewers
every night.

No, the next anchorman would have to be very special,
someone with not only strong reportorial credentials but
someone with an as yet untapped magnetism that would
hold, instantly, as much of Cornwall's ratings as possible and
then, in time, build on them.

He reviewed the possibilities again, moving past Swanson
and McVea to the larger field of staff people. He would have
to take a chance and move somebody up from that group. It
would be a gamble but he had a special kind of faith that even
his son or his wife, Mary Lou, didn't have. It was an
unwavering belief in his own instincts. He would make the
right choice.

His mind began to center on Art Burton. Burton was
doing *Focus* once a week and the show had good ratings. And
he liked Burton's work, had always liked him ever since he
first saw him on that local news show in New Orleans years
ago and had hired him for the network.

It was only a hunch, but Burton might be better than
any of the correspondents who had substituted as anchor
when Cornwall had been on vacation or special assignment.

None of them had ever caught fire as anchors. They
always would be damn good correspondents but they never
would have the combination of reportorial talent—the ability
to report on a summit meeting or a political convention or a
war—along with the God-given ability to read the news to
millions of people and have them believe in you and trust
you.

Burton just might have that combination. He also had all
the right credentials. One of the troops. Good-looking. Good
correspondent. Even won a medal in Vietnam if he remembered correctly.

Yes, Burton could be the fallback if Cornwall stuck to his
decision. Maybe even the solution.

He let the idea roll around in his mind as if it were in his
mouth and he was tasting it. It tasted right, even good.

He pressed the intercom at the side of his desk and
signaled for his secretary, Judy Rosen, to come in.

As Carl Malachek's secretary, Judy Rosen had been part

of his professional life and was familiar with the intimate and oftentimes confidential workings of the News Division.

Letters and memos to White House press secretaries, correspondents, lawyers, agents, officials at other networks, Congressmen, viewers, general managers of affiliates, FCC Commissioners; all of these had run through her typewriter over the years.

Malachek rarely had kept anything from her. But this time he did. He could not tell her about Cornwall's decision. He had to keep this one tight. "What I'd like you to do," he said casually, as if it were not particularly important, "is for you to get Art Burton for me. I need to speak to him."

"Of course," she said briskly.

A few minutes later, she returned with the information that Burton was in New Orleans.

"What's he doing down there? Visiting?"

"His office says he's working on a story," she replied, "and he's also going to make a speech for the affiliate."

"Leave word at his hotel for him to call me," Malachek said.

"Fine," she said, and left his office.

Malachek sat motionless for ten seconds and then he pursed his lips and exhaled deeply. It was a trick he had learned years ago from Robert Miniver, who always let out a deep breath moments before he went on the air.

It would be better if he could speak to Art Burton first—just to make sure he was interested—before telling Rossman about Cornwall. Not that Burton wouldn't jump at the chance to anchor the evening news. Who wouldn't? But there wasn't enough time.

He left his office and walked down a corridor to the main newsroom. He entered the newsroom and walked into a tiny cubicle where rows of Teletypes from various news services— AP, UPI, Reuters, Agence France Press—were stacked like displays in a supermarket. The machines clattered relentlessly, reporting the news from all over the world. Malachek picked the AP wire and began to rapidly scan it, running it through his fingers like a tailor unrolling a bolt of cloth.

Most of the day had gone by and he had no idea of what had been happening around the world. What the hell. When had he had time today to think about the news?

It had been the last thing on his mind.

Chapter 3

"I gotta believe," Frank Baglio said, "that these two are making it in private. Nobody could act that good."

He was looking intensely at a television set mounted on the wall in the corner of a barroom on Magazine Street in the uptown section of New Orleans.

A man and a woman, he bare chested, she in a slip, were lying in bed, the bottom half of their bodies covered by a sheet.

They were locked in an embrace and, just as the man's hand reached under the sheet, the screen went dark and a commercial for a detergent came on the screen.

"Jesus," Baglio muttered to the bartender. "This can really turn you on."

The bartender had been reading a copy of *The Times-Picayune*, which he had spread out on the bar in front of him. "I dunno," he said, "I never look at these programs."

It was shortly after three o'clock in the afternoon and, other than Baglio, the only person at the bar was a young black man seated at the end of the long counter.

Baglio glanced at his watch while the commercial was on and wondered if the black kid knew that he was a cop. Then the soap opera came back on and Baglio stared again at the television set. There was a different scene on now, an elderly woman being pushed in a wheelchair through a hospital corridor.

"Looks real sexy, Frank," Burton said as he walked into the barroom.

The bartender glanced briefly at Burton and then went back to reading his newspaper. The black youth turned to look at him for a moment and continued drinking his beer.

"Hey Armand," Baglio called out, swiveling around on his bar stool to face Burton. "Where y' at, pal?"

"I'm okay, Frank, how are you?" Burton said, unfazed by the familiarity of Baglio's greeting. It was only old friends like Baglio, whom he had known since they'd gone to Warren Easton High School together, who still called him by his given name rather than the name he had chosen for television.

He had been Art Burton for sixteen years, ever since he had legally changed his name after he came back from Vietnam and started in television at WBID.

"Armand Bertrand's all right down here," his first news director at the television station had told him, "but it won't go over if you ever leave. And if you want to get ahead in this business, you've got to move."

At first he had been opposed to the idea, but he had changed his mind. Even he thought of himself now as Art Burton. *Everything changes.*

"I'm glad you let me know you were coming, Armie," Baglio said, motioning him to an adjoining bar stool. "It's good to see you again, pal. What'll you have?"

"A beer," Burton answered. "A Dixie. Miller. Whatever."

"Another Dixie draft," Baglio said to the bartender who quickly filled a frosted glass with beer from a tap and placed it in front of Burton.

"You remember Art Burton?" Baglio said to the bartender. "Used to be on the news here."

"Oh yeah," the bartender said but Burton could tell that the bartender did not recognize him.

"He's on the network now," Baglio boasted.

"What channel?" the bartender asked.

"Channel 5," Burton answered. "WBID. I used to work there."

"Yeah, that's right," the bartender said but Burton could not tell whether the bartender really remembered him.

Burton took a swallow of beer and looked at Baglio. To his eyes, Baglio had not changed since he had last seen him three years ago, when he had come down to do a story on the Mardi Gras.

Baglio was short and overweight and the pencil-thin moustache he had first grown in high school still framed his upper lip. He still had slicked-back black hair that looked as if it would stain your fingers, making them oily and sticky, if you happened to touch his head. Baglio, Burton thought, would always look like somebody who played guard on a high-school football team.

Baglio, however had not been an athlete or much of a student or much of anything. He had just been a good friend, one you could go to Pontchartrain Beach with or drive across the lake with and eat crayfish and drink beer on a Sunday afternoon.

After they graduated high school, Burton went to LSU and Baglio went to a junior college in Mississippi for two years and then came back to join the New Orleans Police Department. He was, Burton knew, honest.

Burton also knew that he and Baglio really had nothing in common anymore other than the years of growing up and being in high school together.

But that was more than enough. Frankie Baglio always would be a friend and that counted for something because, somewhere along the way, he had lost most of his other friends from New Orleans.

It was, he knew, the news business that had isolated him from his roots. It wasn't just that he had moved away from New Orleans and now rarely came back. The break actually had started when he was working at WBID and living in the apartment on Royal Street.

Had he gone into some other business; insurance, banking, retail sales, he would have glided, like the rest of his friends, from high school to college and then into the circumscribed social circle that New Orleans offered; parties, football games, Mardi Gras balls, Civic Club meetings.

But his work had taken him outside the circle.

At Chamber of Commerce luncheons, where his friends were seated at tables in the audience, he would be crouched next to a cameraman, following the text of the guest speaker, nudging the cameraman when it was time to film a brief excerpt.

In the summers, when there were always a lot of parties, he would have to refuse most of the invitations because he had to cover the Legislature, which was meeting in Baton Rouge, ninety miles away.

In time, just like one of the freighters that occasionally broke away from its moorings on a Mississippi River wharf, he drifted away.

It was the same now at the network. There was no

chance to have any real friendships. There was Samantha, of course, but she was special. His only other close friend in New York was Alex Monroe who had been a reporter at WBID in the beginning and then had come to New York years ago to work in the public relations department of one of the big oil companies.

There was nobody else. Acquaintances, sure—a wide range of producers, correspondents, bureau chiefs, and camera crews; people with whom he shared a commonality of work. But, even after eight years at the network, he knew very few of their wives and he did not know the names of any of their children.

"So how are you, Frank?" Burton asked.

"Not bad. Still humping to make a buck."

"And Louise? How are she and the kids?"

"Good. Real good. We still got the place in Gentilly. Couple of blocks from Elysian Fields. Thinking of moving though."

"How come?"

"The blacks. They're starting to come in. Like fuckin' weeds."

Burton quickly glanced to the end of the bar to see if the black youth sitting there had overhead Baglio's remark. Apparently he had not and Burton was relieved. That was all he needed. Trouble in a barroom.

Baglio took a long swallow of beer, finished the glass, and wiped his moustache with the back of his hand. He motioned to the bartender to bring him another beer.

"What about you Armie? Still not married, huh?"

"I don't have the time," he replied. It was true. Before, when he was in the bureaus, there was the constant travel. And now that he was anchoring the magazine show, it consumed all of his time. There was no time for anything permanent.

"So how did your speech go?" Baglio asked, sensing that Burton didn't want to talk about anything too personal.

"It was all right," Burton answered. "Nice crowd, couple hundred people."

"You still knocking 'em dead on the network?"

"I'm trying," Burton answered with a laugh. "But there's a lot of competition."

"What's it like?"

"What? The network?"

"Yeah. You know, working up there with all those people."

Burton was silent for a minute. "When I first came to New York," he finally said, as if he had gone back and looked at it, "a producer called me aside and told me 'This place is a tank full of sharks and barracuda. You've got to keep swimming or they'll tear you apart, piece by piece.' He was right. Most of the time it is a shark tank. So I keep swimming."

"What do you mean?" Baglio asked, unable to grasp the intrigues that had become an accepted part of Burton's life.

"I mean everybody is looking for something else. The producers want to be executives. The reporters want to be anchors. The assignment editors want to be producers. Everybody wants a piece of somebody else."

"What about the anchors?"

"The big anchors? Cornwall and people like that? They don't have to think of going any higher. There's no place higher for them to go."

"What about you?" Baglio asked. "You're doing damn good the way I look at it."

"I'm no different than the others," Burton admitted. "I think about anchoring one of the big newscasts once in a while. So do a lot of others. It's all a big crapshoot. It depends on the timing, whether or not you're in favor, that kind of thing."

"Ah, you're doing all right," Baglio said. "I watch your program every week."

"I'm doing okay," Burton said flatly. He knew that their worlds—his and Baglio's—were so different that there was no way Baglio could ever understand the life he lived; the pressure of the ratings, the worry that he might not succeed, the gnawing fear that somebody else was out there, somebody Malachek would discover on a local news show, somebody who someday might take his place.

It all had turned out differently than he had expected. When he first came to the network, his only desire was to be regarded as a top correspondent. But even though the rootlessness of the life disturbed him, he soon was caught up by its seductiveness; the money, the expense-account travel, the phalanx of support, the professional elitism of it all.

He knew now that he needed and desired all of that. And, with the additional appeal of the weekly magazine show, he also knew that he could not give any of it up. He had become dependent on it as surely as if it were a narcotic.

"I don't have any worries," he lied.

"Tell me something," Baglio said, leaning over to Burton and lowering his voice. "Those people on the soap operas, like the ones on this one," he said, gesturing to the television set on the wall. "Do they fuck on the outside or is all of this just acting?"

Burton laughed and wondered if the bartender, who was at the other end of the bar, talking to the black kid, could hear them.

"How the hell would I know, Frankie?"

"I thought you all worked together up there, in the same building. You must hear things."

"They do most of the soaps in California. I don't know a thing about them."

"That girl who's on the program with you," Baglio persisted. "The blond. What's her name? Stuart?"

"Samantha Stuart."

"Good-looking," Baglio said. "What's she like?"

"Nice person, a terrific reporter," Burton answered. There was no way he was going to tell Baglio about her. She was his one real connection—but hard to hold.

Burton looked at a clock behind the bar and gestured toward a row of booths that lined one wall of the barroom. "Let's sit over there," he said to Baglio.

Baglio said, "Okay, whatever you want," and they walked over to a booth near the entrance. The bartender came over to the booth, wiped the Formica-topped table with a cloth, and said, "The black guy down there wants me to switch to the baseball game. You guys mind?"

Baglio looked up at the set and saw the same elderly woman on the soap opera. "No, go ahead," he said grudgingly.

"Get you anything else?" the bartender asked.

"No. Nothing."

The bartender walked away and Baglio lit a cigarette. There was no noise in the barroom other than the low hum of the air-conditioning unit over the door and the program on the television set.

The room felt oppressive to Burton and he wished that Baglio had picked some other bar, someplace with a little class. This one had none. The paneled walls were bare except for some pictures, one in each booth, of various Tulane University football teams. The one in his booth was of the 1955 team. Fifty white guys all holding helmets in their laps.

"What's up, Armie?" Baglio asked. His police training told him that Burton wanted something but he didn't know what.

"I need your help," Burton said. "We're doing a story on illegal gambling. The mob, where the money goes, what's involved. We want to show what it's all about."

"Not a bad idea," Baglio said admiringly. "How are you going to do it?"

"That's the problem. We can always get a couple of people from Gamblers Anonymous to go on camera and talk. You know, how they bet the mortgage with some bookie because they were hooked. And we've got a Justice Department attorney and some local DAs who will talk about the extent of it. But what we need is somebody big, not somebody who's using the cookie jar money every week."

"Somebody who'll talk?"

"Right."

Baglio thought for a minute and then said, "I don't think you'll find anybody down here, Armand. There's not that kind of money. You've got to go to Vegas or California or the East."

"That's why I wanted to see you, Frank," Burton said quietly. "I read about that raid you made last week."

"The wire operation," Baglio said, nodding his head. "That was a good make. Can you imagine? These guys had a whole house full of phones up on South Carrollton. Right near the Seminary. Beautiful."

"They were booking bets from all over the country according to what I read," Burton said.

"Yeah. It was pretty big. Interstate. They're all going up on federal charges."

"Who were they?"

"The bookies were small fry. The operation was run by Mike Delgado. Remember him? Used to run a string of whorehouses down in Lafourche Parish. I busted him once for beating up on a stripper on Bourbon Street. But he had a cousin in the Legislature and the son of a bitch got him off. I don't know when he got into gambling."

Burton took another drink of beer. "Will any of them talk?" he asked.

"About what?"

"About anything. Who they were booking bets for. How the payoffs were made. Anything."

"Jesus, Armand," Baglio said. "Why should they?"

"You never can tell," Burton said. "Sometimes you tell somebody they're going to be on television, the whole country will see them, and they'll do anything for you. Can you find out for me?"

"What am I going to tell them? That they're going to be famous?"

"C'mon, Frank," Burton said, trying to hide the impatience he was beginning to feel with Baglio. "We're not going to interfere with the case if that's what you're worried about," he assured Baglio.

"Hey, this isn't even going to be our case. The U.S. Attorney is going to take it. We're just holding these guys because we busted them. Now we turn them over to the Feds."

Baglio had been making rings on the booth's table with the bottom of his beer glass. He stopped and wiped them away with a paper napkin. "Be realistic, Armand," he continued. "These guys aren't going to talk. They're not going to sit still and let you set up a camera and pop questions at them. Their lawyers wouldn't go for it even if one of them said he would talk."

"We've done it once in a while," Burton said. "I can think of a couple of stories."

"Look. Here's how it happens," Baglio said. "It works with me telling Mike Delgado that maybe if he gives some information and cooperates with me, I'll drop a good word with the boys on Lafayette Square."

Burton looked quizzically at Baglio.

"Lafayette Square. That's where the Federals are now. They built a new courthouse there."

"Oh. I didn't know that."

"Yeah. Couple of years ago. Anyhow, that's what happens. No cameras. No TV stuff. You stay out of it."

Burton shrugged and said, "If you think it will work, fine. I just want some information, something that all these young researchers we've got on the show wouldn't know how to find."

"So what is it that you want?"

Burton hunched over his glass. "The story I read said the wire operation was taking in half a million dollars a day. Is that right?"

"About half a million," Baglio answered. "Some days a little more."

"So not all of that had to be from little ladies in Biloxi who wanted to bet the daily double at the Fairgrounds. There had to be some heavy bettors in there, bettors with open credit."

"I'm sure there were," Baglio said.

"What I'd like is to get one of those big bettors to sit down for an interview. How much do they bet? How do they collect? What happens if they can't pay off? What's the bite on them? The whole set-up.

"I don't want some insurance guy or car salesman who's gambling every week because he's hooked. I want somebody who bets $10,000 or $50,000 on the Super Bowl and then comes back the next week and bets a bundle on the point spread on the Knicks or Lakers. In their own crazy way, they're all show-offs. Maybe one of them will talk."

"You want a name, right?"

"Yes," Burton said. "A big bettor. Maybe somebody who's into the mob for a lot of money and wants to talk."

"And you think he'll talk?"

"All we need is one. We'll put him in shadows and no one will know who he is. We can disguise his voice with filters, put a funny nose on him. You don't worry about that. He doesn't even have to be connected to your case. Just a heavy bettor."

"I'll see what I can do," Baglio said. He snuffed out his cigarette and signaled to the bartender who brought a check to the booth. "I've got to be going," Baglio said to Burton. "We've got a ceremony over at Headquarters. Cop of the month award. Can you believe it?"

"Public relations, Frank. It's the name of the game."

"So when are you going back to New York?" Baglio asked, reaching into his wallet and putting a five dollar bill on the table.

"Let me pay," Burton offered. "That's what expense accounts are for."

"Think about this, Armie," Baglio said laughingly. "Twenty-five years ago we used to argue about who would pay for the movie down at the Saenger on a Saturday afternoon. Now we're two grown guys arguing over a lousy bar bill."

The mention of the old movie palace on Canal Street stirred a memory in Burton, of a time when he and Baglio had been not only friends but equals. But now it was different.

He had been cajoling Baglio as if the policeman were just another source, one more person who could somehow help the weekly program. It didn't make any difference, really, that Baglio was an old friend. He was just another part of the mix.

A slight shudder went through Burton, so chilling he could almost feel it, and he grabbed Baglio's hand and said, "C'mon Frank. Let's go. You don't want to miss the ceremony do you?"

They waved good-bye to the bartender and stepped out onto the sidewalk and into the afternoon heat.

The barroom was in an old neighborhood. The sidewalks were cracked and the streets were rutted and pockmarked with potholes. Old, wood-framed cottages, called shotguns because they were long and narrow, crowded the streets, the dreary pattern broken only by an occasional grocery store, small drugstore, or laundry.

The Mississippi River was only a few blocks away and there was a coffee plant nearby, its aromatic smell permeating the area.

A beer truck rumbled down the street, its weight seeming to shake some of the homes on the street. Burton, who had been eyeing the decaying, sun-baked scene, waited until the noise of the truck drifted down the street.

"Why did you pick this place?" he asked.

Baglio said, "I used to live around here when I was just starting on the department. I had half of a double over on Coliseum Street. It was a great neighborhood then."

"It's changed," Burton said.

"What the fuck. What hasn't?"

"I'm going to walk over to St. Charles and take the streetcar back downtown."

"I can give you a ride," Baglio offered. "Take us ten minutes from here to get down to the Quarter."

"I've got some time," Burton said, "and it's out of your way. You'll miss the ceremony over at Headquarters."

Baglio said he could at least drive him over to the streetcar stop and Burton said that would be fine, he would like that, and he got into Baglio's car.

"It was great seeing you again, Frank," Burton said as they drove off. "Say hello at home for me."

"I will. And I'll call you as soon as I get something you can use."

"Have you got my number at the network?"

"Don't worry," Baglio assured him. "I'll find you."

Baglio steered the car onto St. Charles Avenue and pulled over to the curb to let Burton out. "There's a streetcar coming now," he said, glancing in his rearview mirror and seeing a streetcar a few blocks away.

"Thanks again, Frank," Burton said warmly.

Baglio leaned out of the car window. "Listen, Armand," he said. "If I come up to New York sometime, can you get me some tickets to some shows and introduce me around?"

"Sure. Whatever you want."

"Get on a quiz show? Take a tour?"

"I'll set it up."

"Okay, old buddy. See you around," Baglio said. He honked his car horn twice, waved good-bye and drove away.

Burton waited by the streetcar stop and idly watched a black maid, dressed in a starched white uniform, push a little white child in a swing in a playground across the street. A few minutes later, the streetcar came. Burton got on, paid the sixty cents fare, and rode it to the end of the line, Canal Street. Then he walked five blocks to his hotel.

When he got back to his hotel room, the red light on the phone indicated that a message was waiting for him. He called the message desk and was told that Carl Malachek wanted him to call.

Jesus, Burton thought, what the hell could he want?

He called Malachek's number in New York and heard Judy Rosen on the other end of the line. "Carl Malachek's office," she said briskly.

"It's Art Burton," he announced. "In New Orleans."

"Oh, I'm glad you called. He was trying to reach you."

"What's up? Something with the program?" He knew that she was privy to the secrets of Malachek's office and he wanted to be prepared in case some sort of a problem had come up with *Focus on America*. Why else would Malachek be calling him?

"I don't know what he wants," she answered. "He didn't tell me. Hang on."

He silently muttered "shit" to himself and waited for Malachek to pick up the phone in his office. He could picture Malachek sitting there, puffing one of those damn cigars, fiddling with the three monitors on the wall in front of him. It was almost six-thirty in New York—time for the first feed of the network newscasts—and Malachek would be getting ready to view them. All three at once.

"Art?" Malachek said in a friendly tone of voice.

"Yes? What's up?" he asked warily.

"Nothing of a crisis nature. I just wanted to know when you were going to be back in New York."

"I'm taking the late flight tonight."

"You'll be in the office tomorrow?"

"Yes. Of course. Is something happening?"

"No. Not at all. I wanted to talk to you about something and I needed an idea of when you were coming back."

"Well, like I said, tonight. Late."

"Fine. We'll get together tomorrow. Have a good flight."

Even before he could say "Thanks," Burton heard the click on the other end as Malachek hung up. What the hell is that all about, he thought. Malachek doesn't call just to be sociable. Not that hard ass. What does he want me for? Well, whatever it is, I'll find out tomorrow.

He looked out the window and saw again the wide curve of the Mississippi River as it arced through New Orleans, splitting the city in two. The river waters were still, as if they were aware of the oncoming evening and were preparing for the night.

He turned away from the window and his eye caught the bowl of fruit on the dresser, the red apples and green pears gleaming in the shafts of sun pouring through the windows. He walked over to the dresser and picked an apple from the bowl and bit it and thought about Frank Baglio.

He wondered if Baglio would be able to help him and provide him with a name. It would help make a damn good piece, one of those stories that people around the network would talk about. It also would help the program get some good press, maybe a couple of column mentions, a good review in *The Times* or *Variety*.

Things like that mattered. Every bit helped. You had to keep swimming.

Chapter 4

Jerry Rossman strode into the network board room, tossed a copy of *The New York Times* on the highly polished mahogany table, and looked around the room at the executives seated around the table.

"I don't know what happens," he said angrily. "Something happens to these goddamn programs once they leave the Coast. They must turn to shit over the Rockies. I don't get it."

The eight men and one woman in the room did not need to ask what he was talking about. Just like every other network executive who worked in New York, they read *The New York Times* every morning as an act of faith.

And, this morning, *The Times* had carried a bad review of *Buttons*, a program the network had premiered the previous night. The program was being tested as a possible series for the fall, when the new season would begin.

The review only confirmed what the overnight ratings from ten major cities already had signaled—the program was starting off as a loser.

"What did *The Times* call it?" Rossman asked. "A crummy little comedy or something like that?"

"So who reads *The Times*?" Barry Kovaks, the head of programming, asked. It was an old joke and Rossman told him so.

"Barry, never mind the old lines. How many more of these have we got?"

"We still have the pilot, the one you saw on the Coast, and four more episodes. We can spot them in the schedule when we want to fill a half hour or we can run them off from now until August."

Rossman walked over to a huge samovar and poured some coffee into a cup. He stood there for a minute, then walked back to the table and sat down.

Rossman's temper tantrums were legendary and Kovaks worried that Rossman was going to explode and start shouting and screaming about how the network couldn't afford to put on a loser like *Buttons*. A piece of shit. A dog.

He had brought the overnight ratings to Rossman as soon as they had come in from the Research Department. Rossman had been upset but not distraught. The figures showed the show had less than a marginal chance of attracting a steady or large audience.

That had been two hours ago but, since then, the pressure had had time to build.

Sales, advertising and promotion, affiliate relations; they all had had time to look at the ratings and, like family members gathering at the bedside of a dying relative, had prepared themselves for the inevitable.

Kovaks shifted slightly in his chair and eyed Rossman, who had taken off his glasses and was wiping them with a monogrammed handkerchief.

"You know," Rossman said quietly, "I thought this show had possibilities. Maybe it wasn't going to be in the top ten, pull a 26–27 share or something like that, but I thought it was a nice little program. Cute idea. Italian tailor. Jewish wife. Nice spin to it. All sorts of character development potential."

Kovaks glanced across the table at Barbara Schumacher, the head of advertising and promotion. He had heard that she already had been hanging crepe on the show, spreading the word that A and P couldn't save this one.

But now Rossman was indicating he still liked the program, despite its dismal prospects. Kovaks decided; it's nut-cutting time.

"So what do you think, Barbara?" he asked in a disingenuous tone. "Do you think a little extra promotion before next week's show might help?"

You prick, she thought, don't put this monkey on my back.

"I don't know," she answered him. "We'll have to see if
we can carve out some promo time from somewhere or cancel
some other spots. I'll take a look at the schedule when I get
back to my office."

Cute, real cute, Kovaks thought.

"Let's wait until the national ratings come in tomorrow,"
Brad Hoskins, the head of network sales suggested. "I agree
with Jerry. This show has a lot of potential. It's family
oriented. My kids liked it."

Jesus, Kovaks thought, this fucking show is going to wind
up as the greatest thing since *I Love Lucy* if this keeps up.
All these goddamn ass-kissers.

The flow of the meeting had Kovaks worried about how
he should play it.

After all, he had recommended *Buttons,* on the basis of
its plot outline and producing team, as one of the shows the
network should commit to for development. What had the
pilot cost—two, three hundred thousand? Whatever the hell
the number was, it had been his decision to buy.

But the same show that had looked so good in the
screening room in LA, the same show that Rossman had
bragged about when they flew back to New York on the
red-eye with the cassette in his attaché case, the same show
that Hoskins and his sales people had pitched to the reps and
the agencies, was not drawing an audience on the air.

So, go figure. The only problem was this: too many
wrong judgments and he would be back at some local station
in Seattle or Milwaukee or East Armpit haggling with syndicators
about reruns rights to *The Love Boat* and worrying about
which game show he would put in after the six o'clock news.

And there was just no way he could ever go back to
being a program director at a local station. No Fucking Way.

"I think," Rossman said, "we need to give this a little
more time. Maybe try it in a different time slot if it doesn't
pick up next week. Maybe we've slotted it wrong. Maybe it
should go on a Wednesday night, position it where we've got
a good upscale audience. Young urbans. That's where it's
going to pull its numbers."

Rossman trusted his instincts on this one. The audience
would build. Capaletti, the main character in the show, could
become a cult hero. That was the way these things happened.
They could slot Lou Ashman, who played Capaletti, into a

guest slot on *American Sunrise*, set up some press interviews around the country, try for a *TV Guide* cover. Maybe change the title from *Buttons* to *Capaletti*.

"Barry," Rossman snapped, "work closely with the producers on this one. See if they can build up the character of Capaletti more. Maybe make him studying for his citizenship papers or something. I don't know. We've got to take this little Italian guy and make him somebody the whole country will love. Even some poor schmuck in South Dakota who wouldn't know an Italian tailor from Chief Sitting Bull. You get the drift?"

Kovaks stroked his thick black beard that, along with a mop of curly hair, made him look like a Talmudic scholar.

"I'll be on the Coast this weekend. I'll set up a meeting," Kovaks assured him.

Rossman got up from the table again and walked over to the windows that opened up on a view of the skyscraper office buildings across the street.

All five and a half feet of him, from the English-made loafers to the styled haircut that made his close-cropped gray hair look as if it had been molded on to his head, seemed to be sagging under the weight of the network's problems. He looked older than his fifty years.

"We should have a good lineup in the fall," Rossman said, turning back to the people around the table. "We'll have more comedies than either of the others and comedy is where it's at this year. This country feels good about itself again. People want to relax, enjoy themselves. They don't want cop shows or action adventure. We are in tune with the mood of the country. We can sell on this. Some of the pretesting looks very strong. And the creative community is coming to us with good ideas. They know out there in Hollywood that we are willing to spend money on development."

Barry Kovaks shifted uneasily in his chair. He knew that the new fall schedule, which would be unveiled to the affiliates at their annual meeting in Los Angeles, looked good. But Rossman was running on faith. He was still the damn film salesman he was when he started out in the business twenty-five years ago, peddling the black and white comedies and westerns. But this was the 1980s, not the 1950s, and some of the new shows hadn't been tested yet. And what if they turned out like *Buttons*? Good on paper but needing help on the air?

One more bad season and Rossman might walk the plank. And he'd be right alongside him.

Rossman glanced at the small digital clocks that were imbedded in the front panels of three huge television sets on the wall opposite him. It was close to noon and he had a luncheon meeting with Jack O'Connor, the president of a major advertising agency, at twelve-thirty.

"If there's nothing else," he said, gathering up some papers in front of him, "we'll wrap it up. Thank you, everybody."

Carl Malachek got up from the table and walked over to Rossman as the others began to leave the room. "Can I see you for a minute?" he asked.

"Can it wait until after lunch? I'm going to be at the Four Seasons until about two."

"It would be better if we spent a few minutes now," Malachek said.

He had wanted to meet with Rossman before the meeting, to tell him about Cornwall before it somehow leaked, but Rossman had been unexpectedly delayed at a breakfast meeting at the Helmsley Palace Hotel and had had no free time.

"It's serious," he told Rossman.

"All right," Rossman said, looking worried. He walked with Malachek out of the boardroom and into his office, a few steps down the carpeted hallway.

Whatever Malachek's got, Rossman decided, it's going to be trouble. The only times Malachek ever came to his office were when the News Division was going to make waves. Breaking a scandal in Washington, or reporting something that would produce an expensive libel suit, or a ton of correspondence with a major advertiser. God, now what?

Rossman sat down behind a boomerang-shaped table that he used as a desk and gestured to Malachek to pull up a chair beside him.

A small tiger-maple cabinet, with a telephone console and three small television sets, was at Rossman's side. The tabletop was bare, except for an appointment book and some yellow legal pads and a silver mug containing perfectly sharpened pencils engraved with the network's initials.

On the wall behind him, there were two framed pictures. The larger one was an abstract painting, mainly bold slashes of blue and green against a field of soft yellow. The other picture was a blowup of an advertisement for the old television comedy, *My Friend Irma*.

The show had been, according to network legend, the first program Rossman had carried from station to station when he started in the business as a salesman for a film syndicator. The modern painting was there simply because, as Rossman had confessed once to someone, he liked the colors.

"I gather there's a problem, Carl," Rossman said.

Malachek nodded. "A big one," he said quietly. "Jack Cornwall is going to leave."

Rossman leaned forward in his chair. He could feel his feet beginning to tingle, as if they were squirming to get out of his shoes.

"You have got to be kidding," he said slowly. "You have got to be kidding," he repeated.

"I wish I was, Jerry."

"When did all of this happen?"

"Last night," Malachek lied. He did not want Rossman to know that he had known since lunch yesterday.

Rossman got up from the table and walked over to a window that took up most of one wall. It looked out over Fifth Avenue and, far below, he could see the massive jumble of yellow taxis, blue buses, and passenger cars inching along the Avenue. The contrast between the everyday quality of the scene below and the news Malachek had just given him jarred him back into the room.

"What did he say? I can't believe this!" Rossman said, distraught. He began to pace nervously back and forth by the window.

Malachek, who had remained seated, watched Rossman. Four steps to the left. Four steps to the right.

"He's tired. He says he wants out. It's as simple as that."

"Jesus, Carl!" Rossman exclaimed, suddenly wheeling around to Malachek, his voice rising in anger. "It's just not that simple. We are talking about a major, major talent. A star. I mean, with all due respect to your people, Cornwall is the glue that holds it together every night.

"He's been doing the show for what, five years now? And we're number one. And he's walking out?" He felt in his pocket to see if he had remembered to bring his blood pressure pills with him. Thank God, he had.

"We can't afford to lose the ratings on the news," he continued. "Are we supposed to go into the new fall season with a new anchor on the evening news?"

He stopped for a moment to ponder his own question. Then: "Jesus, we are going to get the living shit kicked out of us."

Malachek walked over to Rossman and stood by the window with him.

"It's in his contract, Jerry. There's a window. He can get out," Malachek said. He didn't want to remind Rossman that he, Rossman, had agreed to the window in the contract. He'd need that some other time.

"I don't care if there's a window," Rossman said angrily. "There must be a way to get him to reconsider. The affiliates are going to eat us alive."

"I'm going to have lunch with his agent tomorrow," Malachek said.

"Who? Blumberg? I've known Roger Blumberg for a long time. A good agent. Honorable. Knew him when he was just starting out at MCA. We've made a lot of deals over the years. I'll call him myself right after lunch."

"What about Cornwall?" Malachek said. "Do you want to see him today?"

Rossman paused for a minute. "I don't know," he said. "Maybe I'll set up a lunch with him tomorrow or later in the week. You know, so he won't think we've hit the panic button on this. If we are a little more relaxed, maybe he will be too."

Malachek looked at Rossman. He seemed to be calming down. "I think," Malachek said, "we ought to play every card we can."

"I can't believe it," Rossman said, beginning to pace back and forth in front of the window again. "What are we paying Jack now? Seven, eight hundred thousand?"

"Close to a million."

"And he's going to walk away from that!" Rossman said incredulously. "After all these years he's put in with us?"

Malachek was amused by Rossman's priorities but said nothing.

"Listen," Rossman said. "He's not having a problem, is he?" he asked, pointing toward his head.

"He's solid as a rock. He just wants to quit."

"Son of a bitch," Rossman muttered quietly.

"I know this is going to leak soon," Malachek said. "We're both going to get a lot of questions."

"I'll worry about that after lunch," Rossman said. "Not that I'll be able to eat lunch. Christ, I've got Jack O'Connor waiting for me now over at the Four Seasons.

"Let's face it," he said grimly. "We are not going to get good press on this no matter what kind of spin we put on it. The other nets will go to town on this. How many people know?"

"You. Me. Blumberg and Cornwall's wife."

"So who's going to talk? No one. We've got a little time. I'll get to Blumberg this afternoon. He's discreet."

"I think we ought to think a little bit about a replacement," Malachek said.

"Christ, Carl!" Rossman exploded. "You just gave me the news about Cornwall. Now you want to talk about who's going to replace him? Now? At this fucking minute?"

"I just want to throw a name at you," Malachek said. Even though Rossman would try to salvage the Cornwall situation, Malachek wanted to be ready when it failed. It was going to be a struggle with Rossman. He could tell already.

"All right," Rossman said irritably. "So give me the name. Who do you have in mind?"

"Art Burton. We could take him off *Focus* and put him on the evening news. He's a very strong reporter. Good-looking. It could work."

"Look," Rossman said, "I can't think right now. Maybe it's Art Burton. Maybe it's Michael Swanson. Maybe it's somebody we haven't thought of, somebody from another network. I don't know. Maybe we can turn Cornwall around."

At least, Malachek thought, he didn't bite my ass off.

"But I'll tell you this," Rossman said, walking over to a door that opened up to a small, private bathroom. "Whoever it is, we are going to test the shit out of him."

Rossman stepped into the bathroom, left the door open, turned on a faucet in the washbasin and began to splash cold water on his face. Malachek came over and stood by the door.

"He's got to be a newsman," Malachek said. It was a softly delivered warning.

"Ah, bullshit," Rossman said, burying his face in a hand

towel embroidered with the network's initials. He finished drying his face, then continued. "That's the trouble with you news guys. You think every anchor needs to be a journalist. You know what, Carl? The public doesn't give a shit about these guys' qualifications. Do you think they really care that Cornwall used to be at the White House or overseas? Nah, they believe in him. That's all that it is. They believe in him. You could put Paul Newman or somebody like that, some believable guy, on your news and you'd win. Every night."

"And what would you do when it came time for them to do a story?" Malachek asked sarcastically. "How much would they be believed in then?"

"So they wouldn't do stories. Is that such a tragedy? Look at Mark Antin on the morning show across the street. He couldn't carry Michael Swanson's jockstrap when it comes to reporting a story. But have you looked at the morning ratings today? He's killing us."

"Their morning show is an entertainment program. It's not hard news like ours," Malachek reminded him.

"Hard. Soft. All I know is that I'm having lunch with Jack O'Connor today because he wants to shift one of his big accounts over to Antin's show. He's buying ratings points. So don't give me this cockamamie stuff about everybody being a Pulitzer Prize winner before they can anchor the news. O'Connor doesn't give a shit if Antin doesn't know about Iran or whatever. And neither do I."

Rossman stepped out of the bathroom and walked to his office door.

"Listen," he said, putting his arm around Malachek's shoulders as he escorted him to the door. "We'll get the best possible person if we can't keep Cornwall. We're not going to piss away what we've built up in the evening."

Malachek wished he could feel encouraged by Rossman's pledge but he wasn't. He had a feeling that, if Paul Newman were available, Rossman would be signing him up for the morning and evening shows. It was going to be tough. Very tough.

They walked out of Rossman's office and waited for the elevator and then went down in the elevator together. Malachek got off on the seventh floor.

"We'll talk later," Rossman said as the elevator doors closed in front of him.

"Fine," Malachek said, not believing him.

Malachek walked down the Seven West corridor, lit a cigar and walked into the reception area of his office. Art Burton was waiting for him.

Now that he had spoken to Rossman, Malachek wondered how much he should confide in Burton. He decided it was better to take Burton into his confidence. He had to start building his strategy now, making sure there were no weak points that Rossman could attack.

"How are you, Art?" Malachek said pleasantly. "C'mon in."

Burton put down a copy of *Newsweek* he had been reading and followed Malachek into his office. He had been in the office a few times in the past few years and always felt uncomfortable in it. Malachek had a way of not putting you at ease.

"How was New Orleans?" Malachek asked. "One of my favorite cities."

"It was good," Burton replied. Ever since the phone call from Malachek at the hotel yesterday afternoon, he had been trying to figure out why Malachek wanted to see him. He hoped Malachek would get to it.

"You were working on a story, I understand. And giving a speech?"

"Yes. To the United Way campaign. The story is about the mob and illegal gambling. I was just picking up some information."

Malachek pulled on his chin. "Could be strong. Lots of sex appeal."

Burton's eyes fixed on a picture of Richard Nixon and Malachek in a tropical setting. Lots of palm trees. Must be Key Biscayne, he thought. His eyes came back to Malachek and he looked straight at him, as if to ask, "Why am I here?"

Malachek took a long puff on his cigar and blew smoke toward the ceiling.

"I want to ask you something, Art," he said, after watching the smoke trail off and disappear into the air-conditioning vent. "I want to know if you're interested in doing any more anchoring."

Burton felt his heart beginning to race a little faster. What was Malachek trying to tell him? Was he being replaced on *Focus*?

"What do you mean?" he asked in a tentative voice.

"I mean, what if, let's say, I asked you to fill in for Cornwall for a while. Do you think you could handle it?"

"I'm sure I could," Burton answered quickly, not even thinking about what the question meant. It was almost an automatic response, as if he were being asked if he could get on the next flight to Pittsburgh and cover a story.

"I'm talking about doing the show five nights a week," Malachek elaborated, "not just for a day or two."

The significance of what Malachek was saying was beginning to sink in on Burton. Malachek was talking about more than just occasionally substituting for Cornwall. But he never had done even that. What was happening?

"Are you talking about a couple of weeks? Is Cornwall going on vacation?"

Malachek's eyes swept over Burton, making one final inspection, one last check to confirm that his instincts about the man sitting across from him were right.

He liked Burton's demeanor. Not cocky, but confident. He liked that. It came from having come up the hard way, right from the beginning. He wondered if Burton ever had needed money as a kid. He would bet that he had.

He decided to go the whole route and tell Burton everything.

"I'm going to tell you something in absolute confidence, Art," he said. "John Cornwall is leaving. Only a few people, two or three at the most, know this. It just happened within the last day or two.

"I'm considering you as the replacement but I want that to stay right here in this office, between the two of us for the time being. Is that understood?"

Jesus, Burton thought. Cornwall's leaving and he's considering me to replace him! Unbelievable!

For an instant he thought about his conversation with Frank Baglio in the barroom. He had told Baglio he'd like to anchor the morning or evening news someday but that had been only a wistful thought, a daydream. But now, just like that, Malachek was talking to him about succeeding Cornwall and becoming one of the top three men in television news. He was stunned.

"Are you thinking about a try-out period?" Burton asked,

still uncertain about Malachek's plans. "I mean, are there others you are considering as well?"

"No," Malachek answered firmly. "I trust myself on this. Besides, you can't run an on-the-air contest for this job. You have to go with your own judgment."

Burton's mind was racing, trying to absorb everything that Malachek was telling him. He wondered about the other anchors, Swanson and McVea. Why hadn't Malachek picked one of them? And why had he been chosen? Not that he didn't think he couldn't do it. But why him?

He decided not to ask. It was better not to question, even for a moment, Malachek's instincts.

"I don't know what to say," he admitted. "I had no idea about any of this."

"There are a lot of loose ends to be tied up," Malachek said, "but I wanted to talk to you about this now, rather than later. I assumed you would not be adverse to the idea but I just wanted to make sure."

"No, of course not," Burton said quickly. "I just wasn't prepared for any of this. Cornwall, me, any of it."

"Do you think you can do it?" Malachek asked, seeking Burton's final ratification of his own judgment.

"Yes," Burton answered confidently. "I know it's different than anchoring *Focus* but I can do it. I'm not worried about that."

"It's more than just anchoring a different type of program," Malachek advised him. "You anchor the evening news and you're the front man for the whole News Division, the whole network, in a sense. You are our living symbol. You won't be a reporter anymore or even an anchorman. You'll be something beyond that—a celebrity, almost a demigod to some people. You won't be able to go anywhere, do anything, without having people recognize you. Can you handle all of that?"

"I've had a little of that from *Focus*," Burton said. "I can handle it."

"It's a hell of a responsibility, Art," Malachek cautioned him. "You have to be in the spotlight wherever you go. Your life will be different, I assure you."

A tiny smile crossed Burton's face. "That wouldn't bother me either," he said. He knew that, other than his relationship with Samantha, his life was as flat as one of the bayous in south Louisiana where his father had taken him duck hunting as a child.

There had been nothing then but water and swamp grass and an endless sky. That was the way his life was now, a series of news events, stories that, in the end, left him empty. He wanted his life to be different.

Malachek noticed the enigmatic smile on Burton's face and was puzzled by it.

"Is there anything we need to worry about?" he asked. "Are you clean?"

"What do you mean?" Burton responded, uncertain what Malachek meant.

"You know, anything that could be a problem. Drugs. Boyfriends. Anything like that."

Burton didn't stop to even consider the question. "No, nothing," he replied. The response was a reflex, conditioned over the years. There was no need to tell Malachek anything.

"Good," Malachek said, relieved. "Tell me, do you have an agent? I can't remember."

"No," Burton answered. "I negotiated my last contract myself. Just me and Tom Hickson."

"It's better that way," Malachek said. "Agents are the parasites of this business. I never thought I'd see the day when reporters had agents, did you?"

"No, never," Burton answered quickly. Malachek's antipathy to agents was well known and he wondered now what he would do if he actually became Cornwall's successor. A contract for anchoring the evening news would require an agent, he was sure.

"All of this is speculative, of course," Malachek said, reaching for the scuffed baseball that rested on a tiny stand on his desk. He tossed the ball back and forth in his hands and said, "I still have to get Jerry Rossman to sign off on this. I can't anoint you for something like the evening news without the network's approval. I'm sure you understand."

"Yes, of course," Burton answered, his eyes fixed on the faded red stitching on the baseball. When was the first time he had seen it in Malachek's office? Eight years ago? Had it been that long?

"Do you know Rossman, other than to say hello to?" Malachek asked.

"I've seen him in the elevators a few times and at receptions, things like that."

"He'll be okay," Malachek said, as if he were trying to reassure himself. Burton wondered what Malachek meant but he said nothing.

Malachek rose from his chair to indicate that the meeting was over. He extended his hand to Burton. "I'll keep you advised, Art. But hold all of this in confidence. I'll let you know when you can say something."

"Have you any idea when?" Burton asked, hoping that he didn't sound too eager.

"I don't know," Malachek said. "As I said, I need to discuss this with Rossman and, assuming he doesn't throw any curveballs, there will have to be a lot of coordination. You know, Cornwall's resignation will have to be announced and your appointment and then a promo campaign, everything. It will take a little time but it's just too early to think about all of it."

"It's hard for me not to think about it," Burton confessed.

Malachek liked Burton's honesty. He's going to be all right, Malachek thought. He was sure of it.

"I'll let you know when it's all final," Malachek advised Burton again.

"I appreciate your confidence in me," Burton said, shaking Malachek's hand. "I guess I'll still in a state of shock."

"Don't worry about it," Malachek said, walking Burton to the door.

At that moment, Burton wanted to run down the seven flights of stairs to the lobby, get in a cab and get away from the network building.

The knowledge that he might replace Cornwall—even that Cornwall was leaving—was overwhelming and he was afraid that if he saw someone, anyone, he might not be able to disguise the fact that his mind was locked into the idea of anchoring the evening news.

"Listen to this," he was afraid he might blurt out. "Cornwall is leaving and Malachek wants me to replace him." Christ, what a bombshell!

It was going to be hard to keep it to himself and, even though he had told Malachek he would keep it confidential, he needed to tell Samantha. He could hold it for a day or two, he decided, but he wanted her to know. There was no way he could not share the news with her. It was bursting within him.

It wasn't until he was almost out of the office that he realized he never had asked Malachek why Cornwall was leaving. He didn't feel good about that but it was too late now. He would ask the next time.

"I'll keep you advised," Malachek repeated and he closed the door and went back to his desk. He picked up the baseball again and rubbed it in his hands as if he were polishing it.

". . . And Gabby Hartnett inspects the ball before throwing it back to Big Bill Lee on the mound . . ."

He pulled himself back from the sudden reverie he had slipped into—a sunlit day in the bleachers at Wrigley Field when he'd been a kid and there had been no anchors, no problems, no television, and his only worry had been spending a dime on a hot dog.

He thought about his conversation with Burton. It had gone well, he decided. Burton had been genuinely taken aback by the idea of anchoring the evening show but that was just the reaction he should have had.

Burton wasn't a prima donna, he was a newsman. That was obviously how he regarded himself, as a journalist, not like some of the others who came into this business with the sole idea of making a million dollars a year, or even a quarter of a million, and didn't care about the news.

Hell, no. Burton could still cover a three-car accident on a state highway if he had to. He was all right.

Malachek was still thinking about Burton and the evening news when his private phone line rang. He picked up the receiver and said, "Yes?"

"Hello, Carl. It's Charlotte Glover." The voice was that of the network's chief White House correspondent.

"Charlotte. Nice to hear from you."

"I hope you don't mind my calling on your private line," she said. "I didn't want to go through the switchboard."

Malachek began to tap nervously on the floor with his left foot. She was onto something. He could tell.

"Go ahead, Charlotte. I'm listening."

"I think I'd better come up to New York, Carl," she said. "I just wanted to make sure you are going to be there."

"When do you want to come up?"

"I'll take the three o'clock shuttle."

Malachek glanced at his watch. It was not yet one o'clock. Christ, he thought, it must be big. She was a tough old bird who didn't go in for dramatics.

"Big stuff?" he asked cautiously.

"Very, very"

"Big names involved?"

"Oh, yes."

"Like who?"

There was a slight pause. Then she said, "Just for openers, the President of the United States."

Chapter 5

It was late in the afternoon when Detective Frank Baglio left Police Headquarters at Tulane and Broad.

The humidity was in the nineties and there had been a report by the Weather Bureau of a tropical depression in the Gulf. It was still way out there, four hundred miles southwest of Morgan City, but Baglio knew that these things had a way of growing bigger and developing into hurricanes.

It was just like police work. You started out with something small; a tip, a remark overheard on the street, a badass walking along the street trying not to be noticed, and pretty soon you had a full-fledged ugly case on your hands.

He didn't like tropical depressions. They could become ugly.

He wondered if he should stop off at the Winn-Dixie in his neighborhood on the way home and stock up on batteries, candles, and bottled water, but he decided it could wait.

It had been a dull day for him. Most of it had been spent sitting on a rear bench in the courtroom of Criminal Court Judge Frank Bartelme while the judge heard arguments for a delay in a prostitution case. Baglio had made the arrests and would be one of the witnesses for the DA's office.

I could have gotten a law degree for the time I've spent sitting in courtrooms, he told himself as he walked across the street to the Orleans Parish Prison.

It was not yet five o'clock in the afternoon and he knew the shifts of the sheriffs who ran the prison would not yet have changed.

He went to the office of Floyd Gauthier, a deputy criminal sheriff he had known ever since he had been on the force and found him sitting there, listening to WWL radio and reading the final edition of *The Times-Picayune* newspaper.

There was no air-conditioning in the office and the window was open. The fumes of the buses on Tulane Avenue and the noise of the trucks rumbling over the Broad Street overpass poured through the window, adding to the seedy, stifling atmosphere of the tiny office.

"How are you, Floyd?" Baglio asked in a voice loud enough to be heard over the volume of the radio and the noise of the trucks outside. "What's happening?"

The other man put down the paper, switched off the radio and looked up at Baglio, obviously pleased to see him.

"Hey, Frankie! What brings you over here? Things dull at Headquarters?"

"Usual shit. Little of this, little of that. Listen, do you remember the gambling bust we made last week?" Baglio said, taking a chair across from Gauthier. "Guy named Mike Delgado and a couple of others. The U.S. Commissioner set high bail so they're all sitting here."

"Yeah, sure. What about 'em?"

"I need Delgado. I gotta take him down to the U.S. Attorney."

"Got some papers?"

"They just called," Baglio said, hoping that the deputy wouldn't press him too hard. "Something must be breaking. I'll have him back in an hour."

"You gonna sign him out?"

"Sure." Baglio paused for a minute and then he said, "I'm a little short on the squad so I'll have to take him down myself. I could use a wagon if you've got one."

Gauthier looked quizzically at Baglio for a moment. "I'll have to call the garage." He picked up the phone, dialed three numbers and said, "This is Sheriff Gauthier. I need a patrol wagon to transport a prisoner. Have it ready in ten minutes."

He put down the phone and wiped his forehead and said, "Friggin' air-conditioning has been out all day. They'll have a wagon for you. Anything else?"

"Nothing. Just Delgado. Cuffs on the hands and feet. I don't want to take any chances."

"Sure," Gauthier nodded. He reached into a desk drawer and pulled out a form with the heading, Temporary Transfer of Prisoner. He pushed it across the desk to Baglio, told him to sign it on the line marked, Authorizing Officer, and put it back in his desk.

"Thanks for cutting through the red tape," Baglio said. "It's just too late and too hot to go through all the bullshit."

"No problem, Frankie," Gauthier assured him. "I'll have Delgado brought around to the Broad Street entrance. You can pick him up there."

Ten minutes later, as promised, Mike Delgado was standing by the entrance to the prison garage, a short, obese man, sweating in the sun. Lou Costello in a uniform; gray denim, with O.P.P.—for Orleans Parish Prison—stenciled on the back of the shirt. His hands and feet were handcuffed and he was guarded by a huge, ebony-colored deputy sheriff whose face was shielded from the sun by a broad-brimmed trooper's hat.

Sweat was pouring from Delgado's face as Baglio drove out of the garage in a patrol wagon and climbed out of the driver's seat.

Delgado recognized him and said, "Baglio" as if he couldn't stomach the very sound of the name. "What the fuck is this all about?" He shuffled his feet uneasily.

"Hey, Mike," Baglio answered. "Don't get your balls in an uproar. We're just going downtown."

"Like for what?"

"Like the U.S. Attorney wants a few words with you," Baglio said. He motioned to the back of the van, unlocked the back doors to allow them to swing apart, and gestured to Delgado to climb into the rear of the wagon.

A thick metal grille separated the back section of the van from the driver's seat. There was a metal bench running along each side of the van but no rear windows. It was, in effect, a cage in which a prisoner could see, through a closely spaced grating, the driver's seat.

"You want a cigarette, Mike?" Baglio asked.

Delgado moved his arms to wipe the sweat away from his face.

"Yeah, sure," he answered, suspiciously.

Baglio pulled a Marlboro from a pack in his shirt pocket, stuck it in Delgado's lips, and lit it for him. He gestured again to the back of the van and said, "Make yourself comfortable."

Delgado glanced at the black man standing guard by his side and eyed the deeply polished nightstick hanging from his belt. "He coming with us?" he asked.

He had been around too long not to know what went on sometimes.

"No," Baglio answered. "Just you and me. Go on. Get in."

Delgado slowly placed one foot in front of the other until he reached the steps leading to the rear of the van. "I can't make it up the steps," he said.

Baglio gestured to the deputy who half-lifted Delgado, as if he were a keg of beer, and pushed him into the rear of the vehicle. Delgado slid along the metal bench until he was next to the grating that divided the rear of the van from the driver's section.

Baglio locked the rear door of the wagon, thumped on it twice as if he were a magician demonstrating its escape-proof character, and got into the front seat and drove out of the prison.

After a few minutes, Delgado peered through the metal bars and looking through the windshield, recognized the streets they were passing by. South White, South Gayoso, Jefferson Davis Parkway. He realized they were driving uptown, toward the Carrollton section, away from the business district.

"Hey, Baglio," he said anxiously through the grating. "I thought we were going to the U.S. Attorney."

"Little detour, Mike," Baglio answered casually.

What was he up to, Delgado wondered nervously.

The patrol wagon turned left on Carrollton past a small shopping center with a Winn-Dixie, Shoetown, Baskin-Robbins, and a Chinese take-out and then continued along Carrollton.

The avenue had a residential character to it now, old clapboard or stucco houses with wide porches and front steps, lawns bordered with azalea or magnolia bushes, huge oak and sycamore trees shading the avenue.

Delgado glanced again through the grating, past Baglio's head and saw, on the left, the sprawling grounds of Notre Dame Seminary.

"Your old neighborhood, Mike," Baglio said. They were crossing Carrollton and Apple Street and had just passed the house where Baglio had busted Delgado's wire room operation.

"Cut the shit, Baglio," Delgado said, trying to hide the nervousness in his voice. "I don't need no goddamn tour."

"I just want to refresh your memory," Burton said over his shoulder. "I've got some questions for you."

Delgado slouched back and leaned against the side of the van. There was no way, he figured, that Baglio would pull anything on him. As long as that jig with the nightstick wasn't in the wagon, what could happen?

Baglio steered the car off Carrollton and turned right onto Oak Street, still heading away from New Orleans, toward Jefferson Parish, the sprawling suburban area that surrounded the city of New Orleans. Soon they were on the highway that once had been known as the River Road because it shadowed the twists and turns of the Mississippi River between New Orleans and Baton Rouge.

From his seat, Delgado could see the occasional funnel of a freighter in the river. He was worried but said nothing.

The sun was beginning to settle into the river and it blazed in a bright orange color, beating down on the metal roof of the van. Baglio had the window open on his side but little of the air seeped through the metal grating to the rear of the wagon.

Delgado, who weighed about two hundred eighty pounds, was sweating heavily and, because of the jarring motion of the van as it passed over some of the broken patches of highway, he was beginning to feel a bit nauseous.

"Hey, Baglio," he said through the grating. "What I do to you, huh? I mean what the hell is this? I gotta fuckin' lawyer, you know."

"Who? Your cousin in the Legislature?" Baglio said sharply.

"C'mon," Delgado said. He couldn't believe that this was what Baglio was up to. "That was a couple of years ago."

"You tossed that girl around like she was a string of beads

in the Rex parade, Delgado. Man, you beat the shit out of her."

"A cunt," Delgado said.

"I knew her daddy," Baglio said quietly.

Jesus, Delgado thought. He shifted his huge frame down the metal bench so that he was a little further away from the grating. He suddenly was afraid that Baglio would push his fist through the grating, even though the bars were so closely spaced nothing could squeeze between them.

His shirt was drenched with sweat now and, with his hands cuffed, the sweat was collecting on his wrists and falling on to his pants. His mouth felt dry, as if he wanted to vomit, and he rolled his tongue over his lips to catch some of the sweat rolling down the fat folds of his face.

His eye caught the time on a huge electric clock outside a drive-in bank. 5:28. They had been driving for almost half an hour now and Baglio still hadn't made a move. Through the window, he could see the huge frame of the Huey P. Long Bridge spanning the Mississippi River and he wondered how much further Baglio would drive. Where the hell were they going?

A few minutes later, Baglio made a left turn off the highway and drove through a weed-strewn section of warehouses and loading docks. Up ahead, Delgado saw some old railroad tracks of the Kansas City Southern Railroad.

Suddenly, Delgado felt the van accelerating rapidly and then the vehicle bounced at a high speed over the railroad tracks.

Delgado had not expected the sudden jolt as the van hit the tracks and the impact tossed him off the bench and onto the floor of the vehicle. His head hit the side of the van. Sprawled on the floor like a huge, inflated balloon, he tried to struggle to his feet but the handcuffs on his hands and feet made it difficult for him to achieve any sense of balance.

His head was throbbing where it had hit against the side of the van and he could feel a trickle of blood running down the side of his face.

He felt the van slow down and turn around. Then it was accelerating again and he braced himself, as best he could, for the huge bounce he knew would come next.

The wagon hit the tracks and he slid along the floor of the van. This time his head hit the rear door. He was bleeding heavily now and he knew that he was helpless, that he could not even get to his feet.

"You motherfucker," he gasped at Baglio as the car slowed down and turned around again. He waited in fear for the acceleration to begin but Baglio seemed to be idling the car, taunting him. Then, with a sudden burst, Baglio gunned the car again and raced toward the tracks. Delgado clenched his eyes in fear and tried to cover his head with his arms. But it was no use.

The huge thump as the car crossed the tracks raised him from the floor and he careened, like a billiard ball, across the metal floor. The impact seared his testicles as he bounced on the floor and his head cracked into the side of the wagon, the blow made worse by the cuffs on his hands cutting into his face.

Blood was pouring from his face and he was gasping for breath, afraid that he was having a heart attack.

Baglio stopped the car and turned around to look through the grating at Delgado. He was lying near the rear of the van, a fat, crumpled blob with blood streaming down his face.

"Too bad about these brakes, Mike," he said. "They can't handle these railroad tracks."

"What do you want, for Chrisake?" Delgado gasped.

"I want some information. A name," Baglio answered.

"What kind of a name?" He tried to shift position, to get where he could at least see Baglio, but it hurt too much. So he lay on his back and stared at the ceiling of the wagon.

"A player. A customer. One of your big ones."

The fucker's going to blackmail someone, Delgado thought. But he didn't care. He lay silent for a minute, breathing heavily.

"I want a name, Mike," Baglio repeated softly. "Somebody with a big tab."

There was no answer from Delgado and Baglio turned the ignition on and let the motor purr quietly.

"How you gonna get away with this?" Delgado gasped from the floor. "The Feds will fry your ass."

"Get smart," Baglio said grimly to the rearview mirror. "I can't help it if we hit some bad potholes. The sun blinded me. I'm going to take you to the Charity or the prison infirmary. Get you sewed up. Show me where I laid a hand on you."

Delgado tried to wipe some blood away with his arm. He muttered "fucker" again under his breath and tried to spread his legs, as if that would somehow ease the pain in his groin.

Baglio stepped ever so slightly on the accelerator and the car began to roll forward.

"All right, Baglio, all right," Delgado half-shouted in terror. He caught his breath for a minute. Then he said, "I swear to Christ it's true. I mean on my mother's grave."

Baglio did not turn the ignition off but let the motor slowly idle.

"There's a woman in Las Vegas. Jew. Weinstein. That's the name, Weinstein."

"You're shitting me, Mike," Baglio said and he touched the accelerator again.

"No, no, it's true," Delgado pleaded. "Lopez Drive in Vegas. Big house. On a circle. I made a payoff myself once. A hundred thousand."

"A hundred thousand!" Baglio repeated.

"Yeah," Delgado answered. It was painful for him to talk but he had to get it out, to give Baglio whatever the hell he needed.

"She must be loaded," Delgado continued. "The guys I work for tell me not to worry if she runs it up. She's got an open tab."

"How does it work?" Baglio asked, still talking to the rearview mirror.

"Code," Delgado answered. "I'll get a call. Some guy will call and say Mrs. W wants ten on the Lakers. Or Mrs. W wants fifty on the over-under with the Rams. Always the West Coast teams. Big bucks. Once there was a big win, I was sent out to deliver the payoff. Keep her happy, I guess."

"Did you see her?"

"No. Like I said, I only made one delivery myself. Fuckin' maid took it at the door. Like I was a goddamn Federal Express or something."

"She still betting?"

"Yeah. Only she owes seven hundred fifty big ones."

Baglio was incredulous. "Three-quarters of a million?" he exclaimed.

"Yeah." Then: "But I swear to Holy Christ it's true. I swear to you Baglio."

"I believe you, Mike," Baglio said quietly and he slowly

moved the van forward and drove away from the deserted area toward the Airline Highway, one of the main highways leading into the city.

Delgado lay gasping on the floor, crumbled like a broken sack of grain.

Most of the traffic was heading out of the city now and anybody driving along the highway toward the Jefferson Parish suburbs, Metairie, Kenner, Bridge City, would not have particularly noticed the prison wagon heading slowly back toward New Orleans.

Half an hour later, Baglio had Mike Delgado in the prison infirmary where a doctor sewed eight stitches in his face. There was no trace of any force on the prisoner's face and Baglio, almost solicitous, complained to the young intern about the shitty condition of New Orleans's streets. "All these goddamn potholes," he said. Delgado said nothing.

When he got back to his office, Baglio called a number in New York City.

He waited for five rings and then a voice on an answering machine said, "This is Art Burton. I'm not in now but leave your name and number when the tone comes on and I'll get back to you."

Baglio waited for the tone and then said, "Hey there Armie. I got a name for you. Call me."

Chapter 6

Samantha Stuart stepped out of the shower, removed the shower cap from her head, reached for a towel and peered into the mirror over the washbasin.

The mirror was still fogged from the shower's steam and she rubbed it with the palm of her hand in order to provide a clear space where she could see part of her face. She did not like what the jagged space in the mirror revealed. There was a small blemish, the beginning of a pimple, on the left side of her cheek.

She pulled on her skin with her hand in order to isolate the spot where she had detected the first reddish pink traces of the pimple.

It could, of course, be covered by makeup and the camera would not show it. But it was there—a speck of a reminder that no matter how much she thought of herself as the equal of the men she worked with every day, she would always be burdened by the extra requirement television news placed on its women. You always had to be attractive.

Got a pimple? Cover it. Overweight? Lose a few pounds. Hair not right? Get it styled.

There were male correspondents all over the network who worked by different standards. Gap-toothed, balding, sandpaper skin, one of them even had a glass eye, for God's sake, but it didn't seem to matter.

When it came to her, however, it did matter.

Even Carl Malachek had told her once that she looked better when she wore her hair long. That had been when she had been named a correspondent on *Focus on America*.

So she had worn her hair long and the blond tresses falling over her shoulders somehow made her look like a movie star. She wore it that way until one day, soon after she had aired a powerful, twelve-minute piece on coal miners' lung disease, she was riding in the elevator with Sammy Vollman, the executive producer of *American Sunrise*.

"Did you ever see *Out of Nowhere?*" he asked her.

"No. What's that?" she asked.

"Great movie. 1947 or '48 with Lizabeth Scott. It was on the late show last night. You look just like her."

Not a word about the piece, about the work she had done. The long days doing interviews in the grimy hollows of West Virginia with coal miners and their families. The confrontation with the coal mine owners who threatened to shoot her and her crew if they came on the property. The hours and days in the editing room. None of that. Just a remark about how she looked like some movie actress from the 1940s. Je-sus!

She never wore her hair that long again. But it really didn't make any difference. She knew she was judged by a different set of rules. The Golden Girl. That was what they called her. Behind her back, of course. But she knew.

Nobody really cared that she had paid her dues, that she had spent seven years out there in the affiliates, starting out in California at a station so small she had to help the cameraman lug the recording equipment around whenever they went out on assignment.

Nobody really knew that she had made a decision, back in high school in Newton, Massachusetts, that she would carve out her own life and not settle into the mold that seemed to have been precast for her.

It all would have been so easy. Her father was a professor of Greek History at Harvard. She'd been raised in a household where a plaster bust of Agamemnon rested on a pedestal next to the umbrella stand in the hallway and a quotation from the "Funeral Oration of Pericles" was embroidered into a sampler that hung on the living room wall, and there had been no doubt that she would go to Harvard, breeze through the Classics, and go on to graduate school.

Her older sister, Helen, had followed that pattern and now was comfortably settled with a husband, two children, and three published books, thirty miles away as an associate professor of Ancient History at Wellesley.

But Samantha had wanted another life, a life away from the floor-to-ceiling bookcases that lined the walls of her father's study, away from the faculty wives' teas that her mother always was attending, away from the group of former students who came back to the house every year at Commencement to have dinner with her father.

She went as far away as she could—UCLA—and she majored in Modern American Literature. She worked as a volunteer for George McGovern, marched in anti-Vietnam protests, wrote poetry for the college literary magazine, collected rejection slips from magazines to whom she submitted articles, had a feature story on campus politics printed in the California Life section of the *Los Angeles Times*, and went to the UCLA-USC football games at the Coliseum.

("It's the only Coliseum I'm interested in these days," she told her sister in a letter once.)

For four years she reveled in the California lifestyle—the ocean, the beaches, the mountains, the desert, the endless

stream of cars on the freeways. Most of all, she enjoyed being
on her own, as an individual, and not just the daughter of
Professor Keyes Stuart and the younger sister of Associate
Professor Helen Stuart.

Ever since that time, she had not stopped being her own
person.

She moved closer now to the mirror again, squinting as if
she were peering through a microscope. There were no
crow's feet around her gray-green eyes. Her eyes had a soft,
luminous quality that one critic had described as hypnotic.

She frowned at the thought. No critic ever reviewed
John Cornwall's eyes when he was a reporter, dammit.

She switched on the tiny portable radio on the shelf over
the washbasin and moved the dial around until she found an
all-news station she could listen to while she dried herself off.

Moving the towel slowly along her body, she relaxed in
the touch of the soft sleek velour against her skin. The feel of
it was deliciously sensual and she knew as soon as she began
to draw the towel slowly between her thighs that she wanted
Art Burton to make love to her tonight.

She flirted with the idea of staying naked, letting him
open the door to the apartment and discover her with nothing on. There would be some traces of perfume on her body,
something strong and musky, and she would tell him: lick it
off.

She let herself slip deeper into the fantasy, imagining his
tongue darting snakelike over her body while she rubbed his
cock until it was throbbing and surging into her.

An urgent voice on the radio brought her out of it.

"This late story," the announcer said ominously. "There's
been an explosion in a grain silo near Pittsburg, Kansas. First
reports say as many as twenty-two people are trapped inside."

She switched off the radio and, wrapping the towel
around her, walked quickly into her bedroom and picked up
the phone by her bed.

She dialed the network assignment desk and, when a
young voice on the other end casually said, "News," she
asked, "Who's this?"

"Jack Thompson." It was a name she did not recognize.

"This is Samantha Stuart," she said impatiently. "Are you
one of the desk assistants?"

The voice on the other end took on a more deferential tone. "Yes, can I help you?"

"Give me one of the assignment editors, please."

There was a pause and then she heard "This is Bob Portello, Samantha. What do you need?"

"I was just listening to the radio," she said, "and there's been an bad grain explosion out in Kansas. Lots of people trapped. I worked out there for a few years and grain silo explosions can be terrible. I figured in case somebody wasn't reading the wires, you'd want to know about it right away."

"Thanks, Samantha. Appreciate the tip. I'll check the AP now."

"Okay. Good night," she said and hung up the phone.

She knew what they'd be saying downtown. Bob Portello, that lush, he'd be saying, guess who just called in. The Golden Girl. Lois Lane herself. Little Miss Vera Videotape. Still playing newsperson.

Well, fuck 'em all.

She had paid her dues, just like the rest of them.

In 1975, during her senior year in college, Samantha Stuart decided she wanted to work in television. It sounded interesting and exciting, and she didn't want to go into marketing or advertising or public relations, which was where her degree would probably get her an entry-level job.

She knew little about how the television industry worked, but she wrote up a résumé mentioning her work on the literary magazine and the article she had written for the LA *Times*. She mailed the résumé, along with a color photograph of herself, to the news directors at twenty-five small television stations around the country. The accompanying letter read:

Dear News Director,

I am 22 years old and will be graduating UCLA, cum laude, this June with a BA degree in American Literature. I have taken a few journalism courses and have written for campus publications as well as the *Los Angeles Times*.

I am interested in pursuing a career in television news and I am writing to inquire if you have

any openings for beginners eager to learn and work
hard. I will be happy to come for an interview.
Sincerely,
Samantha Stuart

Fifteen news directors never answered her. Nine sent
her form letters rejecting her application. There was only one
positive response. It was from the news director of a television station in Salinas, California.

"We don't pay very much—$155 a week—" he
wrote, "but we are looking to build up our staff and
I would be happy to interview you for one of our
openings. You appear to be attractive enough to be a
reporter someday."

She was offended by the idea that her physical appearance, even in a photograph, was regarded as her primary
qualification for being a television reporter. But she drove up
to Salinas for the interview and, after meeting the news
director, decided that she would take the job he offered her
even if it meant putting up with his chauvinist remarks.
"I always thought girls who majored in American Lit
went into advertising," he said.
How about boys who majored in American Lit, she
wanted to ask. Instead, she shuddered inside, said nothing
and, three weeks after graduation, started her job.
She was bright and eager and didn't mind working long
hours. She covered fires, murders, Chamber of Commerce
luncheons, ribbon-cutting ceremonies by the Mayor, and
court hearings.
She had been at the station for two years when she got a
phone call from the news director of a station in Wichita,
Kansas. He had been on vacation in California, had seen her
work, and wanted to know if she was interested in moving on
to a larger market, up the ladder. She said yes very quickly.
She covered the same kind of stories in Wichita as she had
in Salinas but the station was bigger, the city was bigger, the
weather was colder, and there was one other major difference.
His name was Tom Jacklin and he was twenty-nine and
he was the leading reporter in the newsroom.

"What did you do in Salinas?" he asked her on the first day she came to the newsroom.

"I was a general assignment reporter," she answered. She was struck by his good looks; a leathery, outdoors look that made her wonder if he spent all of his free time on a farm or a ranch. She hoped he didn't.

"Well, we're all faster than speeding bullets here. Let me know if I can help you."

"How long have you been here?" she asked, not wanting this first meeting to end so quickly.

"Five years. It's a good place to work. You'll like it here."

"Is there anyplace where I can go sailing?"

"You're kidding," he said, laughing. "This is Kansas. I hate to tell you this but no matter what ocean you're thinking of, it's a couple of thousand miles away."

"I was thinking of a lake," she said hastily. "A big lake."

"No such luck," he said. Then: "Are you a sailor?"

"Oh yes. Ever since I was a kid."

"Where was that?"

"I grew up outside of Boston but my family has a summer home in Gloucester, on Cape Ann, the opposite side of Cape Cod. That's where I learned to sail."

"Must have been nice," he observed.

"And you?"

"I'm from here. I went to KU. A real landlubber. A homegrown jayhawker."

Jayhawker. She had no idea what a jayhawk looked like but she liked the sound of it. She pictured a huge bird, soaring gracefully through the sky, hovering over her, protecting her.

Months later, when she was lying in his arms one night, she ran her fingers along the bridge of his nose and asked, "Do you have a jayhawk's nose?"

"Where did you come up with that?" he asked.

"I was thinking of the first time I met you," she answered.

"A jayhawk has a long beak," he said. "I don't."

"It's cute," she said.

It was the first time she had fallen in love. There had been a few romances at UCLA but Tom Jacklin was the first man she ever thought about wanting to marry.

She loved him and she loved her job and, eighteen months later, when she was offered a job at a station in Los

Angeles, she thought about turning it down. But the chance
to work in the second largest market in the country was too
tempting to turn down.

"I have to take it," she told him.

He had picked her up at the airport after she flew back
from the job interview in Los Angeles. They had driven out
into the country, out on the interstate until they came to a
state highway that divided huge plantings of wheat.

The tassels of wheat, golden brown in the sun, hung
limply, drained by the searing sun. Driving along the two-
lane highway, bordered on both sides by the motionless fields
of grain, she tried to imagine what it would be like to drive a
huge combine through the wheat and have it harvested and
shipped somewhere. Was that what was happening to her?
Was she coming to harvest again, just like she had after those
first two years in Salinas?

"You don't have to accept the job, you know," Tom said,
taking one hand from the steering wheel and using it to
stroke the back of her head.

"An offer like this . . ." she said. Her voice trailed off as if
she suddenly were immersed in her own thoughts.

"It will happen again," he counseled her. "They'll come
after you again."

"I don't know," she said. "It's so damn flattering, to be
called out of the blue like that, and asked to come to Los
Angeles. I never dreamed I would work there someday. You
should see the newsroom there, Tom. It makes ours look like
a hole in the wall."

"I'm sure," he said flatly.

"I want it, Tom," she said softly, almost to herself. "I'll
never be able to live with myself if I let it go by."

"I want it," she repeated.

He still was stroking the back of her hair but the
tenderness seemed to have left his fingers. The stroking had
become an automatic motion, a nervous gesture, and she
wanted him to stop it but she was afraid he would be hurt if
she told him.

"Maybe we should turn back," she said. "I'd like to
unpack and get out of these clothes."

"All right," he answered and he steered the car off to the
side of the road and backed up onto the edge of the wheat
field in order to cross over to the other lane of the highway.

Looking toward the field on the opposite side of the road, they could see a scarecrow sticking out from the wheat.

"That's one thing you'll never have to worry about, Samantha," he said, pointing to the black-clad stick figure.

"Being a scarecrow?" she said quizzically.

"Looking like one. You will always be beautiful."

"Thank you," she said softly, and he never saw the tears forming in her eyes.

Salinas, Wichita, and then Los Angeles. Seven years and three different cities of covering City Council meetings, murders, fires, teacher strikes, and community protests before Malachek hired her as a correspondent.

Change the names of the cities and it could have been the same story for more than half of the network's correspondents.

All those years out there counted but they didn't count as much as one singular fact about her. She was beautiful.

"You know what people, men, see when they look at you on the program?" Art Burton had said to her once. "They don't see a reporter, telling them a story. They're thinking, 'I'd like to hop into bed with her.'"

Art Burton, the only man she had ever deeply cared about, had told her that.

It was almost nine o'clock in the evening now and her bedroom lamp was on but it did not illuminate the whole bedroom. She was standing in a pool of darkness and, from it, she could see out her windows to the high-rise apartment houses that lined her street on the Upper East Side.

She stood there in the middle of the room, droplets of water still clinging to her like evening dew on a flower, and she thought: I am trapped by my own looks.

It was something she had felt before, ever since that first news director had answered her letter asking for a job.

"You appear to be attractive enough to be a reporter someday," he had written. She still had the letter.

It depressed her that she always would be thought of as an attractive female reporter, not as a reporter who was female and attractive. It was the difference between her and Art Burton. The difference between being a correspondent and an anchor. Someday she would turn it all around.

The digital clock on her dressing table read 8:58. She

hoped Burton would be on time. She wanted him tonight. Badly.

It was five minutes later when he arrived and by then she had pulled on a pair of peach-colored slacks and a light green silk blouse. She'd decided not to wear a bra. She liked the way her breasts felt against the cool fabric.

"How was your trip?" she asked, kissing him lightly on the cheek as she opened her apartment door for him.

"It was all right. Better now," he said, smiling at her. He returned the kiss, but instead pressed his lips to hers.

They walked into the living room and sat down on a long, low, white sofa that faced a 25-inch television set. On a glass-topped coffee table in front of the sofa sat a bottle of white wine and two glasses. Samantha had put them there earlier that evening, when he had called to say he would be coming over.

Scattered around the room, as if they were child's toys, were some of the artifacts of her career as a correspondent for *Focus on America*. A saddle from Amman, Jordan, where she had done a piece on the little King; a bright red and gold Indian blanket she had bought in Arizona while doing a story on American Indians; a beautifully carved, antique footstool from a country store near Natchez, Mississippi. And, on the mantel above the fake fireplace, resting in a silver frame from Tiffany's was an autographed picture of her and Nancy Reagan.

"So what was it like way down yonder?" she said, tucking her legs under her.

"I saw an old friend I've known since high school," he said. "Somebody who might be able to help on that gambling story. Who knows? Maybe he'll come up with something."

"When is that slotted for? Three weeks from now?"

"Whenever we can do it. I'll speak to Durgin tomorrow," he said, meaning the executive producer of *Focus on America*.

"What about you?" he asked, pouring some wine into the glasses in front of them. "What have you been doing?"

Samantha reached for a glass and clicked it against his. "I'm still doing some editing in the tape rooms on that video music piece. I haven't even started to write it."

"What else is happening?"

"Nothing. No rumors, no gossip," she said, tossing her hair back to get it out of her face.

Burton took a sip of his wine. The excitement he had felt ever since his conversation a few days ago with Malachek was still within him and now, with Samantha sitting next to him, looking serene and beautiful, he wanted to share the incredible news with her. Share everything.

But he was caught between his desire to let her know and his pledge to Malachek to keep it quiet.

"What's the matter?" she asked, struck by his silence.

"I was just thinking," he said quietly.

"About what?"

He shrugged his shoulders. "Nothing in particular. Nothing for you to worry your pretty little head over." He reached over and patted her on the head.

"God, Art, I hate it when you pat me on the head," she said, recoiling ever so slightly from him. "It's so damn condescending."

"Don't give me the feminist lecture, Samantha," he said with a laugh. "I meant it as a tender gesture."

"I know you did," she said, smiling at him. "But don't make me feel like a little household pet. I'm thirty-two years old. I like it better when you treat me as me."

"I will treat you very tenderly," he said, spacing the words out, and he leaned over and kissed her with his tongue in her mouth and then he kissed her on her neck, by her ear.

"I like that," she said softly in his ear.

"What else do you like?" he asked. He could feel himself getting hard. He was surprised that it was happening so fast to him.

"I like everything you do," she answered.

He turned off the lamp on the end table by the couch. The room was dark, but they were able to see each other in the occasional splashes of light from the apartments across the street. Otherwise, it was a room of private darkness.

She let out a small sigh as he put his hand on her leg and began to move it slowly up and down, caressing her thigh. Then he rose from the couch and pulled her to him, drawing her closer. He felt an intense passion for her, wanted to plunge inside her and keep thrusting, filling her until she begged him to stop.

"Jesus," he said, "I want you so bad."

"And I want you too," she answered quickly. Her body was beginning to quiver and she could feel his erection pushing against her. She wanted everything to happen fast, to get it out of his pants and into her so that the feeling inside her, the need, could be satisfied.

"You drive me crazy. Do you know that?" he said as he began to unbutton the top of her blouse.

"I want to," she said, and put her hand over the bulge in his pants. "Do you know how much I want you?"

"Not half as bad as I want you," he half-whispered and now he had her blouse off and he was kissing her nipples, softly and sensuously, and he could feel them hardening in his mouth.

She tossed her head back and reveled in the ecstasy of his tongue licking her breasts. "Kiss me lower," she pleaded. She locked her hands behind his neck and pulled his head down to her crotch.

He tugged her slacks down and then her panties, and pressed his lips against the soft hair of her mound, slowly kissing her. Trembling, she spread her legs farther apart and he fell to his knees and began to tease her clitoris with his tongue.

She felt herself getting wet and she urgently whispered to him, "Take your pants off."

Her hands were still behind his neck, pushing his face and mouth against her crotch, but now she released him and moved her hands to his shorts as his pants fell to the floor.

"I love you," she said and she urged him up, away from where his tongue and lips had been caressing her, and she bent down and kissed his cock on the tip.

"Oh, God," he moaned. He shuddered and pulled her up next to him and said, as if it were a desperate order, "Now!"

They both fell to the rug on the floor and he mounted her. She was moaning "Oh God, you're wonderful," and the throbbing in his cock told him that he couldn't hold it any longer. "I'm coming into you" he said. Then he began thrusting inside her in a steady rhythmic pushing that became so intense he was afraid he was going to hurt her.

They reached climax together, both sighing in exhaustion, and for the next few minutes they lay quietly in each other's arms.

"That was wonderful," he finally said.

"Yes," she responded, running her hands over his back. "I wanted it to happen tonight."

"So did I," he answered. "Especially tonight."

"Why especially?" she asked, moving from underneath him as he began to withdraw from her.

He knew, at that moment, that he wanted to share with her what he knew about his future as much as, only a few minutes ago, he had wanted to share his body with her.

"Tell me why," she said, but it was a request, not a demand.

"In a minute," he said. He went into the bathroom and cleaned himself off, and when he came back, he waited until she was finished in the bathroom.

In her bedroom they pulled back the covers and lay down together in the bed. He pulled her over to him so that she was lying in his arms, nestled against his shoulder.

"I will tell you," he said, "but you must keep it to yourself. Really to yourself. It's a bombshell."

"I will," she said, perplexed.

"Malachek called me in. Cornwall is leaving and he wants me to take over the show."

"Permanently?" she asked excitedly.

"Yes. Full-time. Anchor of the evening news. That's what he's talking about."

"That's fantastic!" she exclaimed. "What did he say? How did it happen?"

She rolled over in bed and propped her chin in her hands and faced him. "Tell me everything," she said. "Cornwall. What's happening with him?"

"He's quitting. I didn't ask Malachek any of the details but the bottom line is he's leaving."

"And you will be the anchor?"

"That's what Malachek wants. I still can't believe it. It's too good to be true.

"It blows my mind," he continued, as if he were talking to himself. "Eight years ago I was still a reporter in New Orleans and now I'm up for the biggest job there is. You can't go any higher."

"It's wonderful!" she said. "It's sensational!"

"Malachek's backing me," he said. "I would have thought they would have taken Swanson off *Sunrise* and put him on at night."

"And it's really going to happen?" she asked, unable to contain her excitement.

He did not answer immediately. Ever since his conversation with Malachek, he realized now, he had been thinking about the anchor job only in terms of getting it.

After all, Malachek himself had said Art was his choice. He had not even considered that it might not come true.

"I don't know what I would do if it doesn't happen," he confessed. "I just haven't thought about it that way.

"It's funny, in a way. When I was at WBID, toward the end, I wanted to come to the network as a correspondent because I wanted to move up in my career. You know, just like everybody else. But I never really aimed this high.

"And now, all of a sudden, I'm near the very top and maybe I don't want to think about not getting there."

"You will, darling," she reassured him.

"The problem," he said, unable to let go of the doubt that had arisen in his mind, "is that up until a few days ago, I never wanted it that bad. I mean when I first started out I just wanted to be a reporter. You know, go out and do stories. And sometimes when I think about it, those years in New Orleans were the best of all. Doing stories every night. Big fish in a little pond, the whole thing.

"But you get up to the network and then you get to do a show like *Focus* and then one day the president of the News Division says he wants you to be the anchor of the evening news and you forget that you never really hungered for it. It's as if you don't have a past. Nothing ever happened up until this moment."

"I don't know," she said, recalling the day Malachek had called her in Los Angeles and offered her a job as a correspondent with the network in New York. "I remember everything, from the day I drove up to Salinas to the moment you walked in the door tonight."

"And do you remember when we first met?"

"Of course, I do," she answered. "Like it was yesterday."

"Yesterday minus about four years. And did you ever dream that someday I'd be telling you that I would become the next anchorman of the evening news?"

"No. Did you?"

He was silent for a moment and then he said, "I suppose

I dreamed about in once in a while, being the next Cornwall. Doesn't everyone?"

"I suppose so," she admitted.

She rolled over again and kissed him on the chest. "I think this deserves a special night, don't you think?" she said.

"I'm all keyed up now," he admitted, "about the Cornwall thing. I don't think I can do it again."

He was disappointed in himself. The desire to make love to her again was still within him but it had been submerged by his excitement about anchoring the news.

She moved her hand to his cock and began to stroke it until it got hard. "Sure you can," she assured him. "Just relax."

To his surprise, she was right. It was even better the second time, slower and less frantic, and when it was over he leaned back in bed and said, "You know that I'm in love with you, don't you?"

"I know," she said quietly.

"I just wanted to make sure you knew," he said. Then: "And you?"

"It seems since forever. But only recently. But it's there."

The realization that she was in love with him had been a slow process for her, a peeling away of layers of wonder and self-doubt until she had discovered the truth deep within herself: his love was important to her, as important as her career. She hoped she never would have to make a choice.

"It's there," she repeated.

"I'm glad," he said, and he kissed her hair.

Samantha's apartment was on the twenty-second floor and no noise reached it from the street far below. It was strangely quiet and Burton lay there, staring at the ceiling, listening to her quiet breathing.

The intensity of their lovemaking had surprised him. They had made love many times before but never with the suddenness and passion of tonight.

They had known each other for four years, ever since she had come to the network from California, but they had been seeing each other, quietly and discreetly, for only the past two years.

In a business where everybody talked, nobody knew about them.

But, from the beginning of their relationship, there had been an understanding that marriage would not be discussed.

There just wasn't enough room in their lives for that. There was too much travel, too many programs, too many demands on their time, too many pressures to handle.

"There's nothing permanent about our lives," he had told her once. "We never have time to plant roots, to stick to anything." Then, as if in desperation, he had confessed, "I don't even know who I could invite to our wedding if we had one."

"That's a terrible thing to say," she admonished him, uncertain what he meant.

He sensed her uncertainty. "I mean I don't have that many close friends," he explained. "Do you?"

"I'm close to my sister," she said. "And I still keep in touch regularly with my roommate from UCLA. Maybe a few others, here in New York."

That had been eighteen months ago, when they had spent a day sailing on her Crosby Cat in the waters off of Gloucester.

Now, lying next to her in the darkness, he wondered what would happen to their relationship if he got Cornwall's job. Would there be more permanence to his life, because he would be in the studio five nights a week, or would the pressure of the top job slowly force them apart?

He knew only that he was in love with her, and he did not know what he could do about it.

He turned away from that realization and said to the ceiling, "Malachek said a funny thing to me the other day."

"What?"

"He wanted to know if I was clean. That was his word— clean. If there was anything he needed to know about me."

"What for?"

"Image, I suppose. You know, you have to be perfect, faultless, pure. Over eight million homes get the news from you every night and you've got to be Mr. Believable. They all put all their trust in you.

"It's so ludicrous. I mean, I could be a child molester or have a huge cocaine habit but as long as nobody knew, as long as my personal side was completely unknown, nobody would care. I'd just keep on giving the news every night, the voice of truth and authority. Mr. Believable."

"And what did you tell him?" Samantha asked.

There was a slight pause and then he said, "I told him there was nothing."

She propped herself up on one arm and leaned over and kissed him. He could feel the softness of her hair on his face. "So go to sleep for a little while," she said, soothingly.

"All right," he answered, and he closed his eyes. But he quickly opened them again and stared at the ceiling.

There had been something, once. A long time ago. But that was buried in the secret, locked, innermost recesses of his mind, lost in the tall grass in a field in Vietnam. He had been a kid then, only twenty-two. And he had saved one of them, the black guy, Eddie Johnston. Won a damn medal for it. But what about the other one? Nineteen years had gone by and he still couldn't erase it from his mind. He had told himself a thousand times: How could anyone know? It was over. Long ago. But it was still within him, a sharp, aching fragment of memory imbedded in him as surely as if it were a piece of shrapnel from those mortars.

He rolled over and finally fell asleep.

He woke up three hours later and got dressed quietly in order to let Samantha sleep. It was almost one o'clock in the morning. He wrote her a quick note: "See you in the office. I miss you already. Love, Art."

Twenty minutes and a $5.40 cab ride later, he was back in his own apartment across Central Park on the West Side. He walked into his bedroom, turned on the light and switched on the answering machine.

Despite the tinny sound of the machine's playback, he recognized Frank Baglio's voice immediately.

"Hey there, Armie, I got a name for you. Call me."

The message delighted him and he got undressed and turned off the light and tried to sleep.

But it was no use. The old memory was coming back to him and he knew that if he did fall asleep he would be haunted by the smell and the sounds of the tall grass and the anguished body in the green field in the jungle.

And he knew that when he awoke, his body would be drenched with sweat and he would be trembling and terrified.

Look at me, he thought. Mr. Believable.

Chapter 7

Vietnam 1966. The infantry squad left the base camp at dawn, just as the first hints of sun lit up the far edges of the mountain ranges in the distance.

The squad moved slowly through the forward perimeter, the soldiers' steady pace punctuated only by occasional words of recognition to the other soldiers crouched in the area. Then they were gone, swallowed up by the rain forest.

This was his first combat mission, a reconnaissance patrol ordered by battalion headquarters to search for Viet Cong guerrillas. Five miles out and five miles back.

Nothing had prepared him for this. After an hour, sweat was seeping through every part of his clothing and dripping from his helmet, searing the jagged scratches made on his face by the mass of bamboo shoots, vines, elephant grass, and undergrowth that formed a tangled barricade along the crude trail.

Walking through the jungle, he remembered the words he had read less than two months ago in an OCS manual at Fort Benning, Georgia. "The jungle can be your friend as well as your enemy." Bullshit, he thought, all bullshit.

He knew that the terrain maps with all the hills flat and the land dry and all the topography in perfect shades of brown, green, light green, and blue could give only a one-dimensional picture. But now that he was here, in this rotting, dank wetness, he could not believe how bad it really was.

He tried to remember what it was that reminded him of something, some long forgotten piece of his life, back home in New Orleans. Then he realized that it was the smell in the air. The air had the same humid, rancid odor he had smelled once before, a long time ago.

A hurricane had come up from the Gulf of Mexico, rolling up over the bayous and marshes, carrying a huge surge of seawater that caused the water levels in the land below New Orleans to rise, sending the cottonmouths and the nutrias and the other swamp creatures to the higher ground and blowing away shacks and fishing camps and homes in the coastal areas near the Gulf.

In New Orleans, there had been darkening skies and bursts of rain and then, as the edges of the hurricane approached the city from the south, from the Gulf, there had been an eerie stillness and a strange, putrid smell as if every sewer in the city had suddenly overflowed and emptied into the streets.

It was, he learned later, the smell of the brackish water being pushed up through the land and carrying with it the smell of the land itself. That was what it smelled like now. Humid. Rancid.

He waited until the squad's radio operator, a tall, black man named Eddie Johnston, walked up almost behind him.

"The stink," he said over his shoulder. "Is it always this way?"

"Paddies," Johnston said. "Paddies stink like this. Bad shit."

Overhead, the sun burned the sky but, because of the thick blanket of foliage, little of the sun's light could pierce the jungle roof. An occasional shaft of sunlight broke through, dappling the land so that the earthen floor looked like a canvas flecked with yellow. In this strange closed world where everything, the tall stands of trees, the leaves, the sawgrass, the vines, the bush, seemed to be at once living and dying, the squad walked quietly, each man keeping five paces from the other.

He knew little about the other men in the squad. He had come to Baker Company only twelve days before, fresh from the States, and had volunteered to lead a recon squad on patrol. This was the squad he had been given.

Just from listening to the men talk, he knew that he was the only college graduate among them. Not that it mattered. Several were from the South, he knew, but that was all. They were all strangers.

Of the other men in the squad, four were Negroes, and, as he pushed through the jungle, he laughed to himself at the irony of it all. There had been no Negroes at LSU. None. All of his life, until he entered the Army, had been lived in the white world of New Orleans. Now here he was, a million miles from nowhere, walking through a goddamn jungle, and there were four Negroes with him. Screw it.

Peering ahead through the brush, he saw a bright patch of sunlight and then, as the squad moved another twenty yards forward, there was a huge field of scrub and waist-high grass. They were at the edge of it, still protected by the jungle, but for the first time since the patrol started, there was a clear field of vision.

"What the fuck is this, Lieutenant Bertrand?" a ferret-faced white youth named Ducoin half-whispered to him.

"There must have been crops here once," he answered. He figured the area to be the size of a football field and, at the far end, where he placed imaginary goal posts, there was a low ridge and then the jungle resumed. He signaled the squad to come closer and said, "We're going to cross this. Don't bunch up. Keep your ass down."

"Fuck," he heard one of the soldiers mutter.

"Move it out," he said. He noticed that a muscle was involuntarily beginning to twitch in his arm and he wanted it to stop.

He had gone less than thirty yards when he heard the hiss of the mortar and then the shattering noise of the explosion. At the same time, he felt the bullet tear through his shoulder.

"Oh Christ, Christ," he screamed as if the rapid fire of the words could somehow protect him. He was down on the earth now, hugging the land, and he was surprised at how scared he was. He felt the blood oozing through his uniform and he realized that he had urinated. Got to live, he thought, got to live. He clutched the ground, listening to the *pop-pop-pop* of the snipers' AK-70s splatter the dirt, and he wondered if the mortar fire would resume.

A few yards away, he saw the mangled body of one of the black soldiers, a man whose name he did not even know. His automatic machine gun was sprawled on the ground beside him. Then he heard the moaning of another man and he recognized the voice of Johnston, the radio operator.

"Oh sweet Lord, my fuckin' leg," Johnston cried out.

"Johnston," he said urgently. "How bad are you hurt? Can you use the radio?"

"I can get the radio," Johnston said. "Where the fuck are they?"

"On the ridge. I'm coming to you."

There was another burst of fire from the distance but it was over his head and he prayed that the low-lying scrub and the wild grass would cover him. When the firing stopped, he could hear the crackle of Johnston's radio and the voice of the radioman calling in the coordinates for a helicopter. Please God, he thought, come and get us.

He managed to raise himself to a half-crouch and then crawled toward the area where Johnston's voice was coming from. He saw him lying on the ground and his first thought was of a huge, wounded black bear. He crept up next to him and said, "Can you make it at all?"

Blood was flowing from a gaping wound in the man's leg. He cut a piece of his pants leg off with a knife and fastened a crude tourniquet over the wound. He was surprised at the quickness of his action and then he realized that the bullet in his shoulder must not have hit a bone. The pain was not too intense although he felt weak from a loss of blood.

"Chopper's coming," Johnston said in a pained voice. Then: "They all dead, Lieutenant?"

"I can't tell," he answered quickly. "Happened so fast."

He wanted to yell out to see if anybody else was alive but he was afraid to raise his voice in the stillness of the field. Instead, he motioned to Johnston to lie quietly and, for an instant, he held his breath, hoping to pick up some sound from the clearing.

Over the rapid thumping of his heart and the throbbing in his shoulder, he heard an almost inaudible cry of pain from a distance.

"*Aargh.*" It sounded in weak gasps and it rippled through the grass as if the sound itself had legs and was crawling.

"Someone's alive!" he exclaimed, unable to hide the mixture of elation and panic in his voice.

"Ducoin!" Johnston said. "I know that fucker's sound. He made it."

Oh my God, Burton thought, where the fuck is he? He raised himself to a kneeling position and peered through the reeds but saw nothing. Where the fuck is he??

A moment later, he heard the moaning sound again. It was what he imagined a dying dog would sound like.

"Jesus!" he shuddered. "He's out there!" he half-shouted to Johnston.

"Ducoin!" Johnston repeated. "It's him!"

Burton was still on one knee and now he began to part the grass, hoping that it would provide him a clue as to where the other wounded soldier was lying. They all had been walking within sight of each other when the mortar attack began. Ducoin, wherever he was, could not be too far away.

"Ducoin!" he called out, trying to hide the panic in his voice and hoping that his voice would not carry to the horizon. "It's the Lieutenant. Do you hear me?"

There was a strangled noise about ten feet away. He thought he could make out the word "here."

He began to crawl slowly through the grass in the direction the sound was coming from. Then he saw Ducoin, sprawled on his side, his arm dangling loosely from his side as if it were a marionette's arm, blood oozing from the gaping hole in his arm socket.

Ducoin's eyes were staring at him and he instantly felt that the soldier had recognized him, even though he was gravely wounded. He inched forward and he thought: he won't live.

A mortar round exploded twenty yards away and the ground shook. He inched forward and looked again at Ducoin and realized that the vacant stare in the soldier's eyes was a desperate, silent plea for help.

The bloody, macabre scene of Ducoin lying there, one arm hanging by a shred of bone, froze him. Then, as if he had suddenly come upon a venomous reptile ready to strike, he lurched backward in fear.

I can't do it, he told himself, I can't do it.

He heard a low whir and he looked behind him in the direction of the noise and he saw the tops of the trees in the jungle begin to weave and sway. The grass in the field began to ripple wildly and, in another few minutes, an enormous olive green helicopter was hovering over the edge of the jungle where it bordered the open field.

He continued to edge slowly backward, still staring at the spot, now hidden by the grass, where Ducoin was lying.

His mind kept pounding with the thought: I couldn't do it. I couldn't do it.

He reached Johnston, placed his arm under Johnston's shoulder and slowly dragged him to the edge of the field where a canvas sling had been lowered from the door of the helicopter.

There was too much noise from the chopper's rotor to say anything to Johnston so he rolled him, as if he were a wrapped-up carpet, into the sling and then, with a pumping motion, signaled to the corpsman standing in the door of the helicopter to raise the sling.

He watched as the sling moved through the air toward the chopper and then he looked again in the direction where he had seen Ducoin. He could see nothing except waving grass.

A few minutes later the sling was being lowered again and he hesitated for an instant, as if in that fraction of time Ducoin would rise from the ground like Lazarus and come to the chopper. But there was nothing.

Suddenly he saw dirt kick up in the field and he knew that the sniper fire had started again.

He felt himself starting to tremble and he knew that it was not from the wound but from fear.

The sling was on the ground now and he crawled into it, lying on his side so as not to further increase the pain in his shoulder.

He waved with his hand to signal that he was ready to be hoisted and then he was going up, over the top of the grass into the clear light and he prayed silently, "Make it, make it, make it!"

Then he felt someone lifting him into a stretcher and he knew that he was in the chopper and safe.

"There's another one," he mumbled softly. "Down there. Another one."

But it was too noisy inside the helicopter for anyone to hear him and so he waited for the medic who was treating Johnston's leg to come to him.

A few minutes later, he pushed himself up with one arm and peered out the window. He felt sick and he tried not to think about what had happened down there and how he had crawled away.

They were flying over marshes, and, for a moment, he

had a fleeting memory of a time when he and his father had gone duck hunting in the bayous near Port Sulphur. He remembered the strange, lonely sound of the duck call, the eerie *hawnk-hawnk* echoing over the water and the loud crack the shotgun made when it fired.

He stared, transfixed, through the window of the helicopter, oblivious to the others on the plane.

He no longer was a twenty-two-year-old in Vietnam. Instead, he was searching intensely in the paddies and the marshes and canals for a small boy, clad in a red and black mackinaw, sitting with his father in a duck blind, looking for the sun to come up over the Gulf of Mexico and waiting for its warmth to comfort his trembling body.

Chapter 8

The first thing Art Burton did when he arrived at the *Focus on America* offices in the morning was to place a call to Frank Baglio's home in New Orleans.

It was nine-thirty in the morning—eight-thirty in New Orleans—and he knew that Baglio still would be home. It was an easy drive from Baglio's house in Gentilly to Police Headquarters and Baglio would not have to leave his home for another half hour or so.

Baglio was probably in the kitchen, Burton thought, pouring Tabasco sauce over scrambled eggs and drinking chicory coffee. It was a pleasant thought and, for a moment, he wished that he could be there.

He had been to Frank Baglio's house only once, years ago, and, as he waited for the number to connect, he remembered a white plaster flamingo in Baglio's front yard and wondered if it was still there.

The flamingo was a tacky piece of outdoor decoration, something you would find in the back aisles of a statuary supermarket, if there were such a place.

He had teased Baglio about it at the time, saying, "There must be a hell of a flamingo salesman around here, Frankie."

And Baglio had replied, "We like it. It makes us happy."

Maybe Frankie had the right attitude. It didn't take much to make Frankie happy and that was something that people in the News Division, always wondering about the next move, would never be able to grasp.

It wasn't that easy to be happy at the network.

Baglio's wife, Louise, answered the phone and said, "Yes, Frankie was still at home," and "How are you, Armie darling," and "Nice talking to you, honey," and "You-all wait just a minute while I go get him."

Burton marveled at the natural endearment of her language. Walk into any restaurant or store in New Orleans and the saleswoman or waitress would call you darling. And mean it. It was different down there.

"Hey Armie, you got my message?" Baglio asked as he came on the phone.

"Got it late last night. That was fast work."

"What the hell. If you can't help an old buddy."

"So what were you able to come up with?"

"Like I said, I got a name for you. Weird. But a heavy player."

"Was it easy? I mean did you have to make any promises?" Burton asked anxiously. He was worried that Baglio might have tossed around the name of *Focus on America* too loosely and had guaranteed some money or air time to whomever he had gotten the information from.

"It didn't take much at all," Baglio said and he went on to tell Burton about the Jewish woman named Weinstein out in Vegas. He did not tell him how he got the name, only that he had checked it out through a friend in the phone company and it was legitimate.

"You really came through, Frankie," Burton said appreciatively. "I can't thank you enough."

"Just think about the free tickets for me and Louise when we come up there," Baglio reminded him.

"Anything you want," Burton assured him. "Stay well. I'll call you later in the week if I turn up anything," he said, and hung up.

Frankie had come up with good information, he reflected.

It was a beginning, something he could work on, something that might have a big payoff.

He wrote on a piece of paper the name Baglio had given him and put it in a desk drawer. Then he turned to the morning papers—*The Times*, the *Daily News*, *The Washington Post*—and scanned the television sections to see if there were any items about John Cornwall leaving the evening news.

The Times television page was mainly devoted to a lengthy article on the future of public television. The *News* and *The Washington Post* carried the usual assortment of industry gossip items. There was nothing about Cornwall in any of the papers.

It was hard to believe but Cornwall's decision apparently was being held very tight. Malachek knew, of course, and, he figured, Malachek must have told Jerry Rossman. But who else knew? And when would it start to leak?

Burton knew that gossip was the main currency of the News Division. It was traded everywhere: in the hallways, the production offices, the editing rooms, the bureaus, the bathrooms, everywhere. Tell an assignment editor in Los Angeles that there was going to be a new associate producer on the evening news in New York and the word would spread to Chicago, London, Atlanta, Rome, Houston, in a few hours. It didn't even have to be true. But it was on the grapevine, the A-wire, and so you never could be sure.

Two years ago, when Samantha had been named one of the correspondents on *Focus*, he had heard about it in the cafeteria two days before George Durgin, the executive producer of the program, had announced it to the staff. That was the way things happened.

What do you hear? That was the unofficial motto of the News Division and it had nothing to do with news.

So pervasive and unrelenting was the flow of gossip, that Burton wondered for an instant if he had made a mistake in telling Samantha about the Cornwall situation.

He knew that she would not purposely tell anyone. There was no question of that.

But even last night, in the silence of his own apartment, when he had lain awake replaying their lovemaking in his mind, the thought had occurred to him that she could be having lunch with someone, or talking to a columnist on the phone, or speaking with someone in another division of the network, and somehow it would slip out.

The thought still bothered him but was overwhelmed by the memory of her. God, she was wonderful. Her moans, the thrust of her body, taking him deeper, higher. It all came back to him and he felt an erection bulging in his pants. Christ, it wasn't even ten o'clock in the morning!

He walked across the hall to Samantha's office to see if she was in.

In contrast to the cluttered chaos of his own office, Samantha's office was neat and orderly, as if a maid came in every morning and cleaned it.

Pots of flowers—geraniums, petunias, marigolds—caught the sunlight on a windowsill behind her desk. A cork bulletin board, decorated with plastic yellow and white daisies, was filled with thumbtacked notes about upcoming appointments or stories or people to call.

A large poster from the Museum of Modern Art filled most of one wall. Copies of the morning papers—the same ones that Burton received—were spread across her sofa and, over the sofa, there was a photograph of a small sailboat. It was the sailboat, he knew, on which she had first learned to sail.

Samantha was seated behind her desk and was wearing a brown tweed jacket and a flowing beige blouse and a single strand of pearls. It was obvious to Art she was not planning to go out on a story.

"That's a nice outfit," he said, smiling at her. "What's the occasion?"

"I'm having lunch with Barbara, my roommate from UCLA. She's in town for a few days and I'm taking her to a luncheon at the Waldorf."

"A luncheon?"

"It's a Women in Broadcasting kind of thing. They asked me to be on the panel but I've done a lot of those recently. I just felt like sitting in the audience for a change."

"How long is Barbara going to be here?"

"Till the end of the week. Why?"

"Well, I've heard a lot about her and I'd like to meet her. You know," he added teasingly, "to find out what you really were like ten years ago."

"I've already told you," she said, laughing. "You know all

about me from the day I first learned about the naval victories at Phormio in the Peloponnesian Wars."

"Jesus!" he exclaimed. "Every time you drop your classical background on me, I am astonished. How do you remember all of that?"

"You would too," she said. "Every year at Commencement, a group of my father's former students came back to our house and refought, on the dining room table, the battles of Sparta and Corinth, all of them, complete with little ships and toy soldiers. You don't forget things like that.

"I remember one year, when I was about fourteen or fifteen years old, I had a big collection of photographs of the Beatles spread out on the dining room table and they all got swooped up in order to have the table cleared. It took me weeks to find all of them. It was a yearly ritual, year after year."

"I'm impressed," he said. "I don't carry any intellectual baggage like that. The only war I really know is Vietnam."

The moment he said it, he regretted it.

He loved Samantha but he did not want her ever to know about what had happened in Vietnam.

So he had kept the incident in the clearing secret from her, even though there had been chances, like last night in bed, to tell her. There just was no need for her, or anyone, to ever know about Bobby Ducoin lying in the field.

But he had shared everything else with her; his first exposure to television at the station in Baton Rouge, his life in New Orleans, the day when Malachek interviewed him for a job, his dreams and, now, his chance for the Cornwall job.

In fact, he could not imagine their relationship, other than their actually being married to each other, being any closer than it was now.

It had started with a simple introduction in the New York bureau on the first day she came to the network from Los Angeles.

He already had heard of Samantha Stuart—the news that a beautiful woman reporter was being hired for the network had leaked from the West Coast days before it happened— but he had seen her only on a videocassette that the LA bureau had rushed to the New York bureau.

When he met her in person on that first day, he thought she was the most beautiful woman he had ever seen.

"Hello, I'm Samantha Stuart," she said as Oliver Ryan, the vice president of news coverage, introduced her to him.

He could not help staring at her, and he mumbled, "How was the weather in Los Angeles?" because he could not think of anything to say.

"It's fine," she answered, smiling at him. Years later, whenever they would talk about how their relationship had grown from that first awkward meeting, she would remind him of that introduction and say, "The weather is still fine in Los Angeles."

Seeing her now, so far removed from that first day, he had a desire to spend the rest of the day with her and just talk, talk about anything. Even the weather in Los Angeles. But there never was enough time.

"There was nothing in the papers about Cornwall," he informed her. "I guess it's still being held very tight."

"I imagine so," she said blankly.

Burton could tell by the tone of her voice that his mention of Cornwall had disturbed her.

"Is something wrong?" he asked.

"I don't know," she answered, idly running her fingers through her hair. "Sometimes I get depressed. Nothing to do with you," she added, as if to reassure him.

"Then what?" he asked.

"After we talked last night," she said, "I was thinking about the Cornwall thing. I mean, there's just so far a woman can go in this business. It's like there's an invisible barrier there. This far and no farther. What's the highest I can go? Weekend anchor like McVea? Co-anchor on *Sunrise* with Swanson? Never the real top."

"Lots of things are changing," Burton said sympathetically. He felt sorry for her, sitting in front of him like this, admitting her frustrations, but there was nothing he could do about it.

"Not enough is changing, Art. I'm happy for you but it's still a man's world in television. You know that."

"It's not of my making."

"I know, darling," she said, "but it would be nice if I could dream the same dreams as you do, wouldn't it?"

"Yes," he agreed. "But I never seriously dreamed about anchoring the evening news on the network."

"But it's a dream of yours now," she reminded him.

"Yes," he said. "It's a dream now," he added in a wistful tone of voice.

"I'd better be going," Samantha said.

"I want to tell you about the gambling story," Art said as he walked with her out into the hallway.

"Has something happened since last night?" she asked.

"I spoke to Frank Baglio a few minutes ago," he said. "My friend who's a cop in New Orleans."

As they waited for the elevator, he told her about the lead Baglio had given him.

"Can you believe it?" he asked. "Some woman in Vegas with a debt of over three-quarters of a million!"

"But why do they carry her?" Samantha asked.

"I don't know," Burton answered. "That's what I want to find out."

"Are you going out there?"

"I'd like to. I could go over the weekend. But I don't know what to do about Malachek. I mean, if the Cornwall job is close, I don't want to be out of town. I'd rather be here."

"Let me know," she said. The elevator doors opened and she stepped in. As they closed, she blew him a kiss and said, "I'll tell Barbara you were asking for her." Then she was gone.

Burton went back to his office and dialed Carl Malachek's number. It was better to tell Malachek, he thought, about his plans to go to Vegas. After all, Malachek might have other ideas.

"Carl Malachek's office," Judy Rosen said briskly.

"It's Art Burton," he said, wondering how much she knew about his talk with Malachek. "Is he in?"

"He is," she informed him, "but he's behind closed doors and he left word not to be disturbed."

"Anybody I know?" he asked, hoping that she would tell him.

"Charlotte Glover," the secretary said matter-of-factly. "She came up from the White House."

"Oh," Burton said. "Leave word that I called, will you?"

"Sure," she answered and she hung up.

Burton speculated for a moment as to why Charlotte Glover would be meeting behind closed doors with Malachek. Maybe her contract was up, he thought, but her agent would handle that.

He stared out the window and wondered if he should

hire an agent in case Malachek came to him with a definite
decision on replacing Cornwall.

A contract like that would be too big to handle himself.
He would have to get somebody good, somebody whose ass
Malachek wouldn't chew off, somebody who would help him
do it right.

It's strange, he thought. Up until a few days ago, I never
would have thought about something like this. But now it all
was a tantalizing vision.

"It's a dream of yours now," Samantha had said to him.
She was right. She always was.

Chapter 9

Charlotte Glover would not have been in Carl Malachek's
office when Art Burton called had it not been for a problem at
the White House the previous afternoon.

Because of the problem, she had had to cancel her plans
to take the three P.M. shuttle to New York and had, in fact,
ended up doing a one minute, forty-five second spot that led
the Cornwall show.

The problem at the White House was this: the President
was going to nominate U.S. Senator Harry Dowling of New
Hampshire to be Ambassador to Japan.

It would not be a particularly distinguished appointment. Dowling had served on the Foreign Relations Committee for fourteen years with little distinction and his only
credentials for the job were a wealthy wife, a collection of
Ming vases and an interest in the Far East.

But Dowling had carried a lot of water for the party over
the years and had made no secret about his desire for the job
when it had become vacant upon the death of the previous
Ambassador.

So it was decided that Dowling would be nominated.

The announcement of his nomination, however, would have to be handled just right.

If it was done at the regular ten A.M. press briefing, the Japanese government would consider it an insult. After all, you just couldn't have Press Secretary Jerry Daniels drop in the name of the new Ambassador to Japan along with an announcement about an upcoming trip to Miami and a pitch for a new program for disadvantaged youths.

Worse, a ten A.M. announcement would give the networks all day to work up a story about Dowling if they wanted to. And that was what counted. More than any editorial in *The Times* or *The Wall Street Journal*. Those few minutes on the air. They could kill you.

"We don't want a lot of cameras stuck in Dowling's face," Jerry Daniels had warned the President's advisers. "He is not one of our more articulate Senators."

A noon announcement in the Rose Garden, with the President and the Senator standing side by side, was ruled out because it would appear to be overemphasizing the announcement. It would be good PR for New Hampshire but how many voters were you talking about? You could handle them by opening two new post offices someplace.

In the end, the recommendation to the Oval Office was that the announcement be made late in the afternoon, around five o'clock, and that the President himself come into the White House briefing room and go before the cameras.

That would impress the Japanese, where it would be seven o'clock the next morning. They could make their early morning shows in Tokyo.

Dowling would be in the Senate, where a farm bill was up for a crucial vote, and the ground rules would specify that the President would not take any questions. That way, no network would have time to work up much of a story. The timing of the announcement could always be attributed to the need to give the Japanese government enough advance notice.

And so, just as Charlotte Glover was preparing to leave her cubicle in the White House pressroom, an announcement came over the loudspeaker that the President would have a brief statement at five P.M. He would make it in the briefing room and cameras would be allowed.

She quickly dialed a deputy press secretary and asked,

"Just for guidance. Is this five P.M. thing something we want to go live with?"

The answer was no. She called Wally Gifford, the executive producer of the evening news, and told him that the President would be making a brief announcement at five P.M. There would be cameras allowed but it was not regarded by the White House as important enough for them to seek live coverage.

"Any idea what it's about?" he asked.

"There's been some talk he might make a trip to South America," she said, "but I think he'd save that announcement for a televised news conference."

"Anybody quitting?" Gifford pressed her.

"Come on, Wally," she said. "Give me some time to poke around. They just announced the event ten minutes ago. Besides, I was supposed to be in New York this afternoon to see Malachek."

What was that all about, Gifford wondered. Then he glanced at a list on a yellow legal pad in front of him. Terrorist bombing in Rome. Four killed. Miners' strike in West Germany. The farm bill vote in Washington. A four-minute segment on Alzheimer's disease. A couple of light features as possibilities to close out the show.

"We can make room easily if it's anything good," he told her. "The show is light tonight, particularly on domestic."

"I'll call you," she said. She hung up, then she called Malachek's office and said a story had come up, she would have to cancel her appointment but would be up in New York on the first shuttle in the morning.

Within two hours, she had developed the story about the Dowling appointment from a source in the West Wing.

She asked a videotape archivist in the network's Washington bureau to find some footage of Dowling at a Foreign Relations Committee hearing and of Dowling accompanying the President during the New Hampshire primary four years ago.

She told one of the evening show producers in New York to request some footage of the U.S. Embassy in Tokyo. It could be satellited in on a late bird from Tokyo in time for inclusion in the piece.

Most of the picture elements of the story could be

constructed ahead of time and all she would need to do would be to drop in some sound of the President praising Dowling.

That was the way the story worked out. On the evening news, John Cornwall led into it by saying, "The President paid off a political debt today and nominated Senator Harry Dowling of New Hampshire to the key post of Ambassador to Japan. Charlotte Glover has the story at the White House."

The piece opened with the old footage of Dowling and the President in New Hampshire.

"Sometimes, walking through the snows of New Hampshire with a would-be President in subzero temperatures can have its rewards," Glover narrated. The scene switched to the pictures of the Embassy in Tokyo, pictures that had been transmitted to New York only an hour earlier. Her narration continued.

"This is the reward for Senator Harry Dowling. The U.S. Embassy in Tokyo. A long way from the hills of New Hampshire and probably a shock to the diplomats in the Foreign Ministry in Tokyo."

It was a good, tough story. After the program, Cornwall called her and said, "Thanks for the Dowling piece, Charlotte, it helped the show."

Jerry Daniels, the White House Press Secretary, came by her cubicle after the show and said, "You people really had the hatchet out tonight, didn't you?"

"C'mon Jerry, get off it," she snapped back angrily.

"You were the only ones to do a piece," he said, thankful to himself that the other networks had not been as enterprising as Glover.

"You're lucky," she said, smiling at him and she thought: If only you knew what I've got. But first she had to see Malachek.

Now, the next morning, she was sitting in Malachek's office. She was a tall, thin woman whose graying hair, pulled back straight and ending in a bun at the nape of her neck, framed a face that seemed to be forever ruddy, as if she spent all her time outdoors, facing the wind.

Were it not for the Bergdorf Goodman suit and the handmade Italian leather shoes and purse she had bought during the President's last trip to Italy, she would have looked like a small-town, Midwest farmer's wife, in town on Saturday shopping at Sears.

Although each network had one woman among the three correspondents they assigned to the White House, Charlotte Glover was not like her counterparts from the other networks. They were blonds, younger, prettier, married, and had come up through television.

Her background had been first in newspapers, stringing for a chain of West Coast papers, then the Washington bureau of a weekly news magazine. Finally, in 1972, when she was thirty-five years old, she joined the network's Washington bureau and was assigned to the Hill.

Four years later, she was assigned to the White House as the correspondent covering for the morning show, *American Sunrise*. In 1980, she took over the lead job and started reporting for the evening news.

She loved the White House assignment; the travel, the way the Transportation Office pampered you on overseas visits, the occasional invitations to state dinners, the long trips to the President's ranch, the speeches to journalism groups, the aura of glamour that attached to you as part of the Presidential entourage, even the luggage tags with Trip of the President embossed on them. All of this compensated for what would have been an entirely different life had she stayed in Palo Alto after graduation from Stanford.

She would have been married for many years now, with grown kids, living in a comfortable home near the campus, leading a Great Books discussion once a month or pouring tea for the faculty wives. The young assistant professor of journalism, who had proposed to her so many years ago, probably would be head of the department by now. And writing a textbook on television news.

Looking around Malachek's office, at the pictures on the wall of Jimmy Carter, Gerry Ford, Henry Kissinger, Richard Nixon, Ronald Reagan, she thought: I know all of these people.

The only problem with the White House beat was that you never really got to break a story—a big story. Most of it was all spoon-fed and, particularly with this administration, tightly controlled. Once in a while you could work up something on your own, like getting a jump on the Dowling appointment, but even that was not a big deal.

The really big ones—Supreme Court appointments, summit meetings, changes in the President's inner staff—these were all kept under wraps and nobody, not even *The New York Times* or *The Washington Post*—got a break on them.

There just were not any Watergates or Irangates any more. Everybody had stopped digging and sniffing, it seemed, because there was no place to get your paws under the fence that had been put up around the Oval Office. So all you could do was lift your legs once in a while and piss, like with the Dowling story.

But now, suddenly, she had something, something big. For the first time in her professional life, Charlotte Glover knew she was on the threshold of breaking a huge story.

"It's good to see you again, Charlotte," Malachek was saying in a friendly voice. "I don't get down to Washington as much as I'd like to."

"You ought to visit the bureau more often," she chided him.

"Every time I go down there, I see half the staff sitting on their ass in their offices," Malachek grumbled. "Nobody seems to go out and look for news. They wait for it to come to them. Handouts and press conferences. That's all you get out of Washington any more."

"I don't think that's true, Carl," she said, although she could think of a couple of reporters who spent all their time in the bureau.

"C'mon, Charlotte," he said teasingly. "Don't be so damn defensive." He liked her and she knew it. Theirs was a relationship of mutual respect—one professional to another.

"I've got what may be a hell of a story, Carl," she said, anxious to cut through the small talk and to get to the reason for her visit.

"So I gather," he said. "You certainly got me curious with your phone call yesterday."

She moved her chair closer to his desk so that she could, if she wanted to, lean her arms on the front of his desk.

"Have you ever heard of Tyuratam?" she asked.

He rubbed his eyebrows for a minute as if the answer could be found behind them. "No," he said. "What is it?"

"It's in the Soviet Union," she answered. "It's where the Soviets have their biggest missile launching site. It's called the Baikonur Cosmodrome."

"I assume it's not a secret," he said, a slight smile crossing his face.

"No," she answered confidently. "Our satellites and space-craft have been taking pictures of it for a couple of years. There are references to it all over the technical journals— *Aviation Week, Encyclopedia of Space Technology*, publications like that."

"When did you become an expert on space?" he asked. He was more interested now, impressed with the knowledge she was displaying.

"I'm not. But I've done a lot of reading in the past few days. Here, look at this."

She reached into her purse and took out a piece of paper which she unfolded and lay flat on his desk. It was a copy of an article.

"This is from the U.S. Congress Office of Technology Assessment," she said, pushing it across the desk toward him.

He reached into his vest pocket and put on a pair of bifocal glasses and scanned the article, which featured a highly stylized drawing of a rocket.

"That's an artist's conception of what we think the Russian Type L rocket looks like," she explained.

"What about it?" Malachek asked, pulling his chair closer to his desk.

"It would be the biggest rocket they've ever built. It could go to Mars."

"To Mars!" Malachek repeated.

"And carry cosmonauts," she added. "A manned expedition to Mars. It would put them far ahead of us."

"Okay," Malachek said, trying to pin the story down. "So we know all of this from a couple of hundred miles up. I assume NASA and the Pentagon and everybody else knows it. Not to mention the Russians. What's the angle?"

"The angle is this," she said quietly. "All of these drawings, all of these articles, all of these pictures are, like you said, based on empty launch pads we've been able to see from up in space. Believe me, I've done some checking."

"Go on," he said, chewing on the end of a cigar he had pulled from the humidor on his desk.

She leaned forward and, without even meaning to, lowered her voice. "About a month ago," she said, "the CIA got some ground-level pictures out of the Baikonur Cosmodrome. Close-ups. Launching pads. The monster rocket. Everything."

"Jesus," Malachek said softly. "How do you know?"

"Trust me," she said quietly.

"All right," he said, tacitly acknowledging her request not to divulge her sources.

"We have to assume the Russians don't know we have somebody on the ground at the Cosmodrome," she continued. "It's probably one of their scientists. God only knows how he got the pictures out."

"Whoever it is, it's a gold mine," Malachek said. "Talk about having a mole!"

Charlotte Glover paused to light a cigarette. She was surprised that her hand was trembling slightly.

"You're right. It gives us a front-row seat on their space program. The problem is, the CIA got cute. They wanted to brag a little, make a few brownie points, so they had copies of the Baikonur photos sent over to the Hill, to the CIA Oversight Committee, the one that has to approve of their special spending projects.

"They sent four blowups over to Ramsey of Kansas," she continued. "He's the chairman of the committee."

"I know him," Malachek interjected. "Real hawk. Wants to send troops everywhere."

"That's him," she confirmed. "All of these committee members have top-level security clearances so they're privy to a lot of information. There's never been a leak. But this one was considered so hot, the CIA didn't take any chances.

"They put the blowups in a manila envelope and attached a tiny microchip device, so small you can't see it with the human eye, to the margin of each picture. The microchips were sending devices, homing signals. Wherever those pictures were, the chips would send out a tone that could be picked up at CIA Headquarters in McLean."

"Christ," Malachek said, marveling at what she was telling him. Her source, he figured, had to be someone high in the CIA. Material like this didn't come from low-level types. And it was all plausible. Ever since the story had come out about the CIA bugging Brezhnev's limousine in Moscow, he knew that anything was possible.

Charlotte Glover snuffed out her cigarette in Malachek's ashtray. He had stopped chewing on his cigar. She had his total interest.

"The pictures stayed in Ramsey's safe," she went on, "except for one time when he took them out for a meeting in his office with two other members of the Oversight Committee. But a CIA and NASA official were in the room at the time.

"Then, a few nights ago," she said, "the CIA picked up a tone that indicated the pictures were being moved from the safe again. This was about eleven o'clock at night.

"They sent three agents over to the Dirksen Senate Office Building and staked out Ramsey's office. From the outside. The tone indicated that the pictures were still in the office, but not in the safe. Somebody was moving them around."

Malachek hunched forward in his chair. "Ramsey?" he asked.

"No," she answered. "About an hour later, Ramsey's administrative assistant, a guy named Herman Willows, came out of the office carrying the pictures in a briefcase."

"Weeping Willows!" Malachek exclaimed. "I knew him. Used to be a reporter for a group of radio stations out in the Midwest. I didn't know he was Ramsey's AA."

"He has been for a number of years," Charlotte Glover added. "Anyhow, when they saw him leaving the building they tailed him and called in the FBI. He was easy to follow, particularly with those little chips beep-beeping away. They followed him to a McDonald's in Bethesda, near his home."

"McDonald's?" Malachek said, trying to picture the scene in his mind.

"Yes. But they didn't want to take any chances, so they nabbed him before he went in. Obviously, a meeting had been set up because, just by coincidence, the second press attaché at the Soviet Embassy was inside, having his all-beef burger patty."

"So the top aide to the head of the CIA Oversight Committee was arrested as he was about to hand over top secret pictures to the Russians," Malachek said admiringly. He was in awe of the story. It was a blockbuster all right.

"It's a great story, Charlotte," he said. "Can you back it up?"

"That's the problem, Carl," she said. "Here's the payoff. There were no charges."

"What?" Malachek said, almost rising from his chair. He was incredulous. "How the hell can that be?" he asked, as if he were demanding to know.

"It's true," she said, shaking her head. "He was taken to FBI Headquarters to be held for arraignment until they could get a U.S. Commissioner downtown and then the word came to release him. They let him out at three in the morning."

"I don't believe it," Malachek said angrily. "How good are your sources?"

"Good enough to be pissed off about it. Plenty pissed."

"Who gave the word to release him?"

"The White House. Direct from the President."

"Jesus Christ," Malachek said softly.

"I'm told that national security was given as the reason," Charlotte Glover said.

"Where have we heard that before?" Malachek wondered aloud. Then: "But why protect Willows? He's a nobody."

"Ramsey isn't," she suggested. "He's one of the President's men. Put troops in Central America and Ramsey will be at dockside waving the flag. Push the button on the nuclear weapons and Ramsey will be singing "God Bless America." It's a cover-up, Carl, the worst kind. Everybody wound up bad on this one. The CIA. Ramsey. The White House is throwing a blanket like you've never seen on this one. It never happened."

"Maybe they don't want the Russians to know," Malachek said, groping for a reason.

"What? With one of their spy types sitting there waiting for Willows to show up?"

"Somebody's talking," Malachek said. "Somebody wants the story out. Right?"

"You can figure it out," she said. "But don't push me on my source. Obviously some people don't like what's happened. They think Willows should be nailed on the attempted espionage charge and the national security problem should be handled at the trial. The problem is nobody will talk for the record."

"Do you think the other nets know?" Malachek asked.

"No," she answered confidently. "I've got this one all to myself."

Malachek buried his head in his hands and thought for a minute, trying to find an approach that would at least provide a way for getting at the story.

"Willows," he said. "Where is he?"

"I checked Ramsey's office late yesterday. He resigned.

Personal reasons. He's on vacation, driving through New England."

"Son of a bitch," Malachek muttered softly. "And Ramsey?"

"I haven't tried him yet," she said. "I want to do some more checking around. But I wanted to let you know about it. There's bound to be a lot of pressure if we are able to prove anything."

"The problem is the photos," Malachek said. "That really is top secret stuff. I don't know how much we can get into that."

"I'll let you know how I'm coming along," she said, retrieving the article from his desk and rising from her chair. "Even without the photos," she pointed out, "we've still got the question of why the White House wanted Willows let off."

"Incredible," Malachek said, coming from behind his desk to shake her hand and kiss her on the cheek. "If you need any help," he said, "I'll send somebody else in to work with you."

"Thanks," she replied and added, "I'll keep you posted." Then she left his office.

Malachek stood alone by his desk, rubbing his chin. It could be a great story, he knew. He also knew what would happen if they got close to it even within sniffing distance.

The pressure would begin with a call from Jerry Daniels in the Press Office. Then he'd get an invitation to come down to Washington for an off-the-record briefing by the Secretary of Defense, maybe the head of the CIA. Everybody in Washington would be in line on this one.

He had been through it before. There had been the story about the secret satellite the Defense Department didn't want the network to report on even though the details had been published overseas. And the story about the Army advisers in Guatemala who weren't supposed to be there. And the story about the Air Force reconnaissance wing using an air base in South Africa.

It always came down to the same balancing act—the public's right to know against what the government claimed was national security. Years of experience and instinct had taught him that coming down on the side of the public was usually the wisest course to take.

He knew, however, that the pressure would be intense

this time. There would be heat. Lots of it. If the President was involved, actually ordering the release of Willows, then the pressure to suppress the story, if they could confirm it, would be enormous. The White House would go right past him and lay it on Jerry Rossman.

Rossman would fold, he knew. There were no guts up in those offices. They all operated from fear and the play-it-safe syndrome. Rossman, Barry Kovaks, Sid Neale. All of them. Keep the government off our backs. Thou shalt not offend Congress. That was the first of the network's Ten Commandments.

His instincts told him to pursue the story quickly and get as much of it as possible nailed down before Rossman started getting any heat. That way, he would have some ground to stand on, a story to defend. Most of all, he didn't want to piss off Rossman right now. He needed Rossman's blessing on Cornwall's replacement. The choice had to be his and not somebody foisted on him by Rossman. His own reputation and the integrity of the News Division depended on it.

His thoughts were interrupted by Judy Rosen who walked into his office with a list of phone calls she had taken while he had been talking to Charlotte Glover.

"One other call," she said, handing him the list. "Art Burton called a few minutes ago."

"All right," he answered. "See if you can get him for me."

She nodded and, a few minutes later, Burton was on the line.

"You called me, Art?" Malachek said.

"Yes," Burton answered. "That story I told you we were working on, the one on the mob and gambling. I've got a hell of a good lead and I wanted to go to Vegas this weekend to check it out."

"You don't need my permission," Malachek told him.

Burton was momentarily put off by Malachek's seeming aloofness. "I just didn't know," he plunged on, "if what we talked about a few days ago, about the evening show, would require me to stay in New York. In case something happened."

"Not at all," Malachek said flatly. "That's still a long ways from being settled."

"Well, okay," Burton said. "I just thought I'd check." He

hoped he didn't sound too presumptuous but it was too late now.

"Don't worry about it, kid," Malachek said in a suddenly paternal tone. "I'll keep you posted."

"Thanks," Burton said and he hung up.

He walked down the corridor of the *Focus on America* production offices to the office of the program's business manager.

"I need a flight to Vegas Friday night. Return on Sunday. Can you book me at Caesars Palace?" he asked.

"I'll try," was the response. "Why Caesars?"

"I don't know," Burton answered. "I like Roman art," he said as he walked out of the office.

He suddenly felt encouraged about his conversation with Malachek. Malachek had turned warm at the end, had even called him "kid." It was almost fatherly.

Somehow, Burton felt, it was going to happen.

Chapter 10

The digital clocks suspended from the ceiling of the barnlike studio that housed America's most successful morning show, *Breakfast Time*, moved in perfect synchrony to 8:51.

Mark Antin, the host of the program, glanced up at them and at a stage manager, casually dressed in blue jeans, a sweat shirt, and tennis shoes, standing a few feet away next to a camera.

The stage manager held three fingers in the air and made sure Antin could see them. Three minutes to go, Antin told himself. Three minutes more to keep this damn interview going. He looked down at a white sheet of paper attached to a clipboard he was balancing on one knee.

"Tell me, Senator," he said in a sincere, knowledgeable voice to a white-haired man sitting in an armchair across from him. "You have supported the President on the missile program before. Why are you opposing him now?"

The guest he had been interviewing for the last four minutes, Senator Arthur Claiborne of Utah, looked surprised but smiled pleasantly and said, "Well, I haven't always supported him on this, Mark. The last time around I also voted no."

Antin flashed the toothy, boyish grin that, over the last five years, had propelled him to a million dollar salary at his network and a prominent place in the pantheon of media stars.

"Well, I was thinking back over the years," he quickly ad-libbed, hoping that he had covered his mistake.

"Over the years," Senator Claiborne responded, "I think I've been very consistent on this issue. There was one vote two years ago where I supported the Administration on this but that was on a peripheral issue."

"What was that?" Antin asked, relieved that the digital clocks now showed 8:52. He could always cut it short, get out of this mess and let them go to a commercial.

"That was the rider on the appropriations bill," the Senator explained, staring at the camera just as his public relations adviser in Washington had told him to do.

"Well, I appreciate your taking the time to discuss this very important issue with us this morning," Antin said, indicating that the interview was over. "We look forward to having you with us again."

"My pleasure," Senator Claiborne said, wondering where all the time had gone.

Antin turned to another camera and, as if Senator Claiborne had suddenly vanished, said, "It's coming up on 8:53 and we'll be right back."

He smiled, held the smile until he saw the first scene of a detergent commercial appear on a television monitor by his side, and then he reached over to Senator Claiborne and shook his hand.

"Nice to see you again, Senator," he said. "Sorry about that mix-up on your vote."

"Not at all, Mark," he answered. He paused for a minute to let a stagehand remove the small microphone that had been clipped to his necktie. "I appreciate the airtime."

"Our pleasure," Antin said, and then he stared straight ahead as the stage manager called out "Ten seconds."

Ten seconds later, at precisely 8:54:30, Mark Antin looked into a camera lens and, reading from a TelePrompTer script that appeared above the lens, told four million viewers across the country, "Tomorrow morning, from Hollywood, the stars of the upcoming rock movie, *Catch Fire*, an expert on home safety, actress turned author Jeanne Graff, part three of our series on medical quackery, and, by satellite from London, an interview with the British Cabinet Minister who is seeking Britain's withdrawal from NATO. All that ahead tomorrow. Good morning, everybody!"

He smiled again, waited until the stage manager yelled "Clear!" and then he reached for a phone by his chair. There was no dial on the phone. It connected him directly to the control room and, during the program, served as an emergency umbilical cord tying him to the producers of the program.

"Here comes trouble," Scott MacEwen, the executive producer of the program, predicted as the red phone rang in the control room.

"Yes, Mark," he said wearily as he picked up the phone.

"Scotty, could I see you in my office after we do the promos," Antin said coldly. It was a demand, not a request.

"Sure," MacEwen answered. He did not want to ask the reason. With a prima donna like Antin, it was best not to ask.

Ten minutes later, after Antin had recorded on videotape a ten-second and twenty-second promo for the next morning's show, MacEwen was seated on a beige and yellow striped couch in Antin's office, five floors above the studio.

The colors of the couch were coordinated with the carpeting and curtains in the office. Everything was subdued, right down to the flecked material covering the walls.

It was an office befitting a star but just to make sure that visitors, such as anchormen or news directors from out-of-town stations, columnists, or affiliate general managers, got the right impression, Antin kept current copies of magazines prominently displayed on a coffee table in front of the couch.

The Economist, The New Yorker, Harper's, The Atlantic, even *Texas Monthly,* and *Washington Journalism Review,* were all laid out as if their very presence in his office certified him as a well-read and well-informed newsman.

In addition, a montage of photographs mounted in a large frame on the wall behind his desk showed Antin on various assignments overseas: Northern Ireland, Beirut, Nicaragua.

MacEwen, a young man in his early thirties who was the fourth executive producer of the program in the last five years, thumbed through a copy of *The New Yorker* while Antin washed the makeup off his face in a bathroom that, by contract, was part of his office.

"Good show this morning," he volunteered as Antin emerged from the bathroom.

"Bullshit," Antin snapped. He lit a cigarette and tossed the match toward a clay pot that held a miniature orange tree.

"What's the problem?" MacEwen asked warily.

"The problem is this," Antin said, sitting down on the couch next to MacEwen and stretching out his legs so that his feet rested on the coffee table, on top of the magazines.

"This network pays me a shitpot full of money to front this goddamn show every morning and I don't want to look like an asshole." He paused for a minute to let his words sink in on MacEwen. Then he continued, "That's the problem. I don't want to look like an asshole and this morning I did. In front of a couple of million people."

"Where?" MacEwen asked, his mind racing back over the past two hours, like a videotape rewinding, trying to recall anything in the program that had not seemed right. He couldn't think of anything.

"The interview with Claiborne," Antin said angrily. "I was given the wrong background on his voting record. I felt like a schmuck and feeling like a schmuck is not what I'm paid for."

"You mean the missile vote question?" MacEwen asked, realizing what Antin was referring to. "It sounded like a natural mistake. Not a big deal."

"It is a big deal," Antin insisted, spacing his words for effect. "Frankly, I don't give a shit what you or anybody else in the control room thinks but it's my face that's hanging out there for two hours. And I don't like it when some twenty-two-year-old researcher fresh out of Smith or someplace preps me with the wrong information."

Someday, MacEwen thought, I'm going to tell him to go fuck himself. And his magazines too. But not today.

"I don't know who the researcher on Claiborne was,"

MacEwen said, shrugging his shoulders. "But I'll find out and speak to her."

"Her ass ought to be fired," Antin said harshly.

"It was an honest mistake, Mark," MacEwen reasoned with him. "I mean, overall, the whole two hours were damn good. The others didn't even come close to us this morning."

"Let's keep it that way," Antin said, slapping his hand on MacEwen's knee and rising from the couch to indicate that, as far as he was concerned, their brief talk was over.

"I'll see you at the production meeting?" MacEwen asked as he walked out the door.

"I don't know," Antin answered blandly. "I've got some things I want to do."

He waited until MacEwen had left the office. Then he called to his secretary, "Get me Mickey Schirmer will you, dear?"

She smiled and, a few minutes later, Antin was on the phone talking to his agent.

"Mickey," he said warmly. "How's business?"

"How could it be this early in the morning?" the agent replied. "I caught your show. You're looking good."

"Listen, I want to talk to you about something. You got some time this morning?"

"This morning?" Schirmer repeated in a puzzled voice. He glanced at his appointment calendar even though he knew he would have to make time, if necessary, for Antin. He was too important a client to brush off. "You want to lunch someplace?" he asked.

"No, I just want to talk over an idea I have with you. I don't want to do it over the phone."

"I can come over now if it's convenient," Schirmer said, looking at an eighteenth-century English grandfather clock across the room from his desk. The hands showed it was almost nine-thirty.

He was intrigued by Antin's reluctance to talk over the phone. What the hell. You never knew what these million-dollar egos had on their minds. And, at 15 percent of a million dollars, he would listen to their cockamamy ideas all day if he had to.

Antin said he could use some exercise, it would be just as easy if he went to Schirmer's office, he could walk over now. Schirmer said fine, why not? Antin hung up the phone and told his secretary he'd be out of the office for about an hour.

"I'll be at Mickey Schirmer's if you need me," he told her and he walked out of the office, took the elevator down to the street, and walked briskly down Sixth Avenue to Fifty-fourth Street and turned east toward Fifth Avenue.

Because it was still relatively early in the business day, the street was not yet crowded with a crush of people. The sprinkling of French, Japanese, and Italian restaurants that dotted the north side of the street would not open for business for another two hours. The only signs of activity were kitchen help hosing down the sidewalks in front of a few of the restaurants.

A steady stream of taxis picked up and discharged passengers in front of the Hotel Dorset on the south side of the street but it was still too early for the steady buildup of traffic that, by noontime, would force cars, cabs, and trucks to creep along the street like a slow-moving chain of circus animals.

Antin loped along the sidewalk, recognized by many of the pedestrians and cab drivers. He was a tall man, close to six feet, five inches, and the long strides that less than eight years ago had helped him to All-America honors as end at Southern Cal carried him easily along the pavement.

It took him less than ten minutes to walk from the network building to Schirmer's office, which was on the first floor of a brownstone facing the rear of the Museum of Modern Art.

He nodded hello to the receptionist in the carpeted foyer and then stepped into Schirmer's office. The office was decorated in a style deliberately designed to make a visitor forget about some of the distasteful aspects of Schirmer's work.

As one of the biggest agents in the business, with clients at all three networks, Schirmer occasionally operated in the atmosphere of a grimy, shadowy Turkish bazaar where he had to haggle, on behalf of his clients, for limousine services, hairdressers, first-class plane travel for wives, husbands, children; even free television sets or VCRs for the vacation homes on the Cape or in the Hamptons.

These were the *chotchkas*, the trinkets, the *chazzerei* he had to bargain for—the parts of his business his office decor was designed to obliterate.

It was the other parts; the deferred salaries, the personal

corporations, the tax shelters, the annuities, the big money, long-term contracts he negotiated for his clients in quiet conversations over lunch at the Carlyle in New York or Ma Maison in LA or Le Perroquet in Chicago; these were the elements of his work he wanted his office to reflect.

And so he sat behind a partner's desk he had purchased at auction at Sotheby's on Bond Street in London. The lamp on his desk was a spiderweb Tiffany, the office chairs were chestnut and elm Windsor chairs, and on the wall above his couch there was an early American embroidered sampler that spelled The Lord Bless Us.

Mickey Schirmer: law degree from NYU; street smarts that began with waiting on tables at resorts in the Catskills when he was in his early teens during summer vacations; television experience that began as a junior contract attorney at the William Morris Agency fifteen years ago, when he was twenty-five. Knew how the game was played. Dignified taste. Everything quietly understated. It all added up to power if you played it right.

"How are you, tiger?" he said, rising from the leather chair behind his desk and extending a hand with perfectly manicured nails to Antin as Mark came into his office.

"Okay, Mickey," Antin replied and he sat down on the couch and rested one arm on the side. He felt comfortable in Schirmer's office. It was like a psychiatrist's office, a confessional.

"Helluva show this morning," Schirmer said and offered coffee. Antin said no, then began to explain why he wanted to see Schirmer.

He recounted the mistake during the interview with Senator Claiborne and told Schirmer that it was just one more indication of the sloppiness on the show.

"We've got a kid executive producer who couldn't find his ass with one hand tied behind his back," he complained. "Last year, he was producing some local talk show at a station in Seattle. Highest shares in the country, they told me. So now he's doing network. It's no good, Mickey."

"Can't you get him changed? You've got the clout," Schirmer said.

"For who? Some other hotshot kid?" Schirmer was silent.

"Shit, we're booking guests that the other shows had on a day or two earlier," Antin said, exasperated. "Every day is a goddamn struggle. I can't carry it all by myself."

"But your ratings are stronger than ever," Schirmer pointed out. It was stroking time, he could tell.

"I'm tired of doing this shit," Antin said, rising from the couch. He walked toward Schirmer and said, "I want you to shop me around, see what's out there."

Christ, Schirmer thought, he's serious! "I don't know what's out there," he said, stalling. "Your kind of money isn't easy to get, you know."

Antin strode toward Schirmer's desk and placed his hands on the edge. He leaned forward almost as if he were in a football stance.

"Mickey, for Chrisake, I'm a star," he said with no hint of embarrassment. He was simply stating what, to him, was obvious. "You're telling me," he continued, "that if you let the other nets know I'm available, there's not going to be any interest? C'mon, I don't believe it."

"It's not that," Schirmer protested. He felt awkward sitting there and staring up at Antin. At forty, he was eight years older and a foot shorter than Antin. Antin had a full shock of blond hair and a face that still had a few freckles left from years of exposure to California sun. Schirmer was pasty-faced and prematurely bald with only a fringe of hair. Now, staring up at Antin hovering over him, he suddenly remembered a movie he had seen at Loews Paradise in the Bronx, when he was a kid, and he felt like an aging Mickey Rooney looking up at a young Van Johnson.

"You have to understand," Schirmer said. "There has to be something out there. Look around for yourself. Who do you see who's moving? Nobody. Every network is locked in. What are you going to do? *American Sunrise*? That's lower rated than you are. Besides, Swanson just signed a renewal. I read it in *Variety*. *Wake-up Edition*? C'mon, that's so far down in the toilet you can't find it."

"Who said anything about another morning show?" Antin asked. "I want to do something else. Featured reporter on an evening show. Maybe anchor. Anything but this. My contract is up in another three months. Now's the time to look around."

Schirmer decided to test him, to call his bluff. He couldn't believe that Antin was serious.

"You want me to call Carl Malachek?" he asked, coming out from behind his desk. "Just to sound him out?"

Antin wheeled around sharply. "That prick? After what he did to me on Beirut?"

Schirmer had forgotten, until Antin mentioned it, the Beirut incident. Now he remembered.

Antin's network had sent him, along with two producers from the News Division and one from *Breakfast Time,* to Lebanon in the summer of 1982 during the Israeli invasion. The idea was to hype the show and promote Antin's image as a newsman.

The producers did most of the work, going into the field every day to shoot battle scenes and do interviews that could be edited into the stories to look like answers to questions from Antin.

Antin himself would emerge from the Commodore Hotel, where most of the foreign journalists stayed, once a day to record a stand-upper, the opening or closing part of the piece that showed him on the scene. A different location near the hotel was chosen each day. The rest of the narration, written by one of the producers, was recorded by Antin in his hotel room and the edited story was shipped off to Damascus, Syria, for satelliting to the United States every evening.

To the millions of viewers of *Breakfast Time* the next morning, Antin appeared, tieless and shirtsleeved, standing in a rubble-strewn street, to be a knowledgeable journalist covering the Lebanon war. To those who knew, particularly the other journalists in Beirut, including another correspondent from his own network, it was a farce.

But nobody said anything—it was all part of the show business part of the news business—until Carl Malachek was interviewed by *TV Guide* for a story on network coverage in Lebanon.

"The correspondents covering the war on a regular basis do a damn tough job," the article quoted Malachek, "and it's too bad that a network feels it has to send in a nonreporter just to get some ratings. You know, the 'Commodore Commando' type."

Malachek refused to specify who he was referring to but everybody in television news knew. Mark Antin. The Commodore Commando.

"I forgot about Beirut," Schirmer said apologetically.

"I haven't," Antin said bitterly. "I'd like to rub that son of a bitch Malachek's nose in shit if I could."

"Let's face it. You're not going to get a job over there," Schirmer said. "Malachek wouldn't stand for it."

"Screw him," Antin shot back. "Speak to Rossman. You've got a lot of pull over there. What have you got? Half their damn News Division, not to mention Jarvis Winston and all those other stars?"

"Okay, I'll speak to Rossman," Schirmer said patiently. Rossman would have nothing, he was sure of that, but what the hell. Keep the client happy.

He walked over to Antin and patted him on the shoulder, as if to reassure him. "I don't think the others are going to give you anything better than what you've got now," he said soothingly. "And let's face it. Your contract is coming up and we can probably get a million two, million three this time around. They don't want to lose you."

"And maybe the other nets don't want to see me doing *Breakfast Time* anymore," Antin said.

I've got to hand it to him, Schirmer thought. He knows what it's all about. He's come a long way from that sportscaster's job in San Francisco.

"All right," the agent said, putting his hands in the air as if to say "enough." "I'll call Rossman and set up a lunch. Just to sound him out, to let him know you're available. The three of us. 21. The Four Seasons. It will sure as hell shake up Bart Perrin," he added as an afterthought, referring to Rossman's counterpart at Antin's network.

"Perrin will shit," Antin said.

"What's he going to do? Cancel your contract?" Schirmer said sarcastically.

It all was beginning to form in his mind. The Deal. Get Antin's contract going. Give Perrin a little goose, a little *setz* right where it hurts. He could get a column mention or two about the two of them having lunch with Rossman. That would get the pot stirred up a little, make 'em nervous. Then he'd shut it off by getting a new contract, at much bigger bucks, for Antin on *Breakfast Time*.

"I'll call you, Mark, as soon as I set up the lunch," he said, shaking Antin's hand. Then he added, "And cool it about the program. You're doing a helluva job."

"Okay," Antin said eagerly, accepting his agent's compliments in the same way, years ago, he had welcomed the words of his college coaches. That was what mattered. Playing to your highest level. Getting the most of everything. Yardage. Clippings. Money. Fame.

Twenty minutes after Antin left, Schirmer reached Jerry Rossman's office. He was put through immediately and told Rossman he wanted to discuss an "interesting possibility" with him. He suggested lunch but did not mention that he would be bringing Antin along with him.

Rossman said, "Sure, it's always nice to see you, Mickey," and "How about one o'clock today," since it happened to be open.

This one was going to be easy, Schirmer figured. He'd get Bart Perrin shook up and keep Antin happy. Then he'd squeeze Perrin's balls a little, tell him Rossman was really interested in Antin, and the negotiations on Antin's renewal for *Breakfast Time* could be wrapped up early.

It all was beginning to take shape. It reminded him of a scene from another movie he had seen when he was a kid, *South Pacific*. The way the island, Bali Hai, came out of the mists with Mitzi Gaynor and the Italian guy, Brazzi, looking at it from a distance. This was the same thing. The whole form was visible now, a tangible shape out there in the distance. It was glorious. Rising from the clouds, the sun shining on its top. It was beautiful. The Deal.

Chapter 11

Art Burton came out of the endless night of the main casino at Caesars Palace and into the daylight that surrounded the edges of the covered parking entrance to the hotel.

He gave the ticket for his rental car to a parking attendant and squinted past the shadows toward the Strip a few hundred yards away.

It was eleven o'clock in the morning and the desert sun already was high in the cloudless sky. It had taken a moment for his eyes to adjust to the bright morning sunlight but now the whole scene was coming into view, like a tourist's fold-out postcard.

He could see it, piece by piece: the MGM Grand and the Flamingo across the street, deprived of their glitter in the daylight; the gas stations, betting parlors, fast-food places, the smaller hotels and motels with signs advertising All You Can Eat Breakfasts for $3.00, Jackpot Payoffs, 50-cent Minimum Blackjack, Swimming Pools, BIG PAYOFFS! Pets Allowed, 24-hour Lounge Acts, Free Drinks!

It all was so unreal and yet the unabashed tawdriness of it, the brazen, garish atmosphere had a certain appeal. It reminded him of Bourbon Street in the French Quarter— boastfully cheap and gross and, yet, because of it, no need to be crooked. Just vulgar.

He had flown in the night before, a perfect four and a half hour flight from New York with everybody in the first-class section reading or watching a movie he already had seen.

Nobody, not even the stewardesses, had recognized him but he didn't care. He was tired and didn't want to have to make small talk with anyone.

As always, he had preselected a window seat and even though the flight was to the west, into the darkening night, the vistas from his window had been enough to keep him interested.

Over the Plains, in the Midwest, there had been a huge electrical storm with bolts of lightning so enormous they lit up the massive clouds housing the storm. The storm had seemed to cover the whole far side of the sky. It was a brilliant, and frightening, display and he was relieved that it was happening a hundred miles away.

Then, an hour later, they were over the desert and, in the clear night air, he could see the twinkling lights of towns below.

Staring down at the tiny strings of lights, picking out— by the way the lights were arranged—shopping centers or drive-in movies, he wondered about the people down there.

Who were they? What did they do with their lives? What was it like living there, in the middle of nowhere, tied to the next place only by a thin ribbon of interstate highway stretching for miles across the desert?

He and the people down there lived in different worlds,

never really knowing each other. The single bond linking them—television—mattered only to him.

But they were part of the audience—his audience. And flying above them, staring down from the darkness, he wondered about them. Who was in that ant of a car driving along the highway? Young lovers on the way to a movie? A married couple going to a relative's house? And who was playing in that small, lit-up stadium? A Little League team? Some Class C club? Fierce high-school rivals?

He kept peering out of the window until he saw in the distance the glow of the neon signs from the Vegas hotels and casinos, shining like a ghostly light in the darkness.

By the time he got to the hotel and checked in, it was one A.M. back East and his mind and body were still on New York time.

He walked through the huge casino, past the baccarat tables with the tuxedoed dealers, past the hundreds of slot machines and the bored people pulling the handles, holding big plastic cups in hopes of catching a waterfall of coins, past the roulette, the craps, the lucky buck wheel, the hushed tables where little groups of Chinese or Filipinos were playing a game he didn't understand; he walked past all of that, never stopping, and went straight to his room and fell asleep while listening to someone explain, on the hotel's television channel, how to play blackjack.

Now, as the carhop brought his car to the hotel entrance the next morning, Burton felt energetic and refreshed. Before leaving his room, he had called the Weinstein listed on Lopez Drive in the phone book. A woman with a black accent had answered the phone.

"Weinstein residence," she had said. It was the same woman who had answered the phone when he had called twice from New York the day before. Both times, he had quickly hung up.

But it was enough to go on. Baglio's source, whoever it was, hadn't made up a name or an address. It had been worth getting on a plane for.

It took him almost an hour to get to Lopez Drive, a circular street where a few expensive, sprawling, ranch houses seemed to be squatting in the sun.

He parked the car and walked up a gravel pathway, lined by small shrub cactus plants, to the front door of number 7

Lopez Drive. In the back, he could see a redwood fence, running close to one side of the house. A swimming pool, he figured.

This was not the way he was used to doing a story. Usually, there would be a camera crew and a producer and they all would know ahead of time who they were planning to interview, what they were going to shoot, what the story was. Everything would be arranged.

But this story was just in the embryonic stages. There was no way to follow up on Baglio's lead other than to resort to old-fashioned reporting: get out and ring a doorbell and ask questions, the way he had learned when he was just beginning in the business.

Ironically, he and Samantha Stuart and some of the other major correspondents were the only ones who could still do it the old way. But only because their names and faces provided the entree. The cameras would come later, if there were answers to the questions.

He rang the doorbell. A few seconds later, the door was opened by a black woman dressed in a flower-print dress. He assumed she was the maid who had answered his phone calls.

"Yes?" she asked pleasantly.

"Is this the Weinstein home?" Burton asked.

"That's right." Her face was a blank.

"I was looking for Mrs. Weinstein. Is she in?" he said, looking beyond her to an enormous, white stucco-walled foyer that was decorated with a single painting of a desert scene. The only other furnishing was a bench, in the form of a saddle, underneath the painting. There were some magazines and papers on the bench.

"She is here, but is she expecting you?" the black woman asked.

Burton reached into his back pocket and pulled out his wallet. He took out an engraved card with his name, the words *Focus on America,* and the network logo on it and gave it to the woman.

"I'm a network television reporter," he said. "I wanted to speak to Mrs. Weinstein if I could." This was the long shot he had flown almost 2,500 miles to play and he waited to see if it would come through.

The woman stared at the card and then she said, "You

mind waiting outside for a minute, please?" and she slowly closed the door as Burton stepped back.

Burton assumed there would be some sort of a chain on the inside of the door, something that would impart a sense of security and privacy to the home. But there was nothing between him and the woman and he realized that, had he been a burglar, he could have forced his way past her and into the house.

If this house is owned by a high roller, he thought, something doesn't add up.

He stood outside in the sun, by the doorway, and stared at a tiny lizard scurrying across the doorsill. He tried to picture what Mrs. Weinstein, if he could get to see her, would look like. He imagined that she would be tall, well groomed, sleek; the type you'd see in Miami Beach or LA or New York. Lots of jewelry and expensive clothes. Maybe she was a widow who had all this money and was gambling it away from a home she had bought with insurance money.

The door opened and the maid motioned to him to step inside. She gestured toward the bench in the middle of the room and said, "Mrs. Weinstein will be here in a minute."

Burton smiled his thanks. His heels made a small, clicking sound on the terrazzo floor as he walked quickly to the bench and sat down.

Mrs. Weinstein was not what he had expected. She was a small woman, almost tiny, gray-haired, and she leaned on a malacca cane as she came into the room. The cane was rubber tipped and made no noise as she walked across the floor.

She was wearing house slippers and, because they also made no noise on the terrazzo floor, Burton felt as if she were silently gliding toward him, like one of the tourists he'd see in the wintertime skating on the Rockefeller Center ice rink.

She was dressed in a simple black dress with no trimming other than lace cuffs on the sleeves of the dress. He figured she was close to seventy-five years old.

She reminded him of the women you always saw answering the phones on public television stations' fund-raisers. She belongs on a park bench in the Bronx, he thought, or sitting by the ocean in Miami Beach, or playing cards in an old ladies home. She doesn't belong in any part of Baglio's work. Something is wrong.

"Mrs. Weinstein?" he asked in a puzzled, but pleasant voice, rising from the bench.

"You're from the network?" she asked him in a heavy accent that made the word sound like "netverk."

"Yes," Burton answered. "I am a reporter. I do the program, *Focus on America*. Maybe you've seen it."

"So?" she said as a question. "Vot is it that you vant here? You're a friend of somebody's?"

"I was looking for some help on a story I am working on."

She answered him again with a question. "Help? Vot can I help with? This must be some sort of a joke, a mistake."

"We're doing a story on gambling," he said. He felt embarrassed talking to her. Obviously, she knew nothing. He could tell. It was all a mistake. But how did Baglio's source pull her name out of nowhere? He decided to probe a little further to see if, somehow, it would make sense.

"Gambling on sporting events," he continued awkwardly. "Baseball, football, sports like that."

She gestured with one hand as if she were brushing a fly away from her face. "I don't know from gambling," she said. "Years ago when my husband and I vood go to Miami Beach, stay at the Roney, ve vent a couple of time to the racetrack. Vot's it called? Tropical Park?"

This is a put-on, he thought. Somebody is jerking Baglio off and I am the goddamn patsy. He wanted to get out fast and leave the woman alone.

"Yes, Tropical Park," he answered glumly.

"Look, Mr. Burton," she said, ignoring him and looking at his card. "Maybe this is a joke somebody's playing on you." Then: "Tell me, vot time's your program on?"

"Wednesday night. It must be at nine P.M. here. Same as in the East."

She shrugged. "I only vatch late night," she said, smiling at him.

Burton tried to avoid her look and glanced down at the magazines and newspapers on the bench next to him. He decided to end it without making any more of a fool of himself.

"I'm sorry for bothering you," he apologized. "I feel embarrassed about this."

She shrugged again and said, "It can happen," and then

he was backing out of the room, and the noise of his heels on the terrazzo floor seemed even louder this time. Then, finally, he was outdoors.

Shit, he thought. Of all the wild-goose chases. The flight. The hotel. The rental car. Two days and a thousand bucks wasted on a lousy tip. How could Baglio have been so wrong? Malachek would be pissed but he could explain it away. He didn't need this kind of problem with Malachek. Not now.

It wasn't until he was back in the hotel, tempering his frustration by idly dropping quarter after quarter into a slot machine in the casino, that he realized what had been wrong in the house on Lopez Drive.

The papers on the bench, in the room where he met the old woman. There was the *Las Vegas Sun* and the *Los Angeles Times*. But there also was *Variety* and *The Hollywood Reporter*. Trade papers. And the old lady had said she watched "late night"? Not late at night but "late night." That was a television phrase. It was used in the business.

Maybe Mrs. Weinstein didn't know anything about gambling, he suddenly realized, but she had more than a casual interest in television. But what was the connection? And how did Baglio's contact get her name?

He thought for a moment about going back to her house and asking her some more questions. But what more could he get out of her? She was just an old woman in house slippers with a heavy Jewish accent. Could her husband have been a big mobster? It didn't figure.

No, the answer had to lie with Baglio's source, not out there in the sun-baked whiteness of Lopez Drive.

One thing he was sure of now: there was some sort of a connection and he had to find out what it was.

A few hundred miles to the west, in an office in the network's studios in Hollywood, a man in his early forties sat in front of a television set.

He was dressed casually, in running shorts, a sweatshirt with Magical Mystery Tour imprinted on it and, even though he was indoors, a New York Yankees' baseball cap on his head.

His feet, covered by sweat socks and Adidas running shoes, kept beating rhythmically on the carpeted floor. The door to the office was locked and no one could see him sitting there, almost transfixed, his hands clenched together, the sweat forming between his fingers, an intense look on his face as he leaned forward and stared at the set.

It was early in the afternoon in California but it was almost four o'clock in the East and the baseball game on the television set, the Dodgers against the Mets, was in the bottom of the ninth inning at Shea.

The Dodgers were leading two to one, but the Mets had a man on first and two out.

Valenzuela was pitching for the Dodgers. It was a pick 'em game and he had the Dodgers for twenty-five grand. Straight up. Now all that fat little spick had to do was to get out the last batter. He felt his chest tighten as the first pitch was fouled off. Then another one.

His feet beat more rapidly on the floor. The phone was ringing but he didn't answer it. C'mon you Mexican greaseball, he silently urged the pitcher on the screen. Blow him out!

Then he heard the sharp crack of the bat against the ball and the cameras were cutting from the runners circling the bases to the crowds cheering in the stands and the Mets swarming around home plate and—goddamn it—it was over.

His heart was beating rapidly and he sat very still, clenching and unclenching his fingers, until he felt more relaxed. Twenty-five big ones had just gone out the window but it really didn't matter.

Nothing—nothing in the whole damn world—could give him a high like that. To come so close and then . . . let these other putzes get wired on China White or go crazy over young pussy or do whatever the hell they did. For him, there always had been only one release. Only one big kick.

The action, that's what it was all about. Ever since he was a kid in the Bronx, hustling the football betting cards in high school. Then there were the horses, betting with a bookie in a drugstore on the Grand Concourse, and the gin rummy games in the cabanas at Atlantic Beach, when he was working as a towel boy in one of the beach clubs.

And finally, when he made it big in television and had lots of money, there was the heavy action. He craved it the way a nymphomaniac wanted sex. He couldn't get enough of it.

Nobody knew about it, of course. Nobody at the network, not even his agent, Mickey Schirmer, nobody. He had thought a couple of times over the years of going to a shrink, even Gamblers Anonymous, but he didn't want to stop. What for? It was his own kick and he handled it his own way. Even the betting was disguised. Who could know?

He went to his desk and unlocked the top drawer and took out a black notebook filled with dates and numbers. He wrote down the date and next to it the notation -25. Then he put the book back in the drawer and locked it.

Soon, he knew, the phone would ring and a voice belonging to someone he had never seen would say, "That was twenty-five on the Dodgers. Does Mrs. W got anything else?"

But there was nothing else that interested him. The fall and the winter were the best with the Lakers and the Rams and the Super Bowl and the college basketball. That was when he could bet every day, sometimes two or three different events. The summer was shit. Just some baseball and, once in a while, a golf tournament.

He walked over to his office window, which looked out at the front of the studio entrance, and wondered if a second call would come. That was the call that would tell him which singer, or comic, or musical group the people in the East wanted him to book on his show.

The calls had been coming for three years now, ever since his show had been moved into a prime-time slot, but nobody knew about them. Certainly not Charlie Zagora, the executive producer of the show. Poor Charlie. If he only knew that these acts were worth a lot of money—money he would never have to pay the people back East.

It was better this way. Just tell Charlie that once in a while he wanted to give new talent a break, a little exposure on a network show, and Charlie would go along with him.

Like that singer they had on tonight. The big-titted one who had done the Stevie Wonder arrangement so badly in rehearsal that one of the stagehands had said Wonder would be better off deaf and blind.

What the hell. She was slotted near the end of the show and would get on and off in five minutes. Fifty Gs would come off his tab and three weeks from now she'd be booked in the lounge of some lousy club in the Midwest with a big sign out front saying Direct From Network TV Appearance. Fuck it. Who was to know?

It was a nice little arrangement. The people in the East left him alone, handled his action for him, and leaned on him only to book the acts they controlled and were pushing. And they carried his tab.

He glanced at a tiny clock on his desk and saw that it was time to get dressed. He stepped into a bathroom next to his office and showered and shaved and changed into a light brown sport coat and matching slacks and brown, tasseled loafers.

It was still early in the afternoon and the taping would be over in time for him to drive to his home in the Valley and watch the Atlanta Braves on cable. He was thinking of betting them against the Dodgers next week if the odds were right.

He came out of his office and walked down a flight of stairs to the hangarlike building that housed several studios. Within minutes, he was backstage in Studio B, going over the show routine with Charlie Zagora, a few writers, and an associate producer.

By four P.M., the network's late-night, highly rated Saturday night variety show, *The Jarvis Winston Hour,* was ready to be put on tape for showing in the eastern and midwest time zones three hours later.

Winston glanced at the script, asked if any changes were needed on the TelePrompTer, and told Charlie Zagora he felt good.

"Let's make it happen, Charlie," he said, laughing. "After all, my mother will be watching in Vegas. Late night is all she watches."

Art Burton had been playing the slots for over three hours, moving down one row from machine to machine, dropping half-dollars in robotlike fashion, and coming up a winner only once—for ten dollars and fifty cents. He was behind eighty-five dollars but what else did he have to do?

It was after five o'clock and the huge casino was beginning to fill up. Despite the immense size of the room—it was as large as a football stadium parking lot—the space was not vast enough to muffle the noise of the crowds constantly moving around the gambling tables.

There was a throbbing undercurrent of babble, of indecipherable sounds of people talking; to themselves, to the machines, to the dice, to the blackjack dealers, to the croupiers, to the spinning roulette wheel. Occasionally the unceasing current of noise would be punctuated by the raucous shouts of a big winner at the craps table, urged on by other players who had been betting along with him.

He had been oblivious to the noise but now, frustrated by the whole day, it was bothering him. Everything was bothering him: the noise, the people, their relentless search for action, everything.

Most of all, he knew, he was bothered by the old woman in house slippers on Lopez Drive. He couldn't put any of it together: her, the emptiness of that big house, her name being used by Baglio's source in New Orleans.

It kept spinning in his mind, like the little black ball in the roulette wheel, and finally he decided to go to his room and call Frank Baglio in New Orleans. He'd see if Baglio would go back to his contact and find out more about Mrs. Weinstein and why her name had been given as a big gambler with a $750,000 tab.

There was no answer at Baglio's home and then he realized it was Saturday night and Baglio always took his family to a restaurant in the West End, on the lakefront, for seafood on Saturday night. It would be just after seven o'clock in New Orleans and they'd still be there, sucking on crayfish piled on plastic trays.

It would be an hour later in New York—just after eight—and he dialed Samantha Stuart's number, hoping that she would be at her apartment. She was.

"It's boring as hell out here," he complained to her after they exchanged hellos.

"In Vegas?" she said. "I don't believe it."

"You like Lionel Ritchie?" he asked. "He's playing in the big room here. They're already lining up for the first show. Biggest collection of leisure suits you've ever seen. Every guy in line is wearing polyester slacks and white shoes. That's how exciting it is."

Samantha laughed at his description. "It sounds dreadful," she admitted.

"What are you doing tonight?" Burton asked her.

"Me?" she said, as if she were looking at herself. "Nothing. I've got on an old bathrobe and I just washed my hair and I was getting ready to call Helen, up at Wellesley, when you called."

"How is Helen?" he asked.

"Fine. She asked me to come up there this weekend and I may do it. I haven't seen my nieces in quite a while."

"I don't know why," Art said, "but that sounds so funny."

"What?"

"You talking about your nieces. I have a problem picturing you as 'Aunt Samantha.'"

"So do I," she said, recoiling from an image of herself as a perpetual aunt, bringing presents to little girls dressed in pinafores, then blue jeans, then skirts and sweaters, finally wedding dresses.

Was that the way it would be? She brushed the thought away as if it were a loose, wet strand of hair that had fallen over her face.

"The kids are cute," Art observed, thinking back to a glorious afternoon last fall when they were driving back to New York from Gloucester and had stopped off in Wellesley to see Helen and her husband and their children.

The beautiful old college town was ablaze in autumnal foliage and the front lawn of Helen's house had been covered with leaves tinged in brown, red, and rust.

They had spent the afternoon watching Samantha's nieces, aged eight and nine, trying to collect the blanket of leaves into a huge pile. The little girls had scampered about the lawn, chasing and shouting at the windblown leaves, and Art had joined in the chase, pretending that he could speak to the leaves.

"Hey, Mr. Orange!" he shouted at a solitary leaf tumbling toward the sidewalk. "Stop right there!"

Samantha laughed at the spectacle of Art, playing at the level of a child, hovering over the tiny leaf as if he were reprimanding it.

"We should do this more often," she said at the end of the afternoon.

"Yes," he answered, leaving unspoken what he knew both of them were thinking. It would be this way if we were married and had kids, like Helen and her husband. This is the life we would have. Solid. Rooted. It would be nice.

Thinking of that afternoon again, he tried to picture Samantha and he realized how different it would be to see her the way she was now; in an old bathrobe with a towel wrapped around her head.

Every time they had spent a night or two together, either in Gloucester or in New York, it always had seemed like a cameo honeymoon; everything perfect and in place, like a bridal display in a department store.

He often had seen her openly and freshly natural, her hair falling over her shoulders, her body covered only by a thin nightgown or a slip or nothing at all.

But he never had seen her in an old bathrobe or with her hair still wet from a shampoo or her face covered with moisturizing lotion or her fingernails still damp from freshly applied polish.

It was something he wanted: to know her in totality, but he knew that he would never have that feeling unless they were married.

He put the thought away because he knew it would taunt him for the rest of the night.

"If the audience could see you..." he said, letting his words trail off.

"They wouldn't believe it," she said, finishing his thought. "They only think of us as perfect, always dressed right, always doing something exciting, never bored."

"Like tonight."

"Like tonight," she agreed.

"Is anything happening anywhere?" he asked. "How was the news tonight?"

"The news? Not bad," she reflected. "They had a nice closer from Frankfurt on the old section of the city, and a long segment on farmers' problems in the Midwest. Otherwise, not much. How did you make out on the gambling story?"

"I didn't," Burton admitted and he told her about his visit to the Weinstein woman and how he felt there had to be a connection to Baglio's source. But it would have to wait until he could reach Baglio again. Then he asked her, "Anything else going on?"

Samantha paused for a second or two and he could tell, in the flicker of time, that she was hesitating about something. "What's the matter?" he asked.

"There was an item in the *Daily News* this morning. A little column mention in the TV section," she replied.

"About?"

"Wait a minute. I'll read it to you," Samantha said. He heard the receiver being put down on the glass-topped coffee table and then, several seconds later, she was back on the phone, a newspaper rustling in the background.

"Here it is," she said. "Quote. An interesting trio at lunch yesterday at 21. Mark Antin of *Breakfast Time*, high-powered agent Mickey Schirmer, and rival network prexy Jerry Rossman. Unquote. That's all it said."

Burton was stunned.

"They must be talking to Antin about the Cornwall job," he muttered.

His dejected tone of voice was obvious to Samantha.

"You don't know that for a fact," she pointed out.

"I don't know anything anymore," he said bitterly.

He could not believe that Malachek had intentionally misled him. There had been no question in his mind, after the meeting in Malachek's office, that Malachek wanted him to take over for Cornwall. I have to trust myself on this, Malachek had said. Those had been his exact words.

Was Malachek misleading him? Why would Rossman be meeting, now, with Mark Antin? And how could he do it without Malachek being aware of it?

"I just can't believe that Malachek would go for Antin," he said, trying to convince himself that there was some other motivation for Rossman to meet with Antin and Antin's agent. "Antin's a phony," he said. "Everybody in the business knows it. No news background at all. Even his own network knows that."

"The public doesn't know that. And Rossman probably doesn't care," she said, realizing too late that she was adding to his worry.

"It couldn't be happening this fast," he continued, thinking out loud. "Malachek told me before I left that it was far from settled."

"I don't know what to think," she confessed.

"I don't know what I can do about it, though," Burton said glumly. "I mean, I can't call up Malachek and ask. I'm not in that kind of position. I don't have that kind of power."

"Maybe it's got nothing to do with Cornwall," she suggested.

"It's got to," he said. "Swanson just re-signed for *Sunrise*. Why else would they be talking to Antin?"

"But Malachek wasn't there," she pointed out.

"That's my only consolation," Burton said. What a shitty business, he thought.

"What are you going to do?" Samantha asked him.

"Nothing," he responded. "If they're really serious about Antin, I'm out of it. He's got a following. His ratings are damn good."

He paused for a minute and then, as if he were watching his whole future collapse right in front of him, said softly, "I have a feeling that I'm not going to make it, Samantha. I don't blame Malachek. Maybe he's got nothing to do with it. But I think they're going to make a deal with Antin and I'm just being led down the primrose path."

Samantha could almost feel the frustration and intensity of his anger and she, too, felt frustrated because there was nothing she could do about it.

"I wish we were together. Now," she said impulsively.

"So do I," he answered, his mind leaving Rossman and Antin and Schirmer.

"I think I'll come back to New York tonight," he said. "Just so I can be in the office fresh on Monday morning. I know there's a red-eye out of here every night."

"Will you call me when you get in?" Samantha asked.

"Aren't you going up to Wellesley, to see Helen?"

"I think I'd rather stay here," she said.

"Of course I'll call you," he pledged. He was pleased by the thought that she would be there, waiting to talk to him, when he returned to New York. He needed that.

"Have a good flight, darling," she said.

"Yes," he answered and then he said good night and hung up.

He checked the airline flight guide and found a nonstop to New York leaving at 1:30 in the morning. It would put him into Kennedy at nine, New York time.

Even now—eight hours before the flight—he knew that he would be awake all night, the country asleep beneath him, and he would be sitting there alone, wondering about everything, thinking about what would have happened if he had stayed in New Orleans years ago, looking out through a tiny

sheath of window into the night sky, staring into nothing but
darkness.

Chapter 12

Charlotte Glover had been looking for an excuse to visit
Senator Charles Ramsey and she found it in the *Congressional Record*.

There had been a debate in the Senate on defense
spending and Ramsey had inserted in the *Record* an editorial
from a newspaper in Kansas, linking the need for a strong
national defense to any arms control treaty.

Ramsey, she knew, would be impressed if she mentioned
it to him. Nobody ever really read the *Congressional Record*
and this would flatter him and pave the way for an interview.

Her little subterfuge worked. He would be delighted to
see her, he said, and it was good to know that White House
correspondents didn't spend all their time reading just New
York or Washington newspapers.

She found him in his shirtsleeves, sipping a diet soda,
and eating a sandwich at his desk.

"Good afternoon, Miss Glover," he said politely as a
secretary showed her into his office. A smile creased his face,
revealing a perfect set of gleaming teeth, and as his pale
green eyes fixed on her she could see why the Capitol Hill
press corps had nicknamed him "The Swordsman of the
Senate."

He was strikingly handsome. He was in his late forties,
with prematurely gray hair styled in a crew cut. The color of
his eyes reminded her of the color of seawater she had seen
once in the Caribbean, breaking far out over the coral reefs.

Senator Charles "Chuck" Ramsey was an authentic war
hero who had earned the Silver Star and the Congressional
Medal of Honor in Vietnam and whose office would not let a
visitor forget it.

Pictures of Ramsey during his Vietnam service hung from the walls and the most prominent picture was of Ramsey in stiffly starched fatigues, being decorated in the field by General William Westmoreland. The picture was larger than the others and was prominently displayed behind his desk, framed by the state flag of Kansas and the U.S. flag.

Charlotte Glover was impressed by the display and, for a moment, she felt dirty, as if she were somehow tarnishing his bravery, even years later, by trying to nail him on the Willows story. But the moment passed. She had been in the business too long to be disturbed by the potential damage a story could do to someone's reputation.

What the hell, she had told herself years ago, nobody appointed me God.

Ramsey was warm, almost effusive, in greeting her. With genuine courtesy, he apologized for not having any food to offer her.

"I'm on a tight schedule myself," she said, "and I have to be back at the White House for a briefing and then watch the President go off to Camp David. It's our regular Friday afternoon photo op."

"Oh yes," Ramsey said. "All that shouting and yelling at him when he walks to the chopper. Do you people really think all of that is necessary?"

It was the way he said "you people" that set off a tiny alarm inside her. He said it as if he were referring to a lower class of people. Her initial thoughts about Ramsey and his war record disappeared. He was just another politician who had it in for the media.

"I don't think I've had the pleasure of meeting you one-on-one," Ramsey continued, "although I have seen you many times on stories from the White House. Your network does a good job."

"Thank you," she replied. "We try."

Ramsey clasped his hands together and stared at her. "I must say, however, you don't seem to take much of an interest in Senators such as myself who don't have the glamour positions like Foreign Relations or Finance." He was smiling as he said it.

"We have to go where the news is," she answered defensively. "The CIA Oversight Committee doesn't make much news, by its very nature," she added, hoping that perhaps this line of conversation would provide an opening to obliquely bring up Herman Willows.

But she quickly realized that Senator Ramsey apparently felt he had made his point.

"You came here to talk about arms control," he said, still smiling at her. "So if this is all off-the-record, let's spend some time on that."

He was disarmingly friendly and, as she listened to him, she again felt uncomfortable, as if she were doing something wrong. He is serious about this, she thought, and I am not. She had no real interest in what he was saying, even though he was extremely well informed on the subject of arms control and was quoting everybody from George Kennan to Henry Kissinger. Some other time, she thought. Some other time I'll come back with genuine interest and pick his brains on this. But not now.

She asked a few perfunctory questions and then began a delicate probe, as if she were a surgeon making the first incision.

"I'd like to keep in touch with you on this," she said, trying to sound sincere. "I'll try and call Herman Willows next week to set up an appointment."

"You know Herman?" he asked blandly.

"Not really," she said, looking for some sign that would indicate she could keep probing without raising his suspicions. She went a step further. "I only know him by reputation."

"And what's that?"

"Sharp. Knows his way around the Hill. A good man to have as an AA."

"Oh yes," Ramsey concurred. "Herman is a good man. He's been with me since my first term."

"I understand he's on vacation. I'll call when he gets back next week."

"Fine," Ramsey said, pushing his chair back and extending his hand to her as he rose to his full height of six feet six inches.

"Next week will be all right, then?" she repeated as if she were seeking to confirm the arrangement.

"I assume so. If Herman isn't here, just ask to be put through direct to me."

"That's known as the Capitol Hill runaround, Senator," she said teasingly. "I always used to work through the AAs when I was covering the Hill. They're the keys that unlock the doors."

"Well, my door is always open to you, Miss Glover," he said condescendingly. "You don't need to go through the intermediaries."

"That's very kind of you." She sensed that he wanted to keep away from any discussion of Willows. She decided to make a last attempt to pry some information out of him.

"You don't happen to know where I can reach Herman Willows, do you?" she said, trying to look and sound as unconcerned about the answer as possible.

"No," he answered matter-of-factly. Then: "Why do you need to reach him now?"

"A friend of his—a mutual friend—from the Midwest is in town. He and his wife were asking about him at dinner last night," she lied.

"He's driving through New England. I don't know his itinerary," he rapidly shot back. The bulletlike response was out of character for him.

"That's too bad," she reflected. "Maybe they'll see him the next time they're in town."

"Tell me, Miss Glover," Ramsey said as he showed her to the door. "Do you have much contact with Jerry Rossman?"

"Hardly any," she said. She was taken aback by his question.

"I'm going out to Kansas next week for a luncheon one of our major broadcasters is putting on. Rossman is the guest speaker. I'm going to tell him about our interview."

"That's very kind of you," she said, avoiding his glance. She knew that if she looked right at him, she would be unable to play out the charade.

She suddenly felt that he had caught on, that he was suspicious of her and was putting her on guard. But what had made him suspicious? Everything she had said about Willows could have been taken at face value as nothing more than simple inquisitiveness. She had to find out.

"I hope you don't mind my saying this," she said, "but you seemed a bit put out when I asked about Herman Willows. Is there something wrong with him? Is he ill?"

Ramsey put his arm around her shoulder as he opened the outer door of his office. "I don't know of anything wrong with Herman Willows. Do you?"

"No, of course not," she answered quickly.

He stood by the door and, as she turned to say good-bye, he said, "I'll be seeing the President next Monday morning. I'll tell him how much I enjoyed meeting you."

"There's nothing like having the President of the United States as a mutual friend," she said brightly. His hands felt cold.

"He's a very good man, Miss Glover," he said. "A sincere patriot."

"I'm sure," she responded.

"You ask good questions, Miss Glover," Senator Ramsey said in a nonthreatening tone. "I can see why the President has to be on his toes with the media."

"That's what we're trained to do," she said in a terse voice.

Senator Ramsey's eyes fixed on her as if she were a target he was sighting through a rifle scope. She suddenly felt as if she were drowning in the pale green waters of his eyes.

"Training pays off, Miss Glover," he said sternly. His eyes moved away from her and she could tell he was suddenly thinking of something else. She was grateful. But in a flicker of time he came back to her and said, "In Vietnam, in the jungle, we learned to listen for the sound of a certain bird. It always used to make a distinctive sound—a high-pitched whistle—if there was something out there, something we couldn't see. Somehow, the bird always knew something was there."

He cupped his hands over his mouth and made a slow *ta-tweet, ta-tweet* sound that echoed eerily along the marbled corridor.

"That's what it sounded like," he said. "We were trained to listen for it."

A smile crossed his face, and he said, "Maybe the President and those of us who believe in his programs should have a bird like that to warn us at times about the media."

"I don't think we're the enemy," she said forcefully. She felt uneasy and wanted to get away. She hated his type; superpatriots who classified everybody into two camps: them and us. The news business had taught her the world wasn't made that way.

"I didn't mean to imply that you in the media are the

enemy," he said. "Lord knows most of you do very fine work."

"I think we do," she said.

"But every now and then, I still listen for that bird's whistle," he said.

He was smiling at her as he closed the door.

Chapter 13

An interesting trio at lunch yesterday at 21. Mark Antin of *Breakfast Time,* high-powered agent Mickey Schirmer, and rival network prexy Jerry Rossman.

Item in the New York *Daily News*

Jerry Rossman stared at the item and tried to figure out which son of a bitch—Schirmer or Antin—had leaked it.

He had not read any of the papers on Saturday, when the column containing the item appeared. He and his wife had driven up from their home in Scarsdale to Connecticut to visit their son in prep school and had returned home late at night.

By then, he was too tired to read and Sunday was reserved for the massive edition of *The New York Times* and for some work from the office.

Now, as he sat in his office on Monday morning, he read the item for the first time. It was in the packet of press clippings that the Publicity Department, after culling the New York papers and *The Washington Post,* distributed to network executives every morning.

The item was on the top sheet of the packet. There was no way he could miss it and, he knew, neither could anybody else. It meant trouble.

He tried to remember if anybody he knew had seen him at 21 on Friday when he had lunched with Mark Antin and

Mickey Schirmer. They had dined upstairs, in the more private rooms, and he could not recall anybody saying hello or nodding in recognition. A few people recognized Antin, of course, but that was understandable.

Even when they left the restaurant, they had not walked out together because Antin had gone to the men's room and had caught up with them outside, on the sidewalk.

They had chatted for a few minutes and then they had parted, Antin and Schirmer walking together toward Sixth Avenue and he toward Fifth, to pick up a watch he had left for repair at Tiffany's.

Maybe somebody in a cab coming up Fifty-second Street, or walking out of the Warner Building across the street, had seen them but it didn't figure. There would have been a shout, a wave, but there had been nothing.

No, one of those two had leaked the item and it probably was Schirmer.

Well, let the little prick float stories in order to jack up the price on Antin. That could be a problem up the street, at Bart Perrin's network, not at his.

Thank God he had not even hinted to Schirmer or Antin about the Cornwall situation. Both their tongues would be hanging out if they smelled the opportunity for Antin to replace Cornwall. Jesus, they'd be peeing on his shoes.

Not that he wasn't excited himself. The idea of Antin anchoring the news had a lot of appeal. Antin was a name, he had a track record and he was better known than anybody Carl Malachek could come up with.

Besides, the affiliates would love it. If he could work it out over the next few weeks, he could bring Antin to LA with him for the affiliates meeting. Trot him out like a big-game hunter displaying his prize catch.

He would have to play this one very, very carefully. The price would have to be right, he wouldn't let Schirmer squeeze him, and he'd have to get Malachek on board. That would be the hard part, convincing Malachek. But, what the hell, Malachek was a pragmatist. He had a contract too, just like everybody else.

Rossman walked to his window and looked out to the building across the street. He peered at it as if he could see through it, and the buildings behind it, all the way to the smoke-colored tinted windows of the network building four blocks away where Mark Antin worked.

He was standing there, savoring the idea of silently snatching Antin away, lifting him right out from the building, when Sid Neale came into his office for the meeting that always began the day.

"Don't jump," Neale said to Rossman's back.

"Why should I do that?" Rossman asked, turning from the window and gesturing to Neale to sit down on the couch.

Rossman sat down next to him and repeated his question. "Why should I jump, Sid? This could be an interesting day."

"I read the item in the *News,*" Neale said. "Are we talking to Antin?"

Although his position as vice president of public relations made it mandatory that Neale be constantly apprised of Rossman's thinking and planning, Neale's relationship to Rossman was much stronger than the lines on the network's organizational chart indicated.

In the hierarchy of network executives, Neale was first among equals in terms of access to Rossman. And, in the hidden passageways and subterranean chambers of the network power structure, access meant power.

The power was derived from a long association. Neale and Rossman went back a long way together. They both had come into the business in the early days; Rossman as a salesman for a program syndicator, Neale as a publicist for one of the television production houses that blossomed in Hollywood in the mid-1950s.

In 1958, Rossman began selling one of the programs churned out by the production company for which Neale worked and the two men, then in their twenties, came to know each other.

The items Neale planted in the trade press about the program's ratings success at local stations around the country made Rossman's selling job easier as he moved from station to station in the South and Southwest.

Two years later, Sid Neale got a job as a writer in the network's West Coast Publicity Department. He told Jerry Rossman about an opening in the sales department of the network's station in Los Angeles and Rossman applied for, and got, the job.

From there, Rossman moved steadily through the ranks. Sales manager at the station in LA, then station manager and, in 1965, his first major promotion: vice president and general manager of the network's station in Chicago.

Then, a move to New York to take over the same position at the network's flagship station and eventual promotion to president of the network's group of five owned stations.

All the time, he kept in touch with Sid Neale who had been moving upward through the layers of network press and publicity jobs in Los Angeles.

When Jerry Rossman became president of the network, after three years as executive vice president, he sent for Sid Neale and promoted him from his job as head of the network's West Coast Publicity Department to vice president of public relations for the entire network. He wanted somebody he could trust.

Sid Neale moved east, the first time in his life he had ever lived anywhere but Los Angeles, and it soon became obvious to everyone in the network that Sid Neale was Rossman's right-hand man, even if someone else carried the title of executive vice president.

Because of their personal friendship and professional relationship, Neale could ask Rossman questions, even embarrassing ones, without fear of offending Rossman or, worse, hurting his own career. In asking about Rossman's lunch with Antin, Neale knew that he probably was peeking behind a curtain marked Not for Public Viewing but it didn't matter.

"You know something, Sid," Rossman remarked. "I didn't even know Antin was going to be at that lunch. Schirmer snookered me right into it."

"Beautiful," Neale observed admiringly. "What was the reason?"

Rossman put his hands behind his head and leaned back on the couch in a relaxed position. "Antin's available," he said. "Or he will be, when his contract runs out."

"Is he looking or is Schirmer just jerking us off?"

"Both. Antin wants to do something different, at least he says he does, and Schirmer probably figures he can get more bucks out of Perrin by publicly shopping him around. You don't think that piece in the *News* came from their Publicity Department, do you?"

"I didn't know whether it was Antin or Schirmer who dropped it," Neale said.

"It had to have been Schirmer," Rossman said, as if he were pronouncing judgment after a serious deliberation. "At any rate, if we get any press inquiries, just say it was a social lunch, some bullshit like that. I don't think there'll be any interest."

"I was thinking more about here in the building," Neale said. "Malachek. People like that."

Rossman smiled to himself at Neale's intuitive grasp of where the real problem might lie.

"Malachek," Rossman repeated. "He can be handled."

Neale was silent. He sensed that something had come out of the luncheon, some promise, some tentative understanding, something to indicate that there would be more meetings. Why else would Rossman say that Malachek could be handled?

"We've got a big problem, Sid," Rossman said, confirming Neale's instincts. He rose from the couch and, placing his hands in the back pockets of his pants, slowly began to pace back and forth.

"Cornwall is leaving," he said in an even lower voice. "He's walking out."

"Jesus!" Neale exclaimed in disbelief. "When did this happen?"

"Last week. Wednesday or Thursday, I don't even remember any more. Malachek told me."

"Who else knows?"

"Nobody else here. Roger Blumberg does. He represents Cornwall."

"You've kept it under wraps, I'll say that," Neale said, unable to disguise his irritation that he was being told now, after the fact.

Rossman noticed it. "I didn't want to say anything until I spoke to Cornwall himself," he explained.

"When was this?"

"I had dinner with him Friday night, up here in the executive dining room. Just the two of us, after the show. I didn't want to bring in Malachek or Blumberg. I thought I might be able to turn him around."

"I gather you couldn't," Neale surmised.

Rossman stopped his measured back-and-forth walk and

sat down again next to Neale. The exasperation he had felt after the dinner with Cornwall was coming back to him.

"I don't understand guys like Cornwall," he said. "Never have. He's got the whole world by the balls and he lets go. This network has been awfully damn good to him and what does he do? He walks right out on us."

Rossman's voice was beginning to rise in anger. "Can you imagine him doing this to us? Where the hell is the loyalty in this business?"

"What did he say? Did you mention the loyalty angle to him?" Neale asked. To him, everything had a public relations twist, even loyalty.

Rossman threw his hands in the air. "What the hell could I say?" He paused for a few seconds, as if he were waiting to answer his own question.

"It was a very frank discussion," he continued, beginning to replay the dinner for Neale. "I told him how disappointed I was about his decision and that I hoped he would reconsider. He said he had given a lot of thought to it but it was final. He said something about wanting 'space.' That's how he put it, Sid. 'Space,' like he was a goddamn psychiatrist or something. I asked him to hold off for six months, give us time to decide on a replacement, handle it with the affiliates, with the press, work up an ad campaign, but he wouldn't buy it. He said he was crossing the Rubicon, as if I was supposed to know right away what the hell he meant."

"He wouldn't budge?" Neale asked.

"You know what he said to me?" Rossman responded. "He said, 'I've given this network my blood and sweat for over twenty-five years, starting with Little Rock.'"

"Little Rock?" Neale interjected. "What was that?"

"The school integration. Remember? That Governor they had down there and Eisenhower sent the troops in. It was the first story Cornwall covered for the network."

"That's almost thirty years ago," Neale said.

Rossman nodded. "I tried to tell him that this was no way to end a great career, walking out like this, but he just wouldn't move. I mean he is in cement on this.

"He said to me he's tired, washed out, and he needs to get out. I asked him to think it over for a couple of weeks but even that wouldn't fly. Do you want to hear the topper? He leans over to me and says, 'Jerry, if you've been through this

day in and day out all these years, you'd want out too.' Can
you believe it?"

Rossman's voice steadily began to rise. "What the hell
does he think I've been doing all my goddamn life? Sitting in
some cozy office with a computer and a ratings book, placing
orders for thirty-second spots like some twenty-thousand-
dollar-a-year time buyer on Madison Avenue?"

"The news guys don't understand the business, Jerry,"
Neale said, trying to cool him down. "Even a guy like
Cornwall. All he knows is from the news. They think we're
unclean. Lepers."

"Nah, Cornwall knows," Rossman answered bitterly. "He's
been around the network for a long time. He knows what it's
all about."

"What about his contract?" Neale asked. "Don't we have
a lock on him?"

Rossman shook his head. "He has a window. I gave it to
him when he re-signed the last time around. I never dreamed
he would exercise it. I thought it was just a gesture, a kiss.
You know, keep him happy."

Neale got up from the couch and rested his backside
against the edge of Rossman's desk. He could tell, by the
tone of Rossman's voice, that Rossman had given up on
Cornwall. It was over.

"How soon is this going to happen? How long can we
keep it quiet?" he asked Rossman. He was beginning to see
the dimensions of the problem. It could be a disaster.

"Cornwall says we can work out the timing. But what
difference does it make? We can't keep it under wraps too
long. The minute it gets out we're looking for a replacement,
it's going to be all over the place. And we're in a bind with
the affiliates. We have to make a move soon."

"Cornwall won't hold it for another month?"

Rossman stood up and walked over to his window and
looked out as if the answer could be found out there,
somewhere.

"He'll hold it," Rossman said, turning to Neale. "He's
honorable. But I can't go before the affiliates next month and
say nothing about it and then have them find out later that I
knew all along he was going to leave. Jesus, they'll have me
for dinner. They'll be yelling for my scalp all over the country.
We'll all be out."

"What does Malachek think?"

"He's resigned to it. He wants to put Art Burton in there, from *Focus*."

Neale's eyebrows lifted in surprise. "Burton? Is he strong enough?"

"I don't know, Sid," Rossman said in a despairing voice. "Malachek thinks he is but I wonder. I looked at the research on him Sunday night at home. He's got good demographics—big with the 18 to 49 women and *Focus* gets good ratings but he's not a star, you know what I mean?

"We need a major talent in there, somebody we don't have to build, somebody who will hold the ratings."

"Antin," Neale said. "What are the chances?"

"I don't know. I've dealt with Schirmer for a long time and I still don't trust him. He's not one of us, you know? What's he's got—ten, fifteen years in the business? I was already running the local station here when he was just starting out."

"He handles a lot of people," Neale observed.

"He'll take Antin wherever the best offer is," Rossman said.

"What about putting Antin on *Sunrise* and moving Mike Swanson up to the Cornwall show?" Neale suggested.

Rossman shook his head in disapproval of the idea. "Swanson just doesn't have an evening feel to him. He works beautifully in the morning but I don't think he'll play well at night, night after night. I checked his ratings when he substituted for Cornwall a couple of times. They weren't anything to write home about. Besides, if we get Antin, why stick him on the morning show? We'll put him where we can make the most out of him, where the big chips are."

Neale rubbed his chin with his hands. He knew that his skills did not lie in solving the internal problems of the network. Who should anchor what program, which night of the week was best for comedies, which programs should be renewed or canceled; these were questions for Rossman and Barry Kovaks and Malachek and the others to handle. That was what they were paid for.

His skills, his whole career, had been based on making something—a program, a personality, an executive, a decision—look good even when it was bad.

So deciding on a replacement for Cornwall was not his

problem. But making sure that the fallout from Cornwall's precipitous departure was held to a minimum was his problem. A big one.

"So what happens now?" Neale asked, hoping that Rossman's answer would provide him some guidance on how to control the inevitable damage.

"I've got to speak to Malachek," Rossman said. "I know he doesn't care for Antin—I've heard those stories—but Malachek will have to be a team player if it turns out that Antin is right."

"These guys in news," Neale said disparagingly. "You'd think they were a foreign government the way we always have to negotiate with them. Christ, their paychecks come from the same company as ours do."

"I know, I know," Rossman agreed. "But it's always been that way. The damn News Division thinks everything it does came down with the Ten Commandments. The minute you try to preempt their time, or complain about a story or slot a documentary in a low-viewing period, Malachek is up here screaming his head off. You know, 'news is inviolate.' How many times have you heard that one?"

"So we've got to sit here and let them throw shit in our face, on our own air?"

Rossman knew what Neale was referring to. Earlier in the year, there had been a Congressional hearing in Washington on minority hiring practices of the networks. One of the witnesses, a black minister, had criticized all three networks but had singled out Rossman's network as the worst offender.

The hearing did not receive much coverage on the wires or in the *Times* or *The Washington Post*. But the News Division covered the hearing and broadcast a two-minute story, including the minister's criticism of the network, on Cornwall's program.

Neale had never forgiven Malachek. It was Neale who had to work up the network's statement defending its own record and reaffirming its commitment to equal employment opportunity. The network's Washington lawyers, as well as the New York attorneys, had reviewed the statement, word by word, before it was released. Who needed that kind of problem?

And, just a few weeks ago, the News Division had interrupted an afternoon soap opera, at a very dramatic moment, with a bulletin about a Supreme Court Justice announcing his retirement.

Switchboards at affiliates all over the country lit up like Christmas trees with calls from viewers complaining about the interruption. A couple of television columnists in major cities heard about the flood of complaints and wanted comment from the network. That was another pain in the ass Malachek had created.

"Sometimes I wonder if Malachek knows which network he's working for," Neale said sarcastically.

"Listen Sid. This network has got the biggest problem facing it since Miniver fell off that damn mountain in Alaska. Now I'll handle Malachek. You start thinking about what kind of a statement we're going to put out to the press about Cornwall. It's got to come from us. We're the ones who have to announce it."

"Is Cornwall going to say anything?"

"Work up a statement and then we'll show it to him. He'll cooperate, Blumberg assured me of that. But this whole thing has to have a class look to it. We've got to come out looking like statesmen on this one."

"How much time have we got?"

Rossman stared absentmindedly out the window. His mind was working forward to the affiliates meeting, a month away. That was when he would have to be ready with a plan, something that would indicate to the affiliates that the network was devoting its full attention to the problem.

He began to outline his thinking to Neale. "Antin has got a ninety-day option clause in his contract, according to Schirmer. So he's free to talk to anybody and we can talk to him without having Bart Perrin yell contract tampering at us. The ninety-day period must have just opened up.

"As soon as we make any sort of an offer to Antin, Schirmer will leak it all over the place. So we've got to be ready with the Cornwall statement before then."

"I'll speak to Malachek and stroke him a little before getting to Schirmer. So figure a week, maybe two, before we announce Cornwall."

"That won't give us much time before the affiliates meeting, unless Antin is panting to get over here," Neale cautioned him.

"Listen," Rossman said. "I don't have to have Antin

locked up by the time we get to LA. It would be nice, but it's not absolutely necessary. But it's got to be close to a deal. The affiliates have got to know that we're in serious negotiation—that's the spin we'll put on it—so they won't be climbing all over me. That will buy us some time. As long as it doesn't look like we're sitting on our ass, sucking our thumbs, we can stall for a little time."

"You're sold on Antin?" Neale probed.

"He's damn good and right now he's available. I don't have any other suggestions, do you?"

"Schirmer will want megabucks for him," Neale pointed out.

"I know that," Rossman admitted, no longer trying to convince himself that he would not let Schirmer squeeze him. "All it takes is money." He heaved a sigh.

"You know something, Sid? News is worth a goddamn fortune to us at night. We'll pay whatever it takes. It's a drop in the bucket in the long run."

"And Malachek?" Neale asked.

"I'll handle Malachek," Rossman answered. "If it keeps him happy I'll tell him we'll consider Burton. But between you and me I'm not going to buy his bullshit about how the anchorman has to have a news background. Jesus, Mark Antin could go on the air tonight and say that Hitler is alive and every Jew in the country would start getting nervous. People don't care about somebody's background. They believe him. That's all that matters."

Neale nodded affirmatively. He already was beginning to formulate a game plan. Have Cornwall come to LA for a farewell testimonial by the affiliates. It would go over big, have a nice spin to it, and get good play in the press. Then if, by some miracle, Antin had been signed, Antin could come out for the final banquet and be presented to the affiliates. It would be like passing the torch at the Olympics. It would be sensational.

He thought about telling Rossman his idea right now but Rossman seemed to be wrapped up in his thoughts. He was staring out the window again.

"Anything else?" Neale asked tentatively.

"No," Rossman answered. "I was just thinking what I'm going to say to that SOB down on seven, Malachek."

Then he turned away and, as if he were talking to

himself, said softly, "Malachek will play. He doesn't have a choice. He's got a contract too, just like the rest of us."

Chapter 14

Jerry Rossman had decided that it would be a smart tactic to invite Carl Malachek to lunch so that the two of them, alone, could discuss the Cornwall problem. If the meeting seemed to be going well, then Rossman would raise the possibility of Mark Antin replacing Cornwall.

The network president wanted a quiet place, someplace where Malachek would feel encumbered and speak softly, not start an argument. He decided that his private dining room would be perfect.

It was the same room where, just last Friday night, he had met with John Cornwall. It's becoming a place for summit meetings, he thought. Sid Neale is right, you have to negotiate with the news people as if they were a foreign government.

Rossman, however, had been at the network too long to be aggrieved by the idea that even he, as president of the network, had to deal diplomatically and tactfully with the News Division.

News always had been an object of reverence at the network. It was the pure and unsullied virgin the network could display to the rest of the world, particularly Congress, the FCC, and the print media, as an eternal symbol of purity, integrity, and truth.

The incontrovertible truth was this: nobody could fuck with the news. If the Advertising Department were to ask that one documentary be softened in order to placate an advertiser, if the Public Relations Department were to ask that an invitation to a guest to appear on *American Sunrise* be canceled because he or she was too controversial, if Rossman himself were to order that a story be killed because a heavyweight politician was objecting; if any of these or similar prohibitions were laid down, then the News Division would yell "Rape!" And half of Congress and every damn public-interest group in the country would be at Rossman's door in the morning.

Oh no, Rossman knew better. He wasn't going to ram Mark Antin down Carl Malachek's throat without a lot of preliminary stroking. He also would make sure that Antin was pretested before the final decision was reached.

He would get Antin to a studio, out of New York City, and let him read a Cornwall newscast, complete with tapes, pictures over the shoulder, everything from a previous show. The whole bit.

Then the tapes would be shown to sample audience groups to get their reactions. There was no doubt in Rossman's mind that Antin would test well. The research would help when the discussions with Malachek got down to the nut cutting.

None of Rossman's strategy, however, could begin to be implemented because, when he called Malachek's office to set up the luncheon, the News Division president was not there.

"He just left to make the eleven o'clock shuttle to Washington," Judy Rosen informed Rossman.

"Will he be back today?" Rossman asked, somewhat testily.

"Oh yes. He just went down there for a few hours."

"I'll try to reach him down there," Rossman said and hung up.

When Malachek arrived at the network's Washington bureau shortly after noon, there was a message for him at the reception desk in the lobby to call Jerry Rossman.

Malachek smiled, as if he had won a minor victory. He had wanted to call Rossman himself, as soon as he had seen the item in the press packet about Rossman and Mark Antin, but had decided to wait until he returned from Washington. Rossman, he reasoned, must have guessed that he was upset and was trying to reach him in order to placate him.

He put the message in his pocket and walked down a hallway lined with pictures of the network's Washington correspondents to the main working area of the bureau.

It was a large room with banks of clattering Teletypes

lining the walls. Producers and writers sat at desks littered with newspapers, magazines, Styrofoam coffee cups, and videotape cassettes. The chaos on top of the desks destroyed whatever symmetry had originally been intended by placing the desks in orderly rows.

In the center of the room, there was a horseshoe-shaped desk for the six assignment editors. Computer terminals sprouted from the desk, squatting like mushrooms in a trash-strewn field.

Malachek walked past the assignment desk and down an aisle between a row of desks. He nodded briefly to the people at the desks and went into the office of Bob Lanigan, the bureau chief.

"Nice to see you, Carl," Lanigan said pleasantly, rising from his desk to shake hands with Malachek.

The Washington bureau chief was a stoop-shouldered man whose ill-fitting pants were held up by red suspenders. Because of his posture, beer belly, and thinning hair, he looked older than his age. He was forty.

"Charlotte Glover's on her way here from the White House," Lanigan added. Malachek had told him that he was coming down from New York to have a private lunch with the White House correspondent and Lanigan knew that this stop by his office was simply a courtesy gesture.

It did not offend him. Malachek operated on a different plane than he did. He surmised that Malachek wanted to talk to Charlotte Glover about a new contract. Why else would he fly down?

"Bob," Malachek said. "I have to call Jerry Rossman. Would you mind if I borrowed your office for a minute?"

Lanigan shook his head and left the office, closing the door behind him.

Malachek reached Rossman just as the network president was leaving for lunch.

"I can call back later, Jerry," Malachek said, instantly regretting that he sounded apologetic.

"That's all right, Carl," Rossman responded smoothly. "I tried to reach you to see if you were interested in having lunch today, but I had to settle for second best. Sid Neale."

"I had some business in the bureau down here," Malachek explained. "But I'd like to talk to you when I get back."

"We can get together whenever you want," Rossman

assured him. Then he asked, disingenuously, "Anything important?"

"That lunch with Antin. I read the item in the press packet this morning."

Rossman tried to detect if there was any resentment in Malachek's voice. He did not sound disturbed, only inquisitive.

"Don't worry about it," Rossman said offhandedly. "Mickey Schirmer set it up. He brought Antin along. I didn't know it was going to be a threesome."

"Anything to it?" Malachek asked, probing ever so slightly.

"Nothing that can't hold until we meet," Rossman said.

The moment he said it he knew he had unintentionally given Malachek a signal that there had been something of substance at the luncheon. Something that needed further discussion.

Malachek picked up on it instantly. "Don't tell me Antin's looking," he said dourly.

"Everybody's always looking," Rossman hastily observed. He did not want to get into a long-distance duel with Malachek. They were on the verge of becoming opposing forces firing artillery flares at each other, each trying to illuminate the other's position.

"Call me if you're back late this afternoon," Rossman said. "I'm late for lunch."

"Yes, I will," Malachek said quickly and then they both hung up. Son of a bitch, Malachek wondered, what's he up to?

The item about Antin bothered Malachek but he knew there was nothing he could do about it until he saw Rossman face-to-face.

Now, in retrospect, he regretted coming to Washington. But, when Charlotte Glover had called, asking him to come down he instantly had agreed.

If there was one habit Carl Malachek could not break, other than smoking four cigars a day, it was his insatiable thirst for a juicy story—something he could sink his teeth into and be nourished by for weeks on end.

Put Carl Malachek near a good story, even if only within smelling distance, and he was happy.

It reaffirmed his belief that there were moments of exhilaration and satisfaction in the news business that no other profession could offer.

He had first experienced it when, as a young radio newsman in Illinois, he had been driving down a rural highway and spotted a prison van parked in the driveway of a farm owned by a prominent state senator.

He had asked some questions of neighbors, checked with one of the State Senator's opponents who had some contacts at the prison, and then had confronted the politician at the front door of his farm.

"My name is Carl Malachek," he'd said. "I am a reporter." He had been all of twenty-three years old then, with less than a year in the business, but somehow the words, "I am a reporter" had seemed, to him, to be almost ennobling. They instantly conferred on him a status beyond his years.

"What do you want?" the Senator asked in a hostile voice.

"I want to ask about the convicts working on your farm."

In later years, Carl Malachek could still hear the huge wooden door slamming in his face but he also could still remember the thrill he had felt in uncovering a good story and exposing something wrong.

It was the same thing now.

The cover-up of the Herman Willows spy case had all the makings of a ball buster. It had Malachek's nostrils quivering.

Charlotte Glover was waiting for him when he opened the door to let Bob Lanigan back into the office. He kissed her lightly on the cheek as she followed Lanigan into the office.

"Do you two want to be alone?" Lanigan asked jokingly as she returned Malachek's kiss.

Malachek said, "As a matter of fact, we do. Maybe afterward you and I can spend a few minutes together."

"I've got a lunch appointment over at the National Press Club," he said. "Will you be here around two, two-thirty?"

"The Press Club has the worst food in Washington," Malachek growled. "I hope you're not paying."

"Don't worry," Lanigan assured him. He knew that Malachek fancied himself a gourmet but also was tightfisted with expense accounts. Like many others in the News Division, Lanigan never had been able to reconcile the inconsistency.

As Lanigan waved good-bye, Malachek glanced at his

watch. "It's only twelve-thirty. I can get us a table at Jean Louis or Krupin's or wherever you want."

"No thanks, Carl," she responded. "I have to be back at Pennsylvania Avenue by two o'clock. One of the Under Secretaries of State is coming over to give us a backgrounder on the President's South America trip."

"Has that been announced yet?"

"No. They just completed the advance trip. It's supposed to be announced next week."

Malachek settled in the chair behind Lanigan's desk and idly started linking paper clips. "If you don't have time to go out, I can order some lunch in for us," he said.

"I'm pressed for time," she explained. "That's why I asked if you could come down here today. I've reached the point in the story where I need some firm guidance. I didn't want to do it over the phone."

"What's the problem?" he asked.

Charlotte Glover lit a cigarette and sat down across from Malachek. Her mind flashed back to the time she'd sat in Malachek's office and first told him of the story. Then, she had been flushed with the excitement of uncovering it. Now, the problem of proving the story had left her feeling as if she had been thrown into an ice-cold shower.

"I'll start with Willows," she began, "because that's the easy part. He just hasn't been around. He's still driving around New England, or at least that's the story. His house is closed up and one of his neighbors says he's not expected back until next week. Senator Ramsey's office is playing dumb. All they know is that he's on vacation."

"Who's 'they'?"

"A secretary and Artie Gifford. He's Ramsey's press aide."

"Does he know anything?"

"I don't think so," she said, trying to keep her eyes off the long chain that Malachek had formed with the paper clips. "Ramsey is keeping this one very, very close. I don't think anybody in his office suspects."

"Is there any indication that Willows won't be coming back? That this vacation is going to be an extended one?"

"There's no indication one way or the other. Life goes on as usual in Ramsey's office."

"But you said Willows is expected back next week," Malachek said.

Charlotte Glover snuffed out her cigarette in an ashtray on Lanigan's desk. Malachek was beginning to cross-examine her, probing her for any clues that she might have overlooked. She welcomed it. It kept her sharp.

"He's coming back to his house next week, according to his neighbors. I don't know whether he's coming back to the Hill."

"How did you find out from the neighbors? How did you know who they were?"

"I looked up the number in the cross-reference directory, the one where the phone numbers are listed by the address rather than the person. Then I called and said I was a friend from the Midwest who was in town and was trying to reach Willows."

"And the neighbors bought it?"

"C'mon, Carl," she said coyly. "Don't I sound like an old neighbor?"

"And Ramsey?"

"He's sharp and he's tough," she replied grudgingly. "I never had that much contact with him when I was covering the Hill," she added. "He was just one of those Senators you never had that much reason to go to for comment. I don't think the Sunday panel shows ever had him on during his first term. He was just another Senator.

"But now that he's head of the CIA Oversight Committee at Senate Intelligence, he's the number one hawk up there."

"And I gather he's going to play hardball with us," Malachek said.

"Very hard. That's why I wanted to let you know what's happening with him. It could be rough."

"Go ahead," Malachek said with the equanimity of a priest who had been hearing confessions for years.

Charlotte Glover lit another cigarette and filled him in on her interview with Senator Ramsey, including his references to the President and his imitation of the bird in the jungle.

When she finished, he said, "Maybe you're overreacting. Maybe he mentioned the President only because he really is going to see him. Maybe all that stuff about the bird and the danger signal was just Ramsey being his gung-ho, damn-the-press self."

"It's how he brought it up, Carl," she said. "Out of nowhere. All of a sudden. He wanted me to know that he won't take any meddling. I'm sure of it."

"And so?"

"So if I push him, he'll stonewall. And if I push too hard, ask too many questions, he'll tell the President that we're onto something. Right now, he can't be sure. He suspects, but he can't be sure. But once he thinks we've got something nailed down, he'll be down to Pennsylvania Avenue faster than hell. And then you'll get the warnings about national security and exposing classified material and aiding the Russians and all the rest and it will come right from the Oval Office."

"The President would go to Rossman first," Malachek grumbled.

"That's probably why Ramsey mentioned Rossman," she suggested. "He'll put the pressure on wherever he can."

"I can take the pressure," Malachek assured her. "We won't cave on this one if we can get it, believe me." He leaned back and exhaled slowly. It was the relaxing trick Robert Miniver had taught him years ago.

"The problem is, Ramsey is going to be even more careful now that he suspects we might know something," he said. "So we're drilling a dry hole there."

He paused for a minute as if surveying his thoughts. "What about your source as a last resort? Any chance of breaking something loose there?"

"Not a prayer," she said. "If anything is traced back, it would be a disaster. We have to go with what I've been told and take it from there. Prove it somehow."

"I could ask Gordon Baird to work his sources at Justice," Malachek proposed. Baird covered the Justice Department and Supreme Court beat.

"There's probably an airtight lid on this at Justice too," Charlotte said.

Malachek was silent. He placed his hands in a prayer position and rested his chin on them. Charlotte could almost see him, feel him, thinking. She said nothing but just sat there and watched.

"Here's what we're going to do," he said after a few minutes. "We're going to send you back to Ramsey's office next week just to let him know you're around. Show up at his office when you know he won't be there. Let him hear that goddamn bird whistling in his ears. Let his eyes and ears perk up every time he thinks of you. And as long as you're getting nowhere with him, he'll feel safe and secure."

"And . . . ?"

"And while he's feeling that way," Malachek went on, "one bright sunny morning I'm going to have somebody pop up in front of Mr. Herman Willows when he brings in the cat or the milk or the morning paper and ask some embarrassing questions."

"It could work," she said. "If we catch Willows off guard, really ambush him when he's not prepared, he might cave on us. Ramsey probably will have told him I'm striking out."

"Exactly. And Ramsey thinks that you're the only one who's working the story, and that's the way we'll keep it for a while. You and I are the only ones in the News Division right now who know about this story. So there won't be anybody else asking questions anywhere in Washington. And if you're out of town on that White House trip to Miami, Ramsey will be completely off guard.

"When the timing is right, I'll bring in somebody from New York to do the Willows interview. The Washington bureau is like a sieve." He paused momentarily and then added, "I'll fill the reporter in next week. You keep poking around Ramsey."

"Any idea who you'll use?" she asked.

Malachek rubbed his chin. "Samantha Stuart," he said. "If she's out of New York for a few days, nobody will think it's unusual. People on that show travel all the time."

He looked at Charlotte's reaction. "I'm not big-footing you on this, believe me," he said. Reporters called it that when a reporter higher in the News Division's pecking order was sent in to work on the same story.

Because Samantha Stuart was a featured correspondent on a prime-time program, she outranked even Charlotte, the senior White House correspondent.

"It doesn't bother me, Carl," she assured him. "I've worked with a lot of people."

"It's still your story," he said. "You'll do it on the air."

She smiled at him admiringly. "I never thought otherwise."

Later that afternoon, flying back to New York on the

shuttle, he thought about Charlotte. She's a pro, he reflected. She wants this story as much as I do.

A network limousine picked him up at La Guardia. As the car crawled through the late afternoon traffic on the Grand Central Parkway, Malachek continued to relish the thought of breaking the Willows story wide open, hanging him out to dry and Ramsey along with him. It'd be a helluva blow to the other networks when the story ran on the air.

If the story were true, he'd take whatever heat the President could throw at him. As long as the story were true, he'd stick to his guns.

He knew that Rossman would cave in easily, agree to whatever the President requested, because Rossman really didn't care, deep down like he did, about breaking a big story. All Rossman really cared about was not making waves.

But that didn't matter either. He would handle Rossman when the time came. He would handle him on everything, including Mark Antin if that was what Rossman was up to.

The long black limousine moved across the Triborough Bridge and merged easily into the stream of traffic flowing along the East River Drive. Carl Malachek leaned back in the velour seat and lit a cigar.

The insulated, air-conditioned sleekness of the limousine, the heady aroma of the imported Cuban cigar, the potential magnitude of the Willows story all combined to imbue him with a feeling of power. It elated him and, as the limousine sped toward the midtown skyscrapers, he felt ready to take them all on. Every damn one of them.

By the time he reached his office, it was almost five o'clock but he decided it was not too late to call Jerry Rossman.

"How was Washington?" Rossman asked when he picked up the phone.

"Fine," Malachek replied, waiting for Rossman to make the first move.

"You said you wanted to see me," Rossman said quietly.

What a slick article, Malachek thought, almost admiringly.

"As I told you earlier, I was concerned about that item in the *News* about you and Mark Antin having lunch," Malachek said. "I hope it wasn't about the Cornwall matter."

Rossman gripped the receiver tightly. You stupid schmuck, he almost shouted, what the hell do you know about it? Antin is taking your precious *American Sunrise* to the cleaners every morning and you think he's a loser? But he did not yell at Malachek. Instead, he said, in an even tone of voice, "Antin's ratings are pretty good, Carl. But that's beside the point."

"You're right," Malachek said. "The point is that Antin couldn't report a story if it was happening three feet in front of him. It would be an embarrassment to have him on our news."

Rossman bristled at Malachek's statement.

"Nobody ever said he was a first-class correspondent, although I still don't understand why that's so important. As long as people believe in him, what the hell's the difference? But why are you so worked up about this? We don't have any deals going with Antin."

Malachek didn't know whether or not to trust Rossman. "Good to hear you confirm that," he said.

"He's looking. His contract is up and Schirmer is shopping him around. I told you, we are not going to piss away what we—you—have built up in the evening. Antin's a possibility. Or maybe Cornwall can be turned around."

"I don't think that will happen," Malachek said. "Have you spoken to him yet?"

"We had dinner the other night," Rossman replied smoothly.

"And?"

"And who knows? Maybe in the long run his loyalty to the network will prevail."

Malachek smiled. You don't believe that bullshit any more than I do, he thought. Cornwall's gone and we both know it.

"I still think we need to talk about a replacement," he told Rossman.

"Look, we'll take a look at Burton if that's who you think can do the job," Rossman said. "Swanson too. We're not going to name someone next week, you know," he added sarcastically.

"And Antin?"

"Mark Antin is a major piece of talent, Carl. But we'll look in our own shop first and try to find the replacement."

"We can't cheapen the evening news, Jerry. It's too

important," he said grimly, "and we haven't got much time. The new season is coming up fast."

"Jesus Christ!" Rossman exploded. "Don't you think I know that? I'm the one who's got to go before the affiliates and tell them our number one anchorman is taking a walk. I'm the one who's going to eat most of the shit on this. You think I'm looking forward to that?"

"That's why I'm so concerned that we have a strong replacement in there, somebody we can go to the affiliates and the press with, somebody solid, somebody we won't take a beating on," Malachek said quietly.

But Rossman ignored Malachek's pacifying words. "Don't you think I know the stakes in all of this?" he raged. "You want to know what one goddamn rating point in the news at night means to us? How many millions of dollars Cornwall is going to cost us?"

"I know."

"Yeah, yeah," Rossman muttered. "Well, I don't need any reminders about the fall season. Why the hell is this happening to us? What's the matter, Carl? Can't you keep your people happy?"

"I can't be blamed for Cornwall's decision," Malachek said.

"Well, you'd better damn well try and turn him around," Rossman said angrily. "Or you'd better have the right choice to replace him. There's too damn much riding on this to give me this professional standards bullshit about what we need from an anchorman, damn it!" He slammed the phone down.

Several floors below, Carl Malachek looked at his phone in disbelief. Jerry Rossman had never, never, hung up on him before.

He was convinced now that Rossman would try to sign Mark Antin for the evening news. And that could mean the end for him.

There was no way he could maintain respect within the News Division if Antin were hired to anchor the evening news. Antin symbolized everything that was wrong in television news—people with no news background put in positions of prominence and authority because they were good-looking or personable or tested well in some mysterious survey of women 18 to 49.

No. He wouldn't stand for it. Maybe Art Burton wasn't

another John Cornwall but he could someday be. He had all the right credentials and he came from the news.

Malachek had faith in Burton, an unswerving belief that he'd made the right choice. His was a special kind of faith, strengthened by devotion to the news and by years of experience.

He glanced at a picture on his desk of Francis at his ordination. *I wish I had your kind of faith, Francis,* he said silently. *I just don't have the time or strength or piety for that.*

Besides, God doesn't make anchormen.

I do.

Chapter 15

Like a debutante planning her coming out party far in advance, the network was beginning to prepare for its yearly meeting with its affiliates, a month away.

The meeting would serve, if all went well, as an annual rite of reaffirmation and fealty.

The network would pledge its undying efforts to provide its 205 affiliated stations with the best possible programming, programming that would outperform the competition.

The affiliates, according to custom and tradition, would listen appreciatively, pass a resolution commending the network for its continuing efforts to serve the audience, and then return to their respective cities, convinced that the coming season would be the best ever.

As always, the meeting would be a mixture of substance and hope, as if it were a kind of religious service where even the faithful, at least once a year would get nourishment and reinforcement of their belief.

Every year, with the rhythmic certainty of the phases of the moon, the network unveiled a new schedule for the fall season. The schedule contained a mixture of returning programs, new programs, and, as constant staples, the morning and evening news shows—*American Sunrise* and *The Evening News with John Cornwall*.

If the past season had been a success, then the number of new prime-time programs would be low. If the season had been a dismal failure, then the network would tout the new season as being "innovative" and "fresh" and offer the "hot" new programs.

These new programs were always accompanied by predictions of success along with research to back up the predictions.

Never mind that in any given season, at least seventy-five percent of the new programs would fail, only to be replaced the next season by more "innovative" and "fresh" series.

But you had to believe, to have faith that salvation, in the form of a riotous sitcom, a powerful drama, a new quiz show, and continued leadership in news, was Coming Soon. September.

The "coming together" of the network and its affiliates would be held not in a house of worship but in an empty theater near the network's Los Angeles studios.

The symbol of faith would be the network's logo, hanging, crucifix-like, in the center of a gold-embroidered curtain on the stage and decorating the walls of the theater's lobby and entrance.

Various network executives would serve as acolytes and Jerry Rossman, as always, would minister to the flock with a message of inspiration.

On the surface, the outlook for this year's meeting was good. The past season had seen the network improve its prime-time ratings by half a ratings point over the previous season. And, in an industry where decimal point percentages could mean the difference between success or failure—and the resulting gain or loss of millions of dollars—any improvement was significant.

Overall, the network still ranked second among the big three. But the fractional gain over last year—the only gain achieved by any network—would be the theme of The Message Rossman would deliver to the affiliates.

Actually, most of the new series introduced this past season had flopped. The network had made its gains only because of some expensive and heavily promoted miniseries, but this would be overlooked in the general euphoria. After all, why dwell on gloom when the homily would speak of happiness and joy?

One had to have faith, and faith was rooted in the mutual dependency the network and the affiliates had for each other. The network needed the affiliates to carry its programs and paid them a percentage of the advertising revenue for doing so. The affiliates needed network programming to compete in their home cities.

Once again, *The Evening News with John Cornwall* was the number one evening newscast among the three networks. And, as at all networks, primacy in news was as much a matter of prestige and image as it was of revenue and ratings.

The news was much the same on all three networks. In most cities, all three network newscasts appeared at the same time. And, on most nights, each network reported on the same stories—albeit sometimes in different order—for the first eight or ten minutes of their newscasts. Only rarely did one network have a major story that was not reported by either of the other networks.

Leadership in the news ratings at night, then, depended not on outstanding reportage or on production values, but on the audience's preference for one anchorman over the others. The networks accepted this fact and built their strategies around it. On-the-air promotion, newspaper ads, sending an anchor to China, Moscow, Managua for on-the-scene reporting; all of these were weapons in an unceasing battle to increase the popularity—and the share—of the evening anchorman.

That was where the ratings were; in the face, voice, even the inflection of the anchorman and, above all, in the mysterious process by which the audience placed its faith and trust in one anchorman over the others. And once that transference took place, it was hard to change it.

The network executives involved in planning for the annual meeting had planned what the highlights would be.

Barbara Schumacher, the head of advertising and promotion, hoped to have John Cornwall as a keynote speaker at the main luncheon. After the luncheon, Cornwall would moderate a panel discussion with a few of the network's correspondents.

Barry Kovaks, the head of network programming, was preparing a videotape presentation—twenty minutes in length—of the network's hit shows of the past season.

When the tape ended, thirty stars from the top programs would march on stage, singing an original song being composed for the event. It would, Kovaks hoped, set the affiliates on fire.

And, working through Mickey Schirmer, Kovaks had lined up Jarvis Winston to emcee the big entertainment gala that would climax the three-day event. It would be a very big deal.

The affiliates, spread out across the country like Indian tribes on the Great Plains, approached the annual meeting with a sense of optimism and satisfaction.

The President of the Council of Affiliates, Hap Hawkins, was preparing for the meeting in his own way. One of his major tasks was insuring that there would be no major surprises at the meeting.

So far he had found nothing out of the ordinary. He'd already warned Jerry Rossman that there would be the usual complaints about NFL doubleheaders running over on Sunday nights, pushing back the entire evening's schedule so that the stations' local newscasts were delayed beyond their usual starting time.

And, as always, the affiliates would want more compensation from the network for carrying its programs.

And, as they'd done for a number of years, the affiliates would pass a resolution opposing any expansion of the network nightly news from half an hour to an hour.

Rossman had privately indicated he would welcome such an expression of opinion from the affiliates this year. It would take the heat off from some public-interest groups and several Congressmen who always were badgering the network to put on more news in the evening.

There was, in both Hawkins's and Rossman's opinion, a general sense of contentment and satisfaction among the affiliates. If there were any doubters or nonbelievers among the congregation, they were quiet and keeping their heretic thoughts to themselves.

The meeting in Los Angeles was not going to be one for hellfire and brimstone. This was going to be, so it seemed, a meeting filled with praise, of voices raised in joy and gratitude. Even now, a month away, one could almost hear the singing rising to the heavens and see the joining of hands in an unbroken circle as surely as if a revival meeting were being held in a sunbaked town in the South and the faithful were filling the wooden chairs under a canvas tent.

Only a few at the network knew that this was a hollow illusion, as false as the cures of a backwoods faith healer. Only a few knew the real truth; that hidden beneath the surface, as surely as if the Devil himself had planted it, was the bombshell of Cornwall's departure and the question of his replacement.

And these few would say nothing. They would keep the enormity of the secret—the truth—to themselves until it grew so large that it could no longer be hidden. And by then, they hoped, there would be salvation in the form of a new Cornwall, a new Messiah, to lead them.

In a bar in Chicago, a forty-one-year-old man sat on a stool and scanned the classified ads of the *Chicago Tribune*, looking for a job.

He looked older than his years but that was because his face had a pinched, sallow color and he sat on the stool in a bent-forward position, as if he were afraid someone would strike him on the back.

There didn't seem to be any jobs advertised that would suit him. He shoved two dollars across the counter and walked out into the afternoon sunlight on Rush Street, taking the newspaper with him.

He walked slowly up the street, a scruffy character in blue jeans and a faded denim jacket. Few paid any attention to him and only a couple of people noticed that he cradled the newspaper under his only arm.

PART
TWO

Chapter 16

Oh Lord, look at that Bobby Ducoin! Son of a bitch drives that Corvette with one hand better than you or me with two. Goddamn, he is sure one hell of a good old boy! I heard he won a hundred bucks playing bingo over at the Legion Hall last week and spent it all buying beer for everyone. Oh, he's a pisser all right. Damn near ran into some nigger driving a tractor over on Highway 23 a few years ago. Said he didn't see him coming over the rise. Ole Bobby probably was in too much of a hurry getting up to Memphis. Gets laid up there, I hear. Them whores don't give a damn about his arm as long as he's got a good pecker and the right color money. Ain't that right? Damn shame what happened to him over there in Vietnam but sure makes you proud that he came right back here to Fire Point instead of moving away to Atlanta or New Orleans. Hell, those big cities are no place for him. Whatcha going to do down there except spend a lot of money in the big stores and fancy restaurants? Shit, Clarke County boy like Bobby Ducoin is better off here. Did you see where the County Commissioners voted to put up a portrait of him on the first floor of the courthouse? Hired some artist down in Jackson to do it. Hell, it's the least we can do. That boy damn near gave his life for u Some more like him and this country would be a lot better off. Tearing down Nixon and all that and you got boys like Bobby Ducoin been in that prison camp all those years, all that torturing. No way you can tell me there's something wrong with this country. Not with boys like him. Ain't that right?

* * *

This was the summer of 1974. Bobby Ducoin, left for dead in a field in Vietnam, had been home a year now. But in the southern summer twilight, with the crickets calling each other in the pines and the high heat beginning to climb down to evening and the water in the creeks and the ponds lying smooth as a pane of glass and the sun almost disappearing in the skies to the west, there still would be old men, their faces leathered from years in the sun, who would sit around the Courthouse Square in Fire Point and talk about Bobby Ducoin.

He was back home amongst them, gathered unto them like the granite Confederate soldier whose eternally vigilant gaze stared out from the monument in the center of the square.

There Is No Greater Glory, the inscription at the base of the statue read. Bobby Ducoin had known the glory, in a different war and of a different kind.

POW DUCOIN ENROUTE HOME! *The Record,* the weekly newspaper in Clarke County had exclaimed in a banner headline a year earlier when the Air Force planes carrying the POWs had landed at Clark Field in the Philippines.

All of Fire Point, it seemed, had watched the welcoming ceremonies on television and had seen Bobby Ducoin come off the plane, his right sleeve sewed to his jacket, his left hand in a perfect salute, his knees bending so he could kiss the ground. His mother, Mary Jo, cried for hours after that, it was said.

When he came back to Fire Point, there was a big parade in his honor. He sat in the back seat of an open convertible, squeezed between the Governor of Mississippi and one of the state's two Senators, and waved with his good hand to the crowds lined along State Highway 54, which, for the five blocks it ran through the center of Fire Point, was called Lamar Avenue.

The marching band from Ole Miss, dressed in rebel gray uniforms, was bussed in from Oxford to lead the parade and even the band from Mississippi Valley State, one hundred and ten blacks shining like polished ebony in the midday sun, was brought in for the day.

A huge banner, paid for by the Clarke County Chamber of Commerce and reading Welcome Home Bobby Ducoin, was stretched across Lamar Avenue as if it were a triumphant arch even though the high humidity and the lack of any breeze made the middle of the banner sag like a deflated balloon.

The bands played marching arrangements of "Dixie" and "When the Saints Go Marching In" and "South Rampart Street Parade" and when the parade was over and the speeches were over and Bobby Ducoin had been given the keys to Fire Point by Mayor Tom Mosher and a free weekend at the Magnolia Ramada Inn (just off the Interstate 10 miles W of Fire Point) and a lifetime membership in the Fire Point American Legion Post 118 and the keys to a brand new midnight blue Corvette, courtesy of Lamar Chevrolet (Your Hometown Dealer), Bobby Ducoin went home and got drunk with his Daddy on Wild Turkey bourbon and Dixie beer chasers while his Mama stayed in the kitchen and bottled the green pepper jelly he always had liked.

Home was a three-bedroom, white frame bungalow on Barnett Street, a few tree-lined streets away from Lamar Avenue and the Courthouse Square, where Bobby Ducoin had lived with his parents all his life until he had enlisted in the Army.

To everyone in Fire Point, Barnett Street was in "the downtown." If you lived in the downtown, you lived in a section where lower-income white families always had lived in Fire Point. There was a small white middle class, and the few rich whites—the president of the local bank, the owner of the lumber mill, a retired oil man—lived in estatelike houses on the outskirts of Fire Point in an area called Knollwood.

The blacks lived in "The Pines," across from the Illinois Central tracks that intersected Lamar Avenue at the top of a little hill. The Pines was a rambling collection of wooden houses and cottages that stretched for a twenty-block area of unpaved streets until, as if giving up in despair, it reached one of the rural roads that snaked around Fire Point.

Bobby Ducoin had been across the tracks, as the locals called it, only once. In his freshman year in high school, when he was fifteen years old, he and five of his friends paid twenty-five dollars to get laid by a black girl in The Pines and lose their virginity.

In the downtown, the men in the families worked in the lumber mills or for the IC railroad or as garage mechanics or would drive to Memphis to work for the construction companies or barge lines. It was not unusual to see pickup trucks with gun racks over the rear window parked in the driveways of houses in the downtown.

There would be copies of *TV Guide* and *Reader's Digest* on top of the color television in the parlor—nobody called it the living room—and even though few people in the downtown went past the twelfth grade of the Clarke County Consolidated, the "Three Cs," as it was called, many of the cars and trucks in the driveways had Ole Miss or Mississippi State decals on the windshield.

This was what Bobby Ducoin had come home to: a piece out of time in the red clay of Mississippi; a place where the seemingly endless two-lane state highway and the rolling hills and the blazing sun in the summer and the cold, damp, cloudless skies in the winter emitted a feeling of loneliness and emptiness as haunting as the pine forests that embraced the town. And yet, in some mysterious way, it was as sweet as the jonquils that bloomed on Barnett Street and the rise on Lamar Avenue in the glorious color-burst of spring.

When Bobby Ducoin came back to Fire Point, seven years after he had dropped out of the Three Cs to enlist in the Army, he was a local hero with six thousand dollars in back pay from the Army and a desire to do nothing except, as he told one of his old friends, get laid and get drunk.

Fire Point seemed, at first, the same as it was when he had left it. The Clarke County Bank and Trust, Ackerman's Variety Store, Parks Jewelry, Bob and Al's Sporting Goods (Hunting and Fishing Licenses Sold Here), the Indian Lake Cafe and Package Goods Store, Mooney's Barber Shop, they still were fixtures on the square just as was the statue of the Confederate soldier.

In his childhood, awed by the semiromantic framework in which the War Between the States, as it was called, was taught in the lower grades of the Three Cs, he had developed a reverent regard for the knapsacked and long-rifled soldier in the square. Years later, after the rotting, infested jungle heat of Vietnam and the brutal years in the cramped, corrugated tin hut in the prison camp, he would smile to himself when he passed by the statue in the square. Son of bitch wouldn't know what the fuck war is all about, he would think to himself.

The mythical, martyred, stone hero of his childhood had

become, twenty years later, just another statue splattered with bird shit, staring at the Mississippi sun.

For the first year after his return home, Bobby Ducoin tried to get the war out of him by screwing or drinking and, when there was nothing else to do, talking about it.

You had a bad time, Bobby? his Daddy would ask him and he'd answer, oh, yeah, it was real bad. This would be late at night as they sat in the parlor, his Daddy tired from work at the lumber mill outside of Fire Point, and the two of them sitting there having a beer and there'd be nothing on the television.

There was a lot he couldn't remember, he would confess, like how he got to the prison camp and how his arm got shot off. But he could remember some things.

And he would say: We were on a patrol, I remember that, and there was a lot of shooting and mortar fire but I don't remember much else except lying in the field and calling for help. There was this big nigger radio man, Eddie Johnston, calling out and I thought I saw the Lieutenant in the platoon come for me but I don't remember what happened. He went away and I thought I heard him crawling back through the grass, like one of those old hunting dogs wiping his haunches, but there was too much pain and I must have passed out. And then I remember being picked up from the field, after the helicopter left, and I was on a bamboo stretcher and the VC were chattering like a bunch of god-damn monkeys and they took me to a prison camp.

And his Daddy would ask, as if fearing a reconfirmation of what he already knew: And they beat you real bad?

This would be on other nights, with the story coming out slowly and, again, there would only be the two of them in the room—just him and his Daddy—because his Mama couldn't stand to hear it all. She had cried only twice before in her whole life, when Roosevelt died and when Bobby came off the plane in the Philippines. But she had cried a lot ever since the first time he had started to tell them about the prison camp. The three of them had been in the parlor then but, after the first time, only his Daddy would listen.

They beat us with big bamboo sticks, he would say, and tied our feet with tight leather straps and made us sit with our heads between our knees for hour after hour until we passed out.

And then he would tell how he was kept in solitary confinement for over a year, living on a bowl of rice a day and watching rats scurry over his straw mattress, and how he got dysentery and was sent to a work camp, digging ditches twelve hours a day and how he never knew where he was except that it was somewhere near Hanoi because that was where the planes landed to take him to the Philippines and Hanoi was a three-hour truck ride from the prison camp.

It took Bobby Ducoin almost a year to tell the whole story, bringing it out piece by piece as if he were sewing together the patchwork quilt that covered his bed in the winter.

And when he had told everything he knew, he realized that he still didn't know it all; that there were missing pieces, just as there were tattered fragments on the worn edges of the quilt.

It was all in the past and all he could tell his Daddy was, "I hate what happened to me. Goddamn, I hate it."

In that first year, the permanence of Fire Point, the minuscule rhythms of its life, served to protect him as if he were in a cocoon insulated from the world outside.

The way the thunder would roll out of the bottomlands as a summer storm approached, the brownish yellow color of the soybeans as the autumn neared, the clattering noise of a garbage can being turned over by a hungry possum or coon in the stillness of a winter night, the first sprouting of the cotton Bolls in the spring; they all enveloped him in a warming haze and it took him a long time to perceive and then, as if his eyes were slowly focusing, finally to see what had changed around him.

It was then that he began to feel sorry for himself.

It wasn't that the people in Fire Point didn't still appreciate him and what had happened to him in the war. Shit, they were even going to bring in some artist to paint a picture of him to hang in the courthouse. No, it wasn't that.

It was just that everything seemed to be changing. It was as if, while he had been away, and even in the past year, there had been an enormous silent movement far beneath the earth; a huge sea change that had shifted everything above ground so that now, even though all the buildings and the statue in the square and the buildings in the downtown were still standing, they all were slightly out of kilter.

The more he looked, the more he realized how much
had changed. There were niggers playing on the Three Cs
now. And, on Friday nights in the fall, when most of the town
came out to watch the Fire Point Indians play State Division
A High School football, there would be whites and niggers
sitting in the same sections of the wooden stands that rose
from the field.

And in the cocktail lounge of the Southland Motor Inn
out on the highway, where he'd sometimes go on a Saturday
night to watch the dancing and hear some music, he'd see
guys he'd known since high school sitting there with gold
chains on their necks and wearing shirts with the buttons
open so that you could see the hair on their chests.

It was all changing. A company out of Houston was
building a new movie theater—Cinema I and Cinema II,
they called it—out in the shopping mall and the Pickwood
Theater in the town was going to close. The Trailways bus
from New Orleans to Chicago still came through every afternoon but the IC had closed its station in Fire Point. There
were music groups with crazy names like Led Zeppelin and
Jefferson Airplane on the radio and, at the 4th of July picnic
in Handeman Park, nobody had given a speech. Everybody
had been throwing Frisbees or barbecuing on fancy kettles
and listening to rock music on portable cassette players like it
was just another Sunday.

The whole world, it seemed to him, was changing. It was
marching past him like it was on parade and he was watching
from the sidewalk in front of one of the stores on the
Courthouse Square. It should have been the other way.

At the beginning of 1975, his money began to run out.
There was no job he really wanted in Fire Point. He could
tend bar out at the new Motor Inn going up on the highway
or get a job clerking in one of the stores on the square but
that meant working regular hours and saying yes sir, and yes
ma'am, and he had promised himself back in the POW camp
that, if he ever got out, he would never take shit from no
one.

In June 1975, Bobby Ducoin put on a white shirt and a
new tie and his best suit and drove eighty miles south to
Jackson and applied for a job selling funeral insurance for the
Home and Life Memorial Insurance Company of Mississippi.

You'll make most of your money off the niggers, someone in Fire Point had told him, but it didn't matter.

He'd take their money because, he was learning, it was everybody for himself these days. Besides, he would be his own man, drive his own car, keep his own hours and, if he was any good at it, make some money.

For the first few months, Bobby Ducoin was good at it. He drove all over Mississippi, from Picayune in the south to Batesville in the north, up and down I-55 and the other highways and rural roads, selling peace of mind and a proper burying. He'd stop at the small town funeral homes, the ones with the neat white signs in front and the porch lights on all night and the hearse in the back, and he'd speak to the funeral director and point out how funeral insurance would mean good business.

He'd always get some names of prospects and he'd be sure to attach his business card—Robert Ducoin, Field Representative, Home and Life Memorial Insurance Company— to the religious calendar he'd leave as a gesture of appreciation and he'd promise to stop in again on his next visit.

Only there never was another visit. Even though there was some business in the big cities—Hattiesburg, Meridian, Biloxi, Pascagoula—most of it was in the poor, rural black areas that were unchanged from generations ago.

And you couldn't step in cow shit or chicken shit all your life, walking up dirt lanes to those damn shacks off the road, with the cotton dresses and the overalls hanging out to dry in the sun on a chicken wire clothesline, and the nigger kids staring at you like you were the Sheriff, and telling some fat woman with a gold tooth shining in her mouth that it's just a few pennies a day to make sure that you'll be sent to the Lord in proper style so just sign right here and then driving off with the pebbles in the road sticking in your tires and all the time you're hoping to find a good restaurant on the highway that will sell fried catfish and a cold beer.

Oh no, you can't do that too long before the sun gets to you as it beats down on the two-lane and the cable TV in the motel makes you want to see the Atlanta Braves baseball games in person and the waitresses in the coffee shop all ask if you want a refill, darlin', and all the time they're staring at the sewed up sleeve on your right side and you know they're probably screwing some hairy-chested guy with an open neck shirt and a big gold chain and two good arms. Oh no.

So Bobby Ducoin began to stay off the road more and more and started coming back to Fire Point and the house on Barnett Street on Thursday nights instead of Friday nights.

One day in midsummer, he flew to Atlanta to see the Braves with Hank Aaron play in a night game. When he came back to Jackson the next day, for his semimonthly visit to the Home Office, he was half-loaded because he had drunk too much beer on the plane even though it was only a one hour flight.

He walked into the Home Office of the Home and Life Memorial on Capitol Street, with his coat off, his shirt collar unbuttoned, his tie loose and the sweat forming a dark pocket on the side where he had the butt of an arm. It was ninety-five degrees outside, and the sudden immersion into air-conditioning made him feel sick and he puked all over the desk of the front office receptionist.

They didn't even give him the money he had earned as a draw against commissions for the last two weeks. Instead, the manager told him he was a disgrace and probably needed counseling from the VA.

Bobby Ducoin came back to Fire Point and didn't tell his Mama or Daddy what had happened. I just got tired of all that shit, he told his Daddy, and it didn't bother him that he was lying.

He hung around Fire Point for a few weeks, picking up odd jobs when he could. But, when the money he had saved began to run out, he decided to leave for good.

In late August 1975, Bobby Ducoin drove to Atlanta, sold the midnight blue Corvette he had been given on his homecoming to Fire Point and asked the dealer who bought the car if he needed any help. Lost my arm in Vietnam in the war, he said, and there's not too many jobs around for a one-armed vet.

The dealer asked him for some references and said, if they checked out, he'd give him a job. Bobby gave him his father, the Mayor of Fire Point, and the pastor of the Fire Point Methodist Church.

He spent the next week going to the Atlanta Braves baseball games at night. Other than the one time he had flown to Atlanta to see a ball game when he was working for

the Home and Life, he had never seen a baseball game in
person. It had always been on television.

But now he reveled night after night in the spectacle;
the splashy colors of the different tiers of seats that surrounded
him, the brilliance of the towering stadium lights, the dazzling greenness of the artificial grass, the larger-than-life
replays on the giant television screen that loomed behind the
outfield.

He'd buy a general admission ticket, sit in the upper
grandstand, and drink three or four beers a night, sweating in
the evening heat and swatting away the night bugs attracted
by the radiance of the arc lights above him and he'd stomp
and cheer whenever the Braves scored a run because, in
Atlanta, they were called America's Team and he liked that.

After the game, he would take the shuttle bus back to
the downtown area and then go to the one-bedroom apartment he had rented in an old house near Peachtree Street.
That first week, sotted by beer and drained by the excitement of watching the baseball games in person, he would not
wake up until eleven or eleven-thirty in the morning and
then he would spend the rest of the day walking around
downtown.

He went back to the used car dealer after a week and
was hired. You checked out okay, the dealer, a florid-faced fat
man named Joe McConnell told him. The preacher over
there in Mississippi says you were a POW, is that right?

Yessir, Bobby Ducoin answered, wondering if the young
woman who was answering the phone in the tiny office in the
showroom was Joe McConnell's wife.

Now, a few days later, Bobby Ducoin sits in a folding
aluminum chair with red and white webbing and watches the
little yellow, blue and green plastic pennants, strung out like
tiny diapers on a clothesline, fluttering on the nylon cord that
stretches from the streetlights at the front of "Big Joe"
McConnell's Used Car Lot. If a customer walks onto the lot,
he'll meet him, be polite, try to highball him on a trade-in
and will keep in mind "Big Joe" McConnell's only sales
lesson: Don't let them Jew you down.

After two weeks, he has not sold a car but he has learned
that the woman in the office is McConnell's niece, a twenty-
year-old, honey blond, big-titted girl from Waycross, Georgia

who goes to the University over at Athens and is working for her uncle this summer.

Her name is Katherine, and one Saturday afternoon, when there are no customers on the lot and the pennants are hanging limp on the wire and the TV is carrying the Braves game from Pittsburgh on the cable, Bobby Ducoin asks her if she wants to go to a movie that night.

She says, sure, and they go to a Pink Panther movie and he puts his good arm around her and she says nothing and he knows right then, with her head leaning on his shoulder and those big melons looking like they're going to burst out of her blue blouse, he knows that he is going to score.

After the movie, they stop off for a couple of beers and a pizza and he asks, you want to come back to my room, and she says, flat out, why not, and so they go back to the small apartment off Peachtree Street and she says to him, let's hear some music, but all he can find on the radio is rock music or country and western and he asks her, do you really need to hear music and she smiles and says, I don't need nothing.

He starts to unbutton his shirt, slowly, with one hand, and she says to him, leave the shirt on, I don't want to look at it. He tells her I got one bad arm but one good cock and she says, that's all you need.

He fucks her with his shirt on and everything else off and when it is over she tells him she has been looking at him ever since he drove onto the lot with that midnight blue Corvette. Her uncle thinks she's just a little country girl, she confesses, but she's fucked a couple of guys on the football team, not the niggers, of course, and she came to Atlanta to have some fun. Never fucked anybody with one arm, she says, and suddenly he raises himself from the bed and hits her across the mouth and tells her to get the hell out, she ain't worth shit.

The next day, Bobby Ducoin is worried that she will tell her uncle but nothing happens. Then one day two months later, Katherine comes to him in the middle of the afternoon, him sitting there in the aluminum chair from K-Mart, sitting by a 1974 silver Cutlass with a LOW MILEAGE sticker covering half the windshield, and she says, I missed my period again.

He asks her, what are you telling me, and she answers that she thinks she's pregnant and Bobby Ducoin says to her, not smiling and with his lips twisted into a half-sneer and his

eyes staring right through her, maybe it was one of them
Bulldog quarterbacks you were fucking. And he can see the
tears forming in her eyes and he gets up and walks away.

The next day he is gone, leaving no forwarding address
and not even bothering about his last week's pay. He never
knows whether she is lying or if, as he sometimes wonders in
later years, there is a little kid in Georgia with his face and
her honey-colored hair.

There was no sense in going back to Fire Point—"Big
Joe" McConnell could find him back there—so Bobby Ducoin
went west, taking a Greyhound bus to Denver because he
always had wanted to see the mountains and the snow.

He got a job working as a night cashier in a restaurant at
Stapleton Airfield but he didn't like the work, any more than
he had liked working for the Home and Life in Jackson or
"Big Joe" McConnell in Atlanta. So, six months later, when
he couldn't stand it any longer, and he felt that too many
customers were staring at him as he worked the cash register
with one hand, he quit.

For a few years after that, he drifted from job to job and
city to city, living in a succession of dreary rooming houses,
YMCAs and cheap hotels, always living on the thin edge of a
week's pay.

It didn't seem right that nobody gave a shit about the
fact that he had been a prisoner in a POW camp and it wasn't
fair that he had to scrounge for a living like this—working as a
movie usher in Oklahoma City or stuffing phone bills for the
phone company in Shreveport—while everyone else out there
was making big money. It seemed like the whole goddamn
world was turning against him.

The best job, one that lasted for a year, was on the
midnight-to-eight shift as a dispatcher for a big trucking
company in Rawlins, Wyoming. He'd sit there in a glass-
enclosed office, like an admiral on a bridge, looking out over
the huge tarmac with the big orange and blue Union 76 neon
signs lighting up the night and he'd send those big semis
rolling out onto I-80 and there was a sense of power, of being
somebody. But it all ended when he got drunk in a barroom
in Cheyenne one weekend, tried to beat up a waitress, and
was arrested. He was fired the next day when he returned to
the big lot with the huge trucks.

Fire Point was far behind him now. His Mama, and then his Daddy, had died and he had gone back for the funerals, riding a Trailways bus all night and the next day, but there was nothing there to hold him.

His Daddy had sold the house on Barnett Street after his Mama died and had moved into a new development, Magnolia Gardens, out by the shopping center on the outskirts of town. A two-story, white brick building with phony columns at the entrance and a small swimming pool in the back and not even a second bedroom where Bobby could visit. After his Daddy's funeral, Bobby knew he'd never come back there again.

Even if Bobby Ducoin had come back to Fire Point, even if he had sat right down at the base of the statue in the Courthouse Square and talked to the men who, years ago, had talked about him in near-reverential tones, it would not have been the same.

The years of shiftless wandering, of never having much money, of depending on a weekly paycheck and the monthly GI disability payment, of being rootless in a world where everybody under thirty years old seemed to be making a pile of money; all of that transformed him into a hard-eyed, thin-haired man who physically resembled a field animal—a mole, a ferret—scurrying through an empty field, burrowing yet another hole, foraging for food.

See Bobby Ducoin on the street and you avert your eyes, not because he is physically repugnant, even with one sleeve sewed to his shirt, but because you see a faceless person who carries the smell of old beer and bus station waiting rooms and yesterday's newspaper and cracked plaster rooms in YMCAs and cheap movie houses.

Oh yes, Bobby Ducoin is out there and he doesn't give a shit about anybody or anything because things just didn't work out. Not from day one.

And now, in the late summer of 1985, with his job as a ticket taker at Wrigley Field about to end, Bobby Ducoin walks down Rush Street toward the Loop, a newspaper folded under his only arm, and he knows that soon he will have to find another job.

Oh yeah, Bobby Ducoin thinks to himself, I gotta get

humping. This little ole country boy's got to make a living. Nobody out there gonna do shit for me.

Ain't that right?

Chapter 17

The rehearsal of *Focus on America* had been underway for less than ten minutes in the fourth-floor studio that was the program's on-air home when Art Burton began to let the production talk drift by him, as if he had wandered onto another set and could hear only snatches of conversation through a door left half open behind him.

He never had liked rehearsals but he knew there was too much that could go wrong in a one-hour show, even where many of the segments were pretaped. A tape could be miscued, a camera angle wrong, a graphic appear at the wrong time; all of these needed to be checked and practiced beforehand. It was a necessary evil.

"We'll have to cut down on the map behind you, Samantha," George Durgin, the executive producer, was saying into a control room microphone that carried his words to the set where Art and Samantha were standing.

"Check the lighting on Art's face. . . . Can we bring up the music a little more on the opening title? . . . There's a shadow behind Samantha. . . ."

It was not that he didn't care about the conversation floating around him. There just wasn't any room for it in his mind. His head was filled, as it had been for days, with the despair he'd begun to feel about his failed chances for the Cornwall job.

Everything was being crowded out by one enormous, glaring fact. Despite what Malachek had told him, nothing had happened. Nothing.

He had been waiting for a week now, waiting for some sign, some puff of white smoke from the inner councils of the network, that would tell him he'd beaten the odds, that he would be the next anchorman of the evening news. But there had been no sign.

The whole thing was falling apart in front of him. A gnawing doubt that he would be chosen had plagued him ever since the *Daily News* article about Mark Antin and Mickey Schirmer meeting with Rossman. It had wiped out everything—the Vegas gambling story, the trip to New Orleans, everything.

Durgin began reciting the routine for the upcoming show. Thirty seconds for the opening. First piece runs seven minutes and twenty-eight seconds. Cue to commercial. Intro the second segment. The Gospel According to St. Durgin.

He glanced over at Samantha, who was making some corrections on her script.

He always had admired Samantha's professionalism. She wasn't like some of the women correspondents who, in the network's eagerness to get women on the air, had been promoted too fast from local stations. Most of those women were on minor beats or second-level stories now, rarely getting on the shows, slowly disappearing from sight, like a vanishing species that once had inhabited the earth. When their contracts ran out, they would be gone.

No, Samantha was different. She had earned the right to be here. And even if she couldn't go any higher, here was damn good.

He recalled the first time she'd ever appeared on the show. She had produced a good, solid piece on the decline of the shoe-manufacturing industry in some eastern Massachusetts towns, filled with poignant interviews with families whose incomes were slowly dwindling to the near-poverty level.

The story was followed, as part of the program's regular routine, by an unrehearsed brief discussion. It was the first time Art and Samantha had ever done the cross-talk segment together.

"What do you think, Samantha?" he had asked her. "Is there any real hope for the families we just saw in your story?"

"It isn't just those families," she'd replied. "It's all the families we didn't see . . . all those people who may be sitting there tonight watching this program and wondering about their future. Thousands of men and women who may soon be out of work."

There had been nothing to say after that. It seemed to him that she had said it perfectly.

Now, standing near her on the set, he saw her glance up from her script and look at him; a quizzical look as if she intuitively knew that his mind was elsewhere. A little smile broke out at the corner of her mouth. She tapped her pen across her fingers, as if she were reprimanding him for not paying attention.

He caught the tiny gesture and smiled back at her. The quick exchange of glances, furtively as schoolchildren passing secret notes, only increased his impatience with the rehearsal. He wanted to be alone with her so they could talk.

He heard Durgin asking, "Art, do you want to rehearse the voice-over lead-in for the next segment?"

"Fine," Burton answered. "I'll do it now."

Over the loudspeaker, Burton heard "Five-four-three-two-one ROLL TAPE!"

On a television monitor in front of him, Burton eyed scenes of Sarasota, Florida, and he began to read a script about the economy of Florida's west coast. It was about thirty seconds in length and the last scene, a shot of a yacht anchored at a pier, ended before he finished the narration.

"Recue the tape," Durgin's voice boomed out across the set. "A little faster on the reading, Art," Durgin instructed.

"Whatever you say, boss," Burton responded automatically and, as the scenes came by again, he paced his narration so that his voice and the videotape ended at precisely the same moment.

"That'll do it for now," Durgin said in a satisfied voice. "We'll run through the rest on Friday. Thank you, Art. Thank you, Samantha. Thanks, everybody."

Burton and Samantha walked down the corridor and took the elevator to the *Focus* offices on the seventh floor.

"You looked as if you couldn't care less," she told him as he followed her into her office.

"About you?" he asked, uncertain what she meant.

"No. The rehearsal. I could tell you weren't into it."

"Was it that obvious?" he asked. He pushed aside a

stuffed animal and sat down on her burnt orange suede couch.

She nodded and sank into the chair behind a desk filled with notebooks, newspapers, and several videocassettes.

"A real mess, isn't it?" she said, spreading her hands across the desk to embrace the full range of disarray.

Her words went right by him. "I'm going to close the door."

"People will talk," she said coyly, a smile breaking out at the edges of her mouth.

"Let them," he answered quickly, going to the door.

"What's the matter, Art?" she asked, struck by his abruptness. "Talk to me."

"It's the Cornwall job, Samantha. It's getting to me. It's sitting out there, tempting me, and I can't get to it. I'm beginning to feel that it's not going to happen."

His words came out rapidly, as if a floodgate had opened and all the damned-up frustration was suddenly pouring out. The rush of words engulfed her.

She had wondered what he was going to do when he had closed the door.

The thought had crossed her mind, very briefly, that he was going to pull her onto the couch and make love to her, there, in the office. But the thought had come so quickly, and lasted so briefly, that she had not even fantasized how she would respond.

"Why don't you go to Malachek?" she asked.

"I can't," he said wearily. "I'm not a heavy-hitter like Cornwall. I just can't walk into Malachek's office and say, 'About that anchor job, Carl.' It just isn't done that way."

"Maybe you should get an agent," she suggested. "At least a good agent could find out what's going on with Rossman and Antin."

"I can't do that," he said. "I've never had one. Besides, getting an agent now would be like waving a red flag in front of Malachek. He hates agents. It wouldn't make any sense."

She gave him a comforting smile. "Malachek told you that you were his choice, Art. He obviously wants you or he wouldn't have said so. He knows you want it, doesn't he?"

"Of course he does," he answered. "Who wouldn't want it? Jesus, being one of the chosen few. One of three Princes.

There are only three jobs like it in the whole business, Samantha."

"Oh yes," she said bitterly. "I know."

The minute she said it, he realized how he had unintentionally wounded her.

"Look," he said apologetically. "Someday a woman is going to anchor the evening show every night. God knows you're good enough. I think you're fantastic. But it's not in the cards for you, not now. Maybe not for me, either."

Samantha had been hurt by his inference, no matter how unintended, that she feared being someone who was never going to make it to the very top. Someone like her. But hell, it wasn't her fault that she couldn't go any higher. It was the system, the shitty system, that prevented her from aspiring to anything higher than anchoring the weekend show or co-anchoring *American Sunrise*.

But Art had a chance. "Don't let this destroy you," she told him. "Go to Malachek. You've got a right. That damn item about Rossman meeting with Mark Antin is probably in every desk drawer in the News Division by now. It's no secret."

"Look," he said, "you know the way this business works. You can be terrific, work your ass off, and some lousy columnist writes a two-sentence item that you've got a big ego or your producers don't like you or you're pissing on other correspondents, and all of a sudden there's a quarantine sign on your door even if none of it is true. And it takes a long time to get the sign down. So if it leaks out that Cornwall is leaving and I'm angling for the job, I could be shot down before I take my shot."

"How is it going to get out? It'll be just you speaking to Malachek."

He shrugged. "How do these things ever get out? I don't know. It just happens. Malachek tells Rossman that I'm interested in the job. Rossman tells someone. Maybe Barry Kovaks, someone like that. So Kovaks is flying out to the Coast and he sees somebody he knows, a syndicator, a producer, an executive, and they talk about the business—programs, pilots, ratings, anything—and somehow the evening news comes up and the next day the other guy tells someone at another net, 'I hear Art Burton is making waves.' I'm telling you, that's the way it happens."

"You know what?" she said, getting up from her chair. "We're living in Paranoia Palace. All of us. You, me, Durgin, the people on the assignment desk, everybody in the whole damn network. We're so afraid of somebody saying something unfavorable that we're paranoid half the time. It's crazy, Art, absolutely crazy."

"I know that," he agreed, rising from the couch to meet her. "But what the hell can I do? There's a big difference between the front office and everybody else. Seven West is a different world. There's them and there's us.

"I don't know Malachek all that well," he continued. "I don't know how he'd react if I set up an appointment to talk about the Cornwall job. Maybe he'd resent it, think that I'm too pushy. Up until now, I've been just one of the horses in the stable. Can I walk in and remind him that he wanted me to run in the Kentucky Derby?"

A trace of a curl fell over Samantha's forehead and she brushed it back with her hand. "I don't know," she said resignedly. "You've been in this business longer than I have. Maybe you just sweat it out, even if you don't want an agent, and trust that Malachek is going to come to you. Something's got to happen soon, one way or the other, doesn't it?"

"Yes. Malachek never said exactly but I assume it'll have to be before the new season."

"That's coming up fast. I don't see any harm in just mentioning it to him," she told him. "Tell him you were wondering if anything was happening and let it go at that."

"Maybe I will," he said. Talking to her had made him less fearful of doing anything that would disturb the fragile nature of Malachek's commitment.

Up until now, he had felt like a nature photographer for *National Geographic*, crouching in a grass shelter day after day, waiting for a bird's egg to hatch, afraid to move a tiny blade of grass for fear of disturbing the entire cycle of gestation.

But maybe Samantha was right. In the cycle of the network's life, Malachek was part of the birth process of the anchorman. Without Malachek's approval, nothing could happen. "Maybe I'll go see Malachek," he repeated, as if convincing himself. "I'm going out to Vegas again to give that gambling story another shot. I'll stop by his office before I leave, you know, casually, to let him know what's happening on the story. And I'll mention Cornwall, and see if there's anything new."

"Will you ask him about that meeting Rossman had with Mark Antin?"

"I don't know how far to push it. Yes, if I see a chance to bring it up."

The loose curl fell over her forehead again and she tossed her head back, trying to get the curl in place.

"Here, let me," he said. He put his hand on the shock of hair and brushed it back off her forehead.

"Thank you," she said softly. His tiny gesture erased the previous conversation from her mind, and now he seemed suddenly fragile and vulnerable.

"It will work out," she said, her thoughts coming back to the reason he was standing there.

"I hope so," he said, almost prayerfully. He took her hand and squeezed it and leaned toward her and kissed her on the mouth. "I don't know what I'd do without you," he confessed into her ear.

She nuzzled her nose against his cheek, wanting the tentative touching between them to go on, to escalate. But then she withdrew slightly from him as if to indicate that here, in her office, at eleven o'clock in the morning, this was as far as it could go.

Samantha walked him to her office door. "I should have realized that it was eating you up like this. I should have called you while I was out of town."

"I could have called you," he responded, "but I wanted to talk to you in person. It's better this way."

"When will you see him?"

"Today, if I can. I'm going out to Vegas tonight."

"Call me."

"I will," he promised. "Keep your fingers crossed."

"Yes," she said, smiling. She watched him go across the corridor to his own office, which faced hers. Then she closed her door and sank down on the couch.

She wanted him to succeed, to be chosen for the anchor job, but she knew there was nothing she could do to help him.

She had no real leverage at the network other than her salary—$90,000 a year—and the fact that she was a woman.

The leverage, however, was a paradox. The network paid

her a good salary because she was good but also because the network needed visible women, just like it needed blacks and Hispanics on the air. She was more than a token, but still less than an equal.

She had come to a grudging acceptance of the fact that there really wasn't much she could even talk to Malachek about concerning her career, other than proposing some shots as a fill-in anchor on *American Sunrise*. Or maybe an occasional special. But she knew she would remain where she was, valuable, on display, a shining prize in the network's showcase.

What it came down to was this: she'd take the money and run, just like the rest of them. If Art could make it to the top, great. Both of them, in effect, would make it. The good guys would win.

She idly toyed with the stuffed bear on her couch and thought about Art making love to her there.

It could have happened when he had first closed the door. He could have pulled her over to the couch, right where she was sitting now, and kissed her softly and tenderly. The door would be closed and somehow she would have adjusted the venetian blinds on her window, shutting out the sunlight.

The room is totally dark and she leans back on the throw pillows and raises her skirt and spreads her legs and all the time he is kissing her and moving his hands over her and then he pulls her panties down and his cock is inside her and she feels that warm fluid oozing into her wetness....

The fantasy was so intense that she closed her eyes, as if to isolate herself from everything around her. When she suddenly blinked them open, she looked down and realized that she had instinctively spread her legs apart and she was sitting on the couch as if she were waiting to be fucked.

God, she thought, I feel wet.

She got up quickly and walked to her desk and looked out the window. For half a second, she was puzzled that the venetian blinds were open and shafts of sun were streaking through the slats. It should have been dark.

Then she remembered, and smiled to herself and tried to remember the fantasy.

It was, she thought, good in the dark.

Chapter 18

It was late in the afternoon, an hour before he had to leave in order to catch the flight to Vegas, when Art Burton finally got to see Carl Malachek.

He found the News Division president leaning back in his chair, smoking a cigar, and thumbing through a copy of *TV Guide*.

It surprised him. Malachek was more of a *Time-Newsweek-The Economist* type reader.

"Hello, Carl," he said pleasantly. "Have you got a few minutes?"

"Why not?" Malachek answered in a slightly gruff voice. He wondered whether Burton was going to ask him about Jerry Rossman's meeting with Antin.

He had to know about it, Malachek figured. It had to be all over the division because everybody, down to the lowliest mailroom clerk, read the TV columns in the papers before they read the front pages. That was the way the damn business worked. World War III could break out and most people would read about it after they had checked the television columns.

Well, right now it was none of Burton's business, Malachek decided. If Burton asked, he would tell him so.

"What's on your mind, Art?" Malachek asked.

"I'm going out to Vegas again on the gambling story," Burton answered, "and I'm having some problems with it."

"Tell me about it. Anything major?" Malachek inquired, his level of interest perceptibly rising.

Burton realized that there was now no good way to bring up the Cornwall situation with Malachek. He had triggered the man's interest to a good news story—and it'd be awkward

diverting Malachek's interest to something else. The chance
was gone.

Burton plunged ahead. "There's a hang-up. There's an
old woman out there, Jewish woman, who I was told is
betting heavily with the mob. Big money. Hundreds of
thousands of dollars. But if you saw her, there's no way
you could believe she's a gambler. It just doesn't add up."

"Maybe you got a bad tip," Malachek suggested.

"I don't think so. My source is too good. He's a
cop."

"You think cops have the right information all the time?"
Malachek asked and Burton could not miss the sarcasm in his
voice.

"This cop does," he responded defensively. A picture of
Frank Baglio came up in his mind. Maybe Frankie likes soap
operas, Burton thought, but he's still a hell of a cop.

"If he's as good as you think he is," Malachek declared,
"find another source to back him up. All it takes is time and
money."

"I've got another source," Burton informed him. "My cop
knows somebody on the force out in Vegas. He may be able
to help me. It may take a little time though. I'm going to be
out there for a couple of days. That's what I wanted to tell
you, in case you needed to reach me."

What he wanted to say was, "In case you wanted to give
me some good news." But he didn't. He hoped that Malachek
would realize that he was wondering about the Cornwall job
and would say something to reassure him that it was all going
to work out. But Malachek gave him nothing except a nod of
the head and the words, "Keep at it. Stay in touch."

For Malachek, it was the best way to end the conversation. Clean. Simple. No opportunity for Burton to ask about
Cornwall even though Malachek figured Burton must want to
know. He noted what he took to be Burton's restraint but
there was nothing he could tell him with certitude until he
had worked it all out with Rossman.

It was better this way, better that the subject hadn't
come up.

Burton said, "I'll let you know how I make out," and
walked out of Malachek's office, trying to find some significance in Malachek's final words—"Keep in touch."

But he could find none. Glancing at his watch, he

realized that he had to leave for the airport and wouldn't even have time to call Samantha.

The whole meeting just hadn't worked out the way he had wanted it to.

Now, flying west on the late evening flight, he drifted in and out of sleep. For most of the flight, he had been distracted by an eerie distortion of the figures on the small movie screen mounted on the wall at the front of the first-class cabin.

Something was wrong with the projection of the movie on the screen. The screen could not accommodate all of the picture. Disembodied parts—Clint Eastwood's arm, Sondra Locke's left ear, spilled over the margins of the screen onto the lavatory door.

There was no way he could sleep, with that happening in front of him. Once, a passenger had walked up the aisle to use the lavatory, opened the door, and half of Clint Eastwood's arm had disappeared. Just like that. Gone forever.

The passenger in front of him had kept his reading light on; a tiny beacon shining out of a dark landscape. Burton had asked the flight attendant for an eyeshade but just the knowledge that the light in front of him was on, shining, had made it impossible for him to sleep.

It was almost one o'clock in the morning, New York time, when the plane finally began to descend below the clouds and the neon lights of Las Vegas came into view.

With nothing left but to wait for the landing, he replayed Malachek's words in his mind, probing them for some nuance that would provide him comfort and assurance.

The words, "Keep in touch," he reluctantly concluded, had no significance at all.

A few minutes later, the plane landed. He had brought only a carry-on garment bag and an attaché case and he walked quickly past the baggage claim area and through the airport lobby to the cab line.

"Caesars Palace," he said to the cab driver.

By the time they got to the hotel, Burton was thankful that there had been no conversation. He needed the silence, even if it was only three dollars and twenty cents worth. Plus tip.

In the morning, with the sun pouring through the windows, he felt better.

The meeting with Malachek, the intermittent sleep on the flight from New York, it all seemed to evaporate in the blinding sun.

It rose over the mountains that guarded the western edge of Las Vegas and, standing at the window, he suddenly thought of how the sun had lit up the mountain range in Vietnam the morning they had gone out on that patrol.

Jesus, it was so long ago but he still remembered. He always would. He shuddered slightly and reached for the phone to call Samantha. Then he remembered that it was noon in New York City, and she was speaking at a luncheon. He would not be able to talk to her until evening.

Instead, he called room service, ordered eggs Benedict and a pot of coffee, then dialed the Las Vegas Police Department.

The contact Frank Baglio had given him, a detective named Tyrone Davis, should be at work by now. He tried to picture what Davis looked like. With a name like Tyrone, he probably was black. Whites were not named Tyrone.

A desk sergeant whose name came out as part of a longer announcement—Vegas Police Department Sergeant Angotti speaking—answered the phone and put him through to the Detective Bureau.

"Is Sergeant Davis on duty?" Burton asked.

"Speaking."

"My name is Art Burton. Frank Baglio in New Orleans told me I could give you a call."

"Oh yeah," Davis answered. "Frank called me a few days ago. Said you might be calling me."

"Yes," Burton confirmed. "Frank's an old friend of mine. We grew up together."

"He's a good cop. I worked with him on a narcotics bust once. Big haul. Interstate thing. Big case. Treasury, Vegas police, New Orleans cops. Lasted three months. That's how I got to know him. You from New Orleans?"

"A long time ago. I work in New York now," Burton answered, deciding from the voice that Davis was white.

"Did he tell you why I'm here?" Burton asked, wondering if Davis knew that he was on television. I hope he doesn't think I'm another cop.

"Frank said you were working on a story for that program of yours. *Eyewitness America*. Right?"

"Yes," Burton replied, not wanting to embarrass the detective by correcting him. "I need some information on a woman who lives here in Vegas. Her name is Weinstein. She lives on Lopez Drive, on the outskirts."

"She must have money," the policeman said. "That's the high-rent district out there."

Burton hesitated for a moment, undecided whether or not to tell the faceless voice on the other end of the phone all the details of the story he was working on. What the hell, he decided, if Baglio gave me his name, I can trust him.

"We think she may be a heavy gambler, hundreds of thousands of dollars bet with the mob."

"Here? In Vegas?"

"No, back East. The kind of gambling where you don't report anything to the IRS. The kind where you're betting a bundle every week. We hear she's into the mob for three quarters of a million."

"Jesus," Davis muttered.

"There's a problem," Burton went on. "I met Mrs. Weinstein. And she's not the type."

"Who is?"

"I don't know. All I know is, she doesn't fit the mold. She wouldn't know a point spread from a space shuttle."

There was silence on the other end and Burton wondered if the line suddenly had gone dead.

"Are you there?" he asked.

"I'm here," Davis assured him. "I just was calling something up on the computer, trying to see if we had anything on her in our files."

"And?"

"No. Nobody named Weinstein. I spelled it both ways. *I* before *E*. *E* before *I*. All sorts of combinations. Nothing."

"I don't think she's the type who would be arrested for anything. She's in her late seventies."

"It can happen."

"Listen, Tyrone. Is it okay if I call you by your first name, by the way?"

"Ty is better. That's how I've been known ever since I was a kid."

"Okay, Ty." Burton could not resist the temptation. "That's an interesting name. Family name?"

Davis laughed. "Shit, no. On their first date, before they

were married, my parents went to the movies. *Blood and Sand.* Bullfighting movie. Tyrone Power was the star. So I came along in forty-six and, out of sentiment, they called me Tyrone. If I had been a girl, I would have been Rita. Rita Hayworth. Crazy, huh?"

Burton laughed. "Tyrone Davis. I must confess I can't quite picture it on a movie marquee."

"What the hell," Davis said. "For the movies, I'd change it. Just like half the people in Hollywood."

"How right you are. Look, I'm going out to the house on Lopez Drive again," Burton said, "to see if I can come up with anything. If not, I'll take the late flight back to New York tonight."

"Tell you what," Davis said. "Give me a call when you get back to your hotel. Maybe I'll have something by then."

"That really would be appreciated, Ty," Burton said.

"I'll call you." He hung up the phone and got out a map of Las Vegas from his attaché case and located Lopez Drive on it.

Fifty minutes later, he was on the highway leading to the outskirts of the city.

He drove in silence for miles until the road was no longer bordered by fast-food outlets, shopping malls, Putt-Putt golf courses, cheap motels, and billboards advertising Lake Tahoe or Reno or airline flights to Los Angeles and Hawaii.

Mrs. Weinstein's house was as he had remembered it: low-lying, sprawling over the ground as if it had been built in a series of afterthoughts; put a wing here, add a swimming pool there, add a patio here.

It was a home that obviously was worth a lot of money. Maybe a half a million, he figured, and it was in a neighborhood where, it seemed, the home owners did not have to worry about making mortgage payments.

A few seconds after he pushed a bell that set off chimes somewhere inside the house, a maid appeared in the doorway.

It was the same black woman who had answered the door on his last visit

"Yes?" she asked, looking at him quizzically, as if he were a delivery man or a postman who had come to the wrong address.

"I was here a few weeks ago," he said, "to talk to Mrs. Weinstein. I was wondering if she was in."

The woman's head moved in a slight nod of recognition. "Oh yeah," she said. "The man from the TV. I remember her telling me about you."

"Yes," he answered. "The man from the TV."

"Missus Weinstein not here," the maid said, still standing in the doorway.

"Will she be back soon?"

"No, she's in LA."

"In LA?" he echoed, surprised.

"Her son lives there. She visits him every month."

"Do you know when she'll be back?"

"Three or four days. She takes the first flight in the morning. I drive in and pick her up at the airport."

"That's nice," he said absentmindedly. "Do you think she'll be here in a few days?"

"She left yesterday. So maybe a couple of days from now."

"All right, thanks," he said. He took one of his business cards from his wallet and gave it to her. "Tell Mrs. Weinstein I was here, if you would," he said. "Tell her I will call her."

The black woman turned the card over in her hand as if she were expecting to see something printed on both sides of the card. Burton waited to see if she would recognize his name, or even the name of the program, but she did not. Unless you do a nightclub act here, he decided, you're a nobody.

"Please give her the card," he reminded her over his shoulder as he walked back to his car and heard the door to the house close behind him.

He was frustrated and angry that he had spent all this time only to find nothing. It just never had occurred to him that the Weinstein woman would not be home. And he could not picture her in Los Angeles visiting her son. The woman was too old to drive, and you needed a car in Los Angeles just to go to the bathroom. So what was she going to do, sit around her son's house all day, reading the papers? And she did it once a month?

When he arrived back at the hotel, he was still puzzled by it but his bewilderment was only part of a larger frustration.

The story was going nowhere, and, unless he could come up with something quickly—he would have to abandon it.

Focus on America did that lots of times. Stories just didn't work out, or were not produced well enough to meet George Durgin's standards, and so they were abandoned.

The program's budget could handle it, and illegal gambling would be an easy one to stop. Not a piece of tape had been shot yet, no interviews had been lined up, nothing. This one could be aborted right after conception.

But he knew that there was a story, and if he could pull it all together, starting with the arrests Frank Baglio had made in New Orleans, it could be a big one. It was the type of story that got ink, got attention, and that was what counted.

Get your name and your work in the columns. It was all part of the game, and that's what he needed now—attention that would make people like Rossman notice him more than ever before.

He picked up the phone and dialed the Police Department and asked for Detective Davis.

"Hello, Ty," he said as Davis came on the phone. "It's Art Burton. I struck out. The Weinstein woman wasn't home."

"Well, I got a little information for you," Davis said. "It's not much but it's all I could come up with. I checked the real estate records. She doesn't own the house. It was bought a few years ago by a Jerry Weinstein, who lives in Beverly Hills. Might be her ex-husband."

"Probably her son," Burton said, jotting down the name. "Her maid said she visits her son in LA every month. It must be him. Any address?"

"300 Majorica. Means nothing to me. Except in Beverly Hills, it's got to be good."

"I really appreciate your help, Ty," Burton said. "If there's anything I can do for you in New York sometime, you know, tickets to shows, something like that, let me know."

"That's okay," Davis said. "I never get east. But keep me in mind if you ever do a cop show out here. You know, with a name like Tyrone I should be in the movies, right?"

Burton laughed and hung up.

He stared at the pad. But the name and address meant nothing other than a link to Mrs. Weinstein. He would have to go to Los Angeles to see what the next link in the chain would be.

At least it was a lead, no matter how small, and he felt better.

He switched on the television. The set was tuned to the network's affiliate in Las Vegas and, as a soap opera ended, the network began to run promotions for programs coming up later in the week.

"There's laughter and music every Saturday night," an anonymous announcer was saying. "Top stars visit Jarvis Winston for television's best variety hour. Be watching on Saturday night when Jarvis Winston rings down the week and brings down the house. Ten Eastern, nine Central and Pacific. *The Jarvis Winston Hour.* Here on the Network of America."

How can people watch that shit? Burton had seen *The Jarvis Winston Hour* and it was a dog. But Winston brought in the money and some of it paid the bills for news. In the end, he knew, they all were in the same butcher shop, just making different kinds of sausage.

Samantha, Malachek, the announcer who had done the promo, Winston: their paychecks all carried the network's brown and red logo in the corner. Just like his did.

He picked up the pad of paper again and then he remembered something Davis had said, something about his name.

"I'd change it in a minute to go into the movies," the detective had told him. "Just like half the people in Hollywood."

Like Cary Grant had been Archie Leach. And Tony Curtis had been Bernie Schwartz. And Judy Garland had been Frances Gumm.

And—now he remembered—Jarvis Winston had been Jerry Weinstein!

He had heard it around the newsroom in New York once, when they were joking about names. Some correspondents had changed their names, particularly the Jewish ones. Bill Edwards, one of the correspondents in London, was really Billy Epstein. Robert Forrest, the correspondent at the Pentagon, was really Bobby Greenwald. And Jarvis Winston was really Jerry Weinstein.

Somebody had seen it someplace, in the contract department of the Entertainment Division. Jarvis Winston was Jerry Weinstein. And his mother was being used to get big payoffs in gambling. Only she didn't know. That had to be it. She didn't know!

The money came in hand-delivered packages that she brought to her son once a month. He probably told her it was some sort of an arrangement with the network. Scripts for pilots or something like that.

Jesus. Jarvis Winston, the network's biggest star, betting big, big money with the mob. It was too wild to be true!

Burton reached for the phone and started to call Malachek but then he put the phone down. It was better to wait, he decided, until he had it nailed down. He'd have to prove it, really get it buttoned up, and then he'd break it to Malachek. Malachek would love it.

Burton was elated. For the first time in days he felt free of the depression that slowly had been enveloping him.

Now, with the realization about Jarvis Winston, he had burst through it, like a runner breaking the tape at the end of a long distance race.

He suddenly felt strong and confident. He looked out the window toward the desert that began at the fringe of the city and he pictured himself running through it: his arms churning through the still, blue air; his legs kicking up the sand behind him, leaving a trail of grainy dust that obscured him to the other runners, the sun glistening off his body, his whole body moving forward in powerful strides.

He could run like this forever, to the far edge where they all would be waiting for him at the finish line. Samantha, Malachek, Rossman, all of them, and, at the very end, he would be running surely and swiftly, and he would run to her and hold her and kiss her and he would win. Everything.

Chapter 19

"Hey, baby, give it to me one more time!"

Jarvis Winston took a piece of paper from a notepad by his phone and cradled the phone in his ear.

"Okay," he said, pulling a pencil from his desk drawer. "I'm ready."

He slowly read back the words he was writing down on the pad.

"The economy is getting so bad that my mother-in-law says she's cutting back to call us once a week. I never thought I'd hope for the stock market to crash.

"Hey, I love it!" he said delightedly. "I'll use it in the opening monologue this week. You're great, Mickey."

He hung up the phone and put the piece of paper into a notebook with the words FILLER MATERIAL stamped on the front and silently thanked Mickey Schirmer for calling.

That was one thing about Mickey. He always was good for a couple of one-liners, some piece of shtick he had picked up in New York, maybe from one of his clients. Who knew? That was what made him a good agent. He cared.

What other agent would call every week and give him material? Maybe it was because Mickey was Jewish, like him, and had that Borscht Belt sense of humor. Yeah, Mickey was like him. They both had grown up in the Bronx and they both knew a good joke when they heard one and a good two-handed set shot twenty feet from the basket when they saw one and a good piece of ass when they had one.

Mickey was a lot like him, only Mickey didn't know what he knew. About the betting. The fucking money he was dropping every week and the way he was handling it. That was one thing nobody knew. Nobody.

Jarvis Winston glanced idly at the notebook, tapped his fingers on the top of the book as if it were a bongo drum, and waited for another phone call.

This one would be from his mother. When she was in LA, staying at his house in Beverly Hills, she called him every afternoon.

"Hello, Jerome, you having a nice day? Everything okay?"

And he would answer, "Yes, Mom, everything's fine."

"The shvartze here is fixing chicken for dinner tonight. You'll be here?"

"I'll try, Mom."

In the afternoon, three days a month, he'd get the call and the announcement about what Neddie, his black housekeeper, was fixing for dinner. His mother never called her Neddie. Always the shvartze. The black.

You can't change old Bronx habits, he decided. Not even his.

Anyhow, it was too late for his mother. She had become a yenta, an old woman who padded around in house slippers and read *Variety* and didn't even ask about the package she brought him once a month.

He couldn't stop it. The gambling was like a narcotic, a drug he had been on all his life. He couldn't get off it even if he wanted to. So he'd keep doing it. And as long as his mother didn't know what was in that manila envelope she brought him, what the hell difference did it make?

She had asked him only once and he had lied to her, telling her it was scripts from New York his agent kept sending out to him.

"By messenger?" she asked. "He doesn't trust the mails?"

"Don't worry about it," he had said, as if it were a completely normal occurrence that some guy he had never seen, probably some guinea or, worse, a coal black spade with one of those Marvin Gaye beards, would show up at her doorstep in Las Vegas with a package for him.

The thing was, it didn't bother him. It never did.

Ever since he first started out in the business, ten years ago, doing that noon talk show in Indianapolis and hosting *The Money Movie* in the afternoon, he'd been gambling.

Somebody told him about a bookie running an operation in a cigar store just off the Circle, near the Soldiers and Sailors monument. He bet on everything, including the Sweet Sixteen High School Basketball Tournament, and he figured that he probably was one of two people at the station who was doing something on a regular basis that all those ministers on the Sunday morning religious programs were preaching against.

The other person was the station manager who, he found out, was banging the station's weekend switchboard operator.

It wasn't until he got to the network, five years ago, starting out with a thirteen-week summer replacement variety show, that he realized how easy it all could be.

Shit, they were snorting coke behind the scenery flats in the big studios and nobody gave a damn. A bunch of young kids, all wearing sneakers and T-shirts and baseball caps, were producing and directing the shows and it was like a big summer camp.

Hey campers! Today we're going to have swimming and volleyball and two tapings and a run-through and tonight's marshmallow roast is canceled in favor of some new white stuff just in from Colombia.

That was the way it was and, when he had asked Mickey Schirmer, the agent he had hired and the one who had gotten him the thirteen-week tryout, what the fuck was going on, Schirmer had told him, "That's California, kid. It's different from New York. Out there, they can get away with it because it's away from everything," Schirmer had said.

"Look at them, the hundred-dollar sweatshirts and the designer jeans and the sports cars. Nobody gives a shit about what's a little bit—or a lot—illegal because as long as you're enjoying yourself, and the ratings are good, and you're healthy, and looking good, what's the difference?

"Besides, who's going to tell? All the big network honchos are back in New York, running the network. They don't want to know if some junior writer has got a seventy-five dollar-a-day habit. What the hell difference does it make? He probably works for a production company anyhow. It's their little red wagon.

"A big star gets in trouble, that's something else. But how often do you hear about that? The big ones, they play it very, very close. You got one guy out there, biggest drag queen you've ever seen, and all the executives in New York pray every night he doesn't get knocked off by some jealous queer in Frisco. But you never hear about it.

"What you got out there is a bunch of vice presidents keeping an eye on a bunch of producers who are making a bunch of programs that are making a bunch of money. So everybody's happy."

Mickey had been right. He always was. All it took was one full season, twenty-six weeks with thirteen reruns, for him to realize that as long as he was making money for the network, they didn't care what he did as long as he kept clean in public.

So he kept clean while all the time he was getting in deeper, until he had to start putting some mob-owned acts on the show in order to work off the tab.

The big executives in New York, Jerry Rossman, Barry Kovaks, the rest of them, they didn't know about it. How could they? It was all handled so nicely. Shit, it worked like clockwork.

He wondered for a moment what Rossman would do if he ever found out about his gambling problem. Cover it up, probably. The network couldn't stand a scandal of any kind.

Bad press ruined the network image of good guy citizen, putting on all those programs of culture and news for all those schmucks out there. Who the hell were they kidding? No, they'd cover it up all right. They'd get Sid Neale or one of his high-priced flunkies to put out a story that Jarvis Winston was tired, or the show was losing its punch, or he was having trouble getting big-name guest stars.

He'd be out and he would never get a job in network television again. They'd make sure of that.

He could almost picture Rossman, seated at some industry dinner, flanked by the presidents of the other two networks, seated on the top tier of the dais, and somewhere between the lousy pâté and the chicken Kiev, Rossman would say to the others, "By the way, if Jarvis Winston is shopping around, don't go for it. There's a problem."

That was what would happen. And neither of the other two would ask what the problem was because all they had to hear was the word "problem" and that would be enough. Nobody wanted a problem.

Well, they weren't going to get one with Jarvis Winston because little Jerome Weinstein was too smart to let it all go down the drain. The house in Beverly Hills, the white Porsche, with the JOKES license plate, the shvartze who cooked the meals, the house in Vegas he had bought for his mother after his father Morris, the furrier, had died of a heart attack, right there in the middle of Seventh Avenue and Thirty-eighth Street; his agent, the residuals, he wasn't going to lose any of it.

In a way, it was just another bet he was making. His smarts, his *keppela*, against the habit, the action. The smart money—his money—was on him. Just speculating about his own chances of keeping it all working was a thrill of its own. He tried to calculate the odds on the network ever finding out.

What would they be? 100 to 1? 1,000 to 1? Hey! Give

me little Jerry Weinstein, president of the senior class in high school, and six points against all the network brass. An underlay if ever there was one.

He laughed just thinking about it and he was still enjoying the thought when the door to his office opened behind him.

He did not hear two men walk in and it was only when one of the men brushed up against the leaves of a tall ficus plant by the door that Jarvis Winston turned around and realized that he was not alone.

It took him a second longer to sense that he was in trouble. The old *keppela* was working overtime.

"You guys looking for somebody?" he asked, trying to sound nonchalant. They had left the door open and, for a moment, Winston felt relieved. What could happen with the door open, in an office on the second floor of the network building?

"We just wanted a few minutes of your time," one of the two men said. They both were in their mid-thirties, Winston figured, with sun-streaked blond hair and moustaches. They wore sunglasses and Winston noted that the man who had spoken was wearing brown and white saddle shoes.

They were well dressed. Saddle Shoes had a tan gabardine suit, a white button-down collar shirt and a blue and red striped rep tie.

The other one, the taller of the two, was wearing a sport coat and slacks and an open-necked sport shirt under which he could see a gold chain with a medallion.

Winston couldn't figure them out. They didn't look like California types. They looked like people playing California types and that was what bothered him.

Christ, he thought, this is crazy. It's five minutes past three on a Friday afternoon and I'm sitting in my office in the network building and two guys walk in off the street on me and half the staff is five minutes away in the Commissary. So why am I worried?

He got up to walk to the door when the man with the open-necked sport shirt and the gold medallion moved quickly and effortlessly to the door and quietly closed it and locked it.

It was then that Jarvis Winston knew that his intuition had been right. He was in trouble.

"Like I said," Saddle Shoes said softly, "we just want a few minutes of your time."

Suddenly, his fist shot out from somewhere behind his back and landed in the soft, layered, fat flesh of Winston's stomach.

It's going through me, Winston thought. He sagged backward and crumbled to the floor, his hands wrapped around his stomach as if trying to protect it. Oh my God, he moaned at the intense pain.

The taller of the two men came and stood over Winston. Winston was slowly rocking back and forth, clutching his stomach in agony. From the corner of his eye, he could see only the man's shoes and a little way up his knees.

"Why?" Winston asked pleadingly. "Why are you doing this to me?"

The man bent down and spoke into Winston's ear. He was so close that Winston could smell cigar smoke on his breath.

"Some friends of yours wanted to send you a message," the man said.

The old line from *What Makes Sammy Run* ran through Winston's mind. "If you want to send a message, get Western Union." Oh Christ, he thought, don't hit me again.

"You get the message?" he heard the man ask.

Winston's answer came out as a question. "Who sent you?"

"You're getting too far behind."

He quickly tried to calculate where he was on the tab. Somewhere around two hundred fifty thousand, he figured. But his body hurt too much to think about it. All he could say was, "I'm not behind."

"They say you are," the man said and Winston never saw the swift, vicious kick coming. It was aimed at his rib cage and Winston started to scream in pain but the other man quickly shoved a handkerchief in Winston's mouth to stifle any sound.

No thoughts were going through Winston's mind now. Only pain and a desperate pleading to God to make them stop. Don't let them do it anymore, he repeated over and over in his brain.

The one who had kicked him leaned over him and said, "Now listen carefully, Jarvis. This is just a little reminder that you still owe big money and you can't work it all off by booking the acts. *Capisce*??"

Painfully, Winston raised his head to signify that he understood. Then his head sank back to the floor.

"So maybe you'd better get a little money in, you know, just to show that you're a straight guy. That way, there's never any trouble. You can keep the action going and there's no complaints. Everything's businesslike. *Capisce*?"

Winston moved his head slightly. I'm going to die, he thought.

"We're gonna go now," the man said. "You can tell the cops a couple of cokeheads beat you up or something. Big star like you, there's always lots of dopers looking for money or something. Here's a coupla good-bye kisses from all your friends."

Through terrified eyes, Winston saw the man bend down and roll him over, as if he were a dead, big-game animal being prepared for mounting on a wall. Then he felt the sickening thud of a shoe cracking a rib on the other side of his body and he felt the handkerchief being removed from his mouth just in time to let the vomit come rushing up from deep in his stomach.

The last thing he heard was one of the men saying, "The son of a bitch is puking."

Jarvis Winston, emcee, comic, star of the network's prime-time variety show, lay writhing in pain, his purple and gold LA Lakers sweatshirt covered with foul-smelling vomit, his body seething with the agony of broken ribs, his eyes swollen tight, filled with tears of pain and fear.

Somewhere, in the dark blackness of the back of his mind, he tried to think why this was happening to him. But he couldn't. There was nothing but blackness. The old *keppela* just wasn't working.

It was Charlie Zagora, the executive producer of *The Jarvis Winston Hour*, who found Winston a half an hour later. When he came into the office and saw Winston lying on the floor, half-conscious, he yelled "Jesus!" and felt sick.

The shock of seeing Winston lying there, as if he were dead, froze him and he frantically tried to think of what to do. He was terrified and he ran to the door and yelled into the hallway, hoping somebody would hear him. "Help! Get a doctor! Somebody! Help!"

He ran back into the office and, standing by Winston's side, afraid to even bend down and touch him, picked up the phone and dialed the operator.

"This is Charlie Zagora in Jarvis Winston's office," he said breathlessly. "Get a doctor up here quickly. It's an emergency."

He was surprised at how quickly he had reacted. He had done all the right things, just like the movies. Called for help. Asked for a doctor. Jesus, it was unbelievable.

Not more than a minute had elapsed since he had come into Winston's office. He had planned to discuss the preliminary rundown for this week's show. He had been carrying his stopwatch with the large second hand sweep he used for timing show segments. Now he bent down over Winston and thought: How do I take his pulse?

He could see that Winston was breathing and he put his hand on Winston's forehead as if he were trying to see if Winston had any temperature. It was the only thing he could think to do.

"Jarvis," he said rapidly. "Can you hear me?" There was no answer.

Oh Christ, he thought, what the hell has happened here? The thought crossed his mind—who would do the show that week—but he was ashamed of even thinking it and he quickly shut the thought off as if it had never been there.

Winston moaned slightly. Zagora said, "It's Charlie Zagora. Help is coming."

Winston blinked his eyes to acknowledge that he could hear. His mind was beginning to come back now, as if he were just waking up and bits and pieces of a dream were still floating around his memory.

He tried to remember what had happened, why he was lying on the floor like this. He could remember, in faint outline, the two men and the brown and white saddle shoes but nothing else other than that he had been beaten up. Oh God, he thought, what do I look like?

Through the narrow opening of his swollen eyes, he could see someone—Zagora, Charlie Zagora, that's who it was—kneeling by him. He wanted to speak, to say something, but he couldn't. Everything hurt too much.

Zagora got up and walked over to the phone and called the operator again.

"Is anybody coming up here?" he demanded urgently, not even bothering to identify himself or where he was calling from.

The operator said, "They're on their way," and Zagora walked over to the window and looked out into the vast parking lot of the studio. At the far end of the lot, where the network's security guards were stationed in a wooden booth by the entrance gates, he saw a police ambulance, its amber light spinning in a constant circle.

Hurry up, goddamit.

A few minutes later, three policemen, accompanied by two of the network security guards, rushed into the room. Zagora noticed that one of the men was carrying a stretcher that was folded up like a child's toy that had to be assembled.

"They're from the emergency service, Mr. Zagora," one of the network guards said hurriedly.

"Yes, yes," Zagora said automatically, pleased that the guard knew his name.

One of the policemen came over to Winston, knelt down, and said, "We're going to move you, sir. We're taking you to a hospital."

Winston closed his eyes in relief. He was going to be all right.

Another policeman came over to Zagora and asked, "Is he able to talk?"

"I don't think so," Zagora replied. "He was beaten up pretty good."

"Any idea how long he's been lying here?"

"I don't know. I found him about five minutes ago. Like that."

Zagora watched as the stretcher took shape, complete with casters, and he stepped back, almost out of respect, as the two policemen rolled the stretcher next to Winston's battered body.

"Can you move him?" Zagora asked.

"Oh yeah," one of the policemen assured him. "We've handled worse." Jesus, Zagora thought.

The two officers bent down and slowly began to lift Winston onto the stretcher. Winston looked up at them gratefully and winced in pain.

He was beginning to remember more now. The men who beat him up had been sent by the mob. They wanted more money. Then he realized: I can't say anything. I can't tell. No one knows.

He felt himself being rolled out of the room. He could see the ceiling and the back of the policeman who was walking in front of the stretcher.

They're taking me to the hospital, he thought. There will be questions.

He slowly moved his head to the side and tried with his eyes to communicate to another policeman who was walking alongside the stretcher. It wasn't until the policeman looked down at him, to check his condition, that Winston was able to signal somehow that he wanted to say something.

The police medic bent over and checked an IV in Winston's arm. Winston saw the fluid dripping through the tube into his vein. Then the idea came to him.

He ran his tongue over his lips and struggled to get the words out. They came out fitfully, each word requiring an effort.

"Druggies," he whispered to the ceiling. "Druggies did it."

The policeman walking beside him cocked his head to pick up the words.

"Druggies," Winston repeated faintly.

He heard the policeman tell the others. "He's saying some guys whacked out on drugs did it."

Winston closed his eyes and tried to smile. The old *keppela* was back working again. No one would know.

After Winston was taken to the ambulance, Charlie Zagora remained in the office, feeling as if he were staying behind at the cemetery after a funeral.

The few minutes since Winston had been wheeled out had been enough for Zagora to think about the larger perspective: what did this mean for the network?

It would have to be handled by the network's Public Relations Department. They were the ones who would take over, moving in like an army of occupation.

He knew that by the time the Hollywood police issued their report, the network's PR Department would be ready with its first news release, along with a bio of Jarvis Winston and a packet of publicity stills.

Zagora went to Winston's desk and saw the familiar brown and red cover of the network phone directory. He quickly thumbed through it until he found the number of Milton Stanger, the network's West Coast director of PR.

He dialed the number and, after identifying himself to a secretary, was put through to Stanger.

"Hello, Milton," he said urgently. "This is Charlie Zagora. From the Jarvis Winston show. We've got a hell of a problem here."

"Like what?" Stanger responded quickly.

Stanger's ability to sense an impending problem, ranging from drunken comedians to network executives with exotic sexual habits, was not failing him. The words, "We've got a hell of a problem here," spoken by a man he did not even know, except by name, were enough to trigger the alarms in his system.

"Somebody just beat the shit out of Jarvis Winston."

"Jesus!" Stanger exclaimed. "How is he?"

"He's being taken to a hospital. The cops are taking him."

"Oh my God. How bad is he? Is it critical?"

"I don't know. The emergency squad is handling it."

"Can he talk? Does he know what happened?"

"He whispered something to the cops about guys on drugs."

"Jesus," Stanger repeated, this time in a lower voice, as if the impact of the news had physically weakened him.

"Listen to me," Stanger continued. "I need more information. What hospital is he being taken to ? What precinct is handling it? Can you find out?"

"Yes, of course," Zagora replied, admiring the way Stanger was taking hold. The first wave of the publicity force was already establishing a beachhead.

He had never met Stanger and knew him only by his reputation as one of the repositories of the network's darker secrets. He also knew that the job of West Coast director of PR was, despite its geographical distance from New York, on an equal basis with any of the top network jobs in New York.

California was where the stars were. Not just Jarvis Winston but big-name, prime-time talent; people with as much star value as Clark Gable or Cary Grant or Lana Turner would have had in the days before television. Only more people saw these stars than all the movie audiences combined.

No wonder Stanger got paid a shitpot full of money. *He'll earn it on this one*, Zagora figured.

"All right," Stanger said. "Now, who knows about this? Other than you, that is? Was anybody around? Secretaries, people like that?"

"No. No one."

"That's a break," Stanger commented, relieved. "Whatever story we put out won't get contradicted by some twat who wants to see her name in the LA *Times* or *The Hollywood Reporter*."

Son of a bitch, Zagora thought admiringly.

"You said he told the cops it was some dope heads?" Stanger asked.

"Yes," Zagora answered.

"How long have you worked on the show?" Stanger asked, his voice serious.

"Three seasons."

"Level with me. Is he okay? I mean, has he got a habit? Cocaine, heroin?"

"No," Zagora answered quickly. "He was clean. I'm positive of it. I would have known."

"Anything else?"

"Like what?" Zagora was annoyed at himself. He was almost getting defensive about Winston and yet he really didn't like him all that much.

"Like little boys. Little girls. Or big boys. I don't know what. I just want to make goddamn sure that whoever did this didn't do it because Jarvis Winston has got some nasty habit that somebody else doesn't like."

"I doubt it. I think he's a nice Jewish kid who's probably shacking up with every broad who gives him the come-on. I don't think he's queer, if that's what you're worried about."

"I'm worried about anything that will hurt the network," Stanger said. "Maybe it was druggies," he continued, thinking out loud. Then: "Listen, Charlie. I'm going to call a friend of mine on the Department and find out whatever else I can. Have the cops questioned you yet? What did they tell you to do?"

"Nothing," Zagora answered, realizing for the first time

that he had been left alone by the police and had been given no instructions on what to do. *I thought they always took a statement*.

"They didn't tell me anything," he said to Stanger. "They just wheeled Winston out and left me here like a schmuck."

"They'll be back," Stanger informed him. "Stay there and tell them everything you know. I'll get one of the network lawyers over and somebody from my department will come over too."

"What are you going to do?" he asked.

"I'm going to call Sid Neale in New York," Stanger replied, misunderstanding Zagora's question, "and see what kind of a release we're going to put out on this. Let's face it. A network star gets beaten up, somebody as well known and as popular as Jarvis Winston, and every two-bit paper and 50-watt radio station in the country is going to play it up big.

"It'll be all over the LA papers, probably the *News* and the *Post* in New York. Christ, it might even make the network shows tonight."

"Hey," Zagora said, almost pleadingly. "I don't want to do any interviews. I mean, not even for our network. Let 'em interview the cops."

"I'm telling you right now," Stanger said firmly, and now he was speaking with the implicit imprimatur of the network and Zagora knew it. "If Sid Neale or Jerry Rossman say that you should make yourself available in case any of the nets, or the press, want to talk to you, then that's what you're going to do. This is too big to screw around with. Jarvis Winston is no small-time star. And we've got to take this one and turn it around so that the whole friggin' country is sending him get-well cards and nobody is asking why a couple of cokeheads chose to beat him up or how they ever got in the goddamn building in the first place. All of that is going to get lost in the flowers and candy and get-well cards, got it?"

"Yeah, sure," Zagora said, concealing his sudden anger over the fact that this faceless voice on the phone, this high-priced bullshit artist who probably couldn't produce a fifteen-minute Saturday morning kids' show in Des Moines, this network flack, was concerned only about how the whole thing was going to play.

Meanwhile that poor bastard Winston was probably lying unconscious in St. Mary of Something or Other Hospital, the one near the studio, with a couple of nuns clucking over him, and all that Stanger can talk about is what kind of a story they are going to put out.

Fuck 'em, Zagora thought. I'd have been better off if I had stayed in the locals, away from all this bullshit. No big money talent, no network PR people, none of this bullshit.

He looked out the window at the studio parking lot, at the yellow bordered spaces filled with hundreds of high-priced cars.

The late afternoon California sun was bouncing off the windshields and chrome platings, sending a blinding burst of bright light back at him.

In the distance, through the haze, he could see the Hollywood hills and he tried to pick out his home with the red bouganvillea bushes and the swimming pool and the built-in gas barbecue.

"I'll do whatever you want," he told Stanger.

What the hell, he thought, it's just the way the business works.

Chapter 20

Samantha Stuart sat in the front seat of the rental car, on the passenger side, warmed her hands on a container of coffee that her cameraman, Joe Fleming, had given her, and looked across the street toward Herman Willows's house.

She had been sitting in the car since six A.M., ever since the sun sneaked up on Washington and had begun to bathe the city in a soft morning light. Now, after two hours of waiting, she felt as if she knew every tree, every house, every crack in the sidewalk on the street in the northwest section of the city where Willows lived.

It was a residential neighborhood and the houses were all two-story combinations of wood and brick that reflected the general tenor of the neighborhood. Solid, permanent, and conforming.

Nothing broke the pattern of colonial or federal style houses. They were all of a piece, like the display of some homebuilder who was opening a new development called Thomas Jefferson or George Washington Estates.

Because it was a Saturday morning, there were none of the usual activities that one would normally expect to see in a neighborhood like this.

No children leaving for school while their mothers, not yet made-up and their hair unbrushed, waved good-bye at the door. No husbands backing their cars out of two-car garages, driving off to Government buildings or lawyer's offices downtown.

The final editions of *The Washington Post* had been delivered in the predawn darkness so there was not even a newspaper boy, aiming a rolled-up paper at every doorstep on the street, to break the silent scene.

Other than a Chesapeake and Potomac phone company repair truck, which appeared to have been left by a repair crew on the street overnight, the street was empty.

The tedium of waiting had given her time to review, over and over again, everything Malachek had told her about Herman Willows. Even as she went over the details again, they still retained their explosiveness.

Willows had removed top secret, ground-level photos of the Baikonur Cosmodrome at Tyuratum from a safe in the office of the CIA Oversight Committee. The FBI had arrested him minutes before he was to deliver them to a member of the Soviet Embassy in Washington. And he had been released within an hour on direct orders of the White House. No charges had been filed. It had been completely covered up.

When Malachek had called her into his office—was it only two days ago?—she had sat in stunned silence while he unraveled the entire story for her: how Willows's boss, Senator Charles Ramsey, had stonewalled Charlotte Glover, how Glover had been unable to pry anything out of any of her other sources.

"Charlotte's the only correspondent who knows the story," Malachek had confided in her. "And now you."

It was one of the few times she had been in Malachek's office. To Samantha, like so many others in the News Division, Malachek was a semimysterious figure; a kind of Oz who one never saw but learned about through his comments in the press or through others who did see him—usually the executive producers, or major talents such as John Cornwall. And even though she was probably the network's best-known woman correspondent, along with Charlotte Glover at the White House, Malachek had never treated her as if she were somebody special, somebody to whom attention should be paid.

The equal treatment with her coworkers, male and female, left her with an ambivalent feeling. She wanted to be treated like the others, particularly the men, because she felt like their equal. But a little attention now and then from Malachek would have made a difference.

The closest she had come recently had been a complimentary remark he reportedly had made about one of her stories on *Focus*.

Now, however, he was letting her in on a huge story.

"We want to nail Willows and the White House," Malachek had said determinedly. "If it's true, and I think it is, it's the biggest cover-up since Watergate. The bastards are not going to get away with it."

"I'm flattered," Samantha confessed. It was, in fact, potentially the biggest story she had ever been assigned. She wondered why Malachek had picked her for it. It was not the kind of story she usually did.

Investigative pieces usually took up a lot of time and, with the pressure of a weekly program, she just did not have the luxury of working for several weeks on a single story. Features, personality profiles, human-interest stories—these were more her line of work.

"What angle do you want me to work on?" she asked.

"Just one," Malachek said, leaning forward over his desk as if to emphasize the confidential nature of what they were discussing.

"I want you to confront Herman Willows and push him as hard as you can. Don't accuse him of anything, for God's sake, because I don't want a goddamn libel suit on my hands. You never can tell what somebody is going to do but the first thing they usually do is hire some smartass lawyer who's had a few years at Justice and they file a suit for harassment. So watch how you handle it."

Samantha shifted slightly in her chair. The idea of an "ambush" interview, confronting someone with a camera and microphone when they were not expecting it, always had left her uneasy.

The act of catching people off guard, trapping them in the lens of a camera, seemed to her to be inherently unfair. It meant that a television reporter had the right, the power, to do something that was beyond the bounds of acceptable practice and to do it in the name of the pursuit of the news.

"You don't expect me to ring his doorbell and shove a mike in his face, do you?" she asked, hoping that Malachek would say "No."

He quickly disabused her of the idea. "Of course not," he said. "What I want you to do is this: he walks his dog every morning. Don't ask me how I know, but I know. All right?"

"Okay."

"So I want you to confront him on the street, when he's walking his dog, and see what you can get out of him. Wait for him outside his house."

"You don't think simply asking for an interview would work?" Samantha asked.

"He would say no. And we'd be right back where we are now. Only he'd be on guard. Right now, he probably doesn't suspect anybody is looking into this. So you'll catch him unaware."

"What about Senator Ramsey? Don't you think he's tipped off Willows?"

Malachek leaned back in his chair, in a more relaxed position. "I don't think Ramsey really knows that we're onto this. He got a little suspicious when Charlotte questioned him about Willows but she hasn't gone back to him since then and he probably thinks she's dropped it, that she was just digging.

"No," he said, as if reflecting again on her question, "I don't think Ramsey is aware that we're doing this. Nobody is."

"It's a terrific story," she said, excited by the prospect.

"You realize, Samantha," Malachek said, "that if we break this story, Charlotte Glover will put it on the air. She's the one who got the original tip on it."

"I understand," Samantha said. She had figured that

Glover would do the story on the air. After all, Glover had come up with it. Still, she had a piece of it—a big piece—and it was a plum that Malachek was handing to her. She wondered why.

"I'm glad to be working on this story," she said, "but I'm curious about something. What about the Washington correspondents? Why don't you want any of them in on this?"

"Because if I use somebody else from the Washington bureau, it will get out," Malachek said, his eyes following a small cloud of smoke from a cigar he had just lit. "Those people talk. I don't want this spread around by the watercooler or in the White House pressroom or some bar in Georgetown. I don't even want a Washington crew used on this. You bring a crew down from New York, a crew you can trust. But no producer. I want to keep this to as few people as possible. I've already told George Durgin that I have assigned you to a special project in Washington for a few days. Nobody else knows anything."

I can't even tell Art, she thought. But it didn't matter. She would tell him when it was over and he'd be pleased.

"What about Durgin? Won't he ask me?" she wondered.

"He won't," he told her. The way he said it, with the complete assurance of a Mafia boss who had ordered the silencing of a damaging witness, left no doubt in her mind.

Malachek had been right. When she went to Durgin and requested a crew, Durgin instantly acquiesced with no questions asked. He obviously had gotten the message.

Now, two days later, she sat in the rental car and waited. The crew—cameraman Joe Fleming and soundman Jerry Gerson—sat in the backseat, their camera and microphone equipment carefully placed on the floor where it could be quickly reached and readied for use.

"Who is this clown anyhow?" Fleming asked, as he sprawled against the rear armrest and tried to make himself comfortable.

"Just somebody who figures in a story," she said.

"C'mon, Samantha," the cameraman argued. "We've been sitting on our asses for two hours waiting to grab him. Who is he? Some big-deal politician?"

She turned around in order to see him and watch his reaction when she told him. Up until now, she purposely had said nothing to Fleming or his partner about the assignment

other than it was an investigative story and would require a
stakeout—and then an ambush interview on the street.

She had been afraid of a leak. Now, hoping to see
Willows emerge from his house across the street at any
moment, she doled out some details to the crew.

"He's the administrative assistant to the head of Senate
Intelligence and he's a suspect in a spy case. Okay?"

Gerson lit a cigarette. "A fuckin' spy?" he exclaimed.

"Maybe," Samantha said. "That's the reason for the
interview."

"Ever seen him before?" Gerson asked.

"No. But I've got a good idea what he looks like.
Besides, he walks his dog every morning."

"Jeez, Sam," Fleming said, his boredom swiftly turning
to admiration. "How long have you been working on this?"

"It comes from Malachek," she said quietly. "He assigned
me. It's his story."

Neither of the two men said anything. Her disclosure
that the story was right out of Seven West, from Malachek
himself, immediately impressed them. There was no need for
her to say anything else but she wanted to make sure they
understood the importance of the assignment.

"Look, guys," she said, purposely lapsing into her best
one-of-the-boys manner. "This is not some politician on the
take or somebody ripping off a government program. This
could be a very, very, big story. And we're only going to get
one bite at it."

As she said it, she realized that she was preparing herself
emotionally to do an interview that, she reluctantly admitted
to herself, she wished she could do under different circumstances. In a house, a hotel room, a television studio, anywhere but in the middle of the street on a sleepy Saturday
morning with probably most of the neighborhood peering out
from behind their chintz curtains when she pursued Willows
down the sidewalk.

She rested her chin in her hand and remembered the
very first time she had been uneasy on an assignment.

It had been her first job out of college. She had been a
reporter in Salinas and had been sent to the house of a
policeman who had been killed in a shoot-out with a burglar.

"See if you can get a picture of him," the news director

had told her. "No camera, no interview, just get a picture of the cop."

Driving by herself to the house, she'd pictured all the dreadful possibilities. There would be a tinted wedding portrait— the policeman and his bride holding hands on the front steps of some church—or a posed vacation picture, the two of them at Disneyland or someplace like that; or just a picture of the cop in his uniform.

She had knocked on the door and even now, all these years later, she could see the young woman standing at the door, her bloodred eyes signaling her incredulity that some- one could impose on her grief this way, at a time like this. Samantha could hear the door slamming and could remember how terrible, how wrong, she felt about having gone to the house. She also remembered throwing up next to her car before she drove away from the house.

Interviewing Willows would be different, of course. She was older now. More experienced. A network pro. But some- how she was reminded of that first assignment early in her career. She still was intruding and it bothered her.

Her thoughts were interrupted when Joe Fleming spoke from the backseat. "It's show time!"

She glanced out the front window and saw a man whom she recognized as Willows emerge from his house on the other side of the street. He was holding a chocolate brown springer spaniel on a leash.

Willows was smaller than she had expected and frail looking. Malachek had told her that Willows was about forty-five years old, but, at first glance, he appeared older. He was not wearing a hat and tiny tufts of gray hair spread out from his head as if they had been pasted on before he went out in the morning.

He had a pleasant face, almost cherubic, and as she mentally transformed the plaid slacks and tan shirt he was wearing into a brown cassock, she pictured him as a monk. Friar Willows. A real loser, she thought.

The dog, pausing to sniff at various spots on Willows's lawn, trying to find the right place to urinate, kept tugging at his leash, and Willows let the dog lead him.

"Do you want us to start shooting, Sam?" Fleming asked urgently.

"Not yet," Samantha said, aware that her heart was

beginning to beat a little faster. "Wait until he gets past the car, across from us."

She glanced again at Willows, noticing this time that he wore gray, wire-rimmed glasses. A book reader, she thought.

Willows seemed oblivious to their presence, even though their car, and the phone company repair truck, were the only vehicles on the street. He seemed to be concentrating on the dog, who kept pulling and tugging on the leash, and leading him closer to Samantha's car.

Samantha turned away from the front window, to the two men in the rear of the car.

"We could be anybody talking," she said to them, as if to reassure herself that Willows did not know who they were. "Let me know when he's opposite us," she told them.

Joe Fleming held the camera in his lap, cradling it in his arms like a soldier carrying a weapon. Jerry Gerson kept the microphone, sheathed in a gray cotton wrapping, between his legs, making sure that the umbilical cord of cable that attached his gear to Fleming's camera was not getting snarled in the equipment on the floorboard of the car.

"What if the dog comes over to take a leak on the car?" Fleming asked.

"I don't know. I hadn't thought of that," Samantha answered. She noticed that her mouth felt suddenly dry. Oh my God, she thought, don't tell me I'm going to throw up.

Nobody in the car said anything for a few minutes and then Fleming said, "He's just across from us. The dog is taking a shit in the street."

Samantha looked out the side window and saw Willows bend down and take a little shovel and a paper bag from his rear pocket.

"I knew he was law abiding," Gerson said sarcastically. "This guy's no spy."

Samantha stifled a smile—couldn't a camera crew ever be serious?—and told herself: *Now is the time.*

"Let's do it now," she said quickly and, as she said it, she opened the car door and strode quickly across the street.

The camera crew, reacting instantly to her command, got out of the car at the same time and was one step behind her as she moved toward Willows.

Fleming had the camera mounted on his shoulder, ready for use, and Gerson was alongside him, pointing the microphone at Willows, as if the microphone were a gun sight that could hone in on a target.

Willows suddenly became aware of the trio approaching him from behind and he bolted up and turned around to face them.

"Who are you?" he said in a frantic voice tinged with fear. "What are you doing here?"

For an instant, Samantha felt sorry for the little man. He looked so pathetic, standing there in the morning sunlight, with a paper bag and a tiny shovel of dog shit in his hand; his Saturday morning and, in a moment, his whole world, about to be shattered. Then she remembered why she was there.

"Start rolling," she barked to Joe Fleming and, as she heard him say, "Rolling," she came up to Willows and said, "Mr. Willows, I have some questions I want to ask you."

"Who are you?" Willows repeated and he backed away from her as if he instinctively sensed that everything suddenly had gone wrong.

"What do you want?" he repeated in a voice mixed with bewilderment and fright.

"I have some questions," Samantha said again. "My name is Samantha Stuart. I'm from *Focus on America.*"

"I don't know what you want," Willows said, his eyes darting from her to the gaping lens of the camera. "This is private property," he said and she caught the tone of desperation in his voice.

"It's a public street, Mr. Willows," she pointed out quietly. "I have just a few questions."

Willows began to tug anxiously on his dog's leash but the animal, sniffing with curiosity at Samantha and the camera crew, would not move.

"C'mon, Brownie, time to go in," Willows said urgently, pulling on his dog's leash.

"Were you arrested the other night, Mr. Willows?" Samantha asked quickly.

"I don't know what you're talking about," Willows snapped at her and he jerked at the leash so violently that the dog yelped in pain.

"The other night," Samantha repeated. "Were you held in custody by the FBI?"

"You people are crazy," Willows said loudly and now,

with the dog cowering into obedience, he began to walk in rapid strides toward his house.

Samantha walked briskly alongside him, the crew in front of her, walking backward and facing Willows.

"We understand that you were picked up by the FBI, Mr. Willows. At the McDonald's in Bethesda," Samantha said.

She thought she detected a grimace on his face, as if she had physically wounded him, but he said nothing.

"Why won't you comment, Mr. Willows?" she persisted. "Can't you say anything about it?"

They were only a few houses away from Willows's house now and Samantha realized that Willows was going to get inside his house and be safe before she could get in many more questions.

As they passed a white brick colonial, a door opened and a woman in a nightgown came to the front steps and silently watched the scene. Samantha wondered what the woman must be thinking. At the same time she hoped that Willows's dog would stop and start sniffing again.

But everything was happening too fast. The dog was keeping pace with Willows, as if the animal and its owner were racing each other, and Willows was almost at his front door.

"Is there a cover-up, Mr. Willows?" Samantha shouted at him. "What are you hiding?"

Willows stopped and turned and looked at Samantha. He said nothing but just smiled wanly at her with a sorrowful expression that, for a long time afterward, she would remember at odd times, like a fragment of memory that suddenly had surfaced in her mind.

Then he was inside his house, pulling his dog behind him. He shut the door and she could hear the lock in the door being turned from the inside. She looked down the street but the woman who had been in the doorway of the white brick colonial had disappeared. It was over.

"Did you get it all?" she asked the cameraman as they walked back to their car.

"Every mother-loving frame," Fleming said proudly.

"I don't know what he's done," Gerson offered, "but that's one guilty son of a bitch."

"I got the same feeling," she said. Then she added, to no one, "He's pathetic."

"You feel sorry for him?" Fleming asked, opening the trunk of the car and placing his camera in an aluminum suitcase.

"I don't know," Samantha said wearily. "I just don't like that kind of interview. Maybe I'm not tough enough."

She climbed into the driver's seat and rested for a moment. She was surprised at herself for admitting her self-doubt to her crew but maybe it was better this way. Get it out. Maybe she really wasn't like the men reporters. Maybe she lacked that last bit of toughness, that final steely element that allowed other correspondents to knock on widows' doors or pursue people down the street and not feel bad about it.

"So now what?" Jerry Gerson asked as he slumped in the rear seat and Samantha adjusted the rearview mirror.

"So now we go back to New York and I give the tapes to Malachek. And, as far as you all are concerned, this interview never happened. That's straight from Malachek."

The tension of the encounter with Willows was beginning to catch up with her. She felt drained and exhausted.

"I'm tired," she confessed to the crew. "Would one of you mind switching with me?"

"I'll drive," Fleming volunteered and he moved into the driver's seat. Samantha got into the backseat, leaned against the headrest cushion and, as the car pulled away from the curb, she began to feel sleepy.

Nobody in the car paid any attention to the other vehicle on the street—the phone company repair truck.

But inside the truck, three men were bent over a large reel-to-reel audiotape machine, checking the machine to make sure that every piece of sound made on the street within the past ten minutes had been picked up by sensitive directional microphones implanted in the rims of the truck's headlights.

"Did we get it all?" a young man with the erect posture of a military officer asked the other two.

"We even got the shovel scooping the dog shit," one of the others answered proudly. "Every bit of it."

The military man watched as the audiotape machine in front of him began to rewind at a high speed. Then as it clicked to a stop, he removed the reel from its spindle as carefully as if he were defusing a time bomb.

He placed the audiotape in a large manila envelope and took a letter-size envelope from his breast pocket. The envelope contained a bright red gummed label with the words P3 Classification Only emblazoned in white letters on it.

He placed the gummed sticker on the large envelope and handed it to one of the other men.

"See you around the campus," he said, smiling, and then the other man, placing the manila envelope in a briefcase that he chained to his wrist, got out of the truck and walked around the corner to a parked car.

A few minutes later, the car was weaving its way through the early morning traffic on N Street in Georgetown.

The driver, whose youthful appearance was belied only by the gray patches on the sides of his crewcut hair, steered the car onto Pennsylvania Avenue.

Soon, he was on E Street and then, behind 1600 Pennsylvania, he was waved into West Executive Avenue—away from public view. He parked the car in a reserved space guarded by an agent from the uniformed Secret Service.

Even though it was a Saturday morning, and not yet nine o'clock, he knew that somebody whose name and face were instantly recognizable would be waiting in a basement office to receive the tape.

P3 Classification Only meant the President or three top men in the government: The Secretary of State, The White House Chief of Staff, or the Director of the CIA.

As he flashed his credentials to a military guard standing in the hallway leading to the small room in the White House basement, he wondered which of the three men it would be.

He knew that the call would have gone out from the truck, informing a high-ranking person that the tapes were on the way to the White House.

Somebody, maybe even the President himself, maybe still in pajamas, would have been notified and, within minutes, would have gone down to the tiny, unmarked room in the White House basement.

He quickly ran his hand through the bristle of his crewcut hair, as if to insure that every strand would stand up straight, and then he approached two military officers, wearing pistols in belt holsters, who were guarding the door to the small room.

"I have an envelope for delivery," he said. "P3 Classification Only."

One of the two men nodded, glanced at the briefcase attached to his wrist, and signaled to the other officer to open the door.

He walked inside.

Chapter 21

The President of the United States was sleeping when the call came on one of the three phones—the black one—on the night table next to his bed.

"It's easy to remember. Red for the Russians. White for White House secure. Black because the CIA always gets dirty," his predecessor had told him on that first walk through the living quarters years ago.

The black phone hadn't rung that many times in the past. The most had been during that screwed-up coup in the little African country—the one whose name he never could remember—years ago.

As he picked up the receiver, the President wondered what news the call would bring. There were things the CIA was doing that he didn't know about or want to know about.

Maybe one of their projects had gone wrong and he was about to be confronted with some dreadful news. A submarine had sunk where it wasn't supposed to have been or a plane had been shot down over Siberia or God knows what.

"Mr. President, this is General Beckenham," the voice on the other end was saying.

"Yes, Alfred," the President replied quietly, wondering whether the retired Air Force General, now the Director of the CIA, had four stars sewed to his pajama tops.

"I'm sorry to bother you, sir, but I've just gotten a call

from Langley. There's been a development on the Herman Willows matter that I thought you should know about right away."

For a second or two, the President couldn't remember Herman Willows. Then it came back to him. That little prick in Chuck Ramsey's office who had tried to sell the Cosmodrome photos to the Russians. They had stopped him just in time. Now he remembered.

"What happened?" he asked, staring at the clock on his night table. It was almost eight-thirty in the morning. The reception for the Prime Minister of France had lasted too late last night. He wondered if his wife, in the adjoining bedroom, was still asleep.

"One of the television networks apparently knows something about the Willows story," Beckenham reported. "They sent a reporter out to interview him this morning. Our people got it all on audiotape."

"Inside his house?" the President asked incredulously. He didn't want any bugging of people at any time without a court order. He thought he had made that clear to Beckenham and his people and to the FBI a long time ago.

"It was a street surveillance, sir," the CIA director hastily explained. "It's the constant stakeout we've had outside Willows's house. The TV people got him there."

"Dammit," the President said under his breath. If the Willows story were uncovered. . . .It would have to be stopped.

"I'm having the tape sent over to you, sir, so you can listen for yourself."

"Have you heard it?"

"No. I've only been given a summary. Apparently the network knows something but maybe not enough."

"Which network is working on it?"

Beckenham told him and the President immediately thought of Charlotte Glover, sitting there in the front row at the press conferences, or standing at the South Portico entrance when he came back after Camp David weekends.

Sweet little old maid Charlotte. Stick a knife in his back and smile at him all the time. Christ, you can't trust any of these bastards.

"Was it Charlotte Glover?" he asked. "Who was the reporter?"

"She identified herself to Willows as Samantha Stuart,"

General Beckenham answered swiftly. "The description I've been given is a blond, good-looking. The pictures are being developed now."

"Pictures?"

"Long-range lens. Taken from the same van where the microphones were."

"All right. Send it all down by courier as soon as possible. Do you know this Stuart woman, who she is?"

"One of their correspondents, sir. She works on *Focus on America*."

"All right. When will the tapes be here?"

"At any moment, Mr. President. They are being delivered to the basement situation room."

"Fine. I'll keep you informed."

"Thank you, Mr. President."

The President thanked Beckenham and pressed the buzzer on the white phone that connected him with the Georgetown home of Gordon Allen, his Chief of Staff.

"Yes, Mr. President," Allen answered in a voice that exuded efficiency, even though he had just emerged from the shower and had on only a huge bath towel.

"Gordon, I think you'd better get over here right away," the President ordered.

"Yes, sir. I'll be there shortly," Allen answered briskly. He did not need to ask if a major problem had suddenly arisen. If the President called him at home before nine o'clock on a Saturday morning, there was no need to ask.

"It's the Willows case," the President elaborated. "There may be a leak. One of the networks is working on it."

"How do we know?" Allen asked, drying himself off.

"There are tapes," the President said. "I'll be in the situation room," he informed him.

"Yes, sir," the Chief of Staff said in an automatic response. "I'll leave my house now."

Twenty minutes later, the President of the United States, dressed in loafers, slacks, and white sport shirt with the presidential insignia embroidered on it, stood in the center of a small room in the basement of the White House.

Gordon Allen, a tall, silver-haired man with the tan of a man who played a lot of tennis, or sailed, or both, stood next to him.

Even though it was early on a Saturday morning, Allen

was dressed in one of the black, chalk-stripe, three-piece suits he had favored as a Wall Street banker.

His appointment as the President's Chief of Staff had merely reinforced his conservative taste in clothes as well as politics.

The only other person in the room was an Air Force Captain, wearing a dress blue uniform, who was the duty officer. A badge over his left breast pocket identified him as Captain H. E. Morris.

The President and Allen both wore headsets attached by separate cables to an audiotape machine. The machine was housed in a wall assembly that also included a large television set, a panel that controlled a movie projector and a console that displayed overlays on a huge map of the world mounted at the far end of the wall.

The two men stood for five minutes listening to the tape of Samantha Stuart's pursuit of Herman Willows.

When the tape ended, the machine clicked off automatically. Neither of the men said anything. They removed their headsets and the President turned to the duty officer. "Captain, would you mind stepping out of the room, please? This will only be a minute or two."

The Captain quickly saluted and left.

"What do you think, Gordon?" the President said, a troubled expression on his face.

The Chief of Staff reached for his back pocket where he kept his tobacco pouch. In times of stress, he always liked the comfort of a pipe but, as he reached for the pouch, he realized that the room was too small, and windowless, and smoke from the pipe would be suffocating.

He brought his hand forward and stretched it with his other hand, kneading his knuckles until they cracked with a sudden pop that startled the President.

"It's obvious they're on to something," Allen answered, oblivious to the noise his knuckles had made. "You can't tell how much."

"Do you know this Stuart woman?" the President asked. "Have you ever seen her?"

"She's not in the Washington loop," Allen said. "Certainly not a White House regular."

"What does Beckenham say?" he asked the President, who had moved to a chair by a felt-covered conference table and was doodling on a small pad of white paper. Allen noticed that the reedy little drawings looked like missiles.

"He said she works for the *Focus on America* program," the President responded. "I've only seen it once or twice. It's a *Sixty Minutes* type of thing."

The President drew a line through one of his drawings and put the pencil down.

"We need to get hold of this woman's boss," he said decisively. "This story can't go any further, Gordon. We've got to get it killed."

"I'll place a call to Jerry Daniels at home," Allen said, referring to the White House Press Secretary. "He knows all the news executives up in New York."

"No, it's got to be at the very top," the President insisted. "Who's the president of the network? I can't think of his name."

"Rossman," Allen said. "Jerry Rossman. You met him at a fund-raiser last year. Jewish. I think we've invited him to a state dinner in the last few years. I can check it out. Typical show business," he added condescendingly. "Thinks the whole world is made up of people from California or New York. You'd recognize him if you saw him."

"Is he a friend?" the President asked.

"I can find out."

"Get to him," the President ordered. Then, as an afterthought, he added, "We'd better let Chuck Ramsey know about this."

"Yes, of course," Allen said. "I'll do that right away."

"There's a leak somewhere, Gordon," the President said ruefully, as if he personally had been betrayed.

"It would have to be at Justice," Allen said.

"Dammit," the President said angrily. "We can't be hung out to dry on this one. Whatever it takes, we've got to stop it."

"I'll run a check to see who knew about the arrest," Allen said. "I don't know which of the Attorney General's people was involved in this over at Justice."

"It could not have been too many," the President said. "But we've got to get this stopped. Now!"

"I agree," Allen responded.

"Fine. Let's get started. Now!" the President repeated. The President got up and walked over to the wall assembly, removed the tape from the machine, and placed it in the manila envelope in which it had been delivered.

He put the envelope under his arm and, walking out of the room with his Chief of Staff, snapped a quick salute to Captain Morris and the two guards who were stationed at the door.

Within minutes, word was relayed to the White House kitchen that the President had left the situation room and probably would be wanting breakfast soon.

The President went back to his bedroom and turned on the television set. Switching from channel to channel, he could find nothing but cartoons.

The incongruity between the imaginary figures flashing by on the screen, Tom and Jerry, Donald Duck, and others he did not recognize, and the frightening reality of what he and his Chief of Staff had just been confronted with, left him feeling depressed.

Maybe Gordon can kill it, he tried to reassure himself. These bastards can be stopped. It just takes pressure. Lots of pressure.

He looked again at the little figures chasing each other around the screen with broomsticks, frying pans, and butter-fly nets.

We're all the same, he thought. But we have bigger weapons.

Chapter 22

Art Burton opened his eyes and stared at the ceiling.

Another hotel room. Los Angeles. The Century Plaza. A nightstand with a checkerboard top, a frail-looking chair in front of a reproduction antique desk, a wastebasket with a hunting scene lacquered on it. Within a few seconds, he was fully awake.

He glanced at the digital clock on the table by his

king-size bed and saw that it was almost nine o'clock in the morning. As he stretched, he became aware that he had awakened with an erection.

The trouble was, he did not know why he was hard. He tried to remember what he had been dreaming about, if he had been screwing Samantha, or anyone, in his sleep but he could not remember any dream at all.

Maybe I'm just naturally horny, he decided. He glanced at the mirror across the room, over the dressing table and looked at himself as if the outward reflection would offer some clue to his inner self.

He knew that he wanted Samantha, especially now when he was away from her. At times like this, when they were apart, sex was foremost in his mind, more than the desire to be with her, to be able to confide in her.

I must have been thinking of her, he thought, *and don't even remember it.* What had they been doing—fucking in her soft bed?—the Tent, she called it—that had made him so hard and stiff?

Jesus, he thought, I don't want to live like this forever; going from hotel room to hotel room like some kind of journalist Willy Loman, never catching up with my life, traveling on one more story with nothing to show for it but four or five minutes on the air that will end up catalogued on a News Division computer as cassette number 6,271.

Is this what it's all about—waking up with a hard-on?

He knew where he wanted it to end. The Cornwall job. That would be the ultimate reward, would compensate for everything. But it seemed as elusive as the filaments of sunlight filtering through the window curtains.

He decided to order breakfast from room service and asked for copies of *The New York Times* and the LA *Times* to be sent up with the meal. When the waiter arrived with the breakfast tray, Burton reached first for the New York paper.

Out of habit, he turned to the last page of the paper, where the television listings were carried. But then he remembered that the West Coast edition of *The New York Times* would not carry any television news or listings.

Instead, he unfolded the *Los Angeles Times* and saw the headline TV STAR WINSTON BEATEN BY THUGS. He drew the paper closer to him as if to confirm what he had just read.

"Christ," he said softly. He quickly scanned the story,

which recounted how Winston had been found battered and semiconscious on the floor of his office Friday afternoon in the network building in Hollywood.

The story carried over to the front page of the second section and ran for several columns.

"Network President Jerry Rossman," the story continued, "has offered a reward of $25,000 for information leading to the arrest and conviction of Winston's assailants. The announcement was made in a statement released by Milton Stanger, Vice President of Corporate Relations, West Coast, for the network."

The final paragraph of the story said no replacement had been named yet for the period Winston would be in the hospital.

Burton read the story again, pausing to study a front-page photograph of Winston and another photograph that showed the exterior of the network building in Hollywood.

A tiny white arrow, superimposed on the picture, pointed to a window that the picture caption identified as Winston's office. The caption read, "Scene of Vicious Beating."

This wasn't drugs, Burton concluded. It had to have been connected to Winston's gambling. But how the hell could he prove it, prove anything?

All he had were strong threads but he couldn't weave them together yet into something that could withstand the pulling and tugging of the network's lawyers and, worse, the pressures that would come from the network brass to kill the story.

Rossman must be going crazy by now, he thought. His biggest star gets the shit kicked out of him and, on top of that, Cornwall is leaving the evening news.

He wondered if the Winston beating would eclipse the Cornwall problem in Rossman's mind and somehow push it to the rear, leaving the decision on Cornwall's replacement in the shadows.

He glanced again at the digital clock: 9:35—12:35 in New York. Leo Lane, the executive producer of the weekend evening news show, would be in by now. They would know more in New York than the papers had printed. They always did.

If Winston's gambling problems were a well-kept secret within the network, the beating he had taken would have forced the secret to the surface in New York. Something would have come out, whispers would have started floating in the hallways of the News Division.

But if nobody knew, if Winston's dirty little problem still had not been discovered, then he could pursue the story and, he hoped, break it wide open. The headlines in the papers would read TV STAR BEATEN OVER BIG GAMBLING DEBTS. And the stories would credit him for uncovering it.

He put a call through to Leo Lane and reached the executive producer just as Lane was about to go to lunch.

"I've got a longing for Szechuan beef in black bean sauce," Lane told him from three thousand miles away, "so I hope this isn't going to take too long."

Burton and Lane had known each other for years. Lane had been the bureau chief in Atlanta, when Burton had first come to the network, and they could trade insults with each other in a way that reflected their long friendship.

"I'm in LA, Leo," Burton announced.

"Working on a story?"

"Just beginning. I came out to do a little preliminary shooting."

"What's the story?"

"High-school dropouts," Burton lied, mentioning the first thing that came to his mind.

"So what do you need here?"

"Nothing. I was calling because I read in the papers out here about Jarvis Winston. They're playing the shit out of it in the LA *Times*. What's the real story?"

"It got a big play in the *Daily News* this morning," Lane said. "Big picture on the front page. The works.

"I don't know if there is a real story," Lane added. "I think it's what they say it is, a couple of dopers out for some kicks."

Then: "Why? Do you know something?"

"Not a damn thing," Burton answered, catching the suspicious tone in Lane's voice. "I just find the whole thing interesting. You know, two guys walk in off the street, right past the security guards, and beat the hell out of Winston. No money taken, nothing."

Lane wondered if there was an oblique message hidden in Burton's question, if Burton was trying to point him toward a particular path he could not yet see.

"You got a hunch? You trying to tell me something?" he asked bluntly.

"No," Burton answered, realizing he had gone too far and that he was raising Lane's curiosity to the point where, God forbid, Lane might want to do a story on Winston for the weekend show.

That was the one thing he didn't want—some other show, even the weekend show with its lower audiences, poking around the fringes of the Winston story. He wanted this one for himself.

"I was thinking of doing a profile on Winston," Burton said, "for *Focus*. You know, the price of celebrity, all that bullshit. Big star, everybody knows him and two guys off the street come in and beat him up just for kicks. Could be an interesting twist, if it's done right."

"If you're asking for any rumors," Lane said, "I don't have any. The only thing I've ever heard about Winston is that he screwed a production assistant who used to work on the show here."

"Who was she?"

"Nobody you know. Worked here for years, went out to the Coast and got in with the Entertainment Division and then became the LA Open, if you know what I mean."

"Well, I'm going to try to get something with Winston," Burton said, no longer curious about the anonymous production assistant. He felt sure now that Winston's gambling habit was not known at the network, at least not in the News Division.

If it was known at all, and he doubted that it was, Jerry Rossman, Sid Neale, people like that would know.

"Do me a favor and give me the home phone number of the West Coast PR guy for the network. It's somebody named Stanger."

"Hold on," Lane said. A few seconds later, he was back on the line with the number Burton wanted.

"Thanks," Burton said. Then: "Any word on how the

network brass is taking this? Rossman must be off the wall. Did he come out here?"

"No. He's making a speech somewhere in the Midwest. One of the big affiliates."

"Oh," Burton said. He thanked Lane again and said good-bye. As soon as he hung up, he dialed the network switchboard and asked to be connected to Milton Stanger.

It took several minutes of persuasion to get Milton Stanger to agree to any kind of an interview with Jarvis Winston, even if it wasn't to be used on the air.

There were problems, Stanger said; problems with New York, with Winston's agent, with the trade press, with the police.

"You have to understand," Stanger said. "Jarvis Winston is a very, very big talent. Jesus, we had a *Time* magazine cover in the works for him. A cover story! You know what that means?"

"Sure I do," Burton said, even though he had never really understood why the network, which reached millions of homes every night, was so concerned about how it was covered in the press. In the long run, who the hell read the press compared to television? The number of readers didn't make a dent in the number of viewers on any night but here was Stanger, pissing in his pants, because *Time* was talking about doing a cover on Winston.

"Believe me, interviewing Winston isn't like one of your minute-thirty spots on the evening news," Stanger said. "I got *Time* to worry about, *Newsweek*, *TV Guide*, *The Times*, and *The Washington Post*, I mean, the whole friggin country is interested in Jarvis Winston. Hell, why not? He comes into nineteen million homes every Saturday night. Everybody wants to talk to him."

"Milton," Burton said, striving for the right tone of informality and friendliness. He did not want to push too hard because he did not know Stanger's strength in the network hierarchy.

After all, Jerry Rossman could be Stanger's rabbi. Or Sid Neale. All those West Coast guys stuck together and Stanger could be in heavy with the top network brass.

"All I want," Burton said, "is to talk to Winston. No cameras. I just want to get an idea of what he's like, really like. You know, a preinterview like they do on *American Sunrise.*"

"He's been in the hospital less than twenty-four hours. Why can't it wait a few days?" Stanger asked.

"Because we have to plan ahead on our show, weeks ahead. If Winston doesn't sound like an interesting story, we'll drop it. But we've got to get a feel for him, a sense of what he's all about. After all, he could be a wonderful profile or he could be a loser when he's not performing."

"Believe me, he's no schlepp," Stanger said, almost resentfully.

"Okay," Burton said. "So as long as I'm out here, I thought this would be a good opportunity to meet with him, assuming he's up to it."

Stanger was beginning to relent. What could it hurt if Burton saw Winston? If *Focus* did do a piece on Winston later on, it would look good for his office. You usually had to beg the goddamn News Division to do any kind of a plug or promotion on *American Sunrise* for a network special. And now they were interested in Winston for a whole profile. On a prime-time show. Shit, you couldn't buy that kind of publicity. As long as it came out all right.

"I'll see what I can do," Stanger told Burton, "but you have to understand that Winston is still not in good shape. I mean he took a hell of a beating. So if I get you in, it won't be for more than five or ten minutes. And it's all off-the-record. Like nobody knows. This is just a favor within the network."

Burton heard the implied message in Stanger's words. If it was a favor within the network, then Stanger would want something back, some kind of assurance that a profile on Jarvis Winston would be nothing less than a warm and loving portrait of one of America's biggest stars.

Only there never would be a profile. Just, if his instincts were right, a hell of a story about Winston and his gambling action. *Sorry, Milton,* he thought, *I'm going to have to screw you.*

"I really appreciate anything you can do, Milton," he told Stanger and he said he would wait to hear from him.

It didn't take long. Shortly before lunch Art Burton got a call from Milton Stanger.

It was all set, Stanger told him. Winston had agreed to see him. Sid Neale in New York had cleared it as well.

"This could turn out to be a nice story," Stanger said.

"No question about it," Burton said. He felt funny screwing Stanger but he wasn't going to let go of the story. Not when he had a chance to make some real headway on it.

"I'll be there in about twenty minutes," he told Stanger and he went down to the lobby to get his car.

The hospital was in Burbank, to the north and east of the Century Plaza. He decided to take the long way, up the San Diego Freeway, and then doubling back to the Hollywood Freeway to the Lankershim Boulevard exit near Universal City.

From there, it would be just a short drive past the taco stands, the health-food bars and the drive-in restaurants to the hospital.

He did not like driving in Los Angeles. There were just too many freeways and, if he had to drive five miles out of his way in order to ensure that he would not get lost and be doomed to forever wander the maze of freeways, looking for the right exit, then it was better to do it this way.

Besides, the gray haze that had hung over the city when he arrived last evening had been burned away by a bright, late morning sun.

The sky was a clear blue and, although he could not see the ocean as he drove along the freeway, he imagined that the water mirrored the sky.

Samantha had sailed in that blue water. He remembered the way she had talked about it and the look in her eyes when she described the feeling of being part of the vastness of the ocean.

That had been on one of their first weekends in Gloucester, when they walked on Good Harbor Beach, looking at the white-capped waves rolling in to the shore.

"You have to come sailing with me," she had urged. "It is so beautiful, no matter what ocean you're on, the Atlantic or the Pacific. You get to appreciate everything so much more— the sun, the wind, everything."

"I get seasick," he confessed, remembering the time at WBID-TV when he and the other reporters in the newsroom had chartered a boat to go deep-sea fishing in the Gulf of Mexico.

They had tied up their cabin cruiser to one of the offshore oil rigs and the constant motion of the waves and the swelling and dipping of the distant horizon had made him violently nauseous.

Until Samantha had suggested it, he never had wanted to go on a boat again.

If she were here now, he decided, I would go sailing with her.

Even more tempting was the thought of being with her and living in California.

It was a different world out here; laid-back, leisurely, as far removed from the fast-paced street life of New York City as his own life in television news was removed from everyday, ordinary life.

He played with the idea of giving it all up, coming out here and teaching journalism at one of those junior colleges that seemed to be all over the place, or opening his own business, anything that would give him the chance to escape the pressures of the news. But, by the time he reached the hospital, he had dismissed the thought as idle daydreaming.

The hospital sat in the middle of a manicured lawn, a gently terraced slope that led to one of the main streets in Burbank. The parking lot was shaded by towering palm trees and, as he walked the short distance from the parking lot to the hospital's main entrance, he could tell that it was not a hospital for charity patients.

The gleaming exterior, dazzling in a sun-washed white-ness broken only by green venetian blinds on all the windows, looked as if it had been scrubbed overnight by hospital orderlies.

It exuded health and cleanliness, as if the building itself were immune to any of the illnesses and diseases within its white walls.

Inside, there was an atmosphere of deliberate cheerfulness, which seemed to imply that everybody who came here always got well.

Vases of orange and yellow daffodils dotted the lobby and colorful paintings hung on the walls.

The women volunteers at the reception desk wore bright pink smocks with a button, in the shape of a smiling face, attached to the collar. Even the gift shop, in a corner of the lobby, had a red-striped awning over the door as if it were a tiny boutique.

Milton Stanger apparently had cleared his visit with the

front desk because, when he asked for Winston's room, Burton was immediately given a visitor's pass and directed to the fifth floor.

Jarvis Winston's room looked as if a florist's shop had been squeezed into a theater dressing room.

Vases of flowers were arranged on a shelf by the window and other vases stood on a table next to Winston's bed.

Get-well cards were pasted on the walls and, mounted on a tripod in a corner of the room, there was a huge horseshoe wreath of carnations, dyed in the red and brown colors of the network. A white sash stretched across the wreath read: "From Jerry Rossman and all of your fans."

The display of cards and flowers was so sweeping and colorful that, as he entered the room, Burton did not immediately see Jarvis Winston, lying on the hospital bed as if he were just another part of some huge collage.

Then he saw him, gauze wrapped around his head, an IV dripping into his left arm, an oxygen mask clipped to his nostrils. He won't be able to talk, Burton thought.

There were two men seated in chairs by Winston's bed. Burton had never seen either of them before although one of them, who resembled an aging Mickey Rooney, looked vaguely familiar.

"Hello, Art," the other man said, rising from his chair. "I'm Milt Stanger."

"Nice to meet you," Burton responded. He had figured Stanger to be the balding one, the Mickey Rooney type. Instead, he found himself facing every mother's unmarried son.

Stanger was thin and gray haired and he wore thick, tortoiseshell bifocals. Burton had no idea how old Stanger was but he figured him to be close to sixty. He looked as if he had been born tired.

"You know Mickey Schirmer, Art?" Stanger asked, gesturing toward Schirmer who mumbled "HowareyaArt" and waved his hand in a casual greeting.

"We've never met," Burton said, walking over to shake Schirmer's hand. "But I know a lot of your clients in the News Division."

"Yeah," Schirmer said. "Carl Malachek thinks I have horns and a long tail."

"Malachek's not big on agents," Burton remarked.

Schirmer shrugged as if to say, "Fuck him."

"Jarvis," Stanger said, moving closer to the hospital bed. "You know Art Burton, from the *Focus on America* program?"

"Sure, sure," Winston said in a low voice that reflected discomfort but no pain. "Watch it all the time."

"Sorry to meet you this way," Burton said apologetically and silently thankful that Winston could speak. "I hope you're feeling better."

"My temperature and pulse are okay, it's the ratings I'm worried about." Winston managed a smile as he said it.

"Always with the jokes," Schirmer observed. "Even on his deathbed, this guy's doing the one-liners. Beautiful."

"Jarvis," Stanger interrupted. "Art would like to talk to you about doing a profile on you for his show."

"A profile!" Winston echoed. "What are you? A plastic surgeon? I need a nose job?"

"Hey, who's writing your material, Jarvis? You're on a roll. Beautiful, baby," Schirmer said.

I hate these show business types, Burton thought. Always on camera. Always performing. What the hell do they know about what really goes on? Ask them about anything and they give you jokes.

"I don't know how much Milton told you," Burton said, "but even before this accident, we were thinking of doing a piece on you. Now, of course—"

Before he could finish, Winston picked up on his thought.

"Now, of course, I'm a poor schmuck who happened to get beat up by a couple of weirdos freaked out on heroin or coke. Hey, you want to do a profile on me? Great! But let's wait until I get out of this mummy outfit. Right now I look like I could be playing Loew's Cairo."

Schirmer laughed. "Hey, Jarvis, remember Loew's Paradise up on the Concourse?" he asked.

Burton had no idea what Schirmer meant and looked bewildered.

"You don't know what he's talking about, do you Art?" Winston asked.

"No, I'm afraid I don't," Burton confessed.

"The Bronx," Winston explained. "Loews Paradise was a big movie house. Used to go there on Saturday nights when we were kids. Big balcony. Everybody was copping a feel."

"You two knew each other?" Burton asked incredulously.

"Hey, don't all the Jewish kids in the Bronx know each other? You know, from hanging around, temple dances, things like that," Winston said.

Schirmer jumped in. "We actually didn't know each other," he explained, "but we were around together. Grew up in the same place, that kind of thing. Actually, Jarvis is about ten years younger than I am."

"Yeah, but they held Mickey back in junior high for ten years so we could graduate together," Winston said.

"You're too much, Jerry," Schirmer said.

Burton instantly caught the agent's use of "Jerry" instead of "Jarvis." It confirmed what he had remembered in Vegas: Jarvis Winston's real name was Jerome Weinstein.

"You called him Jerry," he said to Schirmer.

"Sure," Winston interjected. "You think anybody would have a real name like Jarvis Winston? A super-goy name? My real name is Weinstein. *E* before *I*. Jerry Weinstein. And five to one you can't spell it right two times in a row."

"I'm not a betting man," Burton said, hoping to elicit a response from Winston but all Winston said was, "Too bad."

"We don't mention the Jerry Weinstein part," Milton Stanger said to Burton. "It's not that we're trying to keep secret that he's Jewish," he added hastily, "but his name has been changed legally for years now."

"My mother still calls me Jerome," Winston said. "Can you believe it?"

Oh my God, Burton thought. His mother! I saw her, even gave her my card, but I didn't know the connection then. She must not have told him or he'd realize that I've been poking around. But what if she does tell him? Christ!

"Your mother still lives in the Bronx?" he asked.

"Nah, she's in Vegas. Bought her a big house out in the desert so she can make chicken soup for the Indians."

Schirmer laughed again.

"You ever see her?" Burton asked innocuously.

"I bring her down here once a month or so. *Plotz* her in front of the pool, you know, with the orange trees and the maid bringing her the fruit juice and the whole *megillah*. It's good for her."

"Next time I'm in Vegas, I'll say hello for you," Burton said, searching for some way to see if Winston was playing dumb, if he really did know.

"Don't bother," Winston said. "Half the time she's in her own little world." He pointed a finger to his head. "You know, a little *meshuga*, if you understand what I'm saying."

"A little," Burton said, smiling. *He doesn't know that I've seen her*, Burton realized, *and if she ever does tell him, I'll say it happened after this. She got the time confused. It will be easy to get away with.*

"So what do you think, Art?" Stanger said, "Do you think you might be interested in doing something on Jarvis?"

"I would hope so," Burton said, with no regret about lying. Even before the meeting, he had developed a dislike for Winston. Just the idea that he was using his mother as an unwitting conduit for his gambling payoffs was enough to make him dislike Winston.

But now, seeing him like this, buried in flowers and get-well cards, cracking jokes and playing to an audience of three, a real wiseass son of a bitch; now, he really wanted to cut his balls off.

"I'll let you know what happens," Burton said, coming over to the side of the bed and taking Winston's hand. It felt warm and clammy, like a fish. "I hope you get out of here soon," he said.

"With my luck, Medicare will be covering me by the time I'm out of here," Winston said.

"Medicare!!" Schirmer exclaimed. "I love it!"

"Thanks again," Burton said and as he walked over to the door, Mickey Schirmer came over and gave him his card.

"Call me when you get back to New York," Schirmer said. "We'll have lunch."

Burton seized the opening Schirmer had provided him. "I read where you and Jerry Rossman were lunching together," he said offhandedly.

"Oh yeah, the *News* had something," Schirmer confirmed. "I wanted Jerry to meet Mark Antin. He's a client of mine."

"I thought Antin was locked up on *Breakfast Time*," Burton said casually.

"He is," Schirmer said. "Solid. But he's somebody I thought Jerry should get to know. And vice versa. What the hell. It's a small business, right? There's only one hundred people in television news and they all know each other. Right?"

"You're right," Burton repeated and he thanked Stanger again, shook Schirmer's hand, and left the room.

Despite the overpowering cleanliness of the hospital, he felt better when he was outside. The fresh air was invigorating and he rolled the windows of the car down so that he would not need the air-conditioning.

The traffic on the freeway back to the Century Plaza was light by California weekend standards. Burton was thankful because the easy flow of cars meant he did not have to concentrate on the traffic and he could think about where the Winston story went next.

The elements were beginning to take shape in his mind, as if he were already editing the various segments.

They would have to get some pictures of betting slips, with the name "Mrs. W" on them.

And Frankie Baglio would have to get his source to talk, even if in silhouette and with an electronically distorted voice, about the payoffs to Winston's mother. They'd also have to stake out the old lady in Las Vegas, get some pictures of her getting on a plane going to, and arriving in, Los Angeles to show how it all worked.

And then, somehow, they'd have to prove that Winston was actually betting. He might have to confront Winston on it and tell him the News Division had the whole story—even if it didn't—and hope that the bluff would work.

What the hell could Winston do? Sue him? Not a chance.

If I can break this story, he thought, it will be a blockbuster. A scandal in the network's own backyard and I blew it wide open. Malachek will love it.

But even as he savored the satisfaction of knowing that the story was beginning to pay off, he felt the doubts and fears that were rumbling in the far corners of his mind like the distant sounds of a summer storm.

There was another side to the Winston story, a side he knew existed but that he tried not to think about because he did not want to confront it until he had to.

But now he could no longer avoid it.

It always had been there, hovering in the distance; the knowledge that if he could confirm the story and get it on the air, he would ruin his chances of replacing John Cornwall.

Jerry Rossman would never approve of him getting the

anchor slot. The network brass would piss all over him, privately of course, but he would be finished.

And Malachek would be finished too. Maybe not right away, but whenever his contract was up. They'd find an excuse for not renewing it. New blood at the top. New ideas. Something like that. Malachek would be out.

The low, undulating hills that bordered the freeway were gone now and he was close to the exit for the hotel. His mind seemed to be racing ahead of the car, trying to devote his energy to the dilemma he finally had confronted.

Now, for the first time in his career, he was faced with a decision whether to abandon a story for personal reasons. It just never had happened. Until now.

He steered the car into the Century Boulevard exit and drove the few blocks to the hotel.

When he got to his room, he thought about calling Samantha to talk it over with her. But would Samantha understand? Could she?

He was on the threshold of the best and most prestigious job television news could offer. It would change his life, give him permanence, give him more than he ever had wanted or dreamed of. And above all, he and Samantha would be able to live the life they both wanted. A life together, with children, chasing leaves over a lawn.

Would Samantha understand that? That he would bury the Jarvis Winston story in order to safeguard his chances for the Cornwall job and all that it meant?

It was better, he decided, that she did not know anything. She would never have to know, just like she would never have to know about Bobby Ducoin.

To hell with it, he told himself, I'm not going to throw it all away. Not now.

He suddenly felt uncomfortable and he took off his clothes and stepped into the shower, as if standing under the cascade of water would cleanse him and make him feel pure. But, as he dried himself off, he still felt dirty, as if his decision about Winston had left him with a permanent stain, a smear of shit, that would not come off.

To hell with it, he thought again. It's a lousy business.

He could still make an afternoon flight and be back in New York by midnight. He'd tell Malachek next week the story just hadn't worked out. And he'd tell Samantha the same thing. Someday, maybe, he'd go back to Winston and nail the son of a bitch.

He let the towel drop from his waist and looked at himself in the full-length mirror that covered the closet door.

I'll be all right, he thought, I'll live with it.

Chapter 23

Jerry Rossman glanced up from his dessert plate of half-eaten sponge cake, dripping in a pool of syrupy strawberry sauce, and looked around the hotel room from his vantage point on the raised dais.

The walls on both sides of the room were formed by sliding partitions, a subtle device that reduced the size of the room so that the small crowd of three hundred or so people in the room would feel they had filled up the entire space.

Rossman wondered how many people the room would hold if the partitions were removed and the Grand Ballroom, as the sign on the speaker's podium proclaimed, was enlarged to its full capacity. Maybe five hundred, he figured. But what for? What the hell could ever happen in Lincoln, Nebraska to draw such a large crowd?

He looked down at the front row of tables, each with a number jutting out from a metal holder encased in a vase of plastic flowers in the center of the table. He saw Sid Neale, with a carefully concealed bored expression on his face, talking to the person seated across from him.

Poor Sid, he thought. He's stuck with these damn luncheons as much as I am.

He took a small bite from the sponge cake and decided it was easier not to eat at all, even if it meant spending another ten minutes talking to the woman seated next to him—Rosalie Hawkins, the wife of H. H. Hap Hawkins, the luncheon host.

He already had spent the first part of the lunch talking to

her, not because he wanted to but because he had been unable to avoid it.

She had pestered him incessantly with questions about the Jarvis Winston incident from the moment he had taken his place at the head table.

"It's just terrible what happened to him," she proclaimed before he had swallowed even his first spoonful of cream of chicken soup.

"It is dreadful," he said. "I almost canceled my trip out here," he confided.

"Do the police have any idea of who did it?"

"Jarvis told them it may have been some people high on cocaine. Thank God, he could talk to the police."

"I think his show is my favorite on the whole network," she said.

"I'd hate to think that you didn't like the program, Rosalie," he said. Calling her by her first name, instead of Mrs. Hawkins, struck just the right touch of friendliness and familiarity.

Actually, he hardly knew her. They had met a few times over the years at affiliate meetings or when she had accompanied her husband on his network-paid trips to New York.

But, because she was the wife of the chairman of the network's Council of Affiliates, she was one of the family.

So he assured her that Jarvis Winston was doing fine and yes, Winston would be back on the show as soon as possible, and yes, she certainly would see him in September because he was going to host the final banquet at the affiliate meeting.

Rossman was grateful when the luncheon emcee, who was the six o'clock anchorman at Hawkins's station in Lincoln, began to introduce the head table.

Rossman looked down the dais as each person stood up to polite applause. The priest who had delivered the invocation. The publisher of a community newspaper. The chairman of the City Commissioners. A professor of journalism at the University of Nebraska. Mrs. Hawkins, whom the emcee described as "the little woman behind the big man behind the name on our paychecks." There was a murmur of laughter.

Then it was Rossman's turn and he rose quickly from his chair and smiled at the audience as the emcee praised him as "one of the most important men in television today, a man who is tuned to the tastes and values of audiences all over America."

Rossman stared at the anchorman, a young blond, about twenty-six years old, with blow-dried hair, and he thought: the kid wants a job.

The luncheon was in honor of the thirtieth anniversary of Hawkins's station and, following the head table introductions, the waiters cleared the tables of dessert plates and coffee cups and the lights in the ballroom began to dim.

"Ladies and gentlemen," the anchorman-emcee announced in sonorous tones, "As a climax to our luncheon, we are proud to present thirty years of our history, as we reported it and as you saw it on your screens at home."

The ballroom was dark now and the videotape program appeared on television consoles that had been set up around the room.

As the program continued, Rossman, watching on a small monitor set up in front of the dais, became interested in the scenes flashing by on the screen: a devastating drought, a visit by President Kennedy in 1961, a famous play from a Nebraska-Oklahoma football game in 1973, the death of a prominent civic leader, local elections, a tornado, the State Fair, Elvis Presley visiting the city.

The moments in time flashed by as if they were pages from a scrapbook kept by the local historical society.

Sitting there in the darkened room, isolated, as it were, from everybody, Rossman thought for a moment about his own life in Scarsdale, outside of New York City.

Could these people here possibly conceive what it was like—the chauffeured limousine with the phone and the TV set in the back, picking him up every morning and driving into Manhattan along the Bronx River Parkway? The constant cycle of luncheons, banquets, industry conferences he was always attending?

He didn't know from state fairs or Nebraska-Oklahoma football games any more than the people out here—the ones at the head table or sitting out front, beginning to squirm in their chairs—knew about him and the thud of the Sunday *New York Times* on the front doorstep or the headlines in *Variety* on Wednesday mornings or the daily meetings about ratings, budgets, show costs, pilots, affiliates, news problems.

We've got nothing in common, he thought. It did not

matter to him that he was one of the honored guests. It was all part of the business.

After all, it was as much a part of his job to sit at head tables as it was to decide where a new show should be placed in the evening prime-time lineup.

And if he had a feeling for the latter, a finely tuned instinct that told him to slot a comedy at nine-thirty on Thursday nights against the other nets' cop shows, then it really didn't matter if the people out here knew how he lived.

If the comedy was a hit at nine-thirty, that was all that mattered. His taste was in tune with theirs. That was what mattered in the long run.

The program ended and the lights went back on and the audience was standing, applauding vigorously. Rossman leaned over to Hap Hawkins, seated on the other side of the lectern. "That was a hell of an impressive tape, Hap."

"I'm real proud of our folks, Jerry," Hawkins answered, acknowledging the audience's applause at the same time. "You won't find a better station anywhere."

"I've heard that in New York for years," Rossman commented obsequiously.

"I'm glad you could come out for this, Jerry. Especially in view of the Winston thing. It means a lot to us out here."

"I wouldn't have missed it for anything," Rossman said smoothly.

"I'd like you and Sid to drive back with us to the station," Hawkins said, rising from his chair as the audience began to flow out of the room. "They want to tape an interview with you for the six o'clock news."

"Fine," Rossman said, even though he hated the idea of some young kid with a couple of years in the business sitting down and talking to him about "the industry."

He could almost predict what the questions would be. When will Jarvis Winston be back on the air? What do you think about televised presidential debates? What about the level of violence on the cop shows?

Anyhow, he should have been in Los Angeles, checking on Winston, flying the network flag. But he needed to be here to start laying the groundwork for the announcement about John Cornwall. He had to kiss Hawkins's ass. In private.

The luncheon had provided the perfect excuse to come

out and speak to Hawkins, *schmooze* with him, make him understand that the network was not going to let the news go down the toilet, just because Cornwall was leaving.

They'd get the best possible replacement—Mark Antin if he could swing it—and spend a fortune promoting him.

Hawkins had to be on board from the beginning. Without his support, poison would spread through the affiliate ranks and there would be no way to stop it. Let a virus spread among the affiliates and it could become an epidemic.

Rossman gestured to Sid Neale, who had come over to the head table.

"Hap's station wants to do an interview with me," he said to Neale. "We'll go back to the station and then to the hotel."

Neale moved closer and, noticing that Hawkins was shaking hands with one of the head table guests, leaned forward and said, "Have you had a chance to talk yet?"

"No. Not yet," Rossman answered. "We'll talk at the station."

"You'll win him over," Neale said encouragingly.

Rossman smiled. He was glad he had asked Neale to fly out with him because it might take the two of them together to handle Hawkins. It wasn't going to be easy.

The interview at the station went just the way Rossman figured it would. The reporter was a young man in his early twenties who, before the interview began, confided to Rossman that he had gone to journalism school at Northwestern and then taken a job out here, in Lincoln, as a reporter in the newsroom. He had been working at the station for less than a year and was making $20,000,

"I guess network news is what I'd really like to do some day," the reporter told him.

"I'm sure," Rossman answered. What chutzpah, he thought.

When the interview was over, Rossman perfunctorily thanked the reporter and walked over to a corner of the studio where Hawkins and Sid Neale had been watching the interview on a television monitor.

"Sharp kid," he said to Hawkins.

"It was a good interview, Jerry," Neale said. "Very good questions."

"We've got a great bunch of reporters," Hawkins said in a paternal manner. "They'll be your correspondents someday."

Rossman did not respond. Instead, he asked Hawkins if he could spend a few minutes with him and Sid Neale, they had something important they wanted to discuss, and could they go to Hawkins's office?

Hawkins said, "Of course," and, wondering what was so important, led the two network executives up a carpeted stairway toward his office.

The walls on both sides of the staircase were filled with plaques from scores of civic organizations testifying to the public service rendered by the station.

If a visitor got the impression that the station, and its employees, spent twenty-four hours a day supporting the United Way, Volunteers of America, the Red Cross, 4-H Clubs, the Rotary Club, the U.S. Army Reserves, the Firemen's Auxiliary, and other similar groups, then the seemingly unending display of plaques and certificates served its purpose.

The station made millions of dollars a year, hired few minorities, produced one documentary a year, and carried paid religious programming instead of the network's news interview show on Sunday morning. But above all, it was a Good Neighbor.

Hawkins's office was large but simple in its furnishings. There were three television sets mounted in a wall, a print of Norman Rockwell's *The Four Freedoms* on another wall, and a plain desk that was empty except for a phone and a small figure of a Nebraska Cornhusker mascot wearing a red sweater with the letter *N*.

"I gather you're a big football fan, Hap," Rossman said, picking up the tiny plastic toy.

"Never miss the Big Red," Hawkins said, sitting down in a leather chair behind his desk. "I've had season tickets for years."

Rossman began to pace slowly back and forth in front of the desk and then he realized it was a sign of his own nervousness. He quickly walked to a couch where Sid Neale was sitting and sat down next to him, trying to look relaxed.

"Hap, there's been a development at the network you need to know about," he said. He spoke in a low voice, as if to emphasize the confidential nature of what he was about to say.

Hawkins leaned forward over the desk and clenched his hands together.

"What kind of development are you talking about, Jerry?" Hawkins asked warily.

Rossman noticed that he was still holding the Cornhusker figure he had picked up from Hawkins's desk and was squeezing its miniature arm.

He put it in his pocket, hoping that Hawkins would not notice that he had inadvertently twisted one of its arms.

"It's John Cornwall," Rossman said, unable to hide the gloomy tone in his voice. "He's decided to quit."

"I don't believe it," Hawkins said. "You're shitting me, Jerry."

"I wish I was," Rossman said quietly. "But it's true. We're going to announce it soon, before the affiliates meeting. I wanted you to know, now."

Hawkins's face began to redden, as if the heat of his rising anger were beginning to color his skin.

"You people have got to be crazy," he said angrily. "The best goddamn anchor in the country and you're letting him get away? C'mon Jerry, a two-bit UHF in Timbuktu wouldn't let this happen to them. You can't be serious."

"We've tried to convince him to stay," Sid Neale interjected, "but his mind is made up."

"Christ, he was just out here last year at our Volunteer of the Year Award dinner. He did a hell of a job," Hawkins reflected.

"Hap," Rossman said, "It's important that this be kept quiet. You're one of the few people who know." He hoped the last statement would mollify Hawkins and somehow make Hawkins feel that the problem was going to be contained and would be handled.

"We're looking at several replacements right now," Rossman continued. "People who will be strong enough to sustain the ratings even if there is an initial dip. People who will test out well. Good, strong, talent—the best we can find."

Hawkins got up from his desk and, shoving his hands in his pockets, began to scratch his testicles.

"You guys are making my balls itch," he said matter-of factly. "And you're going to make everybody else's balls itch, too. How do you think this is going to go over with the stations? They're not going to like it, Jerry. This is a bombshell you're dropping on all of us.

"One of the most important parts of our schedule—

everybody's schedule—is going to be empty and the new season is coming down awfully fast. You can't let it happen. Throw some more money at him, for Chrisake."

"Cornwall won't change his mind," Rossman said.

Hawkins sat down again, placed his hands behind his head, and slowly began to rock in his chair, as if he were contemplating some private thought.

"Do you realize what this means, just to my own stations?" he asked. "I figure that without Cornwall on there, the network news is going to drop two or three rating points in this market. I'll have to cut my rates, probably have to reduce the price of the spots in my six o'clock news. This is going to be some goddamn mess, Jerry."

He was silent for a moment and then he asked, "Do you have anybody in mind for a replacement?"

"This is also in confidence," Rossman said in the same, low voice he had used to break the news to Hawkins. "But we're talking to Mark Antin about replacing Cornwall."

Sid Neale's eyebrows raised slightly. It was the first time he had heard Rossman say he actually was negotiating with Antin. He did not know whether or not to believe him.

"Mark Antin? From *Breakfast Time*? That would be a hell of a catch, Jerry," Hawkins said admiringly.

"It's strictly in the talking stage, Hap, but that's the other piece of news I wanted you to know about. If it works out, we'll announce it at the affiliates meeting."

Hawkins got up from his desk and walked over to a window. The station had been built on the outskirts of the city years ago when land was cheap and the interstate had not yet come through. Now, there was a huge shopping mall across the way. Looking out the window, Hawkins could see afternoon shoppers walking into the Sears, Wendy's, Firestone Tires, and Jacuzzi franchises that bordered the highway. They were his people.

"Antin's a big favorite out here," he said. "*Breakfast Time* does damn well. Beats *American Sunrise* by a couple of share points every rating period."

"I know it does," Rossman responded. "I checked your rating books before I came out."

"Is Antin a newsman?" Hawkins asked.

Rossman shrugged his shoulders. "What difference does it make? He's good-looking, believable, and has great demographics with the 18- to 49-year-old women. And he's popular. He'll be perfect."

"I think some of the stations might want a stronger anchor, a newsman, you know, in the Cornwall or Robert Miniver mold," Hawkins suggested.

Then he asked, "What does Carl Malachek say about all of this?"

Rossman threw up his hands in exasperation. Just the thought of Malachek and his high-and-mighty attitude pissed him off.

"Let's face it, Hap. Malachek would exhume Miniver if he could and prop him up on the set every night. But a Miniver or a Cornwall don't come along every day. We've got to look to the future. Over the long haul, we may not need a Cornwall type on there anymore.

"Tell me something. Does it matter to Rosalie or your kids if Mark Antin never reported a story in his life? Is that going to make them not watch the news?"

"I hear what you're saying, Jerry," Hawkins conceded. "But some of the old-line conservative stations . . ." His voice trailed off.

Rossman brushed off the warning. "We can handle them," he said. "Show me a station that wouldn't put a Mark Antin on their news and I'll show you a station that's being run by a general manager with his head in the sand."

"I still think there will be resistance," Hawkins said.

"It's different now, Hap," Rossman countered. "People don't care. They don't want some guy's résumé before he comes on with the news, They just want to get the news. They don't have time for anything else. You know, just give us the dirty laundry.

"There're stations all over the country with anchormen who came out of a cookie cutter. Blond. Styled hair, perfect teeth, and they wouldn't know shit about reporting the news. But they sure can deliver it. And I gotta tell you, Hap, that's all that counts. They sure can deliver it."

"What are the chances of getting Antin, realistically?" Hawkins asked. He was becoming convinced by Rossman's arguments.

Neale looked at Rossman. Rossman could tell Neale was waiting to see how he would answer. You can't bullshit a

bullshitter, he thought, but it didn't matter. Hawkins had to
be stroked.

"I'd say pretty good," Rossman responded. "I'm setting
up a meeting with Antin when I get back. His agent represents a lot of people at our network so we've got some
leverage."

A trace of a smile crossed Neale's face. For a moment, he
remembered Rossman from the old days; the film salesman
days when Rossman could take a thirty-minute sitcom that
was a lump of shit and walk into a station and convince a
program director that the program was the greatest thing
since *I Love Lucy*.

He was still doing it, only on a different scale.

Hawkins put his elbows on his desk and rested his head
in his hands. "Is there a timetable on all of this? Are we going
to be set for the new season or will we be sucking hind tit, as
we say out here, beginning in September?"

Rossman got up from the sofa and nudged Neale to get
up as a signal that they were ready to leave.

"It's the biggest single problem we've got," Rossman
confided to him. "As soon as I get back, I'll be devoting
practically all my time to it."

Then, just to insure that Hawkins would be flattered by
being privy to the network's innermost secrets, he added,
"I'd have worked on it this weekend but I wanted to come
out here for your luncheon and to speak to you in person
about it."

"I appreciate your doing this, Jerry," Hawkins said, "and
you too, Sid." Neale smiled, and reminded himself to make
sure that flowers were sent to Hawkins's wife.

"We have to catch a flight back to Kennedy," Rossman
said, "and need to get back to the hotel."

"Fine, fine," Hawkins said. "I have somebody downstairs
who'll drive you over."

Rossman accepted the offer, gave Hawkins the double
handshake, both of his hands clasping Hawkins's in a sign of
firm friendship; thanked him again for his support and walked
down the long staircase, past all the plaques and certificates.

"They left out Hadassah," Neale said, as they climbed
into the waiting car.

"Not enough Jews here," Rossman said, laughing, as
they drove off to the hotel.

Back in the hotel, in Rossman's room, they discussed the meeting with Hawkins.

"Let's face it," Rossman said, sitting down on the edge of his bed. "It's a holding action. If we can keep Hawkins happy until we get this thing settled, we'll be all right. I don't want some general manager from Broken Kneecap calling me up in the middle of the night to complain that he's going down the tubes because we've lost Cornwall and what are we going to do about it."

"Hawkins may be right," Neale said dejectedly.

"About what?"

"About the resistance to somebody who's not a newsman. You know, seriously, how the hell are we going to promote somebody we can't send to a summit meeting or something like that when the others have got their guys there?"

"Ah, bullshit," he said angrily. "Where the hell is it written that the anchorman has got to be some ace reporter? I'm telling you, Sid, it's a myth. The audience doesn't give a shit. Look at Hawkins's anchorman out here, the kid who emceed the luncheon.

"Would you trust him to cover a tornado or whatever the hell else happens out here?"

Neale was silent.

"Of course you wouldn't," Rossman said, taking Neale's silence as agreement. "And neither would I. But you know something? That kid'll come on at six o'clock at night and look the audience right in the eye, as if he's sitting there in their living room, just him and them, and he'll say 'Good evening. There was a huge tornado near Schmuckville today and one hundred people were killed.' And every one of those people out there will sit up and listen and not one of them will care if that kid ever went to journalism school. They'll just keep on watching because he's making love to the women through the camera at the same time.

"And you know what Hap Hawkins will do?" Rossman asked, smiling. "Hap'll raise the prices on the spots in the six o'clock news. That's what he'll do."

Neale laughed and went over to a small bar and poured himself a drink. Rossman sat quietly on the edge of the bed, trying to think how he could reach Mickey Schirmer when he got back to New York tonight so he could start dealing for Mark Antin, maybe as early as Monday.

The phone rang, and Rossman reached over to the nightstand next to the bed and picked it up. He knew instantly from the hollow, faraway sound on the receiver that it was a long distance call.

"Mr. Jerry Rossman, please," he heard an operator say.

"Speaking."

"This is a White House operator, sir."

Rossman could tell it wasn't a joke. He motioned to Neale to come over to him. He cupped his hand over the receiver and whispered to Neale, "White House operator."

"Mr. Gordon Allen will be coming on the line, sir," the operator informed him.

"Fine," he answered. He did not recognize the name. "Gordon Allen," he whispered to Neale.

"Chief of Staff," Neale said hurriedly. He was impressed and he sat down on the bed next to Rossman.

Rossman shook his head back and forth as if to indicate that he still did not recognize the name.

"Mr. Rossman, this is Gordon Allen, the President's Chief of Staff, at the White House."

"Yes, how are you?" Rossman said pleasantly. He was trying to picture what Allen looked like and why he was calling him on a Saturday afternoon, here in Lincoln, Nebraska.

"Mr. Rossman, the President has asked me to call you because of our concern regarding a story your network is doing."

"A story?" Rossman said. He was genuinely surprised. He had no idea what Allen was talking about.

"Yes," Allen said in a serious voice. "One of your reporters, Samantha Stuart, is doing a story which involves an extremely sensitive subject, which I prefer not to talk about on the phone."

"Yes, of course," Rossman said numbly.

"The President would like if either you, or Mr. Carl Malachek, could come down to Washington to discuss this matter with me and perhaps the Director of the CIA."

"The CIA?" Rossman asked, stunned. Jesus, what the hell was happening?

"If you could come on Monday, we could discuss it at length. Would that be possible?"

"Of course it would," Rossman said quickly. The impact

of it was beginning to sink in on him. My God, this was the White House calling, and you didn't say no to the government.

"Do you want both of us to come?" he asked.

"That would be preferable,"Allen said. "The President has asked me to convey his thanks to you in advance for agreeing to this request." There was a slight pause and then Allen added, "We naturally assume you will keep this phone call and your visit entirely confidential."

"I can assure you of that," Rossman said.

"We will expect you in the morning," Allen said. "The guards at the West Executive Avenue entrance will see you through."

"Thank you for calling," Rossman said. "We'll be there."

He hung up the phone, then got up from the bed and walked over to a chair where he had put his attaché case.

"You're not going to believe this, Sid," he said, opening the case. "That phone call was about some story Malachek's people are working on. The White House says it involves national security. Christ, I really don't need this right now."

"What do they want?"

"They want me and Malachek to come down and discuss it. On Monday," Rossman responded as he pulled out a network telephone directory from his attaché case.

"What's the story about?"

"How the hell would I know?" Rossman asked sarcastically, slamming the attaché case lid shut. "You'd think that son of a bitch Malachek would tell me if they're working on something that sensitive but, no, he keeps it all to himself. Like we're not entitled to know, you know what I mean?"

"You know how they are, Jerry. I've said it a million times. The goddamn News Division thinks it's a separate network."

Rossman was rapidly thumbing through the directory and talking at the same time, as if he were in a race with himself to either find the number or complete his thoughts. The thoughts won.

"Can you imagine it?" he asked. "The White House tracks me all the way out here. I mean, to this very hotel room in the middle of Nebraska, on a Saturday afternoon yet, to tell me about some story my own network is doing and I don't know the first fucking thing about it!"

Then he said, "Here it is. Malachek's home number."

He came back to the phone by the bed. Sid Neale got up, as if doing so would in some way give Rossman a sense of privacy. Rossman ignored the gesture.

"Operator," he said into the phone. "I want to place a long distance call—person-to-person—to Mr. Carl Malachek in Rye, New York." He gave the number and waited impatiently, tapping his left foot on the floor, for several rings. There was no answer and he said to Neale, "He's out."

"Try him when we get back to New York."

"Yeah," Rossman agreed and he hung up the phone. "What time's our flight?" he asked Neale.

"Hour and a half. We should get to the airport. Hawkins has that car downstairs to take us."

"Fine, fine," Rossman said nervously and Neale could tell that Rossman was not thinking about the flight at all. "I'll tell you this, Sid," Rossman said. "Malachek can scream his balls off, but if the White House wants a story killed, we're going to do it. I don't care what the hell it is. I'm not going to have all of this and Cornwall too, you know what I mean?"

"Absolutely," Neale agreed. "That's the last thing we need right now. A lot of stories about how the network violated national security or something like that. Christ, we'd be murdered."

"Don't worry," Rossman said quietly. "It's not going to happen. We'll get this over with quickly. I'll go down with Malachek myself on Monday and it'll be over with."

"We might plant a few stories about how we squelched the report," Neale offered. "You know, how we put national security above our own interests." He was beginning to see the public relations possibilities in something like this, if it could be worked out.

"You're right," Rossman concurred. "That kind of stuff goes over well, particularly out here with the Hawkins types."

He was starting to feel more relaxed now. Everything could be handled. Malachek. Mark Antin. The White House. The affiliates. All he needed was time.

He reached into his pocket for a cigarette and discovered that he had absentmindedly taken Hawkins's tiny Cornhusker mascot with him. It was still in his pocket and he pulled it out carefully.

He held it up for Sid Neale to look at. "Look at this," he said to Neale. "I broke the poor bastard's arm."

"We'd better be going," Neale reminded him. He knew that Rossman was seething inside and he was worried that Rossman would boil over and spew out with unrelenting anger. The flight back to New York would be nothing more than an airborne tirade against Malachek, John Cornwall, and anyone else who was bothering Rossman. By the time they got to the airport, however, Rossman's anger had been replaced by a placid, silent mood.

Neale did not want to disturb Rossman's apparent serenity, and it wasn't until they had boarded the jet, and had fastened their seat belts, that he turned to Rossman and spoke. "How come so silent, Jerry?"

"I was just thinking," the network president replied, glancing out the window as the plane slowly began to roll backward from the terminal. "If we can make a deal with Mickey Schirmer and Mark Antin, nobody's going to remember John Cornwall a year from now. Or Carl Malachek."

The two men began to laugh loudly but the noise of their laughter was quickly drowned out by the growing roar of the jet engines.

They settled back in their seats as the plane lifted off the runway, climbed slowly over the city and the surrounding farmlands spreading out below, and then finally turned to the east, to New York.

Chapter 24

Art Burton turned over in bed and looked at Samantha Stuart's body.

She was lying on her back, her breasts rising slowly with each breath, and he reached over with one hand and cupped one of her breasts in his hand.

Then he leaned over and slowly kissed her nipples, finishing the kiss by running his tongue along the edges of her nipples until he could feel them harden.

She lay quietly, not stirring, and he moved his hand down her bare skin until the tips of his fingers were rubbing the soft skin beneath her pubic hair.

She moved slightly, slowly awakening from a deep sleep, and he nuzzled closer to her and said, "It's me and I love you."

There was a sound, nothing more than that, an indefinable sound that told him she was coming out of her sleep.

"I've been going out of my mind for you," he said. "Don't go back to sleep."

There was the sound again, but this time there seemed to be indistinct words hidden within it. He thought it sounded like "I woan" and he brushed his cock against her to show that he understood what she was saying and he wanted to go on.

"It's early," he said, still slowly moving his fingertips back and forth, caressing the sensitive skin where her legs lay open.

"What time is it?" she asked drowsily and, for a fleeting moment, he felt bad about having awakened her. Then he buried his head in her hair, which smelled of some aromatic shampoo, and he kissed her softly on her ear lobe and he didn't feel bad at all.

"About nine o'clock," he finally answered. "In the morning."

She was still on her back, her eyes closed, and he turned over so that he, too, was on his back, facing the ceiling, but his eyes were open.

"There's light coming into the room," he said.

"Close the blinds all the way," she said, as if she were reading from an instruction booklet.

"I don't want to get out of bed," he said.

"Then don't," she said quietly and he could see the trace of a smile across her face, as if she had just thought of something amusing.

"I want to stay right here," he said. "In this very spot."

"And?"

"Make love to you," he answered and then he felt her hand moving tantalizingly down his chest and stomach until she found his erection. She squeezed it lightly.

"So do I," she said softly.

The desire was beginning to pound within him and he

suddenly felt frustrated by the time it was taking her to awaken completely.

"Can't you tell I want you?" he asked, thrusting his tongue between her lips as he finished his words.

Their tongues touched and she began to move her hand along his cock, pulling it gently as if seductively urging it to become even harder. She could feel it throbbing and she put her tongue in his ear and then whispered, "Make me wet."

"God, I love you," he moaned and his finger found her vagina and he began to massage her, slowly at first, then more rapidly. He could feel the moist warmth of her and he heard her say, "I want you now, darling."

He moved over on top of her and she wrapped her legs around him.

All of the love he felt for her was filling him now and he kept his eyes closed tight as a rush of emotion swept over him.

He was still hard within her—stay this way, she pleaded— and he wanted to thrust harder. She grunted, as if to urge her own body to take even more of him into her, and she held him tight in her arms as if she were trying to compress him into her core, force all of him through her skin so that he would be totally within her.

"Oh my God, don't stop, Art," she said breathlessly and he answered very quickly—"I won't, I won't"—as if their very words to each other had been caught up in the rhythmic motion of their love-making and now the words, too, were coming rapidly and without pause.

"I love you, Art," she whispered.

"Jesus, you're wonderful," he said and he felt himself coming and he called her name as he climaxed. He lay breathing heavily, kissing her face, saying nothing, thinking only that it could never be this good again.

"I never knew," she finally said, her hand rubbing his back softly, trying to completely relax him.

"Knew what?"

"That we could be like this, like animals, almost."

"It was wonderful," he said and he moved his body even closer to her, closing the last bit of space between them so that he was huddling on top of her like someone seeking shelter and warmth.

"Stay in me," she said. "Don't get up yet."

"I need you," he said after a moment. "I really do."

"I need you too," she said and she pulled him tight against her to underline what she had just said.

She had been with him since last night, ever since he had returned to New York from Los Angeles.

He had come to her apartment directly from the airport, not even stopping at his own apartment to check his answering machine for messages.

She had been waiting for him and when he came to the door, she was already wearing a sheer silk nightgown.

He said, "I love you," and that was all.

They went into her darkened living room and there was no talk of his trip, or what either of them had been doing for the past few days; just the unspoken understanding that everything could wait until they had made love to each other because, at this one moment, it was what they both desperately wanted.

She had helped him undress, branding his skin with wet kisses as he removed his clothes, until at last he was naked. Then she knelt down and kissed his testicles and he lifted her nightgown over her shoulders and guided her over to the couch.

They made love wildly but it was too quick, as if each needed to get an undeniable yearning out of them so the rest of the night would be free for more leisurely sex. But they both were tired; he from the long flight and she from staying up to wait for him, and so they went into her bedroom and fell asleep.

Now, with the morning light filling the room and the frenzy of their renewed love-making subsiding, they lay quietly, full of their own thoughts.

Samantha wondered when she would have a chance to speak to Malachek about the Herman Willows assignment.

She had tried to reach him at home when she returned from Washington but there had been no answer and she had decided to wait until tomorrow—Monday—before trying again.

But the Willows story was still highly confidential and she felt she could not tell Art about it, even though she wanted to. Instead, she asked him, "How did your trip go? Any luck?"

"I ended up in Los Angeles," he said, stretching his legs,

trying to relax and, at the same time, feeling uncomfortable that he was going to have to lie to her.

"I know," she said. "You called me from there, yesterday. Remember?"

"Yes," he answered. "It's just that I was thinking about the Weinstein woman. She went from Vegas to LA."

"Were you able to get anywhere?"

"No. I got sidetracked by the Jarvis Winston beating." He paused for a moment, waiting to see if she would make any connection between the names—Weinstein and Winston—but she was silent.

"Winston could be an interesting segment on *Focus*," he went on, wondering why he was carrying the lie further.

At least he was not lying to himself. He knew what was happening to him. His desire for the anchor job was consuming him.

It had been growing ever since Malachek had first said he wanted Art for the job. But since then, with the Holy Grail of network news dangling in front of him every day, always tantalizingly just out of reach, he had come to want it and desire it even more.

Now, his desire was so great he was willing to forget everything he knew about Jarvis Winston if it would insure his chances for getting the Cornwall job.

How could he ever explain that to Samantha? She would be repulsed by his decision and, at worst, he might lose her love. And as he lay next to her, feeling the softness of her skin, struck by the beauty of her face, excited by the suppleness of her body, he knew that losing her would be the one thing he could not endure.

How did it get this way, he wondered. How did his feelings for her grow like this, silently, quietly, without his being aware of it every step of the way?

His love for her had grown to the point where, now, he wanted to see her every day and the frustration of not being able to seemed at times to be more than he could bear.

When their schedules coincided and they were in New York together, he would find excuses to see her during the day. A newspaper to be borrowed. A script to be checked, a cassette to be viewed. Anything.

She knew, of course, that he was trying to find ways, innocent to outsiders, to see her. But that was part of the inexplicable magic of it all. They both knew and they both understood.

He never wanted to lose that. She did not have to know about Winston.

He looked at her and smiled, almost paternally, as if he were protecting her from an ugly secret that would destroy her if she discovered it.

She smiled back and closed her eyes. Tomorrow she would see Malachek, give him the videocassettes of the Willows interview, and see what came next on the story.

Maybe then she could tell Art about it. It was a warming thought and she drew it around her like a blanket.

She fell asleep, thinking, *Art will be proud of me*.

Chapter 25

Like many other people in the media business, Jerry Rossman liked the Hunt Room of the Helmsley Palace Hotel for breakfast meetings.

The location of the hotel, on Madison Avenue between Fiftieth and Fifty-first Streets, was convenient. When breakfast was finished, he could walk to the network building, just a few blocks away.

He also liked the ambiance of the dining room; the service on china, the way the captain addressed him by name, even the patterned cozy that kept the toast warm.

Rossman also liked the idea that he could always get a table.

Thus, on Monday morning at eight o'clock, a day and a half after flying back from Lincoln, Nebraska, Jerry Rossman was sitting at a table in the dining room of the Helmsley Palace eating a broiled grapefruit while his breakfast guest, Mickey Schirmer, heaped cream cheese on a toasted bagel.

"A good schmear of cream cheese, Jerry. I love it,"

Schirmer said, moving his knife back and forth over the cheese as if he were an artist preparing a palette.

Rossman extracted a seed from the grapefruit and placed it in an ashtray. "I can't eat all that rich stuff, Mickey," he said. "Doctor's orders."

"Doctor, schmoctor," Schirmer said. "Listen, if you like it, eat it."

"You eat it," Rossman said dourly. "I got problems."

Schirmer reached for another mound of cream cheese and spread it carefully on the bagel.

"Like Jarvis Winston, you mean." It was a statement, not a question.

"Yes, of course," Rossman answered, regretting that he had sounded depressed. "That's one of the reasons I wanted to have breakfast with you this morning," he continued, trying to sound cheerful. "I wanted a firsthand report on Jarvis."

"Let's put it this way. He hasn't lost his sense of humor. That's the most important thing. Second, he looks like shit," Schirmer said.

"Jesus," Rossman muttered.

"C'mon, Jerry," Schirmer said. "Milton Stanger must have told you how Winston looked. He's been playing Dr. Kildare to him ever since they brought him in. He's in the room more than the doctor."

"A second opinion, Mickey. It always helps."

"Yeah, sure," Schirmer said. Then: "So what do you think, Jerry? Another two months? What are they telling you?"

"Who? The doctors? They say a month, maybe six weeks. He'll be back before the new season, that's for sure."

"He's a big talent, Jerry. Don't put him on the air until he's ready."

He's telling me what to do about Winston. What chutzpah, Rossman thought. For a moment, he decided not to tell Schirmer about Cornwall, just bullshit him for the rest of the meeting, because he could smell the kind of trouble he would be buying with Mark Antin doing the news and Schirmer representing him.

But he could handle Schirmer. It would be worth it. He decided to stroke the agent a little, play to his ego, set him up for the real reason he wanted to meet him for breakfast this morning.

"We won't rush Jarvis," he assured Schirmer.

"I'm glad you could make it this morning, Mickey," he continued. "I wouldn't have blamed you if you said no. Those flights from the Coast can wipe you out sometimes."

"Where were you over the weekend? Kansas, some place?"

"Nebraska," Rossman said. "I had a long-standing engagement at one of our major affiliates that I couldn't miss. Long-standing commitment. Otherwise, I would have been on the first flight to LA."

"Poor Jarvis," Schirmer said, beginning to spoon some orange marmalade onto his plate. "Son of a bitch is just sitting there and these scumbags walk in and do that to him. Even if he wasn't my client, I'd shoot the bastards."

Rossman wanted to shift the conversation away from Winston. He had been on the phone most of Saturday night with Milton Stanger, getting a complete report on Winston's condition and on what the police were doing to find his assailants. Stanger had even briefed him on Art Burton's visit.

So he knew everything there was to know about Jarvis Winston and he didn't need any more information from Mickey Schirmer, even if Schirmer was carrying on as if Winston was his closest relative.

"So, how's business, Mickey?" Rossman asked, pushing the grapefruit away from him and turning his attention to a piece of toast.

Schirmer looked at Rossman quizzically, trying to figure out why Rossman had changed the subject. "It's fine," he answered, smiling. "It couldn't be better."

"All of your clients happy?"

"Are they ever happy?" he answered, shaking his head in mock despair at the thought. He still couldn't figure out what Rossman was leading up to.

"Why do you ask?" he asked.

"Mark Antin," Rossman answered, buttering a piece of toast. "I figured he wasn't happy."

So this is what it's all about, Schirmer thought. He poured some more coffee from the silver-plated coffeepot.

"You interested in Antin, Jerry?"

Rossman paused for a minute as if he actually were contemplating the question, trying to make up his mind.

"I could be interested," he finally said and he knew that by saying it he was setting in motion a process that normally would take weeks or months, but now, because of Cornwall's insistence on leaving before the new season started, it would have to be done in a couple of weeks at most.

His only advantage was that he didn't have to let Schirmer know the timing on Cornwall. That could come later, after he found out if Antin really was available.

"I didn't think you had anything for Mark," Schirmer replied, hiding his astonishment that Jerry Rossman was fishing around for Antin. But what could he want him for?

"When you brought him to lunch at 21," Rossman parried, "I knew that it wasn't just a social call."

"I thought you were somebody he ought to know," Schirmer replied.

"It made one of the columns," Rossman observed casually. He wanted Schirmer to know that he knew the agent had planted the item.

"So? So it made the columns," Schirmer responded. He wasn't going to let Rossman lay anything on him.

"Listen, Jerry," Schirmer continued in a best-of-friends tone of voice. "The three of us lunch at 21 and half the business is eating there. You don't think somebody is going to say something? Anyhow, what's the big deal?"

He took a matchbook from his pocket and began to pick his teeth with the edge of the matchbook. Rossman averted his eyes and glanced around the room uneasily, as if he were afraid that others in the dining room would see the vulgar display.

He wished that he had arranged to meet Schirmer in his office at the network, in private, where he wouldn't have to watch him schmear cream cheese or gulp coffee or pick his teeth.

But there was not going to be any time today. After breakfast, he had to fly down to Washington so he and Malachek could go to the White House to discuss whatever the hell story Malachek's people were working on. Thank God he had reached Malachek last night and ordered him to be in Washington today. Not asked him. Ordered him.

The White House thing was bad enough but meeting

with this little prick Schirmer was more important. So he'd sit here and watch Schirmer pick his teeth because he needed to know, now, if there was a chance to make a deal for Mark Antin to anchor the news.

"When we had lunch, you indicated Antin might be looking," Rossman said. "Is that the way it is or were you just blowing smoke?"

Schirmer shrugged his shoulders. "His contract is coming up to the renewal date. He's got a ninety-day option in there, his option, that allows him to shop around if he wants to."

"You got that kind of clause for him?" Rossman asked admiringly.

"Hey, he's good and they needed him. That's what it's all about, isn't it? That's what a good agent is for."

"I never would have approved a clause like that," Rossman reflected.

"Different strokes for different folks," Schirmer said, smiling.

Rossman wanted to see how far Schirmer would go. The agent was acting too cocky, like he was doing him a favor even to talk about Antin.

He signaled the waiter to bring more coffee and hunched forward in his seat.

"I want to talk to you about Antin," Rossman said, staring right at Schirmer, who had a little blob of cream cheese clinging to his upper lip. "I want to know how serious you are, if you're really looking."

"I'm his agent, and I'm looking to make the best deal for him and do what's in his best interests. Does that answer your question?"

I can get him, Rossman thought. *All it will take is money.*

"I think it will be in his best interests to move over to us," Rossman said, as if he were delivering a judgment on some world issue.

"What kind of a deal are you talking about, Jerry?" Schirmer asked, genuinely puzzled. In his mind, he quickly ran through the possibilities but he couldn't come up with anything. *Sunrise* was Swanson's, Cornwall was doing the evening news—what else was there? Unless Rossman was thinking of some new show. But that would be too big a gamble for Antin to make the jump.

Rossman kept staring at Schirmer, as if he were trying to hypnotize the agent into seeing the seriousness of what he was about to tell him.

"I'm talking the evening news, Mickey," he said quietly.

"What evening news? The Cornwall show?" Schirmer asked, trying to contain his surprise and excitement. It was hard to believe that Rossman was sitting there talking about Mark Antin doing the evening news.

"Yes. The Cornwall show." Then he added, "I'm trusting you, Mickey. I don't want this in the papers or at any of the other nets. Very few people know this and if it gets out, you will have a very hard time for your people at our network. A very hard time."

"We're talking business, Jerry," Schirmer said solemnly. "I don't cock around when we're talking business. We've made too many deals together so there's no need to threaten me. You know that."

"All right," Rossman conceded, wondering if he had offended Schirmer. It was hard to trust him all the way. But he had no choice. He had to spell it out for Schirmer, or most of it, and take his chances. There was no other way.

"Cornwall is going to quit," Rossman said. "We're thinking of Antin as the replacement."

Schirmer was stunned. The idea of Cornwall leaving the network was incredible. He couldn't believe it, but here was Rossman telling him so.

Cornwall was their meal ticket, five nights a week, just like Winston was on Saturday nights. Take Cornwall away and their news ratings would go down, their whole image would be tarnished.

Cornwall had to be worth millions to them, he figured, and he began frantically searching his mind, trying to come up with a figure that he could get for Antin as Cornwall's replacement. Not that Rossman would talk money today, but he wanted a figure he could play around with in his mind, some number he could mentally suck on and get a thill from, just as if he were kissing the tits of that redhead who had come to his office last week wanting him to be her agent.

"Antin would be a natural for your news," Schirmer said. "Great demographics. Great believability."

"I don't need a sales job, Mickey. We've got research too. I want to know if you're interested, if Antin's interested?"

"Of course we'd be interested," Schirmer said. "I want to talk to Mark, of course, but if the money's right and we can work it all out, then we might get together.

"You've got to understand we've got a pretty good deal where we are. Lots of perks. Big clothing allowance, seven weeks' vacation, veto on the executive producer. I got a very good contract for him."

He spaced out the words "very good contract" to make sure that Rossman understood that it was not going to be easy.

Rossman understood. *He's starting to squeeze me already,* he thought, silently thankful that he wouldn't be involved in the face-to-face negotiations with Schirmer. Big money contracts were always negotiated by attorneys for the network's Legal Department, although he would be constantly consulted and would give final approval.

"I gotta tell you," Schirmer said, "I can't believe Cornwall is pulling this. If he were my client, I'd talk some sense into him. Best goddamn job in television and he's walking out. It's unbelievable, Jerry."

"Believe me, it's true. He has his reasons."

"What's the matter? He sick or something? Nothing bad, is it? I mean, you know, cancer?"

"Nothing like that," Rossman said patiently. "He's just had enough. It's as simple as that."

"What kind of timing are you talking about?"

"I don't know," Rossman said, forcing himself to keep looking straight at Schirmer. "We're still discussing it with him."

"You mean it's not final?"

"No, he's going. Our interest in Antin is genuine. If we can't make a deal, we'll go with somebody else."

"Not too many anchor types out there, Jerry. You gonna bring somebody in from a local station someplace? C'mon, no way."

Rossman resented Schirmer trying to goad him. "We've got good people," he responded. "Maybe Swanson from *Sunrise.* Or McVay off the weekend news."

Sure, Schirmer thought. *That's why you asked me to meet you at eight o'clock on a Monday morning. Because you've got a whole stable full of talent just ready to take over*

*the evening news. You want Antin so bad your teeth are
hurting.*

"What about Malachek?" Schirmer asked him.

"What about him?" Rossman could feel himself bristling
at the question and he hoped it didn't show.

"C'mon, Jerry," Schirmer said, lowering his voice. "I
know how Carl feels about Antin. The 'Commodore Commando' bit, the whole thing. The whole business knows."

"Carl Malachek works for the network," Rossman said
firmly. "This decision is being made by all of us, including
Malachek."

Malachek must be eating some shit, Schirmer thought,
but he decided not to press the point. Anyhow, Rossman
would have to make the final decision. Something this big
wouldn't be Malachek's call.

Rossman glanced at his watch and motioned for the
waiter to bring the check.

"I have to catch the shuttle down to Washington," he
told Schirmer. "Get back to me soon, if you would. I'd like to
get moving on this."

"I'll speak to Mark when I get back to the office,"
Schirmer replied. He waited for Rossman to sign the check
and then he pushed his chair away from the table and got up.

"I'm glad we got together this morning, Jerry," he said as
Rossman rose to shake his hand. "You know I'll keep this
confidential and I appreciate your interest in Mark. I know
he will too."

"It would be a smart move for all of us," Rossman said.
"Good for you, good for us."

"So we'll see what happens," Schirmer said, smiling. He
squeezed Rossman on his shoulder and the two of them
walked to the dining room exit together.

Rossman nodded his head in greeting at two vice presidents from another network as he passed by their table. He
wondered what they were thinking when they saw him and
Schirmer. Probably that we're talking about Winston, he
decided, and he decided not to worry about it.

"Can I give you a lift anyplace?" he asked Schirmer as he
walked over to the limousine that was waiting on Fiftieth
Street to take him to La Guardia Airport.

"No, I'm going back to the office. Thanks," Schirmer

answered. He waited until Rossman got in the car and then he waved good-bye and walked toward Fifth Avenue.

As the gray Fleetwood limousine moved tortuously in the morning rush hour traffic, Rossman picked up the car phone and dialed Sid Neale's number at the network.

It was not yet nine-thirty but he knew that on a Monday morning, Neale would be in his office, going through the weekend newspapers from out of town.

"Where are you, Jerry?" Neale asked.

"Third and Fifty-eighth," Rossman said, glancing out the window as the car inched by crowds of shoppers converging on the entrances to Bloomingdales. "Traffic is brutal."

"How did it go?"

"He's interested. He's going to get back to me."

"He's probably calling Antin right now," Neale surmised.

"I'm sure," Rossman said confidently. His eyes followed the shapely legs of a tall woman who was walking up Third Avenue in the same direction the limousine was going. He could not see her face but he imagined that she was very beautiful.

"Listen, Sid," he said. "Can you hear me okay?"

"It's a good connection this end," Neale assured him.

"I want you to start working up a release on Cornwall. We'll clear it with him and Blumberg before we release it but I want to get going on it."

"When do you want it?"

"I'd like to see it when I get back from Washington. I don't trust Schirmer to keep this quiet. I'll tell Malachek about it when I see him."

"What about Antin? Are you going to say anything to Malachek about him?"

"You're goddamn right I am," Rossman said. "I've had enough problems from him this weekend. The White House thing is infuriating. I don't need to keep Malachek happy, believe me."

"When do you see this release going out, Jerry?"

"Give it to *The Times* tonight," Rossman answered. "The more I think about it, the more I'm worried about Schirmer leaking this one. I want it to come from us. Make sure there's a lot of praise for Cornwall in it."

"It'll be ready when you get back," Neale said. "Anything else?"

"No. I'll call you when I get back to the office. Thanks."

He placed the phone in its cradle in the armrest next to the window and looked out of the window as the car turned right on Sixty-second Street and headed for the East River Drive.

The traffic was beginning to move more freely now and he glanced at his watch and figured he would make the shuttle with at least ten minutes to spare.

Chapter 26

When Jerry Rossman told Carl Malachek he would meet him at the network's Washington bureau, Malachek's instincts were confirmed. The meeting with Rossman would be rough.

"You don't need to pick me up. I can get there myself," Rossman had told him curtly. That had been at the end of a brusque, almost rude, phone call from Rossman to Malachek at home on Sunday to tell him about the Washington meeting.

"They want to see us at the White House. Tomorrow. There's a problem," Rossman had told him.

"What do you mean, a problem?"

"Just that. A problem," Rossman answered abruptly.

"Who's they?" Malachek asked, unwilling to let Rossman stonewall him about a problem of such magnitude that it involved the White House.

"They is Gordon Allen, the Chief of Staff. I'll tell you more when I see you."

The White House Chief of Staff meant a big problem. Malachek said he would take the first flight down in the morning.

Now, as he sat in the Washington bureau chief's office and waited for Rossman to arrive, Malachek went over in his mind the possible reasons for the call from the White House.

There had been a story a few weeks ago about a failure in

a new weapons system. It had made the Defense Department angry, but not angry enough to warrant a meeting at the White House. Nor would last week's story about how statistics were being juggled to make the war on drugs seem more successful than it actually was. The Attorney General's top assistant had called about that one.

That left only the Herman Willows story. He knew that Samantha Stuart had been planning to confront Willows this past Saturday. The timing of the White House call pointed to the Willows story as the reason.

They're trying to kill it before we dig any deeper, he figured. He did not wonder if Rossman could stand the heat. He knew he couldn't.

If the White House put on a lot of heat, he decided, he would ask Charlotte to go back to her source and push hard for more information. He did not want to fold under the pressure.

His thoughts about what he was going to do were interrupted when Jerry Rossman walked into the office. He noticed that Rossman was dressed in a black, pin-striped suit. Very network presidential, he thought. Very sincere.

"Hello, Jerry," he said. "How was the flight?"

"The shuttle. They pack you in like sardines." Rossman spoke as if he had a sour taste in his mouth.

"It gets you here," Malachek commented. He looked at his watch. "It's almost eleven-thirty," he said, gesturing to a chair. "Do you want to stay here for a few minutes or do you want to get over there a few minutes early?"

"How far is the White House from here?"

"A ten-minute drive. Fifteen at most. Somebody will drive us over."

"We can go in a few minutes," Rossman said. He sat down in a chair across from Malachek and crossed his arms in front of him, as if he were waiting for Malachek to say something.

Malachek looked at him but said nothing.

"Do you mind telling me what story you're working on that's so goddamn sensitive the White House has to call me in the middle of nowhere on a Saturday afternoon?" Rossman finally exploded.

Malachek drew a deep breath, trying to relax. Rossman won't understand this, he thought. It's going to be like

teaching Journalism 101 to him because he doesn't understand what we do. To him, news is just the stuff that goes
between the commercials.

"We got a tip from a very reliable source," Malachek
began softly. "We were told that a Government employee
was arrested trying to sell secret photos to the Russians. But
the arrest was covered up by the White House. The man was
let go. He's free as a bird."

"So maybe he's innocent."

"The whole thing stinks to high heaven," Malachek said.

"You say it stinks. Maybe somebody else says it smells
like roses."

Malachek thought: he really doesn't understand.

"That's why we're doing the story," he said patiently.
"Because we've been given a good tip and we believe it's
true. But we won't put it on the air unless we can confirm it.

"The White House probably doesn't like us poking around,"
he continued, "because if there's a cover-up, for some reason
we don't know about yet, then they don't want us within ten
thousand miles of that story."

"What kind of a cover-up do you mean?" Rossman asked.

"I don't know," Malachek admitted. "But the man who
was arrested, and then let go, is the top aide to Senator
Charles Ramsey, one of the party's brightest stars. It wouldn't
look too good for Ramsey's reelection chances if his office was
discovered to be a spy's nest."

Rossman threw his hands in the air in exasperation. "For
Chrisake, Carl," he said angrily. "You guys smell a rat in
every living room. I don't think our government is going to
cover up a spy arrest for the sake of protecting some senator,
no matter who he is."

"And did you think a President would resign before he
was impeached? Or another President would be screwing a
mistress in the White House? Or a Vice-President would
plead nolo contendere? Anything is possible, Jerry. Anything."

"I'm sorry, Carl," Rossman said, "but I don't share your
suspicious, sarcastic approach to everything. Save it for the
movies, the ones where the guys wear the press cards in their
hats, because it's not going to work with me."

Malachek spread out his hands in resignation. "You
asked me and I told you," he said.

"And I'm telling you if the White House has got a reason for talking to us about this story, and I assume they do, it's probably a damn good reason," Rossman said, getting up from his chair and looking at his watch.

"We should be going," he said, as if he were talking to himself.

"There's a car out front for us," Malachek said, relieved that the argument had ended for the moment. He realized that Rossman was ready to cave in on whatever the White House would come up with.

I'll fight it, he decided, but he was worried he might lose in the end.

The drive to the White House took ten minutes, just as Malachek had said it would. The network's bureau was downtown, on Connecticut Avenue near Dupont Circle. The car maneuvered slowly through the noontime traffic until it reached Pennsylvania Avenue and then turned right on Fifteenth Street.

They drove past the Treasury Building and then turned right again, between the rear of the White House and the Ellipse. At the southwest gate, Malachek gave their names to a policeman and they were waved into West Executive Avenue.

Thirty yards farther, the driver let them out by a side entrance to the West Wing of the White House. A military aide met them and escorted them up a flight of stairs into the White House offices.

They walked down a small hallway until they reached the outer office of Gordon Allen. A few moments later, the double door to the office swung open and the Chief of Staff, dressed in a suit almost identical to the one Rossman was wearing, came out and extended his hand in greeting.

"Hello, gentlemen," he said. "I'm Gordon Allen."

"Jerry Rossman," Rossman said, taking Allen's hand. He added, "You know Carl Malachek, president of our News Division."

"Yes, of course," Allen said congenially. "We've never actually met, although I certainly know your people. Charlotte Glover and the others."

"Everybody knows Charlotte Glover," Malachek commented as they followed Allen into his office. It was a big office, with bay windows that looked out on the South Lawn, and a horseshoe shaped desk that apparently had been custom-built to complement the curved contour of the bay window.

A huge globe on a pedestal flanked the desk and the walls were hung with portraits of colonial military figures.

The carpeting was a soft blue and Rossman noticed that the Great Seal of the United States was woven into the center of the carpet. *I ought to get a carpet like this for my office,* he thought, *with the network logo on it.*

"Please sit down," Allen said, pointing to two red leather captain's chairs in front of his desk. Allen faced them from behind his desk, which was bare except for a manila folder, with P3 stamped on it, and a small pipe rack.

Malachek looked at the folder and tried to remember what the P3 classification stood for, but he couldn't. He sensed, however, that the pressure was about to be applied and he mentally prepared himself to look for the weak spots in whatever Allen would say.

Allen placed his hand on the folder and looked directly at Rossman.

"What I am about to tell you, Mr. Rossman, and you, Mr. Malachek," he said quietly, "must remain in this room. I will not ask you to sign any pledges. We're all Americans and we're all professionals."

Rossman shifted uneasily in his chair and glanced quickly at Malachek, who was sitting impassively, looking at the Chief of Staff.

"I will get right down to it," Allen continued. "One of your reporters, Mr. Malachek—Samantha Stuart—confronted a government employee in front of his house Saturday morning and made several serious allegations."

Malachek remained expressionless but nodded his head slightly as if to acknowledge that Allen was correct.

I was right. Willows must have called the White House.

"The President has asked me," Allen said, pausing for a brief second to allow his words to sink in, "to tell you that your pursuit of this story is jeopardizing national security. This involves a matter of extreme sensitivity."

Malachek reached for a cigar from his breast pocket but decided against it. There were no ashtrays on Allen's desk. He looked skeptically at Allen. "You're already co-opted us, Mr. Allen. You've asked that everything stay in this room. You've invoked the name of the President on a matter of national security. Perhaps I should leave the room before you go any further. This is a story we may well want to pursue and I would not want to violate your confidence."

Rossman gritted his teeth and stared icily at Malachek. *You pompous son of a bitch. You walk out of this room and you're fired. How dare you pull this kind of shit?*

Allen smiled condescendingly at Malachek. He ran his fingers over the edge of the folder and said, "You may well be co-opted, Mr. Malachek. But if I tell you what is involved here, I think you will make up your own mind insofar as any ethical problem you may have with all of this."

Malachek settled back in his chair. *No use fighting it,* he thought. *I have to hear him out.*

"I just want to make it clear," he growled, "that I resent being asked to come here and being immediately told that everything is off-the-record."

Come off it, you asshole, Rossman thought.

"I would like to proceed," Allen said patiently, as if he were presiding over a partners' meeting at the Wall Street bond house he had once headed.

"Please go ahead, Mr. Allen," Rossman said politely, hoping that Malachek's behavior would not reflect on the whole network and cause problems with the administration. *That's all they needed now.*

"There is no doubt," Allen said, "that Herman Willows was going to sell the ground-level Cosmodrome photos to the Russians. You know what I'm referring to, Mr. Rossman?"

"Yes, of course," Rossman answered quickly.

"We know this because we have a very highly placed source within the Russian Embassy. A mole, if you will. It is obviously of enormous value to us to keep this mole in place and not to jeopardize a very, very valuable source of information.

"It was the mole who told us that the proposed sale of photos was going to take place. Neither we, nor the mole, knew who the seller was until Willows walked out of the Senate Office Building that night and the CIA picked up the signals."

"So why wasn't he charged and jailed?" Malachek interrupted.

"Two reasons," Allen answered. He extended his hand and held out one finger. "First," he said, "jailing him and charging him would have given the game away to the Russians.

We didn't want them to know that we knew. The minute charges were filed, and it made the papers and TV, the Russians would have known that we had an inside source. Don't forget, Willows was operating alone. His wife had no idea what he was doing. She still doesn't. So nobody from the outside would have tipped us off. Any tip that Willows was about to make a sale would have had to come from inside the Embassy. So no arrest, no sign to the Russians about a mole."

Rossman was stunned. He knew that things like this happened. But sitting in the White House, being told about top secret matters like this, was incredible.

"The second reason we didn't charge Willows," Allen said, extending another finger, "is that we need to maintain communication with Willows's contact in the Embassy. It gives us two paths—the mole and the man Willows had been dealing with. We want to know what they're interested in."

"So you've turned Willows," Malachek observed. "He's a double agent."

"Not quite," Allen replied. "Herman Willows is a pathetic little homosexual who was being blackmailed by an ex-boyfriend. Standard stuff. The lover threatened to expose him to his wife, to Senator Ramsey. He needed money and so he contacted the Russian Embassy. Just like that. Called them up and said he had something of interest to sell and would they be interested?"

"And they checked him out, found out who he worked for and got back to him," Malachek said.

"Right," Allen confirmed. "Only now, Willows can be exposed for a lot more than a few incidents behind the bushes in Rock Creek Park. We've taken care of his ex-boyfriend. But now Willows has to play along with us."

"So we're the blackmailers," Malachek said sarcastically.

"We prefer to think of it in national security terms, Mr. Malachek," Allen said with a bite to his voice. "When you're in the gutter, you don't always have a chance to wash your hands. We need Herman Willows to string along the Russians, to be the bait that they fish for. He needs us to stay out of jail for the rest of his life and to make sure that his dirty little habits stay buried. It's as simple as that."

"But the Russians knew what he had to sell," Malachek said. "The fact that we even have the photos is of enormous value to them."

"They never knew what pictures Willows had," Allen replied. "They only knew that he had pictures he said they would be interested in. The meeting with the contact was to show the pictures and set a price. The actual sale would have taken place later. That's why we had to stop Willows before he had a chance to show the pictures. They still don't know what he had to sell."

"Aren't they suspicious that he didn't show up?" Malachek asked.

"We've taken care of that," Allen said. He looked across his desk at both men, scanning their faces for any reaction to what he had been telling them. There was none.

"How?" It was Malachek who asked the question. "How did you take care of it?"

"I'll get to that in a minute," Allen responded. "Do you see why this story can't be pursued any further?"

"Of course," Rossman mumbled.

Malachek put his hands behind his head and slowly began to knead his neck muscles with his thumbs.

"Let me try another scenario, Mr. Allen," he said. "Just hypothetically, let's say. But let's say that there was no mole, that Herman Willows was discovered taking the photos out of the Senate Office Building, just as you say he was, and the FBI arrested him before he could make the contact. And the FBI brought him downtown and he confessed to the whole thing—named his contact, everything. And then somebody discovered who he worked for and all sorts of alarms went off right here at 1600 Pennsylvania Avenue.

"I mean, it wouldn't look too good if one of the leading lights of your party had a spy working as his top aide, would it? Not to mention a blackmailed homosexual. So you shut up Herman Willows, protect Senator Ramsey, case closed."

He raised his eyebrows, inviting Allen to respond.

Allen said nothing. Instead, he picked up the telephone on his desk and said, "Miss Elliot, could you ask Lieutenant Stricklin to come in, please."

A few minutes later, a tall, black Army officer entered the room carrying an oversize attaché case. He laid the case on Allen's desk, opened it up, and took out a large audiocassette player.

"Lieutenant Stricklin is with counterintelligence," Allen

explained as the Army officer took a cassette from the case and inserted it into the player.

"This cassette was made in Herman Willows's home," Allen continued. "It's a phone call he placed to his contact in the Russian Embassy. The call was made at our instruction."

He signaled for the Lieutenant to start the cassette.

There was the sound of a phone ringing and then the voice of an operator saying, "Embassy of the Soviet Socialist Republic."

"Mr. Zoropokin, please." The voice was unmistakably American. Both Rossman and Malachek intuitively knew it was Willows speaking.

A slight pause, a humming sound for a few minutes, and then a heavily accented voice said, "Zoropokin."

"This is your friend."

"I waited for you again last night, but you didn't come."

"I am trying to get more material."

"We always pay good prices for raw material. I told you that. But we want to examine your goods. Are they high quality? Good workmanship?"

"The best."

"Then perhaps we can make an appointment to see them."

"I will call you. Good-bye."

There was a click on the recording and then a louder click as the Army Lieutenant shut the player off.

Allen waited until Lieutenant Stricklin placed the machine back in the attaché case and then thanked him and asked him to leave.

"That is the full story, gentlemen," Allen said. "You can see why it's very important that we maintain secrecy."

Rossman suddenly stood up and said, "I think we don't need any more convincing, Mr. Allen. I am very flattered by the confidence you have placed in us. I can assure you that this network will never do anything to place national security at risk."

"I would never think otherwise," Allen said. He was surprised that Rossman was trying to bring the meeting to a close.

"I appreciate your calling us in, sir," Malachek offered.

Allen's disclosure had stunned him. An hour ago, he had been relishing the idea of breaking one of the biggest stories

in recent years. Now it had exploded in his face and it had
happened right in front of Rossman.

He regretted having been so defensive about it with
Rossman. Even worse, this was not going to help him with
the Cornwall problem.

"We would have had no way of knowing," Malachek
added, almost apologetically, to Allen.

"Things are never what they seem," Allen said.

"I'm afraid we've taken too much of your time already,"
Rossman said, hoping to end the meeting as painlessly as
possible.

Allen sensed Rossman's distress. "I can have a staff car
drive you wherever you need to go," he offered.

"We are going to Washington National," Rossman said,
"unless you're staying down here, Carl."

"No, I'm going back to New York too," Malachek said,
already wishing he had thought of an excuse to stay in
Washington. He did not want to fly back with Rossman.

"Fine," Allen said, smiling. "I'll send for the car now.
I'm sorry we can't lunch together but something has come up
that requires my attention over the lunch hour."

"It's perfectly all right," Rossman said. He and Malachek
shook hands with Allen, said good-bye, and walked to his
office anteroom where an aide escorted them to the diplomat-
ic entrance at the South Portico.

They stood on the Portico for not more than a minute,
watching an Army helicopter practice takeoffs and landings
on the South Lawn. Then a staff car drove up to take them to
the airport across the Potomac River.

Even though it was not yet twelve-thirty, the line for the
one P.M. shuttle to New York was already snaking around the
departure gate when the two men arrived at the airport.

"We've got some time," Malachek said. "I need to call
the office. I'll have the limo pick us up at La Guardia."

He found a phone booth and arranged for the pickup.
Then he arranged to be connected to the network's cubicle in
the White House pressroom.

"Charlotte Glover," he said.

In a moment he heard a familiar voice. "Charlotte
Glover."

"It's Carl Malachek, Charlotte," he said.

"Hello, Carl. How are you?"

"I'm fine, Charlotte. I have to make a plane but I'm calling to tell you your tip on Herman Willows is wrong. I can't give you any details but, trust me, it's wrong."

She didn't know what to think or say. Automatically she asked, "Where are you?"

"In a phone booth at Washington National. I've just come from a briefing on Willows."

"A briefing? By whom?"

"Top level. Believe me."

"I believe you," she said. "Was it private? I mean just us—no other nets?"

"Just us," he said, admiring her competitiveness, even now.

"So what is going to happen?"

"Just don't pursue it," he said.

"All right," she answered and he could not tell if she was despondent or bewildered.

"I'm sorry," he said sympathetically. "It had all the makings of a blockbuster."

"What can I say?" she responded.

"You win some, you lose some," he told her. Then he walked back to the gate just in time to make the flight.

An hour later, the two men were back in New York.

Malachek and Rossman had not talked about the meeting with Gordon Allen since they had left the White House. The White House staff car had not been an appropriate setting and, seated three abreast on the shuttle, with a stranger in the third seat next to them, there had not been sufficient privacy.

Now, as Rossman's limousine made its way along Grand Central Parkway toward the Midtown Tunnel, the network president brought up the subject of the meeting.

"Now that we know the real story, I assume you don't need any instructions from me to stop working on this cover-up of yours," he said sarcastically.

"Of course not," Malachek answered blankly.

Ever since they'd left the White House, Malachek had felt awful. It wasn't just that the Willows story had been a wild-goose chase. Over the years, other stories had turned out to be dead ends. That was just part of the business. You win some, you lose some.

The problem was that Rossman wouldn't understand

that. Rossman would never let him forget what had happened today because Rossman would regard the whole episode as a personal embarrassment.

His network, his network's News Division, had almost endangered a national security operation. That was the way Rossman would look at it.

And, because of that, his own position with Rossman had been weakened. The News Division's Archilles' heel, the one it never talked about—the fact that it could make mistakes—had been exposed right in the inner sanctum of the White House.

The only saving grace was that the story had not been on the air.

But that wouldn't matter to Rossman. Rossman would hold it against him anyway. He had been wrong and Rossman was right. And if he had been wrong on this, then maybe he could be wrong on other things too. Like the Cornwall replacement. That was how Rossman would play it.

"We still have the Cornwall problem facing us," he said to Rossman, deciding to test him now.

"I'm aware of that," Rossman said coldly.

"Have you had any more thoughts about it?"

"Antin. I think he's the best piece of talent around."

Malachek detected finality in Rossman's pronouncement. "He can't win for us," Malachek said.

"You've made your feelings clear to me," Rossman said. "We're going to make Antin an offer, Carl. I met with Mickey Schirmer this morning and I told him we were interested."

Malachek was devastated. *Jesus*, he thought, *is this what I've worked my ass off for all these years? To have the most important decision I've ever been faced with taken away from me?*

Was this the way it was going to end, he thought, stuck in a goddamn traffic jam in Queens—twenty blocks from where I lived twenty-five years ago, listening to Rossman tell me that he doesn't care about my opinion, that he has no respect for me or my intuition or years in the business? Is this what it all comes down to?

"Antin is a piece of shit," he said defiantly, "and you are making a hell of a mistake."

Rossman decided to ignore Malachek's outburst. He could handle him now.

"I told you before," he said softly, "Antin is available. This is not some young anchorman from a small market someplace we're talking about. This is a major talent."

"This is a major phony," Malachek said, wondering if Rossman was aware of the shallowness that had been so evident in Antin when he was sent to Beirut a few years ago.

"Don't fight me, Carl," Rossman said quietly. "I know what I'm doing."

"And so do I," Malachek responded quickly. "I've had a lot of years, Jerry, a lot of years, and I know when I'm right. Mark Antin is wrong. He is a lightweight. Burton will do the job for us. He's what we need, somebody good, somebody solid. Somebody from news."

"I obviously did not make my position clear to you," Rossman said. "We are going to make an offer to Mark Antin. It will be very confidential."

"Schirmer will leak it," Malachek said as one final jab.

"I've already counted on that," Rossman said. "Sid Neale is working up a release on Cornwall. It will go out tonight. Make *The Times*, maybe *The Washington Post* tomorrow morning. We'll control the Cornwall story. Schirmer can say what he wants about Antin."

"And you?"

"If I'm asked about Antin, I'll say he's not under consideration. Naturally, I'll mention your people—Art Burton, the rest. I don't want to hurt the morale of the News Division."

Malachek thought: He really doesn't understand. He's going to bring in some lightweight to anchor the evening news and he doesn't want to destroy the News Division's morale!

The limo finally made it past the tollbooth and into the eerie fluorescent daylight of the tunnel. The monotony of the tiles on the tunnel walls seemed to have a silencing effect on both men. They said nothing until finally the limo emerged into the tumult of the East Side traffic.

"The Stuart woman," Rossman said, as if he had been waiting for the daylight before resuming the conversation, "You'd better give her some reason for not going after that Willows guy."

"I will," Malachek said. The limo turned up First and Malachek dreaded the certainty that it soon would turn again, toward the middle of Manhattan and the network building.

*   *   *

At the same time the limo carrying Rossman and Malachek approached the network building, Charlotte Glover got out of a taxicab in front of the Watergate Apartments in downtown Washington.

Ever since she had started coming here, once a month at first and, now, much more frequently, the curved, sweeping facade of the apartment complex had seemed to her like human arms, reaching out to embrace her.

She walked swiftly through the lobby and took the elevator to the eighth floor. If anybody had seen her and recognized her, she would have explained her presence, in the middle of the day, as purely professional.

"I'm doing an interview for a magazine article I'm working on," she would have said—and she would have been believed. Had she told the truth, no one would have believed her.

Even in gossip-hungry, jaded Washington, no one would have believed that straitlaced, mousy-haired Charlotte Glover, the *bête noire* of the last three Presidents, a woman whose biggest thrill in life seemed to come from presiding at the White House Correspondents annual dinner, would be having an affair.

No, not her. If the White House press corps ran an "old maid" contest, Charlotte Glover would win it every year, easily.

As the elevator door slid open, the clandestine nature of what she was doing began to stir a tremor of excitement within her.

There was a thrill just in the secrecy of it, as if the whispered arrangements to be with him, at this time and in this place, carried a sensuous power that rippled through her body like an aphrodisiac.

She knew that his job, his power, were part of it. She would have felt fulfilled by anybody who made love to her as he did but she knew that it was who and what he was that made it even more exciting.

There also was the seductive knowledge of knowing the sex was illicit. She was doing it with him, week after week, and all the time everybody thought of her as the iron virgin. Well, she could secretly smirk at them, all of them.

It was a beautiful and intimate secret and their public lives had never intruded on it.

There had been only one exception. But that single exception—the one time their professional lives had become intertwined—seemed now to be a problem.

She did not, however, want to spoil what lay ahead. She would ask him later, in bed.

She let herself into the apartment with the key he had given her and called out, "I'm sorry I'm late, darling."

He came from the kitchenette off the living room and said, "I was making coffee for us."

He had nothing on but a dressing gown and he took her in his arms and gave her a long kiss. They held each other for a minute, and he said, "God, Charlotte, I thought this afternoon would never come."

"Neither did I," she answered, stroking the back of his head. "I must have looked at the clock in the pressroom a hundred times this morning."

"And it never goes faster."

"Never."

She looked at him. "You are so different. It's as if you are someone no one knows. Only me."

"No one else does know," he answered. "You make me different."

"Do I?" she asked, full of gratitude for what was happening to her. She took his face in her hands and kissed him passionately.

"Charlotte," he said softly when they broke their embrace. "I love you."

He led her into a small bedroom whose window looked out over the Potomac River and the bridges leading to the Virginia suburbs. She could see planes taking off and landing at Washington National and she thought, it's not even two o'clock in the afternoon.

"I'll draw the curtains," he said, as if reading her thoughts, and she sat on the edge of the bed in the new darkness and removed her shoes and stockings. He took off his dressing gown and lay naked in the bed and watched as she stood up and took off her clothes.

"You have beautiful breasts," he said.

They're not, she thought. They are beginning to sag and my nipples are ugly. But she said nothing and untied the bun at the back of her head, letting her hair fall in a tangled mass over her head and shoulders, and stood by the bed.

"I love you, Gordon," she said softly.

Gordon Allen, Chief of Staff to the President of the United States, keeper of the keys that provided access to the most powerful office in the world, looked up at her and said, "Let me love you."

She lay down next to him and he put his lips on hers and began to run his hand along her thighs.

She let out a sensuous sigh and said, "Tell me where you are."

"On your legs," he whispered to her.

"Go higher," she said. "I want you higher."

He moved his hand until it was resting on her crotch and then he kissed her on the fringes of her pubic hair.

"More," she moaned and he kept kissing her until she could no longer stand the ecstasy. She frantically moved on top of him and guided his cock inside her and she could feel it hard within her.

She let out a low murmur of delight and moved around, slowly and sensuously, watching as he thrust his body upward, again and again.

She kept up the surging motion until she felt herself coming. "Fuck me fuck me fuck me!" she kept repeating as if she were commanding him to stay within her forever.

Then it was over.

She bent forward and kissed him on the forehead. "I love it," she confessed. "I love doing it," she said and she did not feel ashamed. It was true and she wanted to tell him.

She raised herself so that his cock slid out from within her. Then she lay down in the bed next to him and rested her head in the crook of his arm.

He looked almost like a child, blissfully near sleep, and she lay there silently, wondering, is this happening to me?

She had never dreamed, even in her private fantasies, that she was capable of having sex like this, doing it with a married man. It had been going on for six months now and she wanted it to last forever. To make love like this, she knew, was the most she could ever have but it was more than she had ever hoped and longed for.

She looked at him, his eyes closed but a troubled

expression on his face, and she wondered if he had fallen asleep and was having a bad dream.

"Gordon darling," she said. "Are you asleep?"

"No," he answered quietly. "I was just thinking of the supreme irony."

"What do you mean?" she asked.

"We had to call Malachek in," he said. "The President knew that Malachek was on to the Willows story."

Oh my God, she thought, it was Gordon who told Malachek the fake story about Herman Willows. But how could it have happened? And why?

She was stunned by the revelation.

"It was you who told Malachek," she said, sadly.

"What do you mean?"

"He called me from the airport. He said he had been told by a top-level source that the story was wrong. I never dreamed it was you."

"I wanted to tell you when you first came in," he said, "but I wanted you so badly. . . ."

"Why, Gordon, why was Malachek called in?"

"The President knew that your people were starting to sniff around. The CIA had Willows's house staked out. They never told me, the bastards."

"Oh my God," she said. Then: "They don't know anything else, do they?"

"No, darling," he assured her. "They don't know how it was leaked. I told the President it might be somebody over at Justice."

"What do you want to do?" she asked him. "What do I do now?"

"I hate this mess," he said to her. "Protecting that son of a bitch Ramsey. Covering the whole thing up just for the sake of the party's image. It's so goddamn wrong. And the President acts as if it was just another little piece of dirt that can be swept under the party's rug."

"Malachek believed you," she said glumly.

"I had no choice. The President had me set up the meeting. I even had the CIA dummy up a phone conversation to make it sound like Willows was talking to an embassy contact. I had no way of letting you know ahead of time."

"But the story is true," she said. "Willows did try to sell

the pictures and it was covered up for purely political reasons. How can we let it die like this?"

He put his arms around her and drew her closer to him.

"For my sake, you have to play the charade through. I thought we could get it out, end Ramsey as a party power, and go on from there. But my credibility is on the line now. If Malachek goes forward, the President will blame me for not having made the national security excuse stick. We have to let Malachek believe what I told him."

"And my credibility?" she asked, unable to disguise her sarcasm. "I'm the one who went right to Malachek's office and laid out the whole story for him."

"If Malachek is convinced, then your credibility is not damaged. How could you know, darling? It was an honest mistake, a bad tip. These things happen, don't they?"

"Of course they do," she answered. "But not like this. Not when they're true. Not when the biggest cover-up since Watergate is happening in front of our very eyes and we know about it."

"There will be others," he said confidently. "They're starting to get in deep with this one, and once you've started—"

"But you're part of it, Gordon. The President has you in with him now," she said desperately.

"Only you know that, Charlotte," he said. He had a pleading look in his eyes.

She shifted her body again so that she was lying on her stomach with her face in the pillow. She hoped he would not see the tears that were starting to wet the pillow.

I need him so badly, she thought. I need his touch, his love.

"I won't say anything," she said, turning over. "I won't say anything to Malachek."

"Thank you, my beautiful Charlotte," he said and he put his hand on her thigh again.

"Go higher," she whispered and she closed her eyes and waited, wondering if she would ever feel good about herself again.

Chapter 27

Within the network's News Division, the A-wire was the nickname for the unofficial grapevine that carried a constant flow of rumors, gossip, and occasional fact.

On this Tuesday morning, with *The New York Times* already carrying a brief item on John Cornwall's resignation, including a statement from Jerry Rossman, the A-wire crackled through the News Division like a high-voltage power surge.

John Cornwall leaving? It was too shocking to be true. But it had to be true. It was there, in *The New York Times,* in the early edition, and the news flowed along the A-wire with incredible speed, setting off sparks in every area it reached; producers' offices, the cafeteria, correspondents' cubicles, videotape editing, the huge sets that housed the news programs, the bathrooms, the hallways, everywhere.

Art Burton heard the news as soon as he came into the building. He stopped by the assignment desk in the main newsroom, as he did every morning to catch up on any late news, and was greeted by Jules Kinnoy, the thirty-year-old man who had been a copyboy for the past twelve years.

"Hey, Art," Kinnoy said as Burton approached the assignment desk. "What do you think of the news?"

"What news?" Burton asked.

"Didn't you hear?" Kinnoy asked incredulously. "John Cornwall's leaving. It's in *The Times*."

He pointed to a stack of newspapers lying on the assignment desk.

"What do you think of it?" Kinnoy continued. "Must be more to it than they're saying. Probably had a falling out with Malachek, don't you think?"

It's out, Burton thought, stunned. It's happened and I don't know a damn thing about it. He felt his stomach starting to churn with tension and he was afraid to find out the rest—if Cornwall's successor had been announced.

"What else, Jules? What else does it say?" He wondered if the slight quiver in his voice was noticeable.

"Here, read it for yourself," Kinnoy said, tossing a newspaper to Burton.

Burton turned immediately to the last page of the third section where television programs were reviewed and news of the business printed. His eye instantly caught the headline over the half-column story:

Network Discloses
Cornwall Leaving

The story read:

> John Cornwall, anchorman of *The Evening News with John Cornwall*, will leave the program within several weeks and will retire after a long career in broadcasting, according to a statement issued last night by Jerry Rossman, network president.
>
> Rossman said Cornwall's decision is a "purely personal one." He said the decision was conveyed to him and Carl Malachek, president of the network's news division, a few weeks ago but was not made public at Cornwall's request.
>
> The decision by the popular anchorman, coming so close to the new fall season, is bound to cause considerable distress at the network and among its affiliates, although Rossman said a successor to Cornwall will be announced in a few weeks.
>
> "We are all saddened by John's decision," a statement from Rossman said, "but we will maintain the high professionalism and quality journalism which have been a hallmark of his broadcast."
>
> There was no immediate indication from network sources as to who might be selected to replace Cornwall, whose program has led the evening news ratings for the last few years.
>
> Efforts to reach Cornwall were unsuccessful last night. Neither Rossman nor Malachek were available for comment.

Burton folded the paper and put it back on the assignment desk.

Why? he thought. Why the hell are they making it public now? They must have picked someone already.

He glanced up at the row of clocks, mounted on a wall behind the assignment desk, showing the time in different parts of the world. It was 9:20 in the morning in New York, 2:20 in the afternoon in London, 3:20 in Frankfurt, 4:20 in Cairo.

What difference did it make what time it was anywhere? All that mattered was that he had to find out, now, what was going on.

He wondered if Samantha was still at her apartment or had left for work. Maybe she had tried to reach him already, to ask him about the story, to ask what he knew.

The problem was, he didn't know anything. He could have been lost in the desert near Vegas for all that Malachek seemed to care. What the hell was happening?

"So what do you think?" Kinnoy repeated. "Real shocker, huh?"

"I assume he wants to retire," Burton responded, moving slowly away from Kinnoy. John Cornwall's resignation just wasn't a subject he needed to discuss with this newsroom character, with his nicotine-stained teeth and his Bruce Springsteen T-shirt and worn-at-the-heels running shoes.

"Stay cool, Jules," he said casually and he walked out of the newsroom and down the hallway to the *Focus on America* production area. He noticed that Samantha's office was empty and he wondered where she was.

He wanted to call her but George Durgin, the executive producer of *Focus*, was walking through the production cubicles and he knew that Durgin would want to talk about Cornwall.

"Hell of a surprise about Cornwall, isn't it?" Durgin said, walking into his office.

"It really is," Burton answered. "I can't figure it out," he added, surprised at his ability to appear shocked at the news.

"Maybe he's had enough," Durgin said. "Malachek must be going crazy. It doesn't earn him any brownie points upstairs to have this happen, that's for sure."

"What really matters is who Malachek puts in there," Burton remarked. "Who do you think?" he asked.

"Who's had the time to figure?" Durgin responded. "I guess Swanson from *Sunrise* stands a good chance." He was silent for a moment, as if contemplating a list of candidates in his mind. "Who the hell knows what's going to happen? It's going to be wild around here until they name somebody." He tossed his empty coffee cup into a wastebasket and wandered out of Burton's office.

Burton heard him saying, "Did you hear about Cornwall?" to one of the secretaries in the hallway as he closed the door.

Burton dialed Samantha's apartment but there was no answer. He sat at his desk and absentmindedly began to draw geometric figures on a yellow, lined legal pad.

He drew a series of hexagons and octagons, randomly scattered over the paper, that looked as if they were snow-flakes that had drifted down from a winter sky. He began to connect the little crystallike figures until they were linked to each other. Now there was no form or pattern to the drawings on the page. There was simply a mass of lines, spreading in all directions, staring up at him from the page, and he thought: This is me, I don't know where I'm going.

He quickly picked up the phone and dialed Samantha's number again, letting it ring ten times before accepting the fact that she wasn't home. Where is she, he thought. Why isn't she at work?

He needed to talk to her, although he knew what she would say: Go to Malachek. Now's the time. The Cornwall news is out. Go to him.

Almost automatically, as if he were actually responding to her, Burton picked up the phone and dailed Malachek's number. For the briefest second, as the dial tone rang, he thought of hanging up but then Judy Rosen came on the line.

"Carl Malachek's office," she announced.

"Hello, it's Art Burton. Is he in?"

"Just a minute. I'll check."

A few seconds later, Malachek came on the phone.

"Yes, Art," he said, his voice friendly.

"Do you have a few minutes free?" Burton asked.

"Just a few," Malachek answered dourly. "I've got a lot of calls stacked up."

"I was wondering if I could stop by your office sometime today. It's about the article in *The Times*. It's all over the place."

It came out quickly and, even as he said it, he realized

that this was the first time he was reminding Malachek, even obliquely, of their discussion about replacing John Cornwall.

"*The Times* story was a tactic," he said. "Sid Neale placed it."

"Oh," Burton said, surprised that Malachek was sharing this kind of information with him.

"Rossman wants the news out now," Malachek continued. "He's trying to soften the blow for the affiliates."

The fact that Malachek was confiding in him gave Burton a feeling of confidence. "I'm obviously calling for my own reasons," Burton said. "Ever since we met in your office—"

"That discussion has to stay between us," Malachek said impatiently. "The Cornwall replacement isn't going to be settled today or tomorrow or next week. These things take time."

"I know it takes time. It's just that I need to know what's going on."

What's he thinking, Malachek wondered. That his whole career is going to end if he doesn't get it?

Potential anchormen were a breed that seemed to appear in the business every five or ten years, as if they were the result of some genetic-journalistic quirk that spawned reporters capable of going to the very top.

Cornwall had been one, and so had Robert Miniver. They both had the same genes. You could tell when they were correspondents that they were capable of more, that they had the innate ability to move up to the anchor level and, ultimately, lead the network by anchoring the evening news.

Burton could do the same. He believed it.

He was better than Mark Antin or anybody else that SOB Rossman could come up with. Better than anybody else in the News Division.

And yet, Malachek knew, he couldn't deliver the job to Burton. Rossman was blocking him, and there was no way to get past Rossman.

His only leverage was his position as head of the News Division—but even that might not be enough.

"You want to know about your shot at it," he said.

"Yes," Burton answered quietly.

"I haven't changed my mind," Malachek said firmly. "It just takes time to work out."

"I appreciate that," Burton said, relieved that Malachek was still backing him. That was what mattered. He was still alive.

"How are you doing on that gambling story?" Malachek asked.

The question seemed to come from nowhere and rocked Burton. Malachek was asking out of journalistic curiosity but it reminded him of his painful decision to bury the Winston story. Now Malachek had opened the wound.

"The story's not panning out," he said. "I can't seem to get anywhere with it."

"What do you mean? Your sources were no good?"

"It's tough to tie all together," Burton said, fumbling for words that would sound plausible to Malachek. "I had a woman in Vegas I thought could make the whole piece for me, but she isn't working out."

"Keep working on it," Malachek told him. "Don't throw it away yet."

"No, I won't," Burton said. "I'll keep working on it."

"Keep in touch," Malachek said and he hung up.

Burton stared at the phone as if somewhere within its white plastic casing, or buried within the matrix of tiny wire filaments inside the receiver, he could find the answer to his dilemma.

Painfully, as if looking at a grotesque sight—a house flattened by a tornado, a soldier with his arm blown off—he confronted again the fact that he had lied to Samantha, and now Malachek, about the Jarvis Winston story.

He could have nailed Winston, he knew it. He could have blown open a big scandal that any correspondent on any network would have loved to have.

He already had the shards of the story. All he had to do was keep digging until he could put the various pieces together, until they were assembled into a story he could deliver to Malachek.

But breaking the story would destroy his chances for the Cornwall job. He would be violating the network's cardinal rule—don't hang out our own dirty laundry.

Time was working against him too. Now that the news about Cornwall was out, a decision would have to be made soon. Pressure from the affiliates and the rapidly approaching new season would inexorably push Malachek and Rossman into a choice.

Art Burton sat in his office, recalled the hotel room in Los Angeles, recalled staring at himself, naked, in the mirror.

He did not recognize himself as the young reporter in New Orleans anymore or even the one in Atlanta, the one who flew to San Salvador one week and Chattanooga the next week and gave a damn about every story in every place.

He did not even recognize the man who, only a few weeks ago, had flown back to New Orleans and had tossed down a few beers with Frankie Baglio.

No, that Art Burton was obscured and distant now, a forgotten face from some old yearbook, somebody he once knew, somebody from a different time.

Now he was somebody else, somebody he was just beginning to recognize, like a person coming toward him along a dark street who passes under a street light; somebody who was suddenly nakedly ambitious and, worse, deceitful. And all because of the tempting vision Malachek had set before him.

He did not like what he saw in himself and yet, even as he recognized it, he knew that he was unable to change. He could not go back—anywhere.

The Cornwall job had changed everything. It had changed him.

Dammit, Malachek, make it happen.
Make it happen for me.

Chapter 28

At the moment, Carl Malachek could not make anything happen. For the last few minutes, ever since he had finished talking to Burton, Malachek had been impatiently pacing back and forth in the large vestibule on the seventh floor, waiting for an elevator.

You can get news from a satellite anywhere in space, he thought angrily, but you can't get a damn elevator in this building.

His rage was increasing rapidly, fueled by irritation about the elevator service and a gnawing apprehension that he would be late for a meeting Jerry Rossman had hurriedly set up in the thirteenth floor executive conference room.

When Rossman's secretary had called him about the meeting, there had been no need to ask what the meeting would be about.

The news about Cornwall was all over the building by now. Rossman, he figured, would have to say something to the network executives, even if it was nothing more than to reassure them that the problem could be handled.

Malachek wanted to be there from the beginning. Finally, an elevator came and he got in quickly, edging his way into the crowd of passengers.

By the time the elevator reached the thirteenth floor, he was alone and, as the door slid open, he straightened the knot in his tie and ran his fingers through his thinning hair in a nervous gesture.

Rossman's going to take us into the toilet, he thought, and I don't know how to stop him. It bothered him that he was nervous.

As he had feared, the other network executives already were seated around the conference table when he walked into the room.

Rossman was at his customary position at the head of the table, flanked by Sid Neale and Barry Kovaks at opposite sides of the table. The King and his crown princes, Malachek thought.

His eyes rapidly swept down the table. They all were there, the top executives from most of the operating departments of the network: sales, affiliate relations, network-owned stations, advertising and promotion, research, radio, even sports. All of them had a stake in the Cornwall problem. The evening news was the fulcrum on which the network's prestige was balanced and now it was openly, publicly, in danger of crumbling.

Rossman gestured to an empty chair near the middle of the table. "Sit down, Carl," Rossman said in a friendly voice. "I didn't want to start without you."

What's he up to, Malachek wondered as he squeezed into a chair between Barbara Schumacher, the head of advertising and promotion, and Marty Merrett, a huge bear of a man who was director of audience research.

Rossman spread his hands in front of him as if he were holding a sheaf of papers and was about to deliver a speech at an industry dinner.

"I assume you all have heard about John Cornwall," he said. He quickly glanced around the room to confirm this and, without stopping, added, "Carl and I have known about this for a few weeks but for obvious reasons we could not share it with any of you."

Malachek leaned forward in his chair, waiting to see if Rossman would continue to imply that the two of them were together on this all the way.

"We were hoping against hope," Rossman continued, "that John would change his mind but he's in cement on this. So we're going to have to make some moves, and rather quickly, and the reason I've asked all of you here this morning is to make sure that we don't look as if we're falling apart. It's very important that the affiliates and the press don't feel that we're panicking, that we're running around with our thumbs stuck up our ass looking for a replacement for Cornwall."

He paused for a minute to gauge the reaction. Everyone in the room seemed somber, even Malachek.

"We hope to announce Cornwall's successor before we go to LA for the affiliates meeting," Rossman went on, "so that we can minimize the effect of this. Even if it takes a little while, it won't hurt. The whole damn country may be hanging on for the announcement by the time we make it. It could turn out to be a very big plus for us, PR-wise."

Why doesn't he run a sweepstakes, Malachek thought bitterly. Let everybody pick a new anchor and draw the winning name out of a huge plastic barrel right in prime time. Turn it into a real spectacle, for God's sake, and to hell with the news.

"Do we have anybody in the wings?" Barry Kovaks asked.

"Carl has somebody he likes," Rossman said smoothly. "Art Burton from the *Focus* show. We'll be floating his name to test the waters."

"Can he do it?" Kovaks asked.

"I think so," Malachek said firmly.

"I can also tell you confidentially," Rossman said, "that we're talking to Mark Antin's agent about the possibility of Antin coming over here to do the show."

Rossman noticed that Kovaks seemed surprised and pleased at the mention of Antin.

"What are the chances?" Barbara Schumacher asked.

"I think they are pretty good," Rossman said.

"He'd be dynamite for us," Kovaks said. "Good-looking, good voice. I don't think we'd lose a rating point."

You son of a bitch, Malachek thought, what the hell do you know.

"There's excellent research on him," Marty Merrett offered. "Very strong demographics, particularly in the target audiences. You can sell on him."

"We've looked at all of it," Rossman said confidently, pleased that his mention of Antin was generating favorable reaction. He hoped Malachek was taking it all in.

Rossman looked toward the end of the table where Jimmy Valeppi, the head of affiliate relations, sat.

"Jimmy, I want your people to make sure that every general manager is called today and kept informed of what we're doing. I want everyone of them to know that we have a number of people we're looking at. Don't get into names beyond Burton and, say, Swanson from the *Sunrise* program."

He looked at Malachek. "That all right, Carl?"

"Yes, of course," Malachek said, hating Rossman for what he was doing. Hating himself for going along with it.

"We have to keep Antin confidential for the time being," Rossman continued, "but you can drop a few hints that we're looking outside the network as well."

Valeppi was taking notes. Malachek looked incredulously at him and then at Rossman. Everything he had feared yesterday afternoon, driving in with Rossman from La Guardia, was coming true. The son of a bitch was going to run right over him.

For a moment, he thought about challenging Rossman, right there, in the boardroom, with the abstract watercolors on the wall and the silver coffee samovar on the antique side-board and the three big television monitors on the far wall and all the network executives sitting around the mahogany table.

But he decided to wait until the meeting was over and he could confront Rossman alone. It would be better that way. Even if it was humiliating for him, at least it would be private.

"This can stir up a lot of good publicity," Sid Neale was telling the group. "You know, like we're getting ready to crown a new king. The anointed heir apparent to Cornwall, that kind of thing."

"Sid's right," Rossman concurred, grateful for Neale's reminder that a good press was essential. The network couldn't look like it was taking a beating. It all had to look like it was being handled.

"Everybody's going to talk," Rossman cautioned, "and we've got to stay out of the speculation. I'll handle Hap Hawkins and the other general managers on the affiliate council. I already spoke to Hawkins when I was out there over the weekend. He'll be okay. Sid will handle the press inquiries. Obviously we'd like to get this wrapped up before we meet with the affiliates in a few weeks."

"Jesus, Jerry," Kovaks said worriedly. "Can you do it that quick?"

"All it takes is money," Rossman said.

"What about Winston?" Barbara Schumacher asked. "Any word on him?"

"He's doing all right," Rossman said. "I tell you," he added, smiling at the group, "between Winston and Cornwall, the other nets will be lucky to get a mention anywhere. That's the upside of all of this."

He slapped his hands on the table to indicate that the meeting was over, and got up. "Thank you, everybody." He stood and watched the other executives drift out of the room. Out of the corner of his eye, he saw that Malachek was staying behind.

"You got a problem with any of this, Carl?" he asked when just the two of them were left in the room.

Malachek's eyes narrowed until they were slits in an impassive mask. He was silent for a moment. "What do I tell the press, Jerry?"

"What do you mean?" Rossman responded.

"I mean, what do I tell the press, when they ask me about Burton or Antin? What do I tell them?"

"Tell them that you have no comment. Is that so difficult?"

"Most of the press knows how I feel about Mark Antin. What do I say when the news leaks out that he's being considered to replace Cornwall? That I changed my mind?"

"C'mon, Carl, climb off it," Rossman answered testily. "You've been around long enough. Don't answer their fucking calls. That's the easiest way to handle it."

"That's not my style," Malachek said quietly.

Rossman began to drum his fingers on the table impatiently. He didn't need to take this from Malachek, not now or any time, but it was important that Malachek be kept under control.

"Listen," he said. "You wanted Burton and I'm giving you Burton. Up front. Publicly. His name is going to be mentioned in all the speculation and his picture will be in all the papers. That should keep all of you purists down on Seven very happy. Now if, by some unpardonable error, the president of this network should decide that somebody else is better to anchor the news, then that's the way it's going to be.

"And if that somebody is Mark Antin, whose goddamn ratings in the morning are climbing into the stratosphere, then that's also the way it's going to be.

"Let's get it straight, Carl. You and I see it differently. You think the anchor has to have all sorts of credentials so the audience will trust him and believe him. And I say it doesn't matter anymore. Maybe it did matter, back in the early days, when people revered the anchor because the medium was new and the anchormen were so damn all-knowing and they gave the news like it came down with the Tablets. We weren't used to it then. Those guys were like new gods. But it's been more than thirty years, Carl. People are used to having somebody give them the news every night. And as long as somebody is there, sitting in a chair behind a desk, they don't care who he is or what he's made of. All they care is that he sounds nice and looks nice."

"That somebody sitting in the chair still has to be a god," Malachek said, his voice rising with exasperation. "He has to be informed and knowledgeable and, above all, when he tells you that your house is safe from tigers tonight, you have to believe him. Don't you see, Jerry? He can't be just a pretty face like Mark Antin or even just a good correspondent like some of our own people in news. He is the sole embodiment of trust, and trust comes out of experience and knowledge.

"My God, there's only three of them for the whole damn country. Bring every newspaper editor or editorial writer in the country together and they'd fill half of Madison Square Garden. But more people in this country get their news every night from just three men you could fit in the backseat of a Toyota. That's why this is so damn important. Don't you see that?"

"We'll mention Burton," Rossman repeated. He didn't want to argue any further. There was no need to.

"I'm serious about this, Jerry," Malachek said softly. "If you sign up Antin, I'll call it quits. I couldn't work here under those circumstances. I wouldn't have the respect of my people, let alone my own self-respect."

"You'd better think that over, Carl," Rossman said, his tone indicating that he didn't take the threat seriously. You pompous ass, he thought.

Then: "The Stuart woman. Have you reached her to call her off that wild-goose chase in Washington?"

Malachek recognized the question for what it was—a heavy-handed reminder that he had almost blown a national security operation and Rossman knew it.

"I couldn't reach her yesterday when we got back," Malachek said, "but I'll call her as soon as I get downstairs."

"Good," Rossman said. "I don't want any further embarrassment for us. No more White House visits like yesterday."

"No," Malachek said, subdued. "There won't be any problems."

"If that's it, Carl, I'll be around for most of this week if you've got any problems with the press on the Cornwall situation. I've got an Advertising Association convention in Boca Raton at the end of the week."

"When will you be talking to Antin or Schirmer?"

"Soon."

"I meant it about quitting, Jerry."

"Anything else?"

"No, nothing," Malachek replied. He stood in silence by the door as Rossman walked out of the room and into the carpeted corridor.

A few minutes later, he was back in his office. He asked Judy Rosen to call Samantha Stuart in her office but the secretary was unable to find her.

"Try her apartment," Malachek grumbled. Again, Samantha Stuart could not be found.

"Then get me Art Burton," he said. "Have him come over."

Malachek was standing by the window when Burton came in. He gestured to Burton to sit down on a couch, and he sat next to him.

"I've just come from a meeting with Jerry Rossman and most of the brass," Malachek said in a tired voice. "What's important for you to know is that you are going to be publicly mentioned as a possible replacement for Cornwall."

Burton clenched his fists.

"Can you tell me anything else?" he asked eagerly.

"It means that your name will be floated, let's say, as one of those being considered for Cornwall's job."

"And am I?" The first doubts surfaced in his mind. Why did Malachek sound so weary?

"Yes," Malachek answered. "But there will be no decision for a while. Press reaction counts, affiliate reactions. And there probably will be focus group testing before it's all over."

"You mean a bunch of people in a room looking at program tapes?" Burton asked, trying not to sound unenthusiastic.

"It's a business, Art," Malachek said bluntly.

"Who else is being considered?"

"Swanson, but we wouldn't take him off *Sunrise*. And Mark Antin."

"Antin?"

"Yes. Rossman is talking to Mickey Schirmer. You know him?"

"I've met him." Burton wondered if Schirmer had told Rossman of their meeting in Winston's hospital room.

Malachek said, "I don't know what will happen on that. Antin won't be mentioned unless they leak it."

"They?"

"Sid Neale. Maybe Rossman himself. It will make good press, I suppose."

If it's between Antin and me, Burton thought, it will be Antin.

"I appreciate your confidence in me," he said quietly, "but I have a feeling Antin is going to be the next anchorman here."

"Don't jump to any conclusions, kid," Malachek said. "It's too early yet."

"Is it?"

"Yes," Malachek said, unwilling to tell Burton that he probably was right. It would be better to let him down gently.

"Where does Rossman come out on this?" Burton asked.

"His natural leanings are to Antin," Malachek said. "It figures. But nothing is locked up yet. Nothing. Just do your job and when the press ask questions, say you're flattered to be considered. In the meantime, keep it quiet until it comes out."

Burton said he would, hoping Samantha would be in her office when he got back. He wanted to share the news with her, now that he had something concrete to tell her.

"Thanks again," he said, and he walked out of Malachek's office.

Malachek watched Burton leave.

Then he reached for the old baseball on his desk. He slowly rubbed it, as if it were a talisman that would take him back, back to the old days, back to when it was easier. And better.

Chapter 29

Neither Carl Malachek nor Art Burton, nor anyone else, could find Samantha Stuart this Tuesday morning because she had left her apartment at six A.M. and had taken the first shuttle flight to Washington.

It was a crazy idea, maybe, but she wanted to confront Herman Willows again, with no cameras, no crew, just she and him.

He was guilty, she was sure of it, and ever since the ambush interview in front of his house last week, she'd wanted to dig further into the story.

The failed interview had distressed her, had left her with a determination to snare Willows and confirm that his arrest for espionage had been covered up.

She was surprised by her own tenacity. She'd spent so much time covering soft news, human interest stories—but she knew that breaking the Willows story would make the whole damn News Division sit up and take notice. She was more than a pretty blond who did tearjerkers on mothers who kill or babies with AIDS.

The problem was that she was on her own. Malachek had not given her any guidance since that first talk in his office and there was no way she could violate Malachek's confidence and speak to Art about it.

She had sent the videocassettes of the Willows interview up to Malachek's office yesterday but there had been no response.

Now she sat in her rental car, a block away from Herman Willows's house, and lit a cigarette and blew the smoke through a half-open car window into the already humid air of a Washington morning.

Other than a black woman wheeling a baby carriage on the sidewalk, the street was empty and the only noise was the low whir of air-conditioning compressors outside some of the houses.

She welcomed the near-silence. It gave her a few minutes to think about Willows and also about Cornwall's resignation being made public.

She had read the story in *The Times* on the flight down to Washington. She had been tempted to call Art when she landed, to find out what he knew about it, but had decided against it.

She did not want him, or anyone, to know where she was. She'd have to wait until later to find out why the network was releasing the Cornwall story now.

No potential successor had been mentioned in *The Times* article and she wondered if the omission meant that Malachek no longer was backing Art. She hoped like hell it didn't.

Her eyes roamed the street, looking for distraction. But there was none. Cornwall, and Art, and Herman Willows were shifting around in her mind and she frantically skipped from one to the other. Finally she thought only about Herman Willows and how she would handle him.

If he answered the door, she decided, she would be friendly and polite, almost apologetic.

"I just wanted to explain about the other morning," she would say and hope that Willows would invite her in. After that, she somehow would pry it out of him. And, if he didn't let her in and stonewalled her again, it would at least reinforce her belief that a cover-up was underway.

I've got nothing to lose but a morning in Washington, she reminded herself. She climbed out of the car and walked to the house where Herman Willows lived. As she approached it, she was struck by how much the house seemed familiar to her. She had seen it only once, just last week, as she chased Willows to the front door.

But now it all came back to her: the curled-up garden hose on the front lawn, lying there like a huge green snake; the rusting black paint on the railing by the front steps; the door knocker in the shape of a lion's head, tarnished and needing to be polished; even the dark blue mailbox with Willows stenciled in white on it.

She rang the doorbell and, a few seconds later, a woman dressed in a faded white blouse and a pink cotton wraparound skirt appeared in the doorway.

She was tall and more anorexic than fashionably thin. Her hair was in disarray, and she peered at Samantha through heavy-rimmed bifocals perched on the bridge of her nose. The frames disappeared somewhere inside her hair.

Her face had a cartoon-character look, as if she were wearing a child's Halloween mask. Despite this, there was something unaccountably sad about her.

"Hello. Are you Mrs. Willows?" Samantha asked gently.

The woman did not move. Her pencillike body, standing erect, seemed to split the doorway. I could walk past her on either side, Samantha thought.

"Yes," the woman answered. Her voice matched her figure. It was thin and reedy and Samantha detected a tremulous quality to it, as if the woman woke up every morning afraid of the day.

"My name is Samantha Stuart. I work for a television program called *Focus on America*."

"You were here last week," Mrs. Willows said.

How much does she know, Samantha wondered. Does she know everything?

"That's right," Samantha said quietly. "I was trying to interview your husband."

"You have a terrible nerve, Miss Stuart," the woman said, but she did not sound reproachful. It was more of a wistful complaint.

"My husband told me how you came up to him, you and your cameras and your microphones, and harassed him, right here on the street."

She continued in a wavering voice, "There should be a law against things like this. It's horrible."

For a moment, Samantha felt embarrassed, as if she accidentally had wounded this gaunt unattractive woman standing rigidly in front of her.

She doesn't know, Samantha decided, she really doesn't know.

"Did your husband tell you why I wanted to interview him?" she asked.

"You wanted some sort of information on Senator Ramsey," he told me. My husband didn't know what you were talking about," the woman continued. "He told me that. It was something about campaign contributions. You frightened him half to death, coming out of nowhere like that. And the poor dog too."

The words were coming out faster and Samantha wanted to stop her, to tell her she was all wrong, that she was going to be terribly hurt, but she could not find a way of saying it.

She pitied the woman, so blind, so vulnerable, and she hated Willows for deceiving his wife like this.

Please, Samantha silently beseeched the woman, please stop.

"May I see your husband, Mrs. Willows?" Samantha asked in a final bid. "I would like to have just a few words with him."

"There is no reason to," the woman answered, with renewed strength in her voice. She began to slowly close the door saying, "You people don't run the world, you know."

Samantha realized that whatever chance she had to meet Willows in private was gone. She would have to find another way.

She suddenly felt tempted to take Mrs. Willows's hand, the way one would comfort a sick patient, and she realized that her desire to expose Willows was momentarily being overcome by her sympathy for this pathetic creature standing in front of her.

Don't weaken, Samantha.

"Tell your husband," she said quickly just before the door closed, "that I have a story. I know everything."

"What do you mean?" the woman asked.

"Just that," Samantha said. "I know the story."

She wondered if the bluff would work. But Mrs. Willows stepped back inside the house without saying a word.

Samantha looked at the door and then walked back down the front steps to the sidewalk. She turned around and thought she saw, for a fleeting instant, both the woman and her husband peering at her from behind oyster-white chintz curtains in a front window.

She was struck by the incongruity of it. This odd little couple, peering out from their front window, the wife so unaware of what he had done; and here, in the bright daylight, everything so normal and serene.

The green garden hose still lying coiled on the lawn, the Dutch elm trees towering over the street, the lawns showing brown patches from the long summer sun, the hedges bordering the lawn still verdant.

She walked back to her car, still trying to reconcile the mixture in her mind. She was so absorbed by it that she did not even notice that the telephone repair truck that had been parked near Willows's house had turned around and was slowly following her down the street.

Chapter 30

The President of the United States was furious.

The lingering euphoria from a tumultuous welcome on a

one-day trip to Lake Charles, Louisiana, had been wiped out
by the "Eyes Only" report that was waiting for him on his
return to the Oval Office.

The Stuart woman, according to the report, had gone
back to Herman Willows's house and had tried to see him.

If nothing else, this new report on the Stuart woman
only confirmed what he always had known: you can't trust the
bastards.

Well, over the years, he had shown them. There was
nothing in the Constitution, he'd said once, that guaranteed a
press conference every week—even when you're President of
the United States.

Who elected the media to anything?

There was no doubt, he was sure, that the big networks
were slanted against him. Anybody with an open mind could
see that. All you had to do was watch them night after night,
look at the way their White House correspondents always
tried to trip him up, or point out his mistakes and never give
him credit for anything.

The anchors were guilty too. With a tiny smile, or by
raising an eyebrow, or appearing to look puzzled after a
White House report, everybody would know what they were
thinking.

In a moment of frustration one night, after all three
network evening newscasts had aired critical reports on one
of his proposals, he had thought: They can make me or break
me; those three bastards sitting there behind their desks,
with all that power, interviewing Kings or Prime Ministers on
news stories as if they actually dealt with them on foreign
policy. And fifty million people listened to them every night.

Right behind them, like the masters of the hounds, were
their bosses, sitting up there in New York, meeting each
other for lunch or at dinner parties, not giving a damn about
the country, caring only about their ratings and what kind of
sensational news they were going to put on every night.

This latest development about Herman Willows just
showed how right he had been all along.

The problem was: what to do about it?

No answer was immediately apparent to the President.
He toyed with a sterling silver model of a space shuttle,
presented to him by the NASA people down at Huntsville,
and looked across his desk at Gordon Allen.

"I can't believe these bastards, Gordon," the President said. "You had them right in your office, didn't you? Rossman and the other one, from News?"

"Malachek," Allen said softly, stunned by the report the President had just shown him. How could Charlotte let this happen? Why had she betrayed him?

"Sometimes I wonder about the Jews," the President said. "They've never been with me."

"I don't think Rossman had anything to do with this, sir," Allen responded. "He seemed very willing to go along with us. There was no doubt in my mind."

"And Malachek?"

"A little skeptical," Allen replied, thinking back to the meeting in his office. "But I think he was convinced in the end. He seemed rather embarrassed by it all. Besides, both he and Rossman have got their hands full with Cornwall resigning."

"Yes, I read about that," the President remarked. "Too bad. Cornwall seemed to be the most fair of the three of them, although that's not saying much." Allen nodded.

"Did you make it clear to both Rossman and Malachek," the President asked, "that we wanted the story stopped, that they were to order the Stuart woman away from Willows?"

"I did, Mr. President. I told them national security was involved. I even had a phony tape of Willows talking to the Russian Embassy played for them. They believed me, I'm sure."

"So how did this happen, Gordon? Why did that woman go back to Willows? You can read the transcript, what she said at the doorway. 'We have the whole story,' is what she said. The whole damn story."

She can't, Allen thought. *Charlotte would not have told her all of it. She wouldn't do that to me.*

"Stuart is bluffing," Allen said calmly.

"Bullshit!" the President exploded. The ferocity in his voice shocked Allen. He searched in his mind for a way out of this. He needed to speak to Charlotte quickly and find out what had happened. How had it all gone wrong?

"We've got to find out how much they know," the President said. "I've made it clear from the beginning that we were not going to let this little fag create a scandal for us that the media would blow up beyond all proportions. We stopped him before he sold the pictures. That's all that really matters. It's not the media's goddamn right to know everything that happens in government.

"Chuck Ramsey is one of the best Senators we have, one of the rising stars in our party, a potential vice president, and his future, and the party's future, is more important than this queery-dearie Willows. And it's a hell of a lot more important than whether or not some network gets a juicy story it can use to throw more shit at us."

"You're right, Mr. President," Allen said.

The President picked up another ornament on his desk, a miniature satellite that, with a tiny push from his finger, revolved in a perfect orbit around a scaled-down model of Earth. He watched the satellite spin slowly and looked at Allen.

"See if you can get to this Stuart woman directly, Gordon," the President instructed him. "Tell her national security is involved. The women reporters are always more willing to go along than the men. And then get to Malachek or Rossman and make goddamn sure they understand."

He gave the miniature satellite a hard push with his index finger, throwing it off its symetrical orbit, and added, emphatically, "These fuckers think they run the country but they're not going to destroy us, believe me."

Allen always felt a slight uneasiness when the President used profanity and he was relieved that the meeting seemed to be drawing to an end. If it went any longer, he knew, the President's temper would spin out of control and the expletives would spew out like bile. And this is the man with his finger on the button, he thought.

"Is there anything else, Mr. President?" he asked.

"No," the President said, seemingly subdued again. "But let me have a report as soon as you can."

"I will," Allen answered as he rose from his chair. He shook hands with the President and walked back to his office.

He had to call Charlotte Glover, he knew, and he didn't care if his office logs would show that he had placed a call to her.

There would be no trouble in reaching her. She would be where she always was at this time of the morning, sitting in her cubicle in the White House pressroom, working the phones to her sources or talking to her producers back at the network bureau.

He got through to her swiftly and said, "Charlotte, I need to speak to you."

The fact that he was calling her like this, coupled with the urgent tone in his voice, told her that something was wrong.

"I'll be free after the briefing," she said. "Can we meet for lunch? Jean Louis, some place like that?"

"I think the apartment would be better, just for half an hour or so."

The officious way he said it, and the reference to only spending a half an hour together, left her worried and depressed. What was wrong?

"Gordon," she half-whispered into the phone. "What's happened?"

"We can talk later," he said. "Is one o'clock all right?"

"Yes," she answered numbly. "One o'clock is fine."

She hung up the phone, disturbed that he was so obviously upset. It couldn't be his wife. She was still out on the West Coast, the society pages of the *Post* had reported that morning.

She dismissed the horrendous possibility that he was being blackmailed. After all, it was perfectly reasonable that the Chief of Staff and a White House correspondent could meet for social occasions away from 1600 Pennsylvania Avenue.

The uncertainty nagged her through the rest of the morning, distracted her during Jerry Daniels's noon briefing and, when she finally got to the apartment at the Watergate, she'd convinced herself that he wanted to see her in order to break off the affair.

It was going to end, she thought, right here in the apartment. In broad daylight with no curtains drawn.

He'd found somebody younger, somebody who could thrill him even more, and it was all going to be over. She promised herself: *I will not cry.*

But when he answered the door, he was smiling and relief washed over her. It was something else, thank God.

"You're smiling," she said, relieved. She squeezed his hand and kissed him on the cheek.

"Does it surprise you," he asked, returning her kiss, but automatically, with no emotion.

"Yes. You sounded so worried over the phone. I didn't know what to think."

They moved into the small living room and sat down on a couch covered with a floral fabric of white water lilies.

Allen was wearing a white linen suit and, for an instant, he seemed to her as if he were sitting in a pond, surrounded by the flowers.

"I am worried," he told her. "I suppose I was smiling because I realize how foolish I am."

"What do you mean?" she asked.

"To believe that you could resist, for once in your life, the temptation to do a story even if the one man in your life asked you not to do it."

"What do you mean?" she repeated, genuinely bewildered.

"I told you, darling," he said, as if he were speaking to a child who had misbehaved, "that my credibility was on the line with the President on Malachek."

"Yes," she answered, "and I understood."

"But the son of a bitch is still pursuing Willows," he said slowly. "That Stuart woman was out at Willows's house again. Yesterday."

"I can't believe it," she said, shocked.

"It's true. There are tapes."

"But Malachek told me, when he called me from the airport, that it was a bad tip, that the story was wrong. He believed you."

"And you haven't said anything to him?" he asked suspiciously.

"Oh God, Gordon, why don't you trust me?" she asked. She was distraught at the way he was questioning her. "I haven't said a word," she argued. "I haven't even spoken to Malachek. I don't know how it happened. He would have told me if we were still working on it."

Allen got up from the couch and opened a cabinet built into a bookcase. There was a small bar and refrigerator and he poured a jigger of Scotch into a glass embossed with the Air Force One insignia.

"Can you find out how much the Stuart woman knows?" he asked, after downing the Scotch in one swallow. "Is there a way to do that?"

"I can try," she said. She paused for a moment. Then she added, "I suppose I could call her to say I'm sorry about the bad tip. She knows it came from me. Malachek told me he told her. So it wouldn't be out of the ordinary for me to call her. Maybe she'd tell me why she's still working on Willows."

"I need to know what's happening," Allen said, as if he were issuing orders to a subordinate. "I can't risk my own standing with the President. Could you do that?"

He came over and put his arms on her shoulders and gazed down at her.

She knew that if she agreed, she would be moving further away from her own world; a world where she always had been an observer, a reporter, the voyeur peeking through windows at other people making news.

She had crossed over into his world when he had told her about the Willows story but, even then, despite their relationship, she still had been a reporter. She was on a story.

But now she had crossed the invisible line. She was becoming part of the cover-up. *For him.*

"Can you do it?" he repeated. "For me?"

"Yes," she replied softly. She lifted her face in an invitation for him to kiss her.

He leaned forward and kissed her softly on her mouth, then moved his tongue between her lips. Their tongues touched and she felt herself responding, getting excited.

His hands were unbuttoning her blouse now and she leaned back on the couch and closed her eyes and waited for him with a desperate longing she did not know existed within her.

She lay there, breathing heavily, thrilled by the knowledge that soon he would be coming into her. The thought overpowered her that, soon, very soon now, she would never be happier.

I will call Samantha tomorrow.

PART
THREE

Chapter 31

Oh Lord, I hate this fucking heat.

This is Bobby Ducoin, thinking to himself, feeling sorry for himself, sitting in a swaying elevated train headed for the Loop in downtown Chicago, squeezed in with a bunch of people who are sweating just like he is and he's wondering why in the hell he ever left Mississippi all those years ago.

This is Bobby Ducoin remembering: remembering what it was like, living there in Clarke County before he went off to the Army and the Nam; remembering—all of a sudden—the Ford Falcon he drove to the Three Cs in his senior year, remembering the cute little blond with the big tits, Betty Lou whatever her name was, swinging the green and white pompoms in front of the splintered wooden grandstands at the Friday night football games, remembering that once upon a time he was just like everybody else.

The fuckin' war changed all of that; him lying there in the high grass with his arm blown off, whimpering like a trapped possum in the bushes—he remembers that—and watching the helicopter fly away like a big green bird covering the whole sky. Oh yeah, he remembers that all right.

It was a long time ago and most of the time it's like he was looking at it through a wrong-way rifle scope; everything so distant and small and hard to make out.

And on days like this, late summer in Chicago, with no pine forests to shade him from the sun and no still-water ponds to jump into, bare-assed naked, scattering the minnows and mosquito hawks with that first knifelike slicing of the surface, Bobby Ducoin feels like he is a prisoner again.

Only this time there's no welcome home parade at the

end. Just a room at the Lawson YMCA on Chicago Avenue
with white walls and a used TV set he bought at Wieboldt's
and the sound of the buses keeping him awake at night.

It just never has worked out for Bobby Ducoin, not
when he was selling for the Home and Life back in Jackson,
bullshitting all the niggers about eternal peace and blissful
sleep in a proper burying; not with any of the two-bit jobs
he's had over the years, drifting from city to city just like the
white petals in the front-yard magnolia tree used to drift away
in the first breeze of morning.

Oh Lord, he misses that now, the way it was back on
Barnett Street, with his Mama and Daddy still alive and his
friends raising hell on the weekends, double-clutching that
old white Falcon until you couldn't hardly see it for the red
dust it was kicking up on the state roads around Fire Point.
That was a time all right.

Sometimes at night, when he's lying on the bed in his
room at the Y, he imagines that he can hear the Three Cs
High School Marching Band, practicing in the dusk, when
the sun was sinking, playing the "American Patrol" march and
"Bourbon Street Parade" and "Alabamy-Bound"; the sounds
coming up from the practice field behind the gymnasium,
rising right over the whole town so that no matter where you
were, you could hear the sound of the trumpets—even the
tinkling chimes of the mellophone—and the thump-tha-
thump-tha of the bass drum with the Indian chief painted on
both sides of it.

And sometimes on those nights at the Y, lying there in
his shorts, with the lights out and trying to hear the music of
the Three Cs Marching Band, he thinks about the majorette,
Corinne Anne, the golden hair falling off her shoulders; the
spangled uniform with the tight-fitting shorts hugging her
crotch, those beautiful breasts pushing forward.

And he remembers the first time they did it, out in the
pine woods about a ten-minute drive from town, with a
blanket spread on the ground so there would be no pine
needles sticking into them, and she had spread her legs so
wide he thought he was going to crawl right in. Do me, do
me, she had whispered with him on top of her, pushing as
hard as he could, and her fingers clawing into his back like
they was trying to find something under his skin.

And just thinking about it, after all those years, gets him

hard and if he can't stop thinking about it, can't think of anything else, he'll reach down with his one good hand and pull his pecker, thinking of fucking her again, until that one-eyed snake is dripping and hanging limp between his legs.

It isn't always this way for Bobby Ducoin. Once in a while, he can make a pickup in one of the bars up on Rush Street, although the last pickup said she wanted money before they started until she rubbed against the stump under his shirt and said she'd do it for free because she felt sorry for him.

She was a nympho, he decided, because there was no way she could not know ahead of time that he was one-armed. Standing at the bar, sleeve sewed to the side of his shirt, drinking and paying with one hand, what the fuck did she think he was—one of those sex freaks who got it off by doing it in weird ways?

Oh no, she was the weird one, all right. Only the trouble was, he couldn't find her again, even though he looked in the same bar—the one with the flashing Miller's Lite sign in red and white bulbs in the window—for a couple of nights afterward.

Now, sitting on the CTA train, Bobby Ducoin is looking hard at a black girl whose tight little black ass is moving to some music because she's got a Walkman strapped over her head and two black earpieces are getting lost in that frizzy black hair.

Want to sit down, baby, he's saying to her with his eyes. Sit down on me and move it and shake it like that nigger girl did when we went across the tracks back in the Three Cs freshman year and got laid for five bucks a head.

Bobby Ducoin is getting hard and he tries not to think about it, but when he thinks of anything else it's the same as when he was in the prison camp: you see nothing ahead.

That's the way it is now because the summer is coming to an end and pretty soon his job as a ticket taker for the Cubs' games up at Wrigley Field on Addison Street is going to end. VA got him the job, like he was a fucking charity case or something, and it pays him enough to live on and eat and drink on and get laid on. It doesn't bother him when the fans look away from him as he clutches their tickets in one hand

and tells them to tear off the stubs as they walk by him to the
turnstiles.

But the Cubs are going nowhere and he's going to have
to start humpin' again.

The bartender in one of the places up on Rush Street
says he should think about getting a job in the winter with
the snow removal people. He can operate one of them snow
plows with one hand, he's sure of that, but you need to know
an alderman or somebody in order to get one of the jobs. And
with a nigger mayor, they ain't about to give any jobs to a
good ole Mississippi boy, that's for sure. No way.

The train is stopping at Franklin and Chicago, his stop, and
the first thing Bobby Ducoin does is stop at the newsstand at
the bottom of the El steps and buy the final edition of the
Chicago Tribune, the one that comes out late in the afternoon,
so he can read the sports pages and check the television listings
in case there's some movie on that he hasn't seen.

Back in his room, sitting on his bed with the overhead
light on, not much light because there are dead moths lying
in the plastic fixture covering the bulb, Bobby Ducoin spreads
out the *Tribune* before him and turns to the television page.

He looks to the listings but there is a man's picture on
that page that somehow looks familiar.

Search On For
New Cornwall

is what the headline over the story next to the picture says.
He reads the story quickly and then puts his finger on the
picture, as if trying to actually feel the skin of the man, trying
to remember.

The name under the picture is Art Burton and he goes
back to the story again and reads it slowly and there, in the
last paragraph where it says that Art Burton is a native of
New Orleans, where he began his television career in 1969
after serving in Vietnam.

Oh my sweet Jesus!

This is Bobby Ducoin remembering: remembering lying
in the tall grass, the blood oozing out of his socket, the
helicopter hovering overhead. And now he remembers what
has been dimmed by the years in the prison camp, by the
months and years in dingy, grimy-walled rooms in Shreveport,

Rawlins, Oklahoma City, Davenport; by the drinking and the screwing and the scrounging for a living.

He remembers lying there and that young Lieutenant crawling near him, saying "Ducoin!" and then the Lieutenant backing away, looking at him like he was a pile of dog shit with flies all around him, and then the helicopter going away with him lying in the grass, looking right up at it in the sky as if it was an angel taking people to heaven and leaving him to hell.

Oh Lord, he remembers it all now. Bertrand, that was his name. Armand Bertrand. Lieutenant Armand Bertrand. No fuckin' Art Burton; just a wet-pants Lieutenant from New Orleans who turned chicken and left a Southern boy out there to die.

Bobby Ducoin runs his fingers over the picture again, trying to make sure in his mind that he's right. No mistake about it, that's for sure. And now he goes to the wooden desk on the wall by the window and takes out a piece of paper with Lawson YMCA printed in blue on the top.

He starts to write and all of a sudden, like it was playing right under his open window, he imagines he can hear the Three Cs High School Marching Band playing again.

Ain't no way you can stop 'em now because they're playing toe-tapping, big-stepping, high-striding music and Corrinne Anne is leading them, that big silver baton hitting the clouds when she throws it over her shoulders and, oh Lord, been a long time since Bobby Ducoin heard such sounds and he's feeling so good he knows he's gonna whack off with Corrinne Anne in his mind tonight. Only first he's going to write this letter because the Good Lord helps those who help themselves.

Ain't that right?

He begins. "Dear Lieutenant Bertrand."

Chapter 32

The *Focus on America* ratings—the sampling that was used to project the program's total number of viewers every

Friday night—were always available on a Monday morning in the network building.

They came by computer from the rating services used by all the networks and were rapidly injected into the life stream of the network.

In the same way that a constant supply of blood keeps the human heart alive, the figures flowed to every branch of the network that needed the information.

The figures represented people and people represented consumers and consumers meant money to advertisers and advertisers meant revenue to the network and its affiliates.

So the numbers, capsulized like a specimen in a test tube, were analyzed and studied as if they were droplets of blood taken from a pin-pricked finger. They provided life.

For Art Burton, the ratings had only one purpose. They were a measure of the program's success and, by extension, his success.

The question of how much money advertisers paid for commercials in the program was not really his concern. That was for the salespeople, the researchers.

How did the show do? That was what counted.

Now, as he sat in his office and looked at the figures from last Friday night's program, Burton was pleased.

Almost a week had gone by since he and Michael Swanson, the host on *American Sunrise,* had been mentioned in columns and news stories as the leading candidates within the News Division to succeed John Cornwall on the evening news.

But even though last week's ratings for *Sunrise* had stayed the same, the ratings for *Focus* had increased by two-tenths of a percentage point over the previous week. The ratings showed, he believed, that people were interested in him and that new viewers had been attracted to the program out of curiosity about him.

"You watch what happens," Billy McIntosh in the Press Office had told him last week. "As soon as the stories start coming out about you and Swanson, people who haven't seen your show before are going to tune in just to see what you're all about."

Well, McIntosh had been right. There they were—a big two-tenths of a percentage point—all those people who had not watched the program a week ago but had tuned in Friday night.

Even the New Orleans *Times-Picayune* had run a long story on him last week, complete with a picture from his days as a reporter at WBID-TV. Frankie Baglio had sent him the newspaper clipping with the old picture of himself, standing in front of City Hall, holding a microphone with a big 5 on it. Is that me? he'd thought. Is that the way I looked, so serious, so caught up in the story about the Mayor or City Council or whatever it was? And why do I look as if I was happier then than I am now?

The story in *The Times-Picayune* was just one of a number of stories that had appeared around the country. And it wasn't just *The New York Times*, *The Washington Post*, the *LA Times*, and the *Chicago Tribune* that were carrying stories.

Both UPI and AP had sent out articles about how the network, on the verge of a new season, was rocked by Cornwall's announcement and was choosing a replacement for him. Papers all over the country had picked up the stories.

He wondered if Malachek had discussed the ratings with Rossman yet. See, Malachek could have said, I told you Burton was strong. Look how the ratings on *Focus* went up Friday night, even with a lousy lead-in. Maybe Malachek could have said it that way.

But it was after five o'clock in the afternoon and there had been no word all day from Malachek or anybody. George Durgin had been the only one to comment on the higher ratings but he'd expected Durgin to say something.

He looked at the figures again, poring over them as if the figures were transparent and behind the digits, behind the 11.3 staring up from the page, he could see himself and his future.

The problem was, he couldn't. There were too many other people in there as well—Malachek and Rossman and maybe Mickey Schirmer pushing for Mark Antin.

Maybe, in the long run, his future would be decided by sample groups of twenty-five viewers, sitting in rooms in Dayton, Ohio, or Charleston, South Carolina, or wherever the network did its market research; watching tapes of him and Swanson and Antin; pushing black or white buttons when they liked or disliked something, filling out questionnaires after they had seen the tapes: Could you understand him? Did he seem trustworthy? Did he understand what he was reading? Maybe they were the ones who would decide it all.

He put the ratings report in his desk and walked across the hall to Samantha's office. They were going out for drinks and dinner—an anniversary celebration. It had been one week since Malachek had told him he was still backing him for the Cornwall job.

Samantha was watching a cassette of the Friday night program when he came into her office.

"Still good the second time around?" he asked.

She pushed the stop button. "I wanted to see the piece you had on the drug-testing program again. I missed it."

"It was a repeat. We had it on the show last April."

"I know. I remembered it from then and I wanted to see it again," she said, removing the cassette from the player. "I was interrupted when it was on Friday night."

"Interrupted?"

"The phone."

"Who would have the nerve to call you at home during the program?" he asked with mock horror. "Don't they know it's a cardinal sin? Don't they believe the show is live?" he added, alluding to the fact that the show was taped every Friday afternoon.

"It wasn't all that important," she said offhandedly. She reached for her purse and switched off the lamp on her desk. "Ready?" she asked, smiling at him.

"Let's make a promise," he said as they walked out of her office to the elevator. "Let's not talk about the business tonight. No talk about Malachek or Cornwall or me or anything to do with the evening news."

"We can't do it," she said, laughing. "Besides, is there anything new on Cornwall? At all?"

"Nothing," he said flatly. Then he added, sarcastically, "But I'm still in the papers."

"We won't talk about the business. It's a promise," she said.

They walked a few blocks to the Waldorf-Astoria Hotel on Park Avenue and walked through the revolving door and up a few steps leading to the movie-set opulence of the huge lobby.

The Peacock Lounge, where they had decided to go for drinks, was off the lobby. They found a small table in the corner, away from the entrance.

"It's nice to get away like this," Samantha said as she relaxed in a plush chair. The semidarkness of the room and the soft piano music were having a soothing effect on her. She was glad Art didn't want to talk about the business.

A waiter brought their drink orders and placed a small silver tray of peanuts in front of them.

"Did you ever realize," Art said, grabbing a handful of peanuts, "that the only place you ever see peanuts is in a bar? I mean, when have you ever seen peanuts?"

"At a baseball game. The circus," she answered.

"Shelled peanuts," he said disapprovingly. "I'm talking about salted peanuts, like these."

"You really don't want to talk about the business, do you?" she said, sympathetically.

He shrugged his shoulders. "No," he said. "It's been such a crazy week and nothing has moved. I just want to get away from it all, even for a few hours."

"It would be nice, wouldn't it, if we could just walk away from it? Live some other kind of life. Country house, kids, pets."

"You're not serious, are you?" he asked. It was the first time she had ever shown regret about being in television news.

"I don't know," she said, looking past him. "Sometimes I wonder what would have happened if I had done something else when I got out of college. I could have gone into advertising, I suppose, or publishing, or whatever American Lit majors did when they graduated."

"I can't picture you in anything but news," he said.

"I can," she answered, almost wistfully.

Maybe it was the Beatles' songs the pianist was playing. "Yesterday," "Hey Jude." The music reminded her of the Beatles scrapbooks in her bedroom closet in the house at Newton. Would the battles of Corinth and Sparta be fought again this year on the table in the dining room? How old would Helen's kids be next year?

"And would you have been happier?"

"I don't know," she answered. She reached over and took his hand in hers. "What about you? Would you have been happier?"

He thought for a minute and imagined being back in New Orleans, graduating LSU, not going into the Army and to Vietnam. What would have happened to him? Maybe he'd be working now for one of the brokerage houses—he had done well in business and finance at college—and would have a couple of kids.

He'd wear seersucker suits in the summertime, join one of the better Mardi Gras krewes, wait for the football season to begin, drive his family to Gulfport or Biloxi on the weekends.

"I don't know," he said, squeezing her hand in return. "Sometimes I wonder."

"Would we have been married?" she asked and he could not tell if she was teasing.

"Would you like to have been?" he asked her, wondering where this was going to take them.

She was silent for a moment and he knew that she was taking his question seriously. He hoped she would say, yes.

"Yes, I think so," she said after what seemed to him to be a very long time. "I think we could have been very happy."

"So do I," he said. "Rainbows every day."

"Rainbows?"

"It's just a phrase from a song I picked up somewhere. Rainbows. Happiness. Love. I look at you and I see rainbows."

"And now?" she asked, although she knew what the answer would be.

"And now," he repeated. "And now maybe we're so damn caught up in the business and our jobs that we'd never have the time to be happy—even if we were married."

"We could quit," she said.

"No, we couldn't. At least not now."

"I know," she conceded, sure what he was thinking. The Cornwall job. Not now.

"Maybe someday," he said, reassuring her. He squeezed her hand again and signaled for the waiter to bring the check.

"Let's get some Italian," he said and she nodded eagerly. She knew that the conversation, even obliquely, had taken them to the edge of thinking about marriage but neither of them had wanted to go any further.

It was easier to say that the pressure of the business made marriage impossible. It was easier not to talk about it at length. It was easier to eat Italian.

They found a small restaurant on Lexington Avenue in the mid-Sixties and kept to their promises not to talk about the business. They talked about writers they both liked, and music, and promised to make time to see Shakespeare in the Park that summer.

It wasn't until they got back to her apartment that the news was mentioned at all and then only because it was eleven o'clock.

"The local news is on," Samantha said. "Do you want to watch it?"

"Why not?" Art walked over to the television set and switched it on. He sat down on the couch and pulled her down beside him.

"Comfortable?" he asked, putting his arm around her.

She leaned her head against his shoulder. "I had too much tortellini," then moved her face close to his and kissed him on the cheek.

"Let's watch the news and go to bed," he said, enjoying the first stirrings of desire in him.

"Mmmm," she answered.

The first few stories were local crime stories—a triple murder in the Bronx; a drug bust in Brooklyn, a shooting in a West Side tenement. After the commercials, the newscaster returned for the second segment of the broadcast.

"Turning now to national and international news," he said. "There's no movement tonight on the tax bill. House Republicans, with an eye on the upcoming Labor Day recess, are still trying to work out a compromise with the Democratic majority."

A picture of the U.S. Capitol behind the newscaster dissolved into another picture. It was the face of a man Samantha recognized.

"In Washington, the top aide to Senator Charles Ramsey of Kansas was found dead of a gunshot wound at his house tonight. Police said the wound was self-inflicted. No note was left by the victim, Herman Willows. Willows was fifty-three."

"Oh my God," Samantha gasped. She buried her head in her hands and began to sob uncontrollably.

Burton leaned over and grabbed her by her shoulders. "Samantha, what's the matter? Tell me, what's the matter?"

She was still sobbing and was gasping loudly, as if she were underwater and needed to come to the surface for air. She shook her head wildly as if to indicate that she could not answer him.

"Tell me," he said urgently. "For God's sake, tell me what's happening!"

He tried to look at her face but it was covered by her hair and all he could see were the tears pouring down her face and wetting the collar of her blouse.

"Please tell me, darling," he repeated. "What is it?"

"Willows," she mumbled. "I did it."

"What do you mean?" he asked in a bewildered voice. He could not understand what she was saying.

"I did it," she repeated. "I killed him."

For a brief, panicked moment, Burton thought Samantha was going crazy. She's having a nervous breakdown, he thought, and she is cracking up right in front of me.

"Please, Samantha," he pleaded in a strained voice. "Tell me what you mean. What's wrong?"

She looked up at him with eyes already reddened from crying. "Willows. The man who killed himself. I was doing a story on him. I never told you. I couldn't. I went to his house last week. I told his wife—"

The rest of the words were caught in her throat and she was unable to speak. She just stared at him, as if she were paralyzed by some horror that only she could see.

Art felt himself beginning to sweat. Tiny beads of perspiration were forming on his forehead. He was worried by her condition and he did not know what to do.

"Stay there!" he shouted. He got up and ran to her bathroom and soaked a washcloth in cold water. He hurried back to the living room and put the cloth over her face.

"Relax," he said. "Try to calm down."

She held the washcloth over her face. Then she let out a deep sigh, as if a tremendous weight had just been lifted from her. "I'm sorry. It was too much of a shock."

Then she told him everything: how Malachek had asked her to do the ambush interview, how she had gone back on her own to confront Willows; how, only last Friday evening, Charlotte Glover had called her to say that Malachek had found out that national security was involved and that the story was wrong.

"What did Malachek tell you?" he asked her when she had finished.

"I never heard from him," she answered despondently. "I never told him that I had gone back," she went on. "Only you know that. And Mrs. Willows. And..." She was beginning to choke up again and Art put his arm around her to steady her. He took the cloth from her and let it drop to the floor.

"You can't blame yourself, Samantha," he said, trying to comfort her. "Willows must have been very mixed-up."

"It's the business, Art," she said, wiping the tears from her face. "It's this shitty business that makes us do things like this. Go after people like they were animals. Hunt them down and put them in a cage and bring them back alive, right on time for the seven o'clock news.

"Feed the public the raw meat. That's what they want, isn't it? Raw meat and blood. There but for the grace of God go I. That's it, isn't it? Isn't that why they watch? It's somebody else's troubles. And we keep right on doing it, going out with our microphones and cameras and recorders and all because we can't bring ourselves to live normal, ordinary lives.

"And we get a high from this. That's true, isn't it? It's like a drug and we're all hooked. Look at you. The Cornwall job has got you addicted. You couldn't walk away from it if your life depended on it. We can't even think about marriage because of it. We're all the same. A bunch of addicts, hooked on news."

Her words were coming out rapidly now, almost in near-hysteria, Burton stood up and took her by the shoulders.

"Stop it!" he shouted. "Stop saying these things. Listen to me, dammit!"

The harshness of his voice jolted her, and she looked up at him like a lost child seeking help.

"We can't play God," he said slowly. "We can't decide what stories we're going to do on the basis of whether or not we're going to hurt people. That's not our role in life. This isn't church. We're not holding confessional among ourselves and handing out indulgences. This one no, that one yes. That's not what we're all about."

She was weeping softly, and he sat down and put his arms around her. She buried her head in his shoulder.

"Please, Samantha," he said. "Don't tear yourself up like this. I admire you for going back to Willows. You didn't kill him, for God's sake. He killed himself because he was a pathetic man who got himself trapped and couldn't see a way out. You were only doing what you had to do—following up on a story. Don't feel guilty about that."

"But I do," she said tearfully. "If I hadn't pursued him, maybe he could have handled it another way. At least he wouldn't have felt like a frightened rabbit with no place to hide. I was the one who made him realize there was no escape, don't you see that? I stood at his door and told his wife I knew the whole story and I really didn't. Charlotte Glover says there was no cover-up. So I was wrong. But what did his wife think? And what did he think when she came back in the house and told him what I had said? Did he think about it just before he blew his brains out?"

"You did nothing wrong, Samantha," he said softly. "You had a job to do. I couldn't be more sincere about that."

"Don't make me sound like a Nazi soldier, Art," she begged. "I wasn't just following orders. I was acting on my own instincts because I wanted to break a big story. Just like you and that gambling story. Just like you want the Cornwall job. It's all the same, just different degrees. We're all addicts. We need the fix."

Her words froze him. He had lied to her about the gambling story because he had never wanted her to fully realize how much he wanted the Cornwall job.

But she was right. He, too, was addicted. Only his addiction was worse.

He had lied to her, and Malachek, because he wanted the biggest fix in the business—to be the anchorman of the evening news.

And he still was lying to her, even as she sat trembling next to him, with her head buried in his shoulders, her hand clutching his.

Seeing her so defenseless, so tormented by self-doubt, he was overwhelmed by guilt, and he knew that he could not go on deceiving her any longer.

God, he thought, I love her so much and yet I'm doing this to her and myself. The addiction had become too strong, and he had to stop it, before it completely consumed him.

"Samantha," he said, forcing the words out. "I have to tell you something."

"What is it?" she asked in a voice so fragile that her words were like teacups falling from a shelf and shattering.

"I lied to you. I kept something from you."

"What?"

"I lied," he repeated quietly, trying to avoid her bewildered gaze but unable to turn away from her.

Then he told her how he had decided against going any further on the Jarvis Winston story because, if he ever got it on the air, it would ruin his chances for the Cornwall job.

"Winston is tied into the mob," Burton said. "I could have proved it, I'm sure. But I didn't want to push because it would have backfired on me. For my own career, the story wasn't worth it. It probably would have ruined Malachek too."

"Oh God, Art," she said. Her tear-streaked face reflected her anguish. He had been so wrong and she hadn't known it. And now he was admitting it and suddenly it was he who needed her help.

"Art," she said. "You have to tell Malachek. You can't do this to yourself. Even if you get the Cornwall job, you'll never forgive yourself for burying the story.

"You can't go against everything you've always believed, everything you just told me, just because you want this job. Is that the compromise you're willing to make? And live with?"

"It's the top of the business," he said numbly. "The gold ring."

"And at what price?"

"What about Malachek? Rossman will crucify him if this goes on the air," he said, putting up the last barrier against her.

"Malachek can take care of himself. At least he can live with himself."

He looked at her with a wounded expression.

"I'm sorry, darling," she said, "but it's true. You have to be able to live with yourself. And what about Winston? Are you going to let him go untouched just because your ambition has been strong enough to silence you?"

He said nothing.

"What about everything you told me? How I can't worry that people occasionally get hurt? But one of the biggest stars in television is going to get off because somebody is going to get hurt. Only this time that somebody is you. That makes it different, doesn't it?"

"I guess I never wanted to admit it to myself," he confessed. He took her in his arms and held her tight, as if the warmth of her body would protect him from the cold emptiness he felt inside.

"I need you, Samantha, and I love you more than I ever have before. I should have told you about Winston. I just didn't want you to know how much the Cornwall job meant. For both of us. I never realized it myself, until recently."

"I know," she said.

"You're right. I can't keep quiet. I'll talk to Malachek about Winston tomorrow morning," he added.

Then he asked, "What about you? Are you going to tell Malachek that you went back to Willows's house?"

"That was a week ago," she said.

"You don't have to," he told her. "It won't mean anything one way or the other now."

"I'll think about it," she said.

He leaned forward and kissed her on the mouth.

"Let's stay here for a few minutes," she whispered. "In the dark." She turned and switched off the table lamp, took off her shoes and lay down with her head in his lap.

He began to run his fingers tenderly through her hair and across her forehead as if he were soothing a tiny baby. Drained by the trauma of what had happened, she fell asleep.

He kissed her on the forehead and sat there looking out into the dark room, and thought about Malachek and Cornwall and Mark Antin and New Orleans and LSU football and the Army and the soldier lying in the tall grass and how the hell did it all happen?

He stayed that way for a while, until her head felt heavy in his lap. He slid out from under Samantha and left her sleeping on the couch.

He went into her bedroom and stripped down to his shorts. He lay down in the bed, his arms wrapped around a pillow as if it were Samantha. The pillowcase held traces of her perfume, filling his head with images of her. Finally, he fell asleep.

Chapter 33

Mark Antin rested his chin in one hand and looked skeptically at the Secretary of the Treasury.

"Do I take it to mean, Mr. Secretary, that the tax bill—if it passes in its current version—could affect the balance of payments?"

A camera zoomed in on the Cabinet Secretary's face and he smiled at Antin.

"That's exactly what I mean, Mark, and I'm glad you asked. There is a correlation between the amount of income available for investment and the strength or weakness of the American dollar overseas. This bill will hurt our balance of payments."

"But the dollar has lost against the pound and the mark, hasn't it?"

Art Burton got up from his desk, pushed the stop and eject buttons on the VCR, and threw the cassette of *Breakfast Time* on an empty chair.

"What the hell do you know," he said to the fading image of Antin as the screen went black. Must have been up all night doing his damn homework.

Still, he had to reluctantly admit that Antin was impressive. The audience would never know that some young researcher had prepped him for the interview and reviewed all the material with him as if he were being tutored for a test.

The son of a bitch is a quick study, Burton conceded. Have to give him credit for that.

He'd occasionally watched *Breakfast Time* in the past

but now that he knew Antin was his competition for Cornwall's job, he had watched it more frequently.

In the past week, he had set the timer on his VCR to tape the program every morning.

He had studied Antin's on camera appearance with the precision of a surgeon examining a patient on an operating room table.

What is he made of? What does he think? How does he look? What is he all about?

He had been unable to come up with an answer. His viewing of Antin had left him with only one, indelible, impression. Antin was slick.

But he wasn't slick enough to get away with it night after night in the crucible of the evening newscast. Antin had never covered a beat for his network or been a reporter at a local station. He had not paid his dues anywhere. He was a reader, not a reporter.

Malachek wouldn't let it happen.

He had made an appointment to see Malachek at noon and now, as he left his office and walked down the long corridor to Seven West, he rehearsed in his mind how he would handle it.

He would simply lay it all out for Malachek, everything he knew and suspected about Jarvis Winston's ties to the mob, and let Malachek decide what to do.

He had a feeling that Malachek would tell him to keep working on the story. That was just the way the man worked.

He found Malachek looking at the packet of clippings that the Press Department sent to all the executives every morning.

"Lots of stories in here about you and Swanson, Art," Malachek said, holding up the sheaf of reprints in his hand. "Makes good reading."

"I'm not used to all this publicity," Burton admitted, taking a chair across from Malachek.

Malachek held up a photocopy that Burton recognized as a reprint of the feature the New Orleans *Times-Picayune* had done on him.

"Nice story in the *Picayune*," Malachek observed. "I had almost forgotten you went to Vietnam. You still got the medal?"

"Of course," Burton replied. He wondered if Malachek was trying to find out more. But how could he know?

"I have it saved somewhere," he said. "In the bottom drawer of my desk, someplace like that. It's been a long time."

"What was it for?" Malachek asked.

A picture flashed briefly through Burton's mind. The soldier was lying in the tall grass, his arm hanging by a fragment of tissue to a gaping hole under his shoulder. There was blood splattered all through the grass, staining the green blades a crimson red. And the soldier was begging with his eyes for help.

Burton looked past Malachek and out the window, as if the memory would dissolve and then disappear into the wall of glass that formed the facade of the office building across the street.

"Our patrol was ambushed. Most of them were killed but I saved the life of one of them by dragging him to a helicopter sling. A black guy from Mississippi. Eddie Johnston. That's what I won the Bronze Star for."

"Ever hear from him?" Malachek asked.

"No. We never kept in touch. Time passed."

Malachek put the sheaf of paper into a desk drawer and lit a cigar.

"I assume you wanted to see me to find out if anything is happening on Cornwall," he said to Burton as a puff of smoke floated, like a miniature cloud, past his face.

Burton watched the cloud evaporate. "I was hoping something might be happening," he admitted.

He wants it bad, Malachek thought, so bad he probably can taste it. He stared at Burton's face, remembering him from eight years ago; fresh from the affiliate, eager, proud to have been offered a network job, willing to go anywhere they wanted to send him, thrilled to be making $50,000 a year.

What happens to these people, he thought. What changes them? The money? The exposure? The power? How do I tell him that it probably isn't going to go any further for him?

"It's like I told you earlier, Art," he said. "There are a lot of factors in a decision like this. The ratings are just part of it."

"I realize that," Burton said, discouraged, remembering how strong Antin looked on the tape.

"Is there anything else you needed to see me about?" Malachek asked. He put his cigar in an ashtray, placed his hands behind his head, and leaned back in his chair.

"I wanted to tell you about that gambling story I'm working on," Burton began. "I got some information over the weekend." It was a white lie but it didn't matter.

"I think I've got a hell of a story," he continued. "But it may be a hell of a problem."

Malachek did not appear to react. He stayed in the same position, hands behind his head, his body rocking slightly in the black leather chair behind the desk. "Go on," he said quietly.

"Do you remember I told you that I couldn't seem to get anywhere with the woman I thought could tie it all together?"

Malachek nodded and reached for his cigar again. "I remember something about a woman," he said.

"She was supposed to have received big gambling payoffs from a mob courier. And she was carrying a three-quarter million tab on their books."

Malachek kept rocking back and forth, and Burton wondered if Malachek's thoughts were someplace else.

"She's a little old Jewish woman who lives in Las Vegas. Her son bought the house for her. The payoffs are delivered to the house."

He paused for a moment in order to make sure that Malachek got the full impact of what he was about to tell him.

"I found out that her son is Jarvis Winston," he said quietly.

The words seemed to hang suspended in the air.

Malachek leaned forward and pointed a finger at Burton, like a prosecuting attorney.

"You're telling me that Jarvis Winston's mother is getting big gambling payoffs. That she's a heavy bettor?" he asked skeptically.

"I think it's bigger than that," Burton replied. "She visits him at least once a month. According to her maid, she takes a package to him when she visits. I think he does the betting and she's the conduit without even knowing it."

Malachek drew a deep breath. All the ramifications of what Burton was telling him were beginning to take shape.

"Conjecture on your part?"

"A gut feeling," Burton answered. "I saw Winston in the

hospital in Los Angeles. I set it up through the Press Department on the West Coast, gave them a phony story that I was interested in doing a profile on Winston. He's a sleaze, Carl, I could feel it.

"I've met the mother. She's an old lady who's probably never seen the insides of a casino in Vegas. There's no way she could be betting big money with a bookmaking operation thousands of miles away."

Malachek had stopped rocking. His hands were folded in front of him now, clenched together as if he were holding something in them and didn't want to let go.

"Can you prove it? That's the bottom line. Can you prove it?"

"It'll take time. Maybe we'll have to stake out his mother's house in Las Vegas, you know, hidden camera in a van, and wait for another delivery."

His words came out rapidly, as if he were caught up in the momentum of Malachek's questions.

"You didn't answer my question. Can you prove it?"

Burton was struck by Malachek's repeated words. *Maybe he doesn't want me to go any further. He's looking for a way out. He doesn't want to touch it.*

"I think I can prove it," Burton said, thinking about Samantha. "I think that the beating Winston took didn't happen accidentally. I think he's in deep trouble with the mob and this was part of it. Somebody will talk, somewhere."

"All right. Go ahead and keep working on it," Malachek said.

Burton was surprised by Malachek's decision. *He's tough,* Burton thought with admiration.

"I know it's a sensitive story," Burton said. "You won't be too popular with Rossman if we can get it on the air."

"Let me worry about that," Malachek said. "Just make sure that it stands up."

He had to ask. "And me? I don't think it will make me too popular with Rossman."

"Don't worry about it," Malachek said. "I'll take care of it."

Malachek was smiling and, in some enigmatic way it seemed, to Burton, to be a smile of triumph, a victor's smile.

"I'll make some phone calls," Burton said. He realized that, despite his ambivalence, the story itself was starting to

excite him again. It was better this way. At least he could live
with himself.

"Keep in touch," Malachek said. He rose from his chair
and shook Burton's hand. "That's what I like about this
business, Art. You never know from day to day, do you?"

Burton smiled. After he left Malachek's office he went
back to the *Focus* area. He stopped to see if Samantha was in
her office. They had not spoken since late last night when she
had fallen asleep on her living room couch.

There was a note thumbtacked to her door: Gone to
lunch. Back at 2:30. With whom, he wondered.

He went back to his office and thought about his meeting
with Malachek. It had gone better than he'd expected. Malachek
was still supporting him and urging him to stay on the
Winston story. And Samantha knew everything.

He felt invigorated, and he began going over the details
of the Winston story just as he had related them to Malachek.
Can you prove it, Malachek had asked. There were only two
possible ways.

Either Winston himself woud have to be squeezed into
admitting his connection to the mob, or Frankie Baglio would
have to push his source for more leads tying Winston to the
busted gambling operation in New Orleans.

Neither possibility seemed likely. Baglio's source, whoever he was, probably didn't know any more than he had
already told Baglio. If he had been holding back, Baglio
would have spotted it. He was too good a cop to have let it
slide.

And Winston? He could picture him, surrounded by all
those flowers as if he were laid out in a coffin, cracking jokes
with his visitors, trying to pat the ass of every nurse who
walked into the room.

Wonder if he's been signing autographs for the orderlies.
He could just see some poor kid, wearing white shoes and a
white jacket and white pants, bringing Winston a new carafe
of water, emptying the specimen bottle, changing the pillowcase, and taking Winston's bets on the Angels or the Dodgers.

The ludicrous picture made him smile. Then it hit him.
Winston was probably still betting! If he had been beaten up
on orders of the mob, then he was in too deep and would
need to be betting even more heavily, trying to get himself
even. He had to be phoning a bookie some place, and he

wouldn't be worried about phoning from his hospital room because, after all, who would know?

Who would be interested in his phone bills? What possible reason would anyone have for looking at Jarvis Winston's phone bill? He was one of the biggest stars on television and if he ran up a thousand-dollar-a-week phone bill, no one would think twice about it. And no one would check the numbers he had called. Unless they had a reason to.

Excited by the hunch, he picked up the phone and dialed Frank Baglio's number at Police Headquarters in New Orleans.

Baglio didn't know about Winston, only about a Mrs. Weinstein in Las Vegas. Frankie had given him the original lead. Now he'd give Frankie something in return.

He reached Baglio just as the vice squad officer was finishing a po'boy sandwich of roast beef piled onto French bread.

"I can call back later if you want to finish eating," Burton said. He could almost smell the aroma of the warm bread over the phone.

"Hey, no problem," Baglio said. "All I got left is a chocolate moon pie and I can eat it later."

"Frankie," Burton began. "I've been doing a lot of work on that gambling story we talked about. I've come up with some information that can be helpful to you."

He paused for a minute and then he asked, "Is this phone safe? I mean is it all right to talk?"

"It's okay. Don't worry."

"Look," Burton said, lowering his voice to a confidential tone. "Your source told you that he delivered payoffs to Mrs. Weinstein in Vegas, right?"

"Right."

"Well, Mrs. Weinstein's son is Jarvis Winston and she visits him regularly, carrying a big manila envelope."

"Jesus!" Baglio exclaimed. "Jarvis Winston! You gotta be shitting me."

"I'm not, Frankie. Believe me. Now, you know about Winston being beaten up?"

"Sure. It was all over the front page of the *Picayune*. Dopers, right?"

"No. I think it was connected to the gambling. And I've

got a hunch he may still be betting big money, trying to get even. And who's going to look at the phone bills from the hospital?"

"You want the phone bills?" Baglio asked.

"Can you get them?" Burton said. "Is there a way you can get them?"

"There will be a record someplace," Baglio said. "Probably in the hospital accounting department. Certainly the phone company. I can get them."

"If there's a pattern of calls to one number," Burton said, "then you can trace the numbers. If it turns out to be a bookie operation, then that information becomes valuable to you, doesn't it? You could trade it to the Feds, couldn't you? I mean, this would be helpful to you too, wouldn't it?"

"You're damn right it would," Baglio said.

"Just let me know if it is a bookie operation before you do anything with it," Burton requested.

"What do you do with it? You can't nail Winston as a big gambler just on the basis of that."

"It will help," Burton said. "If I've got that on him, then maybe I can find out how deep he is into the mob, what kind of a hold they may have on him. Don't forget, nobody knows about his gambling."

"Man, that would stir up some shit, wouldn't it," Baglio said admiringly.

"It really would, Frankie, believe me."

"I need a little while, Armand," Baglio said. "Got to lay a little pipe. You know, call up a couple of contacts in the phone company out there."

"It's a hunch, Frankie, but I think it will hold up."

"I'll let you know," Baglio promised, and said good-bye.

As Burton put down the phone, he realized that, for the first time in the last few weeks, he was feeling good again. There had been a catharsis in telling Samantha, and then Malachek, about the Winston story. And now his initial plunge back into the story was sending a thrill of excitement through him.

There really was a high, a kick, in the pursuit of a good story. It was exhilarating, like a breath of pure, fresh air. It was times like this that reminded him why he loved the news business.

Just as he was about to make another call, Anita Silas, one of the production secretaries, entered his office.

"Some mail came in this morning," she said, holding an envelope. He glanced at it casually. The lettering was printed, like that of a schoolchild.

"It wasn't marked personal so I opened it," she said.

"Anything interesting?"

"Well, I must confess I never knew your real name was Bertrand," she said, smiling.

"What do you mean?" he asked anxiously.

"It's from somebody you knew in Vietnam. Do you remember a Bobby Ducoin?"

Chapter 34

Jerry Rossman had just answered a phone call from Hap Hawkins when his secretary came into his office and placed a piece of paper in front of him.

The note read, "Malachek holding. Says it's urgent."

Rossman glanced at the flashing light on his phone and said, "Can you hold for just a minute, Hap? Carl Malachek needs to speak to me." He put the man on hold, then punched the other line.

"Yes, Carl," he said, sounding annoyed.

"I'm sorry to interrupt, Jerry," Malachek apologized, "but something has come up that I need to see you about. It's important."

"I just got back from Florida last night, Carl. I'm trying to catch up on a lot of work. Can it wait until this evening?"

"I think we need to talk soon," Malachek said firmly.

Malachek's insistence irritated Rossman. What the hell does he want now? If it's about Burton he can forget it.

Rossman glanced at the small, polished brass Tiffany clock on his desk. The time was almost twelve-thirty.

"I'm free for lunch," he said. "We can meet in the dining room."

"Fine," Malachek said. "Half an hour?"

"Yes. One o'clock. See you then," Rossman said abruptly. He got Hawkins back on the phone. "Sorry, Hap. It wasn't a crisis, thank God. Tell me, how's your lovely wife?"

"She's fine, Jerry. She enjoyed your visit out here. Real pleasure."

"Your ratings all right, Hap? The prime time seems to be doing well over the country, despite the summer drop-off."

"Thursday night's a little weak for us," Hawkins commented. "That new sitcom you're trying out doesn't make it."

"We're taking a good look at it, Hap," Rossman answered.

He hated kissing Hawkins's ass. The idea that a broadcaster like Hawkins, coining money out there in the wheat fields, never having worked a day in his life in New York or LA, somebody who wouldn't know a good script if he fell over one, the idea that somebody like this considered himself an expert on network programming was too damn much.

But that was what the business was all about. Hap Hawkins carried a lot of weight and now, Rossman sensed, he was about to throw it around.

"What's on your mind, Hap? The Affiliates Council happy?"

"I just wanted to speak to you about the Cornwall problem, Jerry. A lot of the stations are getting very nervous."

Christ, Rossman thought, it's only been a week since we announced it. Have they got a lynch party out already?

"It's coming along nicely, Hap. These decisions can't be made in a vacuum. You know that."

"Jerry, I know you and the rest of the network people are very conscious of this. But those of us out here on the front lines are very worried. A weak network news would be a disaster."

"It would be a disaster for all of us," Rossman reminded him. "But we're not going to let it happen. We're going out into the field with test groups by the end of the week," Rossman continued. It was a lie but there was no way that Hawkins could know that.

Hawkins pressed him. "Are you close to a decision? Will we be ready for the affiliates meeting?"

"Definitely," Rossman said confidently. "There's no way

we're going to let this drag on, even though we seem to be getting a hell of a lot of publicity in the meantime."

"The papers out here did a couple of pieces on Cornwall," Hawkins told him.

"Did they speculate on his successor?"

"They ran the pictures of Burton and Swanson. Must have come from your Press Department."

"Sid's people have done a good job on this," Rossman observed.

"Jerry," Hawkins said, lowering his voice. "We can't wait too much longer on this. I've been around a long time and I can smell it building up."

"Smell what?" Rossman asked nervously.

"The uneasiness, the worry. We all live or die with the network's fortunes. You know that and I know that even if a couple of affiliates out there act as if they were independents."

"Yeah, you're right," Rossman said, thinking about one station in the Southwest that was running its own movie two nights a week instead of the network's programs. Sons of bitches.

"But we can't walk right up to the first week of the new season," Hawkins continued, "and not know who's going to be anchoring the evening news. It's an incredible prospect. I don't even want to think about it."

Rossman drummed his fingers nervously on his desk. He had been hoping to hear back from Mickey Schirmer about Mark Antin today. It had been over a week since they'd had breakfast but he hadn't heard word one from the agent since then.

He knew the game Schirmer was playing. Schirmer wanted him to be the anxious one. That's what Schirmer was waiting for. And, once he called, Schirmer would pounce on him and mug him on Antin's behalf.

"Hap," Rossman said smoothly, "I have a call in to Mickey Schirmer. The biggest agent in town. He's got Jarvis Winston, a couple of our correspondents, and he's also got Mark Antin."

"Are you still working on Antin?" Hawkins asked. Rossman could detect heightened interest.

"Very much so. I told you when I was out at your station that I was planning to see Schirmer as soon as I got back and I did. We did a breakfast last week."

"And?"

"And I told him we were interested, very interested, in Mark Antin anchoring our evening news. I'm hoping to hear from him this week. Maybe today."

"That's a hell of a piece of work, Jerry," Hawkins said admiringly. "Why have you kept it under wraps like this?"

"We have to," Rossman said. "There may be some legal questions involved, you know, contract tampering, something that we don't know about. Besides, I don't want to tip my hand. I just want to hear them squeal like a stuck pig when we take Antin away."

"It'll play hell with *Breakfast Time*, won't it?"

"That's the Lucky Strike Extra," Rossman said. "We maintain our evening news lead and take away some of *Breakfast Time*'s rating points. It can all work. It can all come together, Hap."

"What about Carl? Is he satisfied?" Hawkins asked.

"Malachek's a team player," Rossman answered. "He won't walk away from good ratings."

"I'd appreciate it if you could call me as soon as you hear something," Hawkins said. "I'd like to tell just a few of the key Council members. It would be dynamite, Jerry."

"I'll let you know immediately," Rossman assured him. "Hope I can call you by the end of this week. Maybe you and Rosalie can come to New York. I'll probably have a little dinner party for Antin. You know, let him meet some of the important folks in an informal setting, rather than just in LA."

"You'd bring him out for the affiliates meeting, of course," Hawkins said.

"He'd be the centerpiece, Hap. The star of the whole damn show." He paused for a moment to let Hawkins savor the prospect. Then he said, "Think everybody will be happy about it, Hap?"

"It'll be the best damn convention in years," Hawkins said enthusiastically. "Call me, will you, as soon as you hear anything."

"You'll be hearing from me. Give my love to Rosalie," Rossman said and then he hung up.

He got up from his desk and began to pace nervously across the carpet. He had not wanted to call Schirmer so soon but Schirmer, and now Hawkins, was putting the squeeze on him.

Schirmer's no fool, Rossman thought. He knows I'm starting to run out of time and he's keeping quiet while we put out the stories about Burton and Swanson. He's just waiting for me to come begging. Guys like him don't belong in the business. Lousy vultures, getting rich off of their clients and picking the bones of every network.

To hell with it, he decided. All it takes is money.

He went to his desk and pressed the intercom for his secretary.

"See if you can get me Mickey Schirmer," he said. "Leave word if he's not in. And tell the dining room I'll be eating with Carl Malachek."

Two minutes later his secretary said that Schirmer was out but she had left word for him to call back.

He'll call back, Rossman decided. Now that I've come to him, he'll call. All it takes is money, he told himself again, and he took the elevator up to the executive dining room, thinking, it's all going to work.

When Rossman entered the twenty-fifth-floor dining room, Malachek was waiting for him, Bloody Mary in hand.

"I'll have a scotch on the rocks," Rossman said to the waiter who went back into the kitchen and reappeared moments later carrying the drink on a sterling silver tray. Rossman took the drink and said to the waiter, "We'll eat now.

"Sorry to keep you waiting, Carl," Rossman said. "I was on the phone with Hap Hawkins."

"The affiliates happy?" Malachek asked, sitting down at the table.

"They're a little anxious about the Cornwall situation," Rossman said. "But I think that's going to work itself out."

"Why?"

Rossman was about to answer when the waiter emerged from the kitchen carrying two plates of crabmeat salad. Rossman paused until the waiter had left the room.

"I love crabmeat," he said. "Baltimore has wonderful crabmeat."

"What did you tell Hawkins?" Malachek repeated.

Rossman wiped his mouth with his napkin and put his fork down as if he had decided not to finish his food. He glared angrily at Malachek.

"I told him that I expected to make a decision this week.

That I'm hoping to sign up Antin. I called Mickey Schirmer before coming up here."

"And what did Schirmer say?"

"He wasn't in. But he'll return my call, believe me. Now you tell me what's come up that's so urgent."

I'll tell you, Malachek thought, and it's not going to be like when you told me, sitting in that limo outside the Midtown Tunnel, sticking it so far up my ass that it hurt. Now it's my turn.

"It's a news story," Malachek said. "It's got a lot of ramifications."

"Look, it's not another wild-goose chase, is it?"

"No," Malachek answered resentfully. Rossman's remark reminded him that he had forgotten to return Charlotte Glover's phone call this morning. He wondered what she wanted.

"There's a story we're working on. It involves the network."

"The network?" Rossman echoed uneasily. "What do you mean?"

"We've got some information that Jarvis Winston may be involved with big-time gamblers. That he owes a lot of money. That it's probably why he was beaten up."

"Jesus," Rossman said softly.

"We're still developing it," Malachek said, turning the screws slightly and enjoying Rossman's discomfort. "But I thought you would want to know about it. If Winston's involved with the mob, it could mean all sorts of things."

Rossman was silent and looked at his plate. His stomach felt queasy.

"Who's we?" he asked, looking at Malachek. "Who came up with this precious little nugget of information?"

"It's a story Art Burton has been working on," Malachek said evenly. He waited for Rossman to react, but there was nothing. He must be dying inside, Malachek thought.

"This is a story you're planning for *Focus*?" Rossman asked.

"Yes," Malachek replied. "We'll run it by legal, of course, before we do anything. And we'll show it to you before it ever goes on the air," he added casually.

"You mean *if* it goes on the air," Rossman said quickly.

"I don't think you meant that," Malachek said.

"I think I did, Carl. I'm not about to sit quietly in the

corner while you and your people down on Seven thrust this network into a scandal," he said heatedly. "Not on our air, you don't."

"What does that mean, Jerry? It should go to the papers?"

This time there was a reaction in Rossman's eyes. They flared with rage. He looked around the room to reassure himself that no one else was there.

"Listen, Carl," he said angrily. "I don't care if Jarvis Winston is doing it with little girls, or animals, or running a whorehouse in Malibu. Whatever he's mixed up in, we'll see that it stops. But we're not going to put it on our air. We're not going to commit hari-kari in public. Got it?"

"What do you expect me to do?" Malachek said defiantly. "Tell Burton to stop working on it? To kill it?"

"Yes," Rossman said, thankful that no one could hear them. "I think that would be a very politic idea, for all of our sakes. Yours, mine, Burton's, the network's, everybody's."

"And you don't think the story will surface somewhere else?"

"What do you mean?" Rossman asked warily.

"I mean it wouldn't look too good in the press if word got out that the president of the network killed a story unfavorable to one of the network's stars. I mean it just wouldn't make good play," he added with undisguised sarcasm.

You son of a bitch, Rossman thought. "And how's it going to get out?" he asked. He wasn't going to let Malachek do this to him.

"These things have a way of leaking out," Malachek said. "Besides, what rationale is there for killing it? It's not like the Herman Willows story. There's no national security involved in this. We're talking about a variety show host who's mixed up with the mob."

"And who happens to bring in millions of dollars a year to this network," Rossman commented sarcastically.

Malachek toyed with the crabmeat on his plate. "I don't think I can tell Burton to stop working on it," he said, as if the idea were something he actually had thought about.

Rossman saw through it.

"You don't want to tell Burton to give it up, do you?" he said, trying to keep his anger contained.

"Word would get out," Malachek replied. "Reporters

don't like it when their stories are killed by the brass, particularly when the stories are sensitive."

"Who do you think signs that paycheck of yours, Carl?" Rossman asked bitterly. "It's this network that does, this network that you want to piss on in public." His frustration was beginning to show in his voice. "Where in the hell is your sense of priorities, of loyalty, for Chrisake?"

"I've got a sense of loyalty," Malachek replied. "Where's yours?"

"Get off it, Carl," Rossman said quietly. "I'm trying to discuss this in a civilized way, just the two of us. I don't think either one of us wants to get into a pissing match. I'm just trying to point out the damage it will do to this network if you go ahead with the Jarvis Winston story—if it turned out to be true. And *if* it is true, we can handle it internally."

He doesn't have any cards left, Malachek decided. He's down to let's-not-fight-over-this. He's finished.

"Look, Jerry," Malachek said. "I told you I would quit if Antin was hired and I meant it. So chances are I'm not going to be around here too much longer, not if you're ready to make a deal with Mickey Schirmer. So let's be realistic. What can you do to me about Winston? Fire me? Tell the press we had a difference of opinion over a story? All the Sid Neales in the world couldn't make that one fly."

What is he telling me? Rossman wondered. He thought he could sense, somewhere in what Malachek was saying, the makings of a deal. But it was still too obscure and veiled.

If Malachek quits because of Antin, he'll tell the press anyhow and it will make good copy for a day or two. But if he says that he quit because of the Winston story and here's the reason...

His fingers began to tap involuntarily on the table top. Malachek noticed the tiny rat-tat-tat drumming sounds.

"I don't think I have any choice," Malachek said, turning the screws a little harder.

"I would hope, Carl, that you could at least hold off until we get the Cornwall problem settled," Rossman offered.

"You want me to hold off on the Winston story until you've signed Antin? Is that it? Is that what you have in mind?"

"I didn't say that," Rossman countered, making one last effort to stave off Malachek. The outline of Malachek's implied threat was becoming clearer and more ominous. "All I said was that the Cornwall situation is unsettled. Lots of things could happen."

"You didn't answer me, Jerry," Malachek persisted, squeezing still harder. "Tell me what happens if I slow down on the Winston story."

"Would you?" Rossman asked anxiously, grasping at the tiny thread that Malachek was dangling in front of him.

"Lots of things can happen," Malachek said. "But I don't think I'd be too happy if I hold off on the Winston story and pick up the paper and see that Antin is signed for the news."

Rossman felt himself starting to slump in his chair but he stopped himself from doing so. He wasn't going to give Malachek the satisfaction of seeing him physically react like this, crumbling like a blob of wet dough that had been twisted and pounded out of shape.

"You didn't answer my question," he said to Malachek. "Would you slow down, hold off on Winston?"

Now, Malachek thought. Now, I got him.

He was going to beat Rossman and win this one.

No pin-striped film producer like Jerry Rossman who had never seen a hit-and-run victim lying in the snow or caught a County Commissioner trying to fix a ticket or seen a President lying on television, nobody like Jerry Rossman, who probably never had to worry whether his father was going to get fired every other week, nobody like that was going to win on his battlefield.

He had fought too many battles, too many wars, to lose the biggest one of all.

"You forget about Antin," he told Rossman. "Make Burton the anchor. That's the way it should have been all along. I'll take care of Winston." He waited for Rossman to react but Rossman stared silently at his plate.

The network president was stunned. Malachek seemed to be unfazed by the brazenness of his demand. It was as if he were discussing a simple clause in his contract.

Christ, Rossman thought. I never knew he could be such a cold-blooded prick.

"Why, Carl?" he finally asked. "Why does it mean so damn much?"

"I believe in the integrity of what I'm doing," Malachek said. "It's as simple as that. Sure, I want to win and beat the other nets any way I can. I want to stay number one just like you do. But I don't want to fake it. I've got to have an anchorman people will believe in. It's the whole point of what we do. People have got to trust that man sitting there and the minute they start to lose that mystical belief in him, he's gone. That's what makes it all work.

"I'm not hung up on Antin," he went on. "But I believe in the audience's judgment more than you do. They would see through Antin. The first time we sent him out on a major story, or put a major figure on the news at the last minute for him to interview, he'd be finished. And so would we."

"And Burton?"

"Burton is the best we've got. He can do the job for us. People will believe in him, trust him."

"And Winston?"

"Winston can wait," he said.

"Winston can wait," Rossman repeated. *He's got me by the balls.*

"You see, Jerry," Malachek said, "I do have a sense of priorities. And getting the right person to anchor the news is more important to me than exposing Jarvis Winston, no matter how juicy the story is. It can wait."

"It had better wait," Rossman said menacingly. He wasn't going to let Malachek hold the Winston story over him forever. Not if he was going to be bludgeoned into giving Malachek the anchorman choice.

Malachek ignored him. "I'm glad we could get together on this," he said quietly. As far as he was concerned, the discussion was over.

"I think we'd better talk about Burton," Rossman said, trying to make sure that Malachek understood that there was a deal and it was firm.

"I'll leave that to you," Malachek said offhandedly. "I'd like the announcement to come from both of us, though. It has a better appearance."

"Sure, sure," Rossman agreed, loathing Malachek.

"If you want to hold off for another week to let the suspense build up, that's no problem either. I recognize the PR value in all of this."

"We may have to do some testing," Rossman said. "The affiliates may need some massaging. How do you think he will do in test groups?"

"I'm not worried," Malachek said. "The research on him for *Focus* has always been strong. Ask Marty Merrett."

Rossman moved his plate away. He still didn't feel like eating.

"I'll announce Burton to the rest of the executives some time next week," he said dourly. "We'll need some time to notify some of the key affiliates ahead of time. We'll also need to set up some press conferences. Probably a couple of cocktail parties here and on the Coast. Sid Neale's people can work it all out." He said it with no enthusiasm but with a sense of finality and resignation.

"We need to do something for John Cornwall," Malachek pointed out.

"We'll give him a send-off at the affiliate convention," Rossman replied coldly. "Your concern is touching."

"It's all part of the business, Jerry. You know that."

Rossman looked at Malachek with incredulity.

He always had known Malachek to be tough, almost arrogant, unyielding in his defense of the News Division. But he had never seen this side before: mean, cunning, brazenly defiant.

But what could he do? Malachek had him by the balls. But he'd remember it. For a long time.

"I've got some calls to make," he said. He pushed his chair away from the table and got up.

Malachek rose at the same time and walked out of the dining room with him.

The two men stood by the elevator, waiting for it to come up to the twenty-fifth floor. They said nothing to each other and, when the empty elevator arrived, they got in and stood in silence until it reached the thirteenth floor and Rossman got out.

He took a step out and then turned around and held the elevator door open.

"I hope you've got a good agent a year from now, Carl," he said, and let the door close.

Malachek looked at the blinking numbers on the wall of the elevator as it started to descend. 12–11–10. He knew that Rossman would mention his contract. 9–8–7. The doors opened and Malachek walked out.

Fuck him, he thought. A year from now, Rossman could

be out. If the news is still on top, I'll be around for a long time. With a better contract.

He was pleased with himself for the way he had handled Rossman. And he had told him the truth. Getting the right anchor on the evening news was more important than Winston. He could have Winston's ass some other time. After Rossman was gone, if necessary.

It was a trade-off, but so what? He had won the big one.

He walked back into his office and told Judy Rosen to find Art Burton for him.

She reported back a minute later that Burton had left for the day.

"Anything wrong?" he asked.

"No. One of the secretaries down there said he told her he was leaving for the day. Something had come up."

"All right," Malachek said, unconcerned. "I'll speak to him tomorrow."

He sat down in his chair, lit a cigar, and relaxed. He felt confident that he could handle the Winston story with Burton. Subtly, of course, but he could handle it.

Everything was working out. Sometimes you had to play hardball. But now, with Burton, he would have to play just a little bit softer.

Chapter 35

Somehow, in some strange, foreboding way, Art Burton always knew that Bobby Ducoin was alive.

It was not simply a premonition; rather, a belief, rooted in certitude, that the soldier he had left dying in the field in Vietman would some day reappear.

It was an uneasy, disquieting feeling that Ducoin was out there, somewhere, waiting in a distant twilight.

It was an eerie feeling that occasionally would pass

through him like the wind snapping a pile of leaves on a still day.

It was unnatural, as if the rustling leaves were a harbinger of some ominous event.

Maybe it was the nightmare that had recurred over the years; leaving him, at times, soaked with perspiration and trembling under the sheets.

It always had been so vivid, as if he had been lifted out of time and hurled backward into the clearing where they all had marched so long ago; the nameless soldiers, broken figures lying lifeless on the ground, and the living ones; him and the big black one, Eddie Johnston; and the dying one, Bobby Ducoin.

How many times had he been back there, staring at Ducoin, peering with horrified eyes through the tall grass at the mangled flesh, hearing again the strangled cries for help.

No matter how much he wanted to, he never had been able to exorcise the memory. It stayed there, year after year, and somehow, because it always was there, he intuitively knew that Ducoin was alive. And waiting.

Now, as he sat in the living room of his apartment, he still was paralyzed by the letter the production secretary had handed him just a few hours ago.

"Dear Lt. Bertrand," the letter began. "I read in the Tribune paper that you may become the newsman on the evening news. Maybe you don't remember me but I remember you. I was one of the grunts on that patrol that the VC shot up in Nam. Me and the nigger radioman, Johnston, was the ones who didn't get killed. And you. I have not been living like you have all the time since then, least like I read in the paper, and I was thinking maybe we could see each other so you could help me out. Maybe it would make up for some things that happened. My phone number is in Chicago. It is 312–684–3029. I am there most of the time in the afternoons after the Cubs games. Your friend from the Army, Bobby Ducoin (Cpl.)"

It all seemed so bizarre, Ducoin surfacing after all these years. He had no concept of Ducoin as a person, only a remembrance of him as a buried memory, a thing, an anonymous somebody who had been part of a time that still haunted him.

But now that formless shape had materialized. Ducoin was alive, and real, and, through some god-awful twist of fate, the reality was threatening to distort and change his life.

His first instinct after reading the letter had been to find Samantha and tell her about it. *You're not going to believe this*, he would have said, *but I got a letter today from somebody I haven't seen since 1966 in Vietnam. Of all the goddamn things to happen*, he would have said, *just when I was so close to the top*.

But how could he tell her what had happened in the jungle? She'd want to know why he'd kept it a secret for so long. *Besides*, he asked himself, *what can Ducoin do to me?*

Maybe Ducoin doesn't remember anything. After all, how could he? Ducoin had been near death when I found him in the grass. He had been losing blood and was weak. How could he remember that I crawled away?

It did not seem possible. And yet his letter referred to "some things that happened."

Oh God, Burton thought, where the hell did he come from? What rock did he crawl out from under?

Maybe, Burton tried to reassure himself, Ducoin just needs some money. He's down on his luck and figures I'll be an easy touch. He's seen my picture in the papers and he's written to me because that's the way some of these ex-GIs are.

But Burton knew it was more than that. Ducoin wasn't looking for a handout. There was a menacing undertone to his letter, an implicit threat that he would not go away until he got an answer.

As Burton looked at the letter once again, he knew that he had no alternative.

He dialed the number Ducoin had given and waited nervously. Ducoin answered on the third ring.

"Yeah?" Burton heard a voice say.

"Is this Bobby Ducoin?" he asked, desperately trying to recall what Ducoin had looked like.

"Yeah, this is me," Ducoin answered flatly.

"This is Art Burton."

"Hey, Lieutenant, you got my letter! How about that?" Ducoin said, his voice rising with pleasure.

Burton was surprised by Ducoin's reaction. He almost sounds friendly, Burton thought. Maybe he doesn't remember. He tried again to recall something, anything, about Ducoin as a person but nothing came to him.

Ducoin had been just another soldier in the patrol that had left the base camp on that morning. They all had looked the same; faceless figures in the early morning light.

"I'm sorry but I don't remember you," Burton said, hoping that the lie would distance him from Ducoin and discourage the man from going any further.

"But you called," Ducoin said.

"I called because you wrote that we served together in Vietnam. That's the only reason I called—out of curiosity. There's no other reason."

"Sure, Lieutenant, there's a reason, isn't there?" Ducoin said, his voice harsh. "Does it sound funny to be called that again? Lieutenant?"

"I don't have time for this," Burton snapped.

"C'mon, Lieutenant Bertrand, is that the way to talk to someone who served under you?" Ducoin asked with mock respect. "I mean I almost gave my fucking life for you, didn't I?"

Burton winced at Ducoin's use of "Bertrand" but he remained silent. He needed to know what Ducoin had in mind.

"Is there something you wanted to know?" Burton asked. "You wrote me a letter. That's my reason for calling."

"Well, I got a little problem and I figured maybe you could help me," Ducoin said. "That's why I wrote to you. I got a little problem."

"Go on."

"Nah, I don't want to talk about it on the phone. I don't trust no one. I was thinking maybe you could come out here, you know, split a six pack or two and talk about the old days."

He's crazy, Burton thought. He's a psycho and he's in trouble.

"That's not going to happen," Burton said firmly. "I'm not traveling anywhere."

"Ah, c'mon, Lieutenant. You can take a trip once in a while, can't you?"

"I said I'm not going anywhere," Burton repeated.

"Well, I don't have the money to come to New York. Unless, of course, you want to send me the ticket."

Burton was starting to lose his patience. Ducoin didn't bother him now. He irritated him. *He's being cute with me, and I don't have to go along with his little games. He's nothing but trouble.*

"Look," he said icily. "I don't know why you contacted me after all these years, but Vietnam was a long time ago. I don't know you and I don't remember you. So I'm going to hang up and I think you'd be a lot better off if you didn't write me any more because you won't get an answer. Do you understand?"

"Nah, I don't think so, Lieutenant Bertrand," Ducoin said, threat in his tone. "I don't think you should do that."

He really was crazy, Burton decided. One of those vets who never got over the war. He remembered doing a story on one of them once; a bearded guy with his hair in a ponytail, living in a small town in Oregon. Guy got up one morning, put on a pair of fatigues and walked into a doughnut shop and killed thirteen people. Just like that. Thought they were the enemy.

Ducoin could be like that, he thought.

"Don't bother me again," Burton said sharply. Then, for a reason he did not understand, he added, "good luck."

"Don't give me no bullshit, Lieutenant Bertrand," Ducoin erupted. "You remember me all right. And I remember you. Only I don't remember you as what you are now, all fancy with your picture in the paper and making all that money, Mr. Art Burton. Oh no, I remember you from the Nam, crawling away from me like a coon-ass snake and me begging for help."

Burton was unable to hang up the phone. It was as if the words spewing out from Ducoin had sapped his strength, his will. He sat, immobilized, clutching the receiver.

"Now what's all these people out there gonna think when they find out that you're no fucking hero?" Ducoin asked mockingly. "That you got the Bronze Star for leaving me lying there? You don't think I'm not gonna tell them? You think I've been eating shit just so you could make that fancy salary they're talking about in the paper? No way, old buddy. I spent too long in that damn prison camp, Lieuten-

ant. So I think you had better take care of me, real good.
Ain't that right?"

Burton's jaw was clenched so tightly that he felt his teeth
pushing into his gums. He can't do anything to me, he told
himself. He's a mixed-up, crazy vet, and nobody will believe
him. There's nothing he can do. Nothing.

"You're all fucked up," Burton said. "Now don't bother
me any more. Good-bye."

He slammed the phone down, holding it so tightly in his
hand that his knuckles seemed to rise like little foothills from
under his skin.

How in the hell did this happen to me, he thought.
Where did Ducoin come from, where has he been all these
years? How can he suddenly appear like this, from out of
nowhere, to destroy everything I've worked for?

Burton tried again to remember what Ducoin had looked
like, but there was nothing. The only memory was the one he
never had been able to expunge from his mind; Ducoin lying
sprawled in the grass, moaning for help. Even now, as he
thought of it again, a slight shudder went through him.

I have no idea what he looks like, Burton realized. I
don't remember anything about him before that day. But he
knows me. And he remembers. Everything.

Burton stared at the phone again, half-expecting it to
ring but then he realized that Ducoin could not call him at
his apartment. The number was unlisted and, besides, Ducoin
did not know where he lived. Only that he worked at the
network.

And if Ducoin called him at the network, he could be
fended off forever. Burton eagerly pursued the thought.
Ducoin would never be able to get through to him; he'd be in
a meeting, on assignment, out of the country, in conference,
anywhere.

Maybe, after a while, Ducoin would simply give up and
go away.

Nobody is going to pull that shit on me, Bobby Ducoin is
telling himself, sitting there in his room in his shorts and
T-shirt, sweltering in the late afternoon heat, looking again at
the picture in the *Tribune*, waiting for the radio to give the
ball scores after the rush-hour traffic reports, wondering what

the Lieutenant must have thought when he opened the letter.

Must have scared the shit out of him, he's thinking, like some jackrabbit in the burrows, thinking he's safe until he hears that first blast from the shotgun and then it's too late.

Oh yeah, that's what the Lieutenant must have felt like all right. Called right away, didn't he, like he wanted to know what the reason was for me writing to him.

Bullshit! Bobby Ducoin is thinking to himself. Nobody's gonna tell me to fuck off, trying to brush me away like I was some sort of skunk smell you can get rid of by dumping your clothes in Coca-Cola. Oh no, that ain't the way it's gonna happen.

It's been an hour now since the Lieutenant hung up on him, slamming the phone down like he was trying to crawl away again, and all this time Bobby Ducoin has been sitting there, looking at that picture in the *Tribune* like it was one of those prayer cards he used to give out to the nigger funeral-home owners. That's what it is, all right, a ticket to Gloryland, right there staring up at him from the page.

Only it really don't matter what Lieutenant Bertrand, or Burton like he's called now, thinks because things are different now.

It's almost five o'clock in the afternoon in Chicago and Bobby Ducoin has got the window in his room open, letting in the heat and the noises of the buses rumbling up State Street, and the radio is still on, but none of it is bothering him.

He's pulled down the yellowing shade with the stringy fringed tassel in order to keep out the light and he's lying on his bed, thinking about how his life has changed. Just like that.

All this time he's been out there humpin' and he sees one picture in the paper and he knows the good Lord has been looking after him. And he's thinking about all that money he'd better be getting and wondering if the women will come to him once he's got a fancy sports car, maybe one of them foreign ones, and some good clothes from one of the stores on Michigan Avenue.

Oh yeah, that'll be nice, all right.

He reads the article again, thinking about how the Lieutenant hung up on him, and he's telling himself, just like his Daddy told him, there's more than one way to skin 'em once you've got 'em.

Then he goes over to the wooden desk and takes out some writing paper and starts writing another letter.

Oh yeah, Bobby Ducoin tells himself, I'm through taking shit. Forever.

Chapter 36

Charlotte Glover's day in the White House pressroom was almost over.

All that remained, other than the perfunctory check with the assignment desk back at the bureau, was to make a few, final revisions in the script she had been working on for an upcoming feature segment on *American Sunrise*.

The feature was a story on behind-the-scenes arrangements for White House state dinners. Aside from attending the two daily briefings by White House News Secretary Jerry Daniels, Charlotte had spent most of her day developing information for the story.

Now, as she moved the words around on the screen of the small computer terminal on her desk, she decided that the rest of the script could wait until tomorrow.

The cubicle where she worked, littered with mimeographed handouts from the White House Press Office, newspapers, old copies of the *Congressional Record* and releases from various government agencies, felt oppressive and confining.

Although to most people in the profession the tiny cramped space represented the most coveted job in television reporting, besides anchoring the evening news, Charlotte Glover did not regard it in the same way. At least not today.

On this afternoon, anxious to see Gordon Allen and irritated that Carl Malachek had never returned her phone call, Charlotte felt as if her work space was nothing more than a cage, a holding pen, a cell.

She wanted to be elsewhere, at the apartment in the Watergate, testing—because she knew she had to—the limits of her desire for Gordon. But first she had to speak to Malachek about Herman Willows.

The problem was, Malachek had not returned her calls.

She had tried reaching him in the morning but he was busy. Then, when she tried again around lunchtime, Judy Rosen told her that Malachek was in the executive dining room with Jerry Rossman. At three o'clock, he still was not available.

She decided to make one last attempt to reach him. She thought again about what Gordon Allen had said last night when he called to tell her that Willows had committed suicide.

"Don't let me down with Malachek," he had said, almost pleadingly. "The story's over. Willows is dead. You have to go along with me in what we told Malachek."

Then he had asked: can you keep everything you know to yourself, and she had said yes, as she always did when he asked, because she could not help herself.

Now, as she dialed Malachek's private number in his New York office, she wondered if she could maintain the charade that Gordon, with her troubled acquiescence, was playing out.

"Carl Malachek's office."

"This is Charlotte Glover again," she said. "Is he free now?"

Malachek got right on. "I owe you an apology, Charlotte. I should have called you earlier but I was tied up with Jerry Rossman for a good part of the afternoon."

"The Cornwall thing?"

"Yes, Cornwall."

"Have you made a decision yet?"

"We will, soon. Tell me, what's on your mind?"

"I was trying to reach you earlier because I didn't know if you had heard about Herman Willows."

"Heard what?" Malachek asked.

"He committed suicide last night."

The news jarred Malachek, but it did not particularly disturb him. Things like this happened in the real world. The pressure of being a double agent had been too much for the little bastard, he thought.

"Was it in the papers?" he asked. "I didn't read *The Times* all the way through this morning."

"There was a brief item in the final edition of the *Post*. He didn't leave a note."

"I wonder how the White House feels," he said absent-mindedly.

"Why?" she asked.

"They were the ones who briefed me. When I called you last week, I had come from Gordon Allen's office. Allen told me that Willows was being used as a dupe for the Russians. He had been arrested but the cover-up was for national security reasons. They had turned him."

"You didn't tell me that," she said, hating herself. "You only said that the tip was bad."

"I couldn't, at the time. I just wanted you to know that your source was wrong. Nobody was being protected."

Nobody, she thought, except the President and Senator Charles Ramsey. And Gordon Allen.

"I understand," she said quietly.

"I'll have to tell Samantha Stuart," Malachek said. "I finally got a chance to look at the cassettes of her Willows interview. It was pretty damn good. Too bad we got nowhere with it."

"I called Samantha last week," she told him. "She was surprised to hear it was a bad tip."

"You shouldn't share this information on Willows with your source, whoever he is," Malachek said. "It was given to me in confidence and I'm giving it to you only because you're a pro and you're entitled to know. But it shouldn't go any further. If your source asks about Willows, just tell him he was wrong and let it go at that. Okay? I'm sorry it didn't pan out."

"Yes, of course," she answered numbly.

She heard him say, "Thanks, Charlotte, stay in touch. You're one of the best." Then he hung up.

Oh God, she thought, *how can I keep pretending like this?*

Ever since she had told Gordon that she would go along with the fake story about Willows, she had been troubled. Not being able to tell Malachek that she had been right, that the Willows incident was a cover-up, was an open sore that would not heal.

And now that she had remained silent while Malachek innocently parroted the fake story Gordon had told him, the wound bled.

How had she let this happen?

She knew the answer. She loved Gordon and she needed him. But now, more aware than ever before of what her love was doing to her, she wondered how long she could bear the pain. She knew only that she would find out the answer very soon.

She signed off on her computer and called the network assignment desk at the bureau.

"I'm leaving 1600," she said. "I'm on my beeper. The lid is on until the morning."

She walked to the parking lot where, every day, she parked her powder blue Chrysler in the same reserved space. She had picked out the car's color because it seemed so incongruous with everybody's perception of her. It should have been gray, with no trim; or olive green, any color but bright, luminous, powder blue.

She loved the car and what its bright color secretly meant to her. But now, as she drove toward the Watergate apartment, the almost sensual pleasure she usually derived from driving, even for as little as fifteen minutes, was absent.

In its place was the torment produced by the widening conflict between her love for Gordon Allen and her professional ethics and loyalty to Carl Malachek.

Until this afternoon, the conflict had lain beneath the surface of her emotions. She had been aware of it and it had troubled her, even pained her at times, but she had been able to tolerate it because of her passionate need for Gordon.

But the conversation with Malachek had forced her to realize the truth: that if she continued to stay silent, she would lose her self-respect.

Gordon was waiting for her when she let herself into the apartment. He was wearing a light blue and gray plaid suit that matched the soft gray of his eyes. His silver streaked hair was perfectly brushed and everything about him, including the sheen of his highly polished black loafers, was immaculate.

He looked very handsome to her and as he took her in his arms and kissed her, she could smell the faint traces of after-shave lotion.

"How are you, darling?" he asked.

She stood there for a minute, her arms hugging him, holding on to him for support, and said nothing.

"Look at me, Gordon," she said in a distressed voice. "I'm nearly fifty years old and I don't know what I'm doing anymore. I feel so damn helpless."

He looked into her eyes and took her face in his hands. She was near tears.

"Charlotte, darling," he said anxiously. "Tell me what's wrong. I've never seen you this way before."

She pulled away from him. "I spoke to Malachek a little while ago," she said. "I told him that Herman Willows committed suicide."

"And?" Allen asked, a slight edge of anxiety creeping back into his voice.

"And he believed you. He thinks the cover-up was for national security, just like you told him, not to protect Ramsey and the party."

"I'm sorry that I've upset you like this," he said and he kissed her on the mouth.

"I feel so terrible lying to Malachek like this," she said when the kiss ended. "I wish you never had told me, that this could have been kept out of our lives. It all seems so wrong now."

His face showed his concern. "I never dreamed it would backfire like this," he admitted. "The CIA taping the Stuart woman and the President calling in Malachek and Rossman. I never wanted to put you in a position like this, believe me."

"But it happened, Gordon," she said quietly. "And for your sake, I went along with it. I just feel so terrible deceiving Malachek."

"Don't put it that way, Charlotte, me on one side, Malachek on the other. I asked you to protect me because I love you and trust you. Otherwise, I never would have asked."

"It hurts me, what I'm doing," she confessed.

He was silent. Then he kissed her again, and this time she felt the first stirrings within her.

"Do you love me?" she asked tentatively, suddenly afraid.

"I do, darling," he said. He put his hand on her lower back and drew her closer to him. "I love you very much. I want you."

His words aroused her, sensuously working their way

through her body. I want you too, she thought. I need you more than I ever realized.

His hand was caressing her breast and she wanted him to keep it there, to tell him that nothing hurt anymore, the pain from the wound was fading. But as she opened her mouth he pushed his tongue into it and snaked it around her tongue.

A wave of desire rippled through her and she pulled away from him. Quickly removing the jacket of her suit, she tossed it on the sofa. Then she began to unbutton her blouse.

"Let me, Charlotte," Allen said tenderly.

"No, I want to," she answered softly, surprised at herself.

He did not move but watched her, almost hypnotized, as she removed her blouse and then her brassiere. She cupped a breast in each hand and displayed them to Allen, as if she were offering them to him.

"Do you like my breasts?" she asked plaintively.

"Yes, yes," he answered and he ran his fingertips over them.

She reveled in his touch and whispered, "Kiss my nipples. Suck them."

"Yes." He obeyed excitedly, knelt down and moved his lips over her nipples, teasing them with his tongue. She felt herself getting wet and she stepped out of her skirt and panties and stood completely naked in front of him.

"Oh God, Charlotte," he moaned and she pushed his head lower, lower, until she felt his tongue darting around her pubic hair.

"I want you inside of me," she said. "Always. Will you?"

She was thrilled by his near-frenzy. He lifted his face up and said breathlessly, "I want to."

The feeling of power over him was lifting her to new heights. She felt as if she were somebody else, somebody only she had been aware existed within her.

"Please, darling," she said. "Take me," and she felt him gently urging her down to the floor until she was lying on the rug, her legs spread wide and he had pulled his pants down and was pushing inside of her.

"Love me, love me, love me," she moaned wildly. She could feel the swelling of his cock filling the emptiness. Her arms and legs were wrapped around him in a fierce ecstasy and she knew, now, that nothing else mattered as long as she could always have this.

It wasn't until she left the apartment and was driving back to her own apartment in Georgetown that the thought occurred to her. It was all like whoring. Only this was different. She was the one who needed it and was willing to pay for it. With her conscience.

But it was worth it and she pushed the accelerator as if making the car go faster would make the rest of the day and night go faster and bring her closer to tomorrow—and to him.

Chapter 37

Even though he told himself that Bobby Ducoin could not hurt him, Art Burton was not convinced. He lay awake most of the night, afraid that if he fell asleep, deeply asleep, the nightmare, summoned from his subconscious by his conversation with Ducoin, would be more vivid than ever before.

He dreaded the possibility and so he allowed himself only short periods of sleep: so short that nothing—not even a dream, or a nightmare—could take root in them.

He spent the night that way, sporadically opening his eyes to watch the shadows fall across his bedroom and waiting for morning light to push its way through the curtains.

He got out of bed at seven A.M. and went into his kitchen to watch the first segment of news on *American Sunrise*. No major news stories had developed overnight, other than a train derailment somewhere in Arkansas, and so he switched the dial to *Breakfast Time* with Mark Antin, poured a glass of orange juice, and made some instant coffee while he watched Antin's program.

You're good, he told Antin, addressing the TV screen. But you're not good enough.

He felt again as he had when he had watched Antin's cassettes: as if he were scouting a football player, sitting in a press box high above a stadium, analyzing a future opponent;

watching the moves, noticing the eyes, the studied pose with the chin in his hand coming out of a dramatic piece of tape.

"You won't be able to fake it," he said aloud. "People will know."

By the time he finished his coffee, *Breakfast Time* had reached the first half-hour mark and Burton switched the dial back to *American Sunrise* in time to watch Michael Swanson interview an author plugging another diet book.

That's what Swanson does best, he decided, interview authors.

By the time he finished breakfast, showered, shaved, and dressed, it was almost nine o'clock. He left the apartment building near Columbus Avenue and walked down Ninety-second Street to Central Park West.

Years ago, the street had been an unbroken stretch of four-story brownstone buildings, each approached by a flight of mottled gray steps whose monotonous symmetry only accented the undistinguished quality of the street.

In later years, however, some of the brownstones had given way to high-rise apartment buildings, like the one Burton lived in, and the few brownstones that were left, relics of another age, gave the street an architectural polyglot flavor that mirrored the mixture of people in the neighborhood.

Hispanics, blacks, elderly Jews, yuppies, low-income families, they all could be found on this street, or on parallel streets, between Central Park West and Columbus Avenue in the Nineties.

That morning, the urban mix of the street was invigorating, despite the rows of double-parked cars and the sacks of garbage waiting to be collected.

Burton sensed it, and it made him feel alive. He thought about entering the Park at Ninety-third Street, walking through the park to Central Park South and to the network building.

It would take about thirty-five minutes. But he was anxious to see if Ducoin had tried to reach him. He hailed a cab and was in his office twenty minutes later.

There were two messages, both left from yesterday.

"Malachek wants you to call," the production assistant said, "and somebody named Baglio in New Orleans. He said to tell you he got a list."

"Thanks," he said. "Anybody else?" he asked casually.

"No. Nothing."

"Fine." He felt relieved. There had been no call from Ducoin.

He dialed Malachek's extension immediately, but Malachek was in conference and couldn't be reached.

He had better luck with Frank Baglio, who was eating breakfast when Burton called.

"I got your message, Frankie," Burton said. "You didn't waste any time."

"Hey, all it takes is a little doing," Baglio replied.

"What were you able to find out, Frank?" he asked.

"I'm going to get the whole list sometime today," Baglio answered. "Cop I know is going to read it off to me. But it looks like Winston made a lot of calls from his hospital room to an out-of-state number. A lot of calls."

"To where? New Orleans? Vegas?"

"No. Moline, Illinois. I'm asking that a trace be put on the number."

"Can you do that? Legally?"

"No, but I'm doing it."

"Be careful," he told him, then felt foolish for saying it.

"No problem, Armand. You build up a lot of contacts over a while."

"What do you make of it?"

"I think your hunch is right about Winston still betting. A pattern of calls to an out-of-state number from a suspected heavy bettor is a pretty good clue in my book. I mean, you don't have to be Perry Mason to figure this one out."

"How did you get the number?"

"Let's just say somebody owed me a favor. And somebody owed that somebody a favor. That's how it works, Armand. You'd be surprised at the amount of information that flows around. It happens all the time."

"So if I want to find out where's he calling, what that number in Moline is, you can get it?" Burton asked, skeptical.

"Shouldn't be hard," Baglio assured him. "You got to understand, Armie, I'm not talking about putting a tap on the phone. You're talking court orders from a judge or something like that. But, yeah, I can get a trace." He paused for a moment.

"I don't want to tell you how to do your story," Baglio went on, "but you still got to prove it, you know. You still got to show that Winston is heavy into the mob."

"I know," Burton said. "But remember that old Southern recipe for rabbit stew? The one that begins, 'First you catch a rabbit'? Well, I've got a feeling Winston will fold if I can confront him with enough hard facts."

"Why don't you try?"

"Try what?"

"Give him a call. You said you met him already out there in the hospital. Shake him up a little. Drop it on him that you're working on a gambling story. See what he says."

Burton was struck by the simple ingenuity of Baglio's suggestion. He was silent for a moment. Then he said, to himself and to Baglio, "I may just catch myself a rabbit."

"I'll call you later when I get the list," Baglio told him, and said good-bye.

Burton dialed Malachek's number again but Malachek was still in conference. That's always the way, he thought. Malachek is always "in conference." Maybe this time, he speculated, it's about me.

"Leave word that I called again, will you?" he asked, and hung up.

At least Bobby Ducoin had not tried to call this morning. Maybe Ducoin had been testing him, seeing what he could get. Maybe last night was a one-shot.

He eyed the phone on his desk, daring Ducoin to call, and decided to spend the rest of the morning catching up on some reading. He did not want to be out of the office in case Malachek called.

By twelve-thirty he had read the latest issues of *Time* and *Newsweek*, last week's edition of *Variety*, the television columns in *The Washington Post*, the New York *Daily News* and *The New York Times*, and the weather page in *USA Today*. Malachek still had not called.

He had decided to wait until after lunch before calling Jarvis Winston. By the time he returned from lunch, he figured, it would be eleven o'clock on the coast. It would be easier to talk to Winston once the hospital's morning routine was finished.

But now, still anxious to hear from Malachek, he decided to stay in his office and call Winston even though it was only nine-thirty in the morning in California.

Winston was lying on his stomach, having an alcohol rub, when Burton called.

"Yes?" Winston answered in a relaxed voice.

"Jarvis, this is Art Burton. We talked about our show doing a profile on you. How are you feeling?"

"My Nielsen was sagging but I've got a nurse rubbing my back now. It just shot straight up."

Burton could hear a girlish giggle in the background. He wondered for a moment if Winston was getting laid, right there in his hospital room.

"Is it a good time to be calling you? Are the doctors there?"

"Nah, just me and Nurse Elsworthy. You should see her. She is in very good physical shape."

He never stops, Burton thought. He's always on.

"I saw in the trades that you may replace Cornwall. Is that going to happen?" Winston asked.

"I don't know," Burton answered, surprised that Winston followed that part of the business. "Malachek and Rossman haven't decided yet."

"You got an agent?"

"No."

"You should get one. You'll need one. First rule of the business. Big money means agents."

"I figure that's the least of my worries," Burton replied, privately amused at the irony of his statement.

"You know Mickey Schirmer, my agent?"

"I met him when I saw you out there," Burton answered. He wondered if Winston would bring up Mark Antin.

"You ought to think about letting Mickey represent you," Winston advised. "Just a piece of advice. He carries a lot of clout with Rossman."

How much clout, Burton wondered. Enough to get Antin the anchor job?

"It's something to think about," Burton lied, certain there was no way he would get an agent now. Malachek would never forgive him.

"So, it's nice to hear from you," Winston said. "What's on your mind?"

"I just wanted to tell you that the profile is still in the planning stage for one of the *Focus* shows in the fall, once the new season starts. At the moment we're working on a couple of other big pieces. Investigative stuff."

He waited to see if Winston would come back at him. He did. *"60 Minutes shtick?"*

"Sort of. Pentagon waste, used-car racket in the Midwest, big-time gambling ring, that type of thing."

Burton said it casually, but he noticed a heartbeat of a pause before Winston began to talk again.

I've connected, Burton thought.

"Sounds interesting," Winston said. "You spend a lot of time on this stuff?" he asked, almost too casually, Burton thought.

"We have field producers doing some of the groundwork," Burton said offhandedly. "I'll do some of the stories. Samantha Stuart probably will do one of them. She's the featured correspondent on the show."

Burton was curious to see how far Winston would probe, how much he wanted to know. *Maybe he'll go right where I want to take him.*

"I'll probably do the gambling story if it works out," he said. "Stories like that are always juicy. You know, mob money, big payoffs." He wondered if he had gone too far.

"Sounds good," Winston responded after a moment's silence. "It must take a lot of work to do a story like that."

He's still fishing, Burton decided, and he decided to let Winston go in a little deeper. Shake him up, Frankie Baglio had advised him. See what happens.

"A lot of it is just old-fashioned legwork. You know, researching phone records, things like that."

"Phone records?" Winston said, and Burton could hear an undercurrent of anxiety in Winston's voice.

"They're tough to get but sometimes you can," Burton said. I hope the bastard's squirming.

"Phone records must be interesting, if you find out who's being called," Winston said.

"Sometimes you can," Burton said.

"How?"

"Trade secret," Burton said lightly.

"Yeah? Well, that's entertainment," Winston replied but there was no humor in his voice. "Listen, if you see Jerry Rossman tell him the flowers are beautiful, even if he did send me a funeral wreath."

"I will," Burton promised. "We'll let you know about the profile," he added.

He hung up, excited by Winston's reaction. The man wasn't asking questions just out of curiosity.

He wants to know how much I know. How do I get the phone records? How can I tell who's being called? How much work does it take? Those weren't innocent questions. Winston's worried.

He checked to see if there had been any calls. None. Nothing from Malachek. Nothing from anybody.

Maybe he'd gotten rid of Ducoin after all. It was a comforting thought, and he carried it with him as he walked to the elevator. Maybe Malachek would see him when he got back.

In his hospital room, Jarvis Winston rolled over on his back.

"Do me a favor, baby," he said to the nurse. "Look in that address book and get me the number of Mickey Schirmer, S, C, H, in New York. I want to make a call."

He closed his eyes and waited for her to find the number.

Mickey could find out, he was sure, what kind of story those clowns in network news were working on. That was the way to handle it. Find out if the story involved a bookie operation in New Orleans or Moline, Illinois. That was all he needed to know. Then he'd figure a way out of it. The old *keppela* would take care of the rest.

Chapter 38

It was almost four o'clock in the afternoon when Malachek finally summoned Art Burton.

Malachek had spent most of the day discussing with Barbara Schumacher and her people the outlines of a major promotion campaign that would run as soon as the new anchorman was announced for the evening news.

There would be a big budget, well over half a million dollars, she told him, with full-page ads in major newspapers and a series of thirty- and sixty-second promotional spots running in prime time for a three-week period leading up to the new season.

"It's hard to grasp this without a face in there," she said as they looked at a mock-up of an ad showing pictures of major news events surrounding a blank space in the middle of the dummy page.

He Shares The World With You was the boldly lettered headline at the top of the page. In the empty white space in the middle, Malachek knew, there would be a picture of Art Burton. But even Burton did not know that yet. Neither did Schumacher.

She would have to wait until next week when Rossman would make the formal announcement to all the executives. Until then, everything had to be held tight.

"Has Rossman seen this yet?" he asked her.

"Yes, he likes it," she answered quickly, knowing that invoking Rossman's approval would forestall any objections from Malachek.

"Don't worry," she added. "He didn't tell me who it's going to be."

"The ad's good," he said gruffly, ignoring her remark, and he asked to keep the mock-up for a day or two in case it generated any new ideas.

Now, alone in his office, he studied the pictures in the ad—a space shuttle launch, a bombing in Beirut, the President at an Economic Summit, a guerrilla group in Nicaragua, a hurricane in Florida—as if the pictures and the headline in the ad were visual proof of his victory in the struggle for the anchorman.

He was still savoring the idea when Judy Rosen informed him that Art Burton was waiting outside.

He rolled up the ad and went out to greet Burton and escorted him into his office.

"I've been in meetings all day," he explained as Burton sat down, "but I'm glad we're finally getting a chance to talk."

He walked over to a cabinet underneath the stack of three television monitors and opened a door to reveal several bottles of scotch, bourbon, vodka, tonic water, Perrier, and cans of diet drinks.

"You want a drink?" he asked Burton.

Something's going to happen.

"No," Burton answered. "It's a little too early for me."

Malachek opened another door in the cabinet and dropped some ice into a glass and splashed some scotch over it, then sat down next to Burton.

He eyed Burton as if he were sizing him up for some yet-to-be-revealed mission. Burton knew that Malachek was scrutinizing him but the man's face was impassive. It was impossible to tell what Malachek was thinking. It made Burton uncomfortable.

"You wanted to see me?" Burton asked.

"I have very good news for you," Malachek said slowly. "Jerry Rossman and I have agreed that you should replace Cornwall on the evening news."

Oh my God, Burton thought. I've got it! He was aware that his heart was beating wildly and he felt embarrassed by his own excitement. He could hear himself a voice inside shouting, It's me! It's me!

He leaned across the desk and impulsively shook Malachek's hand.

"I won't let you down," he said. "I'm going to give it everything I've got."

"I know you will, Art," Malachek said, almost benignly. He was pleased at Burton's attitude. It was just the right mixture of confidence and humility. He liked that. It was what he expected from Burton.

"I don't know what to say," Burton confessed. "I guess you never can be fully prepared for something like this, no matter how much you think about it."

"Did you think much about it, before this?" Malachek asked. He was curious about Burton's professional genes. Had the anchor always been in his blood?

"Doesn't everybody?" Burton said. He thought for a moment about his early days in television news, sixteen years ago, sitting in WBID's newsroom every night, watching Robert Miniver.

Even then, he'd wondered what it was like to be on the network every night, with all those millions of people watching you, being so damn famous that everybody recognized you. And now it was all going to happen to him.

"I told you the first time we discussed this that your life is going to be different," Malachek cautioned.

"The anchorman of the evening news is the symbol of the network. You are what we, the network, are to the public. You make a speech, it's the network talking. You write an article, it's the network writing. You're more than the front man for the News Division. You're the network's best foot forward. With the public. With advertisers. With opinion makers. With the whole damn shooting match out there. It's a hell of a responsibility, Art. I know you won't take it lightly but just keep in mind, always, that it's a hell of a lot more than just reading the news for twenty two minutes a night."

Malachek's vision of the anchorman's role sobered Burton. Hearing him talk about it made it suddenly, seriously real.

"We've never talked about money. We should settle that as quickly as possible," Malachek said. "Do you have an agent?"

"No," Burton said. "But I'll get a lawyer to handle the contract."

He never had been able to understand the elaborate minuet that required correspondents and producers to negotiate with Tom Hickson, the News Division's contract attorney, even though everybody knew that Malachek called the tune from Seven West.

"The announcement will be made next week," Malachek informed him. "I went over some of the promotion plans with Barbara Schumacher today. You want a preview?"

Burton nodded and walked over as Malachek unfurled the mock-up ad. Malachek pointed to the white space in the middle of the page.

"Your picture will go in there," he said. Burton could visualize it, just as he could almost see his picture, in full color, going up on the wall in the corridor leading to Seven West.

"There probably will be a press conference some time next week," Malachek continued, "and a couple of cocktail parties. Sid Neale likes 21 so we'll probably be there. Neale's people will take care of everything once the announcement is made. And you should plan on going to LA for the affiliates meeting, of course."

"It's all happening so fast," Burton said.

"Yes, it came together very quickly," Malachek agreed, glad that Burton would never need to know how it all had happened.

"What about the test groups? And Antin?" Burton asked eagerly. "How did that all come out?"

"You don't have to worry about the test groups," Malachek assured him. "And Rossman finally realized that Antin wasn't right."

"Can I tell anybody about this?" Burton asked, thinking only about Samantha.

"Hold off until the final announcement," Malachek said. "It's only a matter of another couple of days."

Malachek sat down, then added, casually, "Anything new on the Winston story?"

"Yes, some interesting developments," Burton replied. He told Malachek what Frank Baglio had come up with and the anxiety he had detected in Winston when he had spoken to him.

"You called Winston? Today?" Malachek asked.

"Yes. Why?" Burton perceived a slight edge to Malachek's voice, as if Malachek had been offended by something he had said. He did not understand it and it bothered him.

"What kind of reaction did Winston have?" Malachek asked.

"Nervous. Curious. I think he's worried we may come up with something. At least I hope he is."

"It's risky," Malachek mused aloud. Then, catching himself, he added, "You don't want to press too hard this early."

A tiny alarm went off in Burton's mind, as if Malachek had inadvertently tripped a sensory wire alerting him that something was wrong.

"I thought it was a good idea."

"It is," Malachek said. "But I don't want to push too fast on this without checking it all the way. We both know how sensitive it is."

Yes, Burton thought, but yesterday it didn't seem to matter. *If you can prove it, we'll go with it*, Malachek had told him. Now subtly he was suggesting that Art slow down. Don't push too hard. Don't rock the boat.

"Have you lined up any interviews yet?" Malachek asked.

"You mean with Winston?"

"Yes."

"I haven't gotten that far. I'm still in the digging stage. I'd like to see the phone records first. And I want to find out if the number he's calling is a bookie operation. You know, start putting the elements together."

"This may take some time," Malachek said. "Don't rush into it. Don't be too hasty."

Burton was concerned by what Malachek seemed to be telling him. Somehow, Malachek did not seem to be as fully committed to the story as he had been yesterday.

"Are you saying I should hold off for a while?" he asked. Could it be what he suspected? Winston for him? A trade-off?

Malachek eyed Burton warily. "We'll do the story," he said grimly. "Winston's not going to go away."

Burton was silent. He did not want to believe what Malachek seemed to be saying. He could not believe that Malachek had, in effect, blackmailed Rossman on the anchorman choice by threatening to put the Jarvis Winston story on the air.

He thought back to the first time he had sat in this office, hoping that Malachek would like him enough to offer him a job with the network. He had been so eager then, so willing to believe in the integrity of the network and all that the News Division represented.

And now, years later, he was learning the truth. The Emerald City was just another small town in Kansas and Oz was just another carnival barker, playing a power game for his own personal reasons.

It had been less than a day since he had told Malachek everything he had found out about Jarvis Winston. And Malachek had said that, "It all came together very quickly."

Was that the way it happened up here in the executive suite?

It was all so disillusioning and yet he knew that he would not say anything.

He would tell Samantha, of course. He could not keep it from her.

But everybody else—George Durgin, Charlie Lane, Mark Antin, everybody in the whole damn business—would think he had been chosen to replace John Cornwall purely on his own merit.

What a shitty business.

"I'll keep checking around on Winston," he said, knowing that Malachek would interpret his words as "message received."

"Fine, I'll keep you posted on everything," Malachek said, rising from his chair. He walked with Burton to the door of his office, wondering what Burton was thinking, if Burton was genuinely suspicious of what had gone on between Rossman and him.

If he is, Malachek decided, *he's not showing it. He'll be fine.*

"Thanks for backing me," Burton said, shaking Malachek's hand. It felt like a cold, wet fish.

Burton walked down the corridor of Seven West and glanced at the color pictures, enlarged to poster size, of Robert Miniver and John Cornwall that hung from the walls.

The pictures were formal poses; each man in a dark suit, white shirt, conservative necktie; a sincere, trusting expression on the face, looking straight at the camera lens.

This is it. The line of succession. Miniver. Cornwall. And now me.

What if he'd never told Malachek about Winston and his gambling ties? What if he had kept it buried? Would it still be his picture going up there on the wall? Or somebody else's, such as Mark Antin's?

He wanted to believe that the outcome would have been the same, that he still would have been chosen to succeed Cornwall. But he knew now that he could never be sure and that Malachek would never tell him.

When he got to Samantha's office, she was lying on her couch, her feet propped up on throw pillows, and reading a copy of *Yachting.*

He closed the door and said quietly, "I've got news."

She moved to make room for him on the couch.

"What is it?" she asked eagerly.

"The Cornwall job," he said, smiling slightly in anticipation of her reaction. "I've got it."

"Oh Art!" she exclaimed. "Is it really true?"

She threw her arms around him and hugged him. "I can't believe it! I'm so happy!"

He brushed her hair back off her forehead and kissed her on the mouth, lingering for a moment.

"It's hard for me to believe, too," he said, with no show

of emotion. "It's going to be announced next week. I've just come from Malachek's office."

"What did he say? Tell me everything!"

He kissed her again, wanting to share with her not only his love but, now, his disillusionment as well.

"Let's take a walk," he said, suddenly desperate to escape the network building and be alone together.

"Something is bothering you," she said, clearly worried.

"I feel like I've been cooped up all day. I need some fresh air."

"Aren't you going to tell me what Malachek said?"

"Yes, of course. We can sit and talk in the park."

They left the building just as the first wave of the two thousand network employees began to empty out of the elevators and into the streets to begin their journeys home.

Within minutes, Art and Samantha were in the maelstrom of Fifth Avenue at five o'clock on a sweltering summer afternoon.

The crowds of shoppers, tourists, and homeward-bound commuters surged past. Carried along by their momentum, and withered by the heat that was made even more oppressive by the sun reflecting off skyscraper windows to the sidewalks below, Art and Samantha moved rapidly toward the park.

By the time they crossed the great circular plaza facing the east entrance to the Plaza Hotel between Fifty-eighth and Fifty-ninth Streets, they both felt as if they had been walking for hours.

"This wasn't such a smart idea," Samantha said as she took a handkerchief from her purse and wiped her face.

"I didn't realize it was so hot," Art said and he motioned to a park bench whose only other occupant was a bearded young man idly throwing bread crumbs to a gathering flock of pigeons.

They sat down and Art took his jacket off and stretched his arm behind Samantha's back as if to shield that part of her body from the sun and the heat.

"You were going to tell me about Malachek," Samantha said. "What did he tell you? Aren't you pleased?"

"I told him about Winston," Burton began. "I told him yesterday, everything I had, everything I suspected, the works."

"I'm glad," she said approvingly. "What did he say?"

"It went fine. He was shocked, I think, about Winston but he didn't flinch from the story. He told me to keep working on it and if I came up with the proof, he said he would back me on it. There was no doubt about it."

"That's what you wanted, wasn't it?"

"Of course. That's the way I always figured him to be. No favorites. Straight down the line."

"And when did you ask him about the anchor job? Yesterday?"

"Indirectly. I asked if getting the story on the air would jeopardize my chances with Rossman."

"And?"

"He said I shouldn't worry about it. If I was named to succeed Cornwall, he would take care of the Winston story."

"Well, it worked out then," she observed happily.

"Not really," he said in a voice that instantly deflated her. "Today, when he told me that I had been chosen to replace Cornwall, he also told me to go slow on the Winston story. He wanted me to play it very carefully, to really cool it."

"Maybe he wants to be careful for legal reasons. You know, Winston will probably file a huge lawsuit if he thinks you're libeling him."

"Malachek wasn't saying that, Samantha. He never mentioned lawyers or anything. He was telling me to watch myself. That's what it was, to watch myself, don't spoil anything for myself."

She was silent and he wondered if she understood what he was telling her.

"Don't you see what's happened, Samantha?" he asked in a frustrated voice. "It's all a big game. All the work I've put into the Winston story, the trips to Vegas, to LA, to New Orleans. Malachek probably laid it right on Rossman's desk and said, 'I pick the anchor or else.' And Rossman gave in to him because he couldn't stand the idea of the Winston scandal. Add the Winston story on top of Cornwall leaving and Rossman would be out at the next stockholders' meeting."

"You don't know that's what happened," she argued, trying to convince him and herself.

"I'll never know," he said, "unless I somehow wrap up the Winston story and try to get it on the air. But once I start anchoring, it's going to be hard to keep working on Winston.

Malachek knows that as well as I do. In a few weeks, I'm
going to be tied to the studio every night. My professional
life will completely change.

"I can't ask Malachek how it happened," he continued.
"He's backed me from the beginning. Besides, what's the
point? I wanted the anchor job and I got it. It's just that I'll
wonder if I got it for the wrong reason."

"Maybe Malachek thought you were more important
than Winston," she said finally. "Doesn't that count for
something?"

He shook his head. "No," he answered quietly. "When
you and I talked the other night, about the ethics of the
business, we both agreed I could never live with myself
unless I told Malachek about Winston. Even if it meant
risking the anchor job. But now it's Malachek who wants to
soft-pedal it. The biggest hard ass in the business. Expose his
own grandmother if she was a crook. He's the one who wants
to go slow, for his own personal reasons. That's what I find so
hard to accept."

He was silent for a moment and then he said, "At least
my conscience is clear. I didn't bury the story, like he's doing
now."

"Will you still keep working on it, now that this has
happened?"

"I don't know," he admitted. "Maybe there's a way it can
be done. I don't want to double-cross Malachek on it, go
behind his back. Maybe it will have to wait for a while."

His eyes followed the flock of pigeons edging along the
pavement toward the scattered bread crumbs.

"Happy as a lark, isn't that the phrase?" he said, as if
talking to himself. "Happy as the pigeons, free as the birds,
all that bullshit. It doesn't quite work out that way all the
time, does it, Samantha?"

"Don't be so hard on yourself, darling," she said. "You've
done the right thing all through this. You shouldn't feel bad
about yourself."

"Then why can't I be happy?" he asked her. "Today
should have been one of the biggest days of my life and, for
all of about one minute, it was. I was floating on air up there
in Malachek's office, Samantha. I was being named to the
biggest on-the-air job in the business. And now I'm sitting

here on a park bench with you, watching pigeons nibble on bread crumbs, and I don't feel happy at all."

"You're just guessing all of this about Malachek," she said.

"I'm putting one and one together and I'm getting two," he answered, "and I'm doing it without the help of anything other than my own intuition. And when Malachek tells me, one day after I've told him about Winston—and after waiting all these weeks—that I'm the anchorman—but, oh by the way, Art, maybe you should slow down on Winston, I get two every time. Don't you?"

She didn't respond.

"You would have thought he would have been a little more subtle," he went on. "You know, waited a day or two to ask me about Winston. But he was as subtle as a battering ram. I got the message, believe me."

He noticed the distressed look in her eyes and he took her hand. "Look, maybe you're right. Maybe I should feel better about it. What the hell. It's everything we've been talking and dreaming of ever since Malachek first came to me about the Cornwall job.

"So maybe a week from now, when the publicity starts and then, later, when I start doing the program, all of this will seem less important than it does now. But right now, I feel like I've been had. It should have been great, Samantha, but it's empty."

"Think about it, Art. Malachek didn't tell you to kill the Winston story, did he? He didn't order you off the story."

"Maybe you're right," he responded, still unconvinced.

She squeezed his hand as if to say, believe me.

Ever since he had first told her about the Cornwall job, in the intimacy of her bedroom, she had wanted it for him. But the Cornwall job would mean more than just the professional rewards for Art. It also would mean a change in their lives.

With Art anchoring the evening news, there would be a stability to his life. He would not be on the road as he had been, doing stories for *Focus*, then returning to New York to edit the pieces and anchor the program each week.

Other than stories of great magnitude, such as summit meetings or Presidential trips abroad, he would be in New York, permanently. And, even if she had to travel for *Focus* once every few weeks, there still would be an orderliness to their lives.

They could plan for dinner, movies, weekends, anything, with a reasonable certainty that their plans could be realized.

They could, at last, seriously consider marriage.

Up until now, they had been forced to squeeze and adjust their personal lives in order to accomodate the demands of their careers.

She would be off in Mississippi on a story or he would be in California and they would see each other for a day or two surrounding the taping of *Focus* and then it would be another cycle of sporadic chances to be with each other.

Last month, after they had planned for weeks to spend a weekend at her cottage in Gloucester, he had been forced to cancel at the very last minute. A light plane carrying a rock band had crashed somewhere in the early morning hours and George Durgin had wanted him to fly to the scene to start working on a story tracing the band's meteoric career.

That was the way it'd always been. The very unpredictability of the news business itself had made their own lives unpredictable.

But anchoring the evening news would mean that Art would have a pattern to his life; a symmetry framed by five nights a week in the studio, and that could mean more to both of them than all the money and the prestige of the evening news.

"Don't be disillusioned," she told him. "It's still going to be wonderful for you, for the both of us, even if Malachek is playing games."

He smiled at her and, in the brief tenderness of the moment, he thought about telling her about Bobby Ducoin, finally telling her everything.

Maybe she would understand. But why should she have to worry?

"C'mon," he said to Samantha, trying to wipe Ducoin from his mind. "Let's go back." They got up and walked along the sidewalk. Frightened by Art and Samantha's approaching footsteps, a flock of pigeons huddled together. Then, in frantic formation, they rose toward some trees in the distance.

Art loosened his grip on Samantha's hand and looked at the sky.

The birds were flying away. Maybe it was an omen.

Maybe all of the problems were going to disappear and vanish just like that: Malachek, Rossman, Winston, and . . . Bobby Ducoin.

He looked at the sky again and smiled. The birds were gone.

Chapter 39

A letter from Bobby Ducoin to Carl Malachek arrived on Friday morning, stamped Special Delivery and marked "CONFIDENTIAL."

Because of the Special Delivery label, the envelope lay on top of the pile of letters, interoffice memos and the daily press packet on Malachek's desk when he arrived at his office.

Malachek opened the letter and read it in stunned silence. Then he read it again, trying to cope with its devastating impact.

"Dear Mr. Malachek," it began. "I saw your name in the same newspaper article about Art Burton so I'm writing to you because it says you are his boss.

"I was in the Army with Art Burton only his name then was Armand Bertrand. But he is the one and the same. The outfit was Baker Company of the 1st Battalion, 23rd Infantry in Vietnam. I'm sure you have ways of checking it out.

"What I'm writing to tell you is that Bertrand turned chicken and left me dying on the day we were attacked by the VC in July, 1966, in the Nam. He pulled the radioman away but he left me there to die with my arm all blown off but I got taken prisoner and spent seven years in the prison camp.

"I never knew about him until I saw this story

in the paper that also says he got a medal. I know that's bullshit, for sure. The only reason he's got the medal is because I never knew what happened to him until now.

"I'm telling you all this now because I think a lot of Americans would like to know about him but you can find out for yourself. The nigger radioman was named Eddie Johnston and he lived in Mississippi, just like I did. He was from Grovedale, near the Memphis line. Maybe you can check him out too.

"I have been thinking what to do with this. I have thought about it for a long time. Maybe you should call me at 312–664–3209 so we can meet somewhere and talk about it.

"Sincerely, Bobby Ducoin."

"Oh my God," Malachek groaned aloud.

He leaned his elbow on the desk and rested his head in the palm of his hand. He held the letter in his other hand and stared at it as if he had just caught a scabrous, scaly insect crawling out across his desk.

He read the letter again, the details battering him like hammer blows wielded by an unseen assailant.

The Army unit in Vietnam. The name of the radioman. Even the claim that Burton's real name was Bertrand.

It was devastating.

If it ever became public that Burton had a tarnished war record, one that he had kept secret all this time, there would be no way Burton could anchor the evening news.

Burton never would be accepted in the anchor role. In the eyes of the viewers, he would be less than perfect and the anchor had to be spotless.

He needed another choice for anchor.

The impact of Ducoin's letter was magnified because, Malachek knew, if Burton's chances were finished, there would be little time to start over, to take on Rossman again.

But what if nobody found out?

It would take money to keep Ducoin quiet, of course. But what if it did? Ducoin, Malachek reasoned, was a piece of scum. Five or ten thousand—even twenty—would be enough to shut him up. The network pissed that away on one lousy cocktail party.

He would not even have to tell Rossman. The money could be written off as a payment to a free-lancer—an option on footage from Angola or Afghanistan or Iran. It would be easy.

For a moment, he pictured himself making the payoff to Ducoin, meeting under the El or at the Lincoln Park Zoo or by the lions at the entrance to the Art Institute, handing him an unmarked envelope, saying nothing, walking away.

Jesus, he thought, repulsed by the realization that he even had considered paying off Ducoin. How the hell did all of this happen?

Hell, how could he have known that Burton was covering up something that happened a long time ago? The man had sat here in his office and told him there was nothing in his background to worry about.

How could he have known that Burton was lying?

And yet he felt he should have known. There should have been some signal, triggered by years of experience, to warn him that he was making a mistake in judgment. But there had been no flashing lights, no alarms. Nothing.

The truth was, he had misjudged Burton's character and he could not forgive himself.

Cornwall's walkout had surprised him, but in that his judgment had not been mistaken. In a way, it had been confirmed. He'd always figured Cornwall for a dilettante, wandering through the news business like a member of the landed gentry inspecting his estate. Cornwall's decision to leave was just the final proof of his basic lack of commitment.

It did not weaken Malachek's faith in himself.

But he had also been certain about Burton. Burton was solid. He had come up the hard way, like he had. He was a good reporter who liked a good story.

Look at the way he had dug in on Jarvis Winston, like a dog gnawing at a bone. He had been the perfect choice to replace Cornwall.

Christ, how could he have been so wrong?

The first thing he needed to do was to check on the statements in Ducoin's letter.

First he would have Robert Forrest, the correspondent at the Pentagon, run a check on service records. There would have to be a record somewhere, probably on a computer by now, of a Bobby Ducoin and an Armand Bertrand and an Eddie Johnston of Grovedale, Mississippi.

That would be the first step, the key to everything else, to see if those men had served together in Vietnam. Then he'd get the Atlanta bureau to check the Grovedale, Mississippi, phone book on the chance that an Eddie Johnston was listed. If there was such a person, he would call him.

And then, if it all checked out, he would confront Art Burton.

Malachek got up and walked over to the window, rage growing that one letter from some scumbag was threatening to destroy everything he had achieved.

Who is this Ducoin? Who the hell is he? Does he live in Chicago? Does he take the El? Does he know what it's like to see the snow turn piss yellow after it's been on the sidewalk for three months in the winter? Does he know what it's like to see the boats moored in Belmont Harbor by Lake Shore Drive and wonder who's rich enough to own them? Who is this man who's stinking up my city?

He strode back to his desk and quickly dialed the number in the letter. After two rings, it was picked up.

"My name is Malachek," he said angrily after hearing a dull "Yeah?"

"Are you Ducoin?" he barked.

"Yeah, that's right," Ducoin answered slowly. "I'm Ducoin."

"This letter that you wrote. I'm calling to tell you that it's dangerous business. You can get in trouble for this."

"Can I?" Ducoin asked, mocking him. "Only thing is, it's true. Every damn word of it."

"We get letters like this all the time. Anything further from you and you'll hear from our lawyers."

"No one else knows what I know," Ducoin warned. "Just you and me and one other person—and that one is yours."

"Forget it," Malachek barked.

"Nah, I ain't gonna forget it," Ducoin shot back. "How the hell can I? Would you? Son of a bitch left me to die. You don't forget things like that."

Malachek winced at the thought of Burton as a coward. It couldn't be true and yet there was a bitterness to Ducoin's voice that was too genuine. He was becoming harder to disbelieve.

"You're wrong about this," Malachek said.

"You got a lot of reporters. Go on and check it out. See if I'm telling the truth or not.

"You ain't afraid of that, are you?" he added tauntingly.

"Don't play games with me, mister," Malachek shouted.

"Hey! What makes you think your shit shines, huh? You wanna know something? Your shit stinks just like the rest of us."

Malachek slammed the phone down. "Son of a bitch," he muttered.

Ducoin's arrogance infuriated him but he knew that it was an arrogance bred of certitude.

All that remained was to verify what Ducoin was saying.

It would have to be done quickly. Time was important. The announcement about Burton was scheduled for next week and, if Ducoin's charges were true, he would have to tell Rossman right away. By Monday, at the latest.

After making a call to the Pentagon correspondent and requesting a check into the service records of the three men, Malachek dialed the network's Atlanta bureau and told the bureau chief, Larry Shienfeld, what he wanted.

"I never heard of Grovedale," Shienfeld admitted. "Is it on the map?"

"It's south of Memphis," Malachek said. "It may be in Neshoba County. Do you remember, where those three civil rights workers were killed?"

"That was before my time, Carl," Shienfeld said.

Had it been that long? Twenty, twenty-one years ago?

"Wait a minute," Shienfeld said. "I found it on a highway map here. You're right. It looks about seventy miles south of the Tennessee state line. Neshoba County."

"Give me a call if you can find a number for Johnston," Malachek told him. "Eddie Johnston."

Ten minutes later, Shienfeld had a number for Malachek. Malachek glanced at his watch. Ten o'clock in the morning, nine in Mississippi. It was not too early to call.

He called and a man answered.

"Is this Mr. Johnston?" Malachek asked.

"Yes. That's me."

"My name is Carl Malachek, Mr. Johnston. You've never heard of me, I'm sure, but I'm with one of the television

networks in New York. I'm president of the News Division.
I'm in charge of the news.

"I'm calling from New York, Mr. Johnston. I trust I'm
not disturbing you."

"This some kind of a joke?"

"No, no, it's not a joke," Malachek hastily assured him.

"Why are you calling?"

"We're doing a program on the Vietnam War," Malachek
said, wondering what Johnston looked like. "Somebody told
us to talk to you."

"You are joking."

"You served with the 23rd Infantry Division, that right?"

"Yes."

"First Battalion, Baker Company?" Malachek asked
anxiously.

"That sounds right."

Malachek felt his stomach churning.

"We were told you were injured by mortars. In 1966."

"That was a long time ago. How do you know stuff like
that?" He sounded suspicious.

"We've been doing a lot of interviews," Malachek said.
"Do you remember a Lieutenant Bertrand?"

There was a long pause. Malachek waited, dreading
Johnston's answer.

"Haven't thought of him in a long time. You talked to
him?"

It was the answer he had feared.

"No. But we have his name too. Was he your commanding officer?"

"Oh, you're going back a long time, mister. I remember
that the Lieutenant and me were in the hospital together
after the attack. I was in a different outfit after that. But he's
the one who got me in the chopper. You know where he is?"

"I think so."

"I haven't thought about him in a long time. New
Orleans boy, I think."

Jesus, Malachek thought. "How about a Bobby Ducoin?
Do you remember anyone named Ducoin?"

"Who?"

"Ducoin."

"You go back a long time like that and it's hard to
remember much of anything. I mean, you're talking a long

time ago. You know, like I was a kid then. So I don't remember too many names or faces any more. The Lieutenant, of course, I remembered his name once you mentioned it. But Ducoin don't mean anything to me."

Malachek looked again at Ducoin's letter, lying on his desk next to the phone. "He was from Mississippi," Malachek said.

The pause seemed unending. Then, finally, Johnston said, "Oh yeah, that runty little guy. He the one?"

"I don't know," Malachek said. "I've never seen him. Can you remember anything else?"

He waited for Johnston to answer and, when there was nothing, he said, "I was told he was badly injured in the mortar attack that day. That he was lying in the field near you after the mortars hit. Does that come back to you at all?"

Johnston murmured a long, soft "Oh," and Malachek realized that whatever had happened long ago, Johnston was beginning to recall it.

"Oh yes, I remember who you're talking about," Johnston said. "He was crying like a low dog howling in the night. I remember telling the Lieutenant he was alive. He's alive, I kept saying, as plain as I'm talking to you now."

Malachek felt slightly ill, the same way he had when Cornwall had first told him he was leaving. He nervously tapped his foot on the floor, waiting to see if Johnston had anything more to say. But he already had heard enough.

"He alive?" Johnston asked.

"Ducoin? Yes, he's alive," Malachek said.

"Never did like him, now that I think about it. You know, I could tell he didn't care much for my kind but I felt much the same about him too."

"Did Lieutenant Bertrand try to save him too?" Malachek asked, making a fist of his hand to steady it.

"Tell the truth, I don't remember too much about that day. I remember there was me, and the Lieutenant, him crawling around near me, and Ducoin moaning out there for help. The Lieutenant got me on the sling and they got me up in the chopper. I guess I thought he did it for Ducoin too. I mean, got him out of there, like me."

"Lieutenant Bertrand never mentioned him?"

"Might have, but I wouldn't remember something like

that. Could have been on the chopper but I was hurt too bad to remember anything. That was a long time ago."

"Yes, it was," Malachek said sympathetically. He felt sorry for bursting in on Johnston like this, a stranger calling him at nine o'clock in the morning, lying to him about a program about Vietnam, pumping him about things that happened almost twenty years ago.

"What are you going to do with all this stuff? I mean, why do you want to know all these things?" Johnston asked.

"We may be doing a television program about the war. We are looking for interesting stories. What kind of work do you do, Mr. Johnston?" Malachek asked.

"Chicken farmer. I got a couple of big sheds, couple a hundred layers. I sell the eggs to one of the chains up in Memphis."

"I appreciate your taking the time to talk to me," Malachek said.

"You going to see any of those people you been asking me about? Ducoin? Lieutenant Bertrand?"

"Maybe. Maybe Lieutenant Bertrand," Malachek said. "I don't know."

"Well, maybe they'll remember me if you ask them," Johnston said.

"Yes," Malachek agreed. "I'll ask about you if I see them. Good luck to you." Then he said good-bye and hung up.

God, he thought, what a mess.

Everything Ducoin had said in his letter was holding up. Ducoin had been injured in the attack. Johnston remembered him, "howling like a low dog in the night." And Johnston remembered a Lieutenant Bertrand.

Burton himself, in this very office, had talked about the medal he had won in Vietnam. I've got it in a desk drawer someplace. Isn't that what he had said? Jesus, he thought, poor bastard.

I should do it now, Malachek thought. Call Burton up here and ask him just one question—did you have your name changed from Bertrand?

But he decided to wait until Robert Forrest called from the Pentagon.

Two hours later, he called.

There had been an Armand Bertrand, a Robert Ducoin, and an Ed Johnston who served in the 23rd Infantry. Division. Bertrand had been awarded the Bronze Star and Ducoin had been a POW for seven years. Johnston had been discharged with a medical disability.

Nothing remained but to meet with Burton.

He would have to tell Burton that it was over. Burton still could remain a correspondent, of course. There were several correspondents at all the networks whose personal problems did not limit their acceptance on the air, even though their drinking or drugs or marital problems had been publicized at one time or another.

After all, even Bill Mack, one of their best foreign correspondents, had spent six months in a rehabilitation center after getting hooked on drugs in Beirut. And then he had written an article for *TV Guide* about it.

But it was different for the anchors. They had to be clean, unsullied. Burton would have to understand that.

And beyond Burton, there was his own problem—his future at the network.

The thought depressed him. He was beginning to feel shaky, as if a fault line, hidden below the hard bedrock of his confidence, was shifting and starting to split him apart.

He pushed the intercom for Judy Rosen and informed her, "I'm leaving early today. I'll be at home."

"I'll tell the assignment desk," she said. "Anything else?"

"Yes," he answered "Leave word for Art Burton to call me at home. I need to speak to him."

He decided against requesting a car from the limousine pool and instead walked over to Grand Central Station and took the 12:10 local to Rye. By one o'clock, he was home.

"Why are you here so early?" Mary Lou asked, surprised and worried as he came into the room. It was unlike him to come home this early, even at the start of a weekend. Usually, even with the limousine, he did not get home until eight o'clock at night.

"Is there something wrong?" she asked. "Are you feeling all right?"

She knew the pressures he worked under and, over the last few years, she had noticed the metamorphosis in him.

There had been more than the physical evidence of change: the graying hair, the occasional weariness in his walk, even the lessening of his ability to perform in bed.

She also had been aware of a more disturbing change.

His passion for the news business had slowly been seeping out of him.

He was a different Carl Malachek than the one she had fallen in love with almost thirty years ago and, even though she knew change was inevitable, it pained her to see it.

She hated the network for what it had done to him. And to her.

"What's the matter, Carl?" she repeated.

He came over and kissed her on the cheek.

"I got hit by a bulldozer this morning, Mary Lou," he said wearily. "I just didn't feel like spending the rest of the day downtown, bleeding all over the office." He sat down in a leather chair. His body seeming to sag as if it were carrying extra weight that needed to be absorbed by the crinkled folds of leather in the chair.

"It's Art Burton," he said, unable to hide a trace of bitterness in his voice. "The kid lied to me."

It seemed strange to her to hear him refer to Burton as a kid. She had met Burton once or twice and he appeared to be about forty or forty-one years old. He was not a kid.

"Lied about what, Carl?"

"I got a letter from somebody today," he went on, "somebody I never heard of in my life. He said he served with Burton in Vietnam and that Burton lost his nerve in some battle and left him out there to die."

"Go on," she said quietly. "What else did he say?"

"He had some other details. You know, to prove that he wasn't making it all up. The worst part is that Burton won the Bronze Star out there for rescuing somebody else in his platoon but he did nothing to save this one. Turned his back on him. This guy was picked up by the Viet Cong and spent seven years in a prison camp."

"And what does Burton say?"

"I haven't spoken to him yet."

"So how do you know it's true? Maybe this man is a psychopath or something. Maybe he's fantasizing all of it. People like that can be very convincing, you know."

"Because I had some checks run, Mary Lou," he said dejectedly. "Everything checks out. Everything. It happened."

"And now what?" she asked.

"What do you mean?"

"It happened a long time ago," she said. "If it happened

at all. But what if it did? How old was Burton then? Twenty-two? Twenty-three?"

"Don't you see what it means? Burton can't anchor for me with this on his record. The public will crucify him. A coward in wartime? My God, I don't even want to think about it."

The mixture of sorrow and frustration in his voice tore through her.

"I don't know what to tell you, Carl," she confessed. "Maybe I'm more forgiving than you."

"It isn't a question of forgiving," he said. "I can't have somebody anchoring the news who isn't a clean, blank slate. That's what the public wants. That's what they need; some totem they can worship before that twenty-one-inch shrine every night. Somebody who will keep them safe by telling them the truth night after night. And his believability rests in the fact that he himself is truthful. He's Captain America, all dressed up in a rep tie and a Ralph Lauren suit and a button down shirt.

"It wouldn't matter if Burton were divorced or even a recovered alcoholic because the public would accept all of that. It's a part of today's world. But they won't accept somebody who was a coward and kept it secret and lied about it all these years up to and including accepting a medal for false bravery."

"And what if it never came out?" she asked.

He smiled, pleased by the realization she'd had the same thought as he had.

"I still would know, wouldn't I?" he asked.

"I gave him the break of a lifetime, Mary Lou. I was handing him the whole damn world on a golden platter. Just like that. I picked him right out of the ranks, laid my whole damn reputation on the line for him, fought Rossman tooth and nail for him but he didn't level with me."

"Carl, you're not going to punish him because he lied to you. That's not what it's all about, is it?"

"No," he said. "I never would have offered him the anchor job in the first place if I had known that he had covered up his war record. But now that I know, I can't rationalize it all away. It matters to me, Mary Lou, because I can't make myself ignore everything I've always believed about the network news; that it works only if the front man, the anchorman, is a true straight-shooter, the man in the white hat.

"That's what I believe and I can't suddenly tell myself that it isn't true."

"God, Carl," she said. "Sometimes I wish you weren't so damn unbending."

"So do I. But I've been in the business too long to change."

"What will you do?" she asked.

"I left word for Burton to call me. I'll go into the city and see him in the office tomorrow. I don't want to wait until Monday."

"And you'll tell him it's over?"

"Yes."

"And then?"

"And then?" he repeated. "And then," he said again, coming over and throwing his arms around her in a protective hug. "I guess we'll have to figure out what we're going to do with the rest of our lives."

"I suspected that," she said.

"I have to be realistic, Mary Lou," he said. "I'll be a good soldier and give Rossman a couple of more names for anchor—Swanson, McVea, whoever, but it will be a gesture. The truth is that my best choice turned out to be the wrong choice and I'll never be able to live it down, particularly now, this late. Rossman would never let me forget it.

"And if Rossman puts Mark Antin on the news, I won't be able to tell people I had a better choice but it fell through. I couldn't do that to Burton. No matter what happens from now on, I'll always be a eunuch at the network. Powerless. The man in the empty suit.

"I've got too much pride for that, Mary Lou. I can't work under those circumstances."

His kissed her again, this time on the lips, and put his hands on her shoulders.

"Don't worry, sweetheart," he said, smiling at her. "There's one thing you've got to remember about this job. It ends. It always ends."

She knew what he was referring to. In the years he had been at the network, there had been five other presidents of the News Division. One had committed suicide. The other four had been fired. At least he would be going out on his own terms.

She leaned forward and returned his kiss to show that she understood.

"We've got time to talk about it," he said. "But I'm going to quietly start putting some feelers out. Journalism schools, foundations, things like that. We won't have to worry."

"I know," she said quietly.

Malachek went over to a humidor on a small butler's table and picked a cigar.

He lit it and was just beginning to enjoy it when the phone rang. He knew who it would be.

Chapter 40

The possibility that Bobby Ducoin had contacted Malachek was gnawing at Art Burton's mind.

It hadn't occurred to him until just now that Ducoin would be brazen enough to contact Malachek after their conversation and tell him everything.

After all, how long had it been since he had spoken to Ducoin? Three, four, days? Would Ducoin work that fast? Was he that vindictive?

Now, sitting across from Malachek, he knew what he would say if Malachek confronted him about Ducoin. He would have to admit it and hope that Malachek would understand.

Malachek was standing by the window when he came in. He walked back to his desk and sat down. Then he picked up the old baseball and idly tossed it back and forth.

"How are you, Art?" he asked pleasantly.

"I'm fine, thanks," Burton answered.

Malachek put the baseball down. "I have something to ask you, Art, and I want you to level with me. It's important," he said grimly.

At that moment, Burton knew that Malachek had heard from Bobby Ducoin. He felt the life going out of him. He stared numbly at Malachek and hoped that Malachek would not pick up the baseball again.

"I got a letter yesterday morning from somebody named Ducoin," Malachek said quietly. "Do you know who I'm talking about?"

"Yes, of course," Burton answered. His throat felt dry and he cleared it, the noise echoing through the room.

"Is it true?" Malachek asked softly.

"What does his letter say?"

"That you left him to die in the jungle in Vietnam. You saved Eddie Johnston and you left him to die. You never deserved that medal."

It sounded so matter-of-fact. Burton could not believe Malachek was reciting everything like this, so routinely.

"I did not leave him to die," Burton said, all of it coming back.

"I didn't leave him to die," he repeated. "I just couldn't save him."

"You didn't try?" Malachek asked.

"No," Burton answered quietly, feeling, with that one word, that finally he had expiated the shame he had carried within him for years. "I didn't try."

"Is there more?" Malachek asked.

"No, nothing," Burton answered without even thinking about it. "I crawled away from him and went back and got Johnston in the sling to the chopper."

"Did you see Ducoin from the chopper?"

A brief image flickered in Burton's mind. It was so quick that he couldn't capture it and hold it there. Tall grass, receding beneath him, and, for an instant, a body sprawled helpless in the grass. He was in the helicopter, looking down.

"I might have seen him from the chopper," he said. "It's hard to remember."

Jesus, Malachek thought, what a way for it to end for him.

"Did you have any idea Ducoin was alive?" he asked.

"No, not until I got a letter from him earlier this week. I couldn't believe it."

"Did you contact him?"

"I called him in Chicago, told him not to bother me again."

"What did his letter say?"

"He wanted to meet me. He said I should take care of him because of what happened back there in Vietnam. It was pretty obvious he wanted money or he would tell what happened."

"Didn't that bother you?"

"What?"

"That he would tell, that he would go public with the story?"

"I didn't think he would," Burton said. "I just couldn't believe he had written me like that, you know, after so many years, and was making these threats. I never thought he would keep at it. Or contact you."

"He'll go public," Malachek predicted.

"I don't know," Burton said dejectedly. "I guess he could write a letter to a newspaper somewhere, call a local television station, something like that."

"Yes, he could. And it would spread from there."

Burton grimaced. He took a long breath and said, "I don't know what to say. It's something that happened a long time ago. I've always felt guilty about it but it was my own personal guilt, something on my conscience. Nobody else was affected, if you know what I mean."

"I understand," Malachek said, realizing at the same time that Burton did not fully grasp the significance of Ducoin's threat.

"We will have to drop the idea of you replacing Cornwall," Malachek finally said. "It won't work."

Burton was stunned. He could not believe Malachek was reacting like this. If Ducoin went public with his disclosure, it would be painfully embarrassing but he could survive it. It had happened a long time ago. It could be explained.

For Malachek to cast him out like this was incredible.

"I don't understand what you mean," he said, dazed by Malachek's pronouncement.

"To anchor the evening news, Art," Malachek said, "you have to be a demigod, above suspicion. You have to be one of the most trusted people in the whole country, more than the President of the United States.

"You know why? Because the President can lie, or try to

mislead the public, or even whore around, but when it all comes out, the people are going to look to you—and the others at the other nets—to tell them the truth. And if you're not up there on a pedestal above everybody else, if you've lied or done something wrong yourself somewhere along the line, then they won't trust you and you've lost your effectiveness."

"But I don't think of myself as being impure, tainted," Burton argued. "I made a mistake a long time ago. Does that make me an outcast, for God's sake? I don't believe it."

"You got a medal for saving Johnston," Malachek said, "but you left Ducoin out there to die. And you carried that around inside you, because you were ashamed, didn't you? You were ashamed of that, ashamed of getting the medal."

"Yes, I was ashamed," Burton admitted. "But are viewers going to hold that against me, something that happened twenty years ago?"

"They want to believe in you, Art," Malachek responded. "They need to believe in you. But if you've got that blemish, you'll never be fully trusted."

"And because I was a twenty-two-year-old kid who fucked up, I'm less than perfect. Is that what you're telling me?" Burton's voice was rising in anger.

Malachek pointed a finger at Burton. "What if you learned today, now, that John Cornwall had been dishonorably discharged from the service during the Korean War and served two years in the stockade? What would you think when you saw him? Wouldn't you think about it once in a while, wouldn't it take away from your trust in him?"

Burton was shocked. "I don't believe it," he said.

"No, it's not true," Malachek admitted. "You thought for a moment, didn't you, but you knew that if it were true, Cornwall wouldn't be anchoring."

"But what if it was true?" Burton flared. "What the hell difference would it make as long as the public didn't know? That's all that counts, isn't it? Whether they know or not. I could be a goddamn drug addict or a porno dealer as long as the viewers didn't know."

"And what if they found out?" Malachek asked. "Then what?"

Burton got up and walked over to Malachek. "You're willing to forget about Winston, keep him from being exposed. He's doing something that's illegal as hell and it's happening now, today," Burton said accusingly. "Isn't that worse?"

"He's a variety show host, a performer. He doesn't mean a pimple on the public's ass. There's a lot of them around. But there are only three anchors, and they'd damn well better be perfect in the public's eye. There's a mysterious bond there, between them and the public, and one flaw will weaken it and destroy it."

Burton turned away and went back to his chair. He stood behind it, his hand gripping the leather covered frame.

There was no use arguing anymore, he realized. No matter how hard he chipped away at Malachek's argument, he never would be able to change Malachek's position.

It was over.

He would have to tell Samantha, but maybe it was better in the long run. He could not have kept Ducoin a secret from her forever. Someday, long after they had been married, he would have told her.

"I guess I don't have any choice," Burton said bitterly. "Not that there's anything I could do about it anyhow."

Malachek came over to where Burton was standing. "I wish I had a different answer for you, but I don't. I'll have to tell Rossman."

"Jesus," Burton murmured. He wondered whether he should quit, right now, and walk away from it all.

"It's not all over for you, Art," Malachek said, reading Burton's thoughts. "You can keep on doing what you've been doing. The viewers will forgive a lot of things, maybe even this. But not from the man on top of the totem pole."

"So what happens now?" Burton asked.

"I'll have to go to Rossman," Malachek said, "and tell him the whole story. God only knows what his reaction will be."

"Do you think I'll be fired?" Burton asked nervously.

"No, of course not. Rossman will figure out something with Ducoin. He'll probably lay some money on him—he's stupid enough to do something like that—and hope that he'll stay quiet. We'd all have to assume he'd go away but we never could be sure, could we?"

"No," Burton agreed, finally conceding Malachek's point. "What will happen now?"

"I don't know," Malachek said wearily. "I haven't even

thought that far. Rossman will go for Antin, I suppose. There's nothing to hold him back on that now."

"There was, though, wasn't there? It was Winston, wasn't it?" Burton asked.

"We would have gotten Winston down the line," Malachek said, indirectly confirming Burton's suspicions. "The important thing was to get the right anchor. That's what really counted. That's where it's all won or lost."

Burton's throat was dry again and he felt weak, as if his strength was draining out of him.

"I'm sorry that all of this happened," he said. "I never saw a reason to tell you, or anybody. You asked me a long time ago, in our first talk about this, if I was clean. I said yes. I felt remorse about what happened but I never thought of myself as dirty."

"You were up for a job where the people need to think of you as a thousand percent clean. One hundred percent isn't good enough," Malachek said.

It's strange, Burton thought. This room, where it all began, is where it's all ending.

"Is there anything I need to do?" Burton asked. "I mean about Ducoin."

"No," Malachek said. "I think it would be smarter if you just ignored him. Let Rossman worry about him. Or I will."

"Do you think Rossman will really go for Antin?" Burton asked.

"I don't want to think about it," Malachek answered, wondering if he would be able to reach Rossman this afternoon. He'd heard that Rossman was out of the city, getting an award from some state broadcaster's association.

"Maybe I'll keep working on Winston," Burton said. "What the hell have I got to lose?"

"You may have to leak it to the papers, *The Times* or somebody," Malachek advised him. "Rossman won't let it get on the air. He'll be able to stop it this time."

Burton was beginning to sense the depths of Malachek's depression. He's going to quit, he thought. Because of this, because of me. But he did not feel close enough to Malachek to ask him.

"It's ironic," Burton said. "I've never really hated anyone in my life. And here I am hating Ducoin for what he's doing to me, and I don't even know what the son of a bitch looks like."

"You never know, do you?" Malachek said, almost wistfully, sitting behind his desk again. He was silent for a moment. Burton noticed his silence and he felt awkward standing there.

It just added to the emptiness he felt inside. He wanted to leave, to be alone with Samantha and to flush the rage out of him.

"Unless there's anything more—" Burton said.

Malachek shook his head. "No, I think we've covered it all. There's no need for you to say anything to anybody. After all, the announcement hasn't been made yet."

"A real stroke of luck," Burton said bitterly.

He shook Malachek's hand formally, then walked out of the office.

It wasn't until he reached the end of the long hallway that he realized he had not even glanced at the framed pictures of Miniver and Cornwall hanging on the walls.

Malachek watched him walk down the corridor. Then he picked up his phone and called home.

"Hello Mary Lou Hennesy," he said when his wife answered the phone. Calling her by her maiden name was a special sign of affection.

She was glad he was calling her that now. It meant that he was relaxed, that he'd made peace with himself.

"How did it go, Carl?" she asked.

"It went all right," he answered. "He didn't like it but he had no choice."

He was silent for a moment and she asked, "Are you coming home soon?"

"Yes. I'll see you in about an hour. I'm finished here."

He said good-bye before he realized the unintended irony of his last words.

Chapter 41

It is all over, Art Burton is thinking.

He has felt this way for the last few hours, ever since his

climb to the evening news anchor position had abruptly ended in Malachek's office.

It all had happened so quickly, almost with perversity. Just when, with Malachek's oblique blessing, he had reached the very threshold of the summit, Burton had been crudely pushed back. Now, in his mind, he was falling backward, tumbling and sliding, bleeding; desperately trying to find something to hang on to in order to stop the fall.

The sudden plunge had left him an automaton, numbed and neutered, stumbling robotlike through the landscape; seeing everything, absorbing nothing.

He remembered walking out of Malachek's office, taking a taxi to La Guardia, buying a ticket on the shuttle to Boston, renting a car at Logan, driving to Route 128 and then to the final exit—Gloucester—but all of this had been done mindlessly, as if he had been programmed by a computer to go directly from the network building to Samantha's cottage.

Now, as he stood on the wooden porch that ran along the rear of the cottage, waiting for Samantha to change into her sailing clothes, he still was devastated by all that had happened. He dreaded the possibility that, once he had told Samantha everything, there would be an even greater distance to fall, an even steeper slope to tumble down.

She had been waiting for him when he arrived at the cottage but he'd already decided not to tell her immediately about his meeting with Malachek.

When he saw her, dressed in a blue pleated skirt and a red silk blouse, with her hair gathered in a golden mass behind her head and held there by a butterfly-shaped clasp, and her smile showing her delight that they were together, he knew that he had made the right decision.

There was no way he could suddenly tell her, at that moment, about Bobby Ducoin and Malachek and the end of his chances for the Cornwall job.

It would have to wait a little while longer. Instead, he wrapped his arms around her and kissed her and said, "I'm so glad we've got this time together, Samantha. I promise on my Sea Scouts honor not to get seasick this afternoon."

"Darling," she said reprovingly. "The boat is a twenty-two-foot centerboard sloop. You're not going to get sick on it. Besides, look out there."

She pointed to the ocean, a few hundred yards from the cottage, separated from the cottage by a thread of a two-lane road and the sand of Good Harbor Beach. "The water is very smooth today. It will be like sailing on glass, I promise you."

"If you say so," he said.

"I say so," she responded. Then: "Do you want to have some lunch first or should we go out on the water?"

He was hungry but he could not handle the idea of sitting across from her, trying to be casual, deceiving her, even now, into believing that he was as tranquil as the water lapping at the edge of the beach.

"I'm really not hungry," he lied. "How about you?"

"I can wait. Maybe we can drive over to Ipswich after we come back in and pick up something to eat. There's that wonderful little clam shack just off the main highway. Do you remember it?"

"I don't think so."

"I do," she said. "Wait here while I change into my Captain Ahab outfit."

"It's sailing, not whaling," he called after her as she disappeared into the bedroom.

Now, waiting for her, he wondered when to tell her about the meeting with Malachek. About everything.

He momentarily toyed with the idea of waiting until they were out on the ocean, where the vastness of the sea and the sky might dwarf the problem. Against that endless backdrop, it might seem puny and insignificant.

He shielded his eyes from the sun and stared out to sea. In the distance, he could see the graceful silhouettes of sailboats, their triangular patches of sail floating on the horizon, as if they were kites skimming the surface of the water.

No, he decided. Telling her out there, when she loved sailing and the water so much, would only add to the pain. It would despoil the beauty of the ocean for her, linking it with unhappy memories.

It would be better if he told her now. He walked back into the cottage and sat down on a wicker couch in the living room. The surroundings were familiar, and relaxed him.

Pieces of scrimshaw were scattered around a lamp, resting on a side table, and a Winslow Homer print was on one wall. Across from him, on a paneled wall, there was a row of photographs of Samantha.

There was Samantha as a youngster, sitting next to her sister Helen in a rowboat; the two of them facing the camera. The man holding the oars, he knew, was her father; even then, twenty-five years ago, marked by a shock of white-maned hair.

Another photograph showed Samantha, in shorts, at sixteen or seventeen, standing by the mainsail of her boat, smiling enigmatically at an unknown photographer on the shore. The picture revealed the beginnings of her physical maturity; the long blond hair falling uncombed over her shoulders, the small breasts, the few remaining bits of baby fat around her thighs.

What had she been then? A senior in high school?

Next to it, there was a picture of an older Samantha, in a powder blue UCLA T-shirt, sitting on a pier in Marina Del Rey. The picture had been taken in her junior year of college.

His favorite picture completed the symmetry of the row. It showed Samantha, standing at the edge of the water on the beach across from the cottage. She was ten years old, he knew, when the picture was taken and she was holding a sopping wet dog in her arms. The dog was Plato, the family pet, and she was clutching him the way that little girls held onto rag dolls. The dog had gone too far out in the water and Samantha had rescued him.

The picture always had fascinated him because he could see in her child's expression the same mixture of confidence and wonderment that had enchanted him on the very first day he had met her in New York.

Oh God, he thought, how had it come to this? Sitting here, surrounded by her past, waiting to tell her that his whole future, and hers as well, had been shattered because of one secret he'd kept from her—Ducoin.

Samantha came out of the bedroom then, and at the first sight of her his despair seemed to vanish.

She had changed into white shorts, a blue and white striped gondolier's shirt and white tennis shoes. Her hair was tied behind her with a blue and white bandanna dotted with tiny anchors.

She looked incredibly beautiful, as if she already had

spent hours on the water and the sun and the spray of the waves had left an incandescent glow on her face.

She sat down in a yellow sling canvas chair across from him. "Ready?"

Looking at her, reclining in the low slung chair, her legs curled under her like a kitten, Art wished he could freeze the moment and make the day end now.

If he did that, they could sit there silently, frozen in time, just looking at each other. He would not have to tell her anything.

But he knew he could not postpone the moment any longer.

"Samantha," he said softly, "I'm not going to get the Cornwall job."

He spoke slowly but the words flew past her, too fast for her to feel anything but a fleeting sense of shock. She was on a speeding train and everything was going by too fast, blurring her senses.

She looked at him, dumbfounded. "I don't understand."

"I'm not going to get the Cornwall job," he repeated. "Malachek told me this morning, in his office, before I came up here."

"What do you mean?" she asked in a bewildered voice.

He groped for a way to explain but he was unable to, even though, on the shuttle flight to Boston and then, the hour's drive to Gloucester, he had tried to prepare, rehearsing in his mind what he would say.

It happened in Vietnam a long time ago, he would begin. Or: This will be hard to understand, Samantha. Or: There was this GI in my platoon. Or a million different things.

But now that the moment had arrived, he could not arrange everything in his mind, collect all the details so they would form a logical pattern.

He remembered a phrase from high school in New Orleans: "the *tout ensemble.*" That was what his history teacher had called the French Quarter with its ten square blocks and perfectly defined boundaries. The whole assemblage.

That was what he needed now. But all he had was a crazy quilt of fragments, with no boundary he could point to and use as a reference point.

And then he thought of the medal, resting in a recessed

fold of white silk in a small, velvet-covered box, buried in the bottom drawer of his desk in his living room, covered by old bank statements.

"It has to do with a medal I won in Vietnam," he said, deliberately forcing himself not to look away from her.

"What medal?" she asked, puzzled.

"It was a long time ago," he said. "It's not the type of thing you talk about. No reason to, now, so long after the war. It was mentioned in a couple of the newspaper stories about me. It was the Bronze Star for bravery."

"But the job," she said. "I still don't understand what this has to do with it."

"My squad was ambushed in a mortar attack. I saved the life of someone who was injured by dragging him to a helicopter sling so he could be rescued. That's what I got the medal for. In 1966."

His matter-of-fact recital of the battlefield incident, coupled with his apparent unwillingness to answer her questions, filled Samantha with confusion.

What did all this have to do with the Cornwall job? Why was he telling her this? What had happened to him?

"I don't understand," she told him again, worried now that he was falling apart. She had never seen him like this, seemingly detached from the present, like an old man in a nursing home, wandering irrelevantly through old family history. It scared her.

"You said you weren't going to get the job. Why?" she persisted.

After a moment, he said, "I got the medal for saving someone. But I didn't save somebody else. I left him out there to die. I didn't try."

She looked at him pleadingly, as if saying, help me to understand.

"I didn't deserve the medal, Samantha," he continued, not meeting her eyes. "I was a coward out there. I couldn't help myself. I froze. But all these years I thought that no one could possibly ever know, that it would never matter. I buried it. But something happened—and everything got screwed up." Then he told her about Bobby Ducoin, about the letters from Ducoin to him and Malachek, and Malachek's feelings about the role of the anchorman and why he wasn't going to get the job.

She sat, stunned and silent, and, when he had finished, she murmured, "Oh my God."

"It's true," he said bitterly. "Every bit of it. That's what happened."

"Oh Art, it's so unfair," she said. Her voice was starting to break and tears were forming in her eyes. She didn't want to cry but she couldn't help it. She could feel the teardrops starting to slowly roll down her face.

Art was distraught by her reaction. "Jesus, Samantha, don't cry, darling. Please don't." He put his arms around her and nestled her face against his shoulder. He could feel his shirt getting wet from her tears.

"You were so young, Art," she said, still shaken, "and you've carried it around all these years. Why didn't you ever tell me? It wouldn't have mattered. It's nothing to be ashamed of."

"I never felt right about it, Samantha. I've been haunted by it for a long time. It mattered to me."

She looked at him and said, in a quivering voice that tried to be defiant but couldn't, "It just isn't right. How can Malachek be so damn high and mighty like this? He can't play judge and jury, twisting people's lives like this, like the great puppet master of the News Division."

Art sighed. "I don't think he thinks of himself that way," he said. "For him, it's a matter of principle. He believes the anchorman has to be some kind of a God. And I'm not. I'm not spotless."

"No, Art, don't feel that way," she comforted him. "Cornwall, the ones at the other networks, maybe they're not perfect either."

"We don't know that though, do we?" he answered. "All we know is that they come across as Mr. Integrity, Mr. Trustworthy, Mr. One Thousand Percent Clean and Trustworthy. And if it ever comes out that they're not, then they're finished as anchor. That's why Malachek is dropping me. He's worried that the Vietnam thing would come out and my credibility would be destroyed."

"Oh God," she said, wiping the tears from her face with the back of her hand. "It was all going so wonderfully. I was so happy for both of us. Our lives were going to be so different."

He knew what she was thinking.

The anchor job would have changed everything. For the first time since he came to the network, his nomadic life, a life dictated by the unpredictability of the news, would have been over. Even with the pressure of anchoring the evening news, there still would have been a stability to his life, moored five nights a week to Studio 2A with the curved anchor desk and the row of television monitors and the bank of phones.

Because of that, it would have been so much easier for Samantha and him to have a life together. Now, all of that had vanished.

"It will be all right," he said, patting her on the back as if soothing an infant. "It will be all right," he repeated, reassuring himself as well.

"What are you going to do about that man, the one who wrote the letter?" she asked, her face still pressed against him.

"I don't know," he said. "Malachek said they'll probably buy him off."

"God," she muttered, unable to hide her disgust.

"It's shit, isn't it?" he asked, not needing an answer.

"Will they—fire you?" she asked hesitantly.

"Malachek said I can keep doing *Focus*."

"And Cornwall? What are they going to do now? Who's going to get it?"

He shrugged. "Who knows? Antin, I guess, if Rossman has his way. Malachek probably will quit if Antin comes over."

"Well, I can't feel sorry for Malachek," she said.

"We'll be all right," he said again. "I'm still going to keep working on the Winston story, just to see what happens," he added as an afterthought, though without any enthusiasm.

"Art, I know it hurts. But you'll get past this," Samantha said, still trying to comfort him.

"I know. I told you before, I never really aspired to the anchor job. But everything else—I never wanted you to know about Bobby Ducoin, and now I feel dirty because of how it came out."

"I told you, darling. It doesn't matter to me. I understand."

"Do you?" he asked pleadingly, pulling her toward him. "Do you?"

"Of course I do," she said softly.

He threw his arms around her. "I'm sorry I fucked it all up. I love you so much."

She opened her mouth to him and drew his tongue inside to touch hers.

"I think I have always loved you," he said when the kiss ended. "Even when you were the little girl in the rowboat in that picture on the wall."

"Thank you," she said quietly.

"Do you still want to go sailing?" he asked.

"Do you?"

"No. I think I'd rather just go to the beach."

"So would I," she said.

He kissed her again and they changed into bathing suits and walked out of the cottage. When they got to the beach, they waded by the water's edge. It was low tide and the wet sand, washed by the final ripples of surf coming ashore, felt cool and good under their feet.

At the southern end of the beach, there was a large formation of rocks rising up from the ocean, like deformed, granite sea monsters, and they walked toward it, weaving their way between children making sand castles and ducking Frisbees flying by.

They sat down on the sand in the shadow of the rocks and let the water run over their toes.

"I used to do this when I was a teenager," Samantha said. "I would sit here for hours and watch the water come in."

"I wish I had known you then," he said.

"Maybe you wouldn't have liked me," she said teasingly. "I was a brat."

"I can't imagine it," he said.

"Not a real brat, just somebody who grew up in a house with smart parents and a smart sister. Some of it rubbed off on me."

"A book brat."

"Yes, that's it. Do you know, I was reading *The Republic* and *On Logic* when I was sixteen or seventeen? Thank God I had this," she said, extending her arm to the sea as if it all belonged to her.

"We still have time to go sailing, if you want," he offered.

"No, let's stay here. It's so peaceful and nice."

They both were silent for a moment, and then he said, "I'm glad I got everything out of me, Samantha."

"Tell me," she said. "Would you have told me anyhow, someday, even if you didn't know that that man was alive?"

Her question stunned him. She seemed to be testing his integrity, probing into the deepest caverns of his conscience, places that he himself rarely explored.

"Yes," he answered. "I couldn't have kept it from you forever."

"I'm glad."

"And you?" he asked. "Is there a hidden part of your life that I don't know about?"

"No," she answered, staring out to sea as if some long-buried incident would come rolling into her mind like one of the far-distant waves that were relentlessly moving to the shore. But there was nothing.

"Nope. You know all about me, from Newton to UCLA to Salinas to Wichita to LA to here. No skeletons in the closet. My life has been, well, just a life."

"But not dull."

"No," she reflected. "Not dull. Sometimes exciting. But just a life."

It was true. Until she had fallen in love with Art, there had been no meaningful shades or nuances filling out the texture of her life.

Just a few brief affairs, none of them lasting more than a month or two, during college and after. And there had been the romance with Tom Jacklin in Wichita.

But her passions and emotions had never been aroused the way that Art had moved her.

If she had to encapsulate her life, up to this very moment, she would think of a wide-angle photograph, one of those pictures spread across two pages of a magazine, where everything in the foreground was magnified.

In the foreground, there would be a clear image of herself, at work, but the background would be unclear and not yet in focus.

It was that part of the picture, the broad background of her total life—her life as a woman—that only now was beginning to emerge.

Her love for Art, she knew, was sharing the space that—until now—always had been dominated by the challenges

of work; her life as a series of stories: an interview with the
First Lady, an encounter with a policeman's widow, a face-off
with a coal mine owner, an ambush interview with Herman
Willows.

These, and hundreds more, had been in the foreground,
but always she had known they were only part of the story.

But now, with Art's career thrown into turmoil, she
wondered where she would go from here. My life, she
thought, has been placed on hold. A phrase came to her from
the newscasts. *Still to come*. That was where her life was.
Details to follow.

A wistful smile crossed her face and Art noticed it.

"What are you thinking about?" he asked.

"You," she answered. "How much I love you and need
you."

"Then why the sad smile?"

"It wasn't meant to be. Maybe it just came out that way."

He put his arm around her and said, "Don't worry,
Samantha. Together we'll get through this."

"I hope you're right, Art. But what happens now?"

"I don't have many choices, Samantha," he said with a
trace of bitterness. "I can't go back to New Orleans. To do
what? Anchor the local news? Cover City Hall again. Not
after all these years at the network. I'm too old.

"I couldn't step back like that and you wouldn't want me
to. So local news is out. What else is there? PR? Can you see
me hustling stories to news directors or program directors?
I'm not cut out for that either, Samantha.

"And I don't want to end up on some college campus,
teaching News Writing 104, waiting for Saturday to come
around so you and I can go to the football game, assuming
you don't have a story to cover and can come to Baton Rouge
or Tuscaloosa or Austin or wherever.

"So I'll stay here until I can figure out what it is I want to
do. Maybe just being a damn good reporter is the answer. It
used to be, once upon a time."

Samantha nodded her head dejectedly. It all sounded so
simple, a winnowing of alternatives.

God, she thought, why can't we just be happy?

"Let's go for a swim," she said impulsively and she got
up and ran to the water's edge.

"C'mon," she called back to Art. "The water looks fine."

He got up and ran down to meet her, relieved that she seemed to be shedding her worries. He grabbed her hand and, as if she were a child, led her into the water.

Because of the low tide, they walked a few hundred feet out until the water was almost waist deep.

Samantha bent down and, with both hands, playfully splashed Art's face and body with water. He yelped at the cold soaking.

She laughed. "That's what's known as a Gloucester baptism."

He shivered, cupped his hands so that they formed a scoop and threw water onto her.

"You're crazy," he said, "but I love you."

"And I love you," she echoed. She came closer then and, standing skin to skin, kissed him.

They broke apart and walked farther out in the water until their feet no longer touched the bottom. Then they started to swim, lazily, almost sensually; the sun playing off their bodies, their arms almost touching as they slowly sliced through the water, their legs kicking in unison in a slow metronomelike rhythm.

They swam for almost a half hour circling each other, diving and coming up for air like playful dolphins. Then Art said, "Race you back!"

Samantha swam fluidly, breathlessly, and reached the beach a stroke ahead of Art.

"We forgot to bring towels," she said, shaking herself like a wet puppy.

"Let's run back to the cottage," Art said.

"Will you dry me off?" she asked teasingly.

"Yes. Every delectable part of you."

"It's still early in the afternoon," she said, laughing. "You might upset the neighbors."

"I'll close the shades in the bedroom," he promised, caught up in a growing need for her. He could feel the beginnings of an erection.

"Yes," she said, starting to feel wildly aroused. "Close the shades. Love me hard in the dark." In the cottage they took off their bathing suits and lay down in bed.

Everything that had happened in the last few days, in the last few hours, was swept away by their lovemaking, and when it subsided and their passion had ebbed, like the last edge of surf receding from the beach, he lay on top of her, his lips joined to hers just as the rest of his body was.

He brought his hand up and brushed her hair back with a constant movement of his hand, weaving his fingers through the golden strands.

"We're going to be all right," he said to her in the deep, safe darkness. "We're going to be all right."

Chapter 42

Jerry Rossman paced across his carpeted floor, his eyes riveted on Carl Malachek.

"What the hell are you telling me?" he shouted angrily. "Is this some kind of a goddamn joke?"

He had figured there was going to be trouble from the moment Malachek had asked to see him as soon as he came in.

Winston, he had figured. Or Cornwall. Or maybe some new trouble with the White House. But this? This was goddamn unbelievable.

"It's not a joke, Jerry. Unfortunately, it's true," Malachek answered. He kept his voice low and spoke calmly, trying to not enrage Rossman any further. "There's no alternative. We'll have to drop Burton as the anchor choice. I'm sorry for this."

"Sure, sure," Rossman said impatiently. "Why the hell didn't you wait until we had the promos running and the ads placed and we had told all the affiliates? It's goddamn Monday already!"

"I tried to reach you over the weekend," Malachek said. "You were out of town."

"Sure, sure," Rossman repeated, oblivious to Malachek's explanation. "You've been throwing up Burton's name to me for weeks now, ever since Cornwall said he was leaving.

Couldn't you check him out, for God's sake? *Now* you find out about this Vietnam thing! *Now!*"

"There would have been no way of knowing," Malachek said.

"Who is this character who wrote the letters? What's he about?"

"I don't know. I spoke to him for about two minutes on Friday," Malachek said. "He wants money. I'm sure of it."

"Son of a bitch," Rossman muttered. "So now we're going to be blackmailed by some piece of scum."

"We shouldn't do anything," Malachek said. "We don't want to get in the gutter with him. That's the worst thing we can do."

"He'll talk. He'll destroy the whole network with the Burton story," Rossman said.

"Burton won't be anchoring the news. Ducoin's lost his platform."

"I don't know," Rossman said, as if talking to himself. "I'll speak to Sid Neale about it." He stopped pacing, wheeled around and glared at Malachek.

"I may have to go on my hands and knees, my hands and knees, goddamn it, and beg Cornwall to change his mind. And if I do, you're going to be right there with me. We're running out of time, goddamn it."

"I don't think Cornwall will change," Malachek said.

"He said from the beginning that he wanted out. He told you the same thing, didn't he?"

"I don't know. Maybe he'll change his mind. Or delay it for a little while. He can't walk out on us like this, not now."

"There's still a few weeks left before the affiliates meeting and then a little time before the new season begins. There's time," Malachek said.

"Bullshit!" Rossman exploded. "There is no time. We need an ad campaign, a promo campaign, we've got to sell the affiliates, we've got to promote the hell out of this. This is not some afternoon game show, for God's sake! We need to go to the ad agencies, to the street. We've got a major, major problem, Carl. You, me, the whole network.

"Your number one choice for anchoring our number one news program has just gone down the toilet. Got it? And my number one choice, the guy I should have tried to sign up from the start, may not be available because I haven't heard from his agent in ten fucking days. So where does that leave us? You got any other recommendations, maybe somebody you've checked out better than Burton? Somebody from the other nets maybe, or a hot local anchor somewhere, or our own people? What about the foreign bureaus? Believe me, we are not going to wind up with shit all over our face on this but our goddamn backs are against the wall."

Malachek silently cursed Bobby Ducoin. Burton always had been his first choice. Rossman was right, he had backed Burton from the start. But, ever since ruling Burton out, he had reviewed in his mind other potential anchors. He figured he owed at least that much to Rossman and to himself. He had been able to come up with only three names.

"Michael Swanson from *Sunrise* has always been a possibility," he told Rossman. "He's got good ratings and he's a decent newsman. We should definitely consider him now, I think."

"Antin kills him in the morning," Rossman said dourly. "Who else?"

"McVea from the weekend. He's solid, tests well with the yuppies, but has never really taken off."

"Who else?"

"Samantha Stuart," Malachek said slowly, waiting to see what Rossman's reaction was. "She's got a hard news background. She substituted on *Sunrise* a couple of weeks last year and did very well."

"From *Focus*?" Rossman asked. "The one who pissed off the White House?"

"Yes," Malachek answered. "She works with Burton on the show."

"There's no way a woman's going to solo anchor the evening news, Carl," Rossman said firmly. "I don't care how good-looking she is. The public won't buy it, not when she's up against two men at the other nets. Swanson's a better idea than she is."

"It's a suggestion," Malachek said, reviewing her tapes in his mind. Why the hell not? She was a pro, so it wasn't a case of style over substance. He wondered if she ever had thought about anchoring.

"That's all you got, Carl? Three people who you think might be able to do it? Have you ever spoken to the Stuart woman?"

"No, not about anchoring," Malachek admitted.

"What about the other nets?" Rossman asked. "What are the chances of signing somebody first-rate from another network?"

Malachek thought for a moment before answering. "The best ones are locked up on long-term contracts. I know that for a fact. We'd have to take a chance on somebody and build a following. We'd be better off with somebody from here, somebody our viewers know and like."

"This fucking mess you created, Carl," Rossman suddenly erupted, annoyed by Malachek's use of "we." "You and your precious standards. Look where they've gotten us."

Malachek was silent. He knew there was no way he could control Rossman's fury. He would just have to sit there and be careful.

"If we can't get Antin, we'll go with somebody," Rossman muttered. He walked over to the couch where Malachek was sitting. "When this is all straightened out, Carl, I think you'd better think about working off your contract. We'll make whatever arrangements are necessary. I don't think either one of us would feel comfortable with your staying here, after what's happened. I assume you agree."

"Yes," Malachek said. He already had made some phone calls over the weekend, subtly probing to see what was out there in the way of jobs. As soon as this meeting with Rossman was over, he planned to follow up an inquiry at a top journalism school.

"We can talk about it whenever you want," Malachek said coldly.

"Later," Rossman answered sharply. He thrust his hands into the pockets of his suit coat and began to pace again.

"Goddamn mess," he repeated. "I'm going to call Mickey Schirmer," he decided, stopping in the middle of the room. "I'll call you if I need you."

"Whatever you say," Malachek said, unconcerned, rising from the couch and walking to the door.

He left the room, closing the door behind him, without saying anything.

Just like that, his years at the network were ending.

* * *

Rossman glared angrily at the closed door, wishing his eyes could pierce the door and drill right through Malachek's back. Then he went to his phone and called Mickey Schirmer.

After a few minutes' wait, Schirmer greeted him with a warm, "Jerry, how are you?"

"I'm fine, Mickey," Rossman answered, trying to figure out what Schirmer was up to. His greeting was too friendly, too warm.

"I was hoping to hear from you," Schirmer said smoothly. "You know, follow up on our breakfast."

I've lost Antin. He's setting me up.

"C'mon, Mickey, let's not cock around," Rossman said testily. "I made you an offer. I haven't heard back from you."

"Hey, Jerry. What kind of an offer?" Schirmer asked. "We didn't discuss any deal makers, not that I can remember. You said you were interested in Antin for the evening news. I said I was interested. So who owed who a call?"

"I think you'd said you'd get back to me," Rossman said. "But let's not chew on bones. I'm calling because I want to know where you stand. Have you spoken to your client? Does he want to make a move?"

"What can I tell you, Jerry?" Schirmer asked.

He's gone. Rossman knew it.

"You can tell me what you want to do," Rossman said, dropping any pretense of friendliness. *What was this little prick getting at?*

"We're staying where we are," Schirmer said.

"What happened?" Rossman asked.

"I made a very good deal for Mark. Four years, no cut. A big increase in the money. You couldn't have matched it, Jerry. Besides, every time I picked up a paper, all I read about was how you were considering people from your own ranks."

"C'mon Mickey, you knew we wanted Antin. And I bet you let that slip out in your negotiations over there, didn't you? You must have played them like a violin, getting four years, no cut."

"It's business, Jerry," Schirmer said.

"Yeah, sure," Rossman said. *What the hell was he going to do now that Antin definitely was out? Jesus!*

"I hear your News Division is working on some interesting stuff," Schirmer said casually.

"I don't know what you're talking about," Rossman snapped, genuinely puzzled by Schirmer's statement.

"There's talk on the street that Malachek's got a big investigation going. Something to do with gambling."

Rossman froze. He's fishing for Winston, he immediately suspected. Winston must have suspected that something was going on. But where did he get it from? The story was dead. Malachek had promised him.

"You're hearing wrong, Mickey," Rossman said firmly. "If Malachek had anything big going, I'd know about it."

"So maybe I'm wrong," Schirmer said but Rossman could not tell if Schirmer believed him. "It was just something I picked up."

"From where?"

"From nobody in particular. Just talk. You know how people talk sometimes. Maybe they got it wrong."

"It's wrong," Rossman said, wanting to make sure that Schirmer felt reassured. That's all he needed now, to have Jarvis Winston panicking on him. "There's no investigation like that going on," he repeated, hoping that Schirmer would get the message. That story was going to stay dead, along with Malachek.

"Good talking to you, Jerry," Schirmer said. Then: "You spoken to Jarvis recently?"

"I was going to call him today," Rossman replied, wondering if Schirmer really had those kind of balls, bringing up Winston now. "Milton Stanger says he's coming along fine. He should be out of the hospital this week."

"I know he's looking forward to doing the affiliates convention for you," Schirmer said.

"Yeah, sure. Barry Kovaks wants him to do a whole shtick."

"God bless, Jerry," Schirmer said.

"And you, Mickey," Rossman responded. He hung up, already trying to think of his next move. He looked at the piece of paper where he had scribbled the three names Malachek had suggested but the names, by themselves, were no help.

A twinge of panic was beginning to work its way into his gut. The start of the new season, the need to keep the affiliates in line, the potential revenue loss on the evening news, the inquiries that were starting in the trade press; they all were piling up too quickly, a wall growing higher and higher, brick by brick, until, now, it was threatening to topple over and bury him in the rubble.

He had to come up with an answer before the bricks started crashing down on him. But time was running out.

Maybe Sid Neale could help. He trusted Sid more than anybody else in the whole network, even though he had never told him why he had gone along with Malachek's choice of Art Burton for the evening news. It would have been too humiliating to have told him the truth.

Instead, he had told him that Burton seemed the most logical choice and there would be no resistance from any of the old-line affiliates who would have objected to Mark Antin's lack of news credentials.

Yes, maybe Sid could help. He asked his secretary to find him. Five minutes later, Sid Neale stood in his office, resplendent in a gray, pin-striped suit he'd had made-to-measure by a tailor in Beverly Hills.

"Nice suit, Sid," Rossman observed, admiringly.

"It's the same tailor I've used for years," Neale said, sitting down on the couch and crossing his legs carefully so as not to ruin the crease in the trousers. "It's worth the money, Jerry. He does beautiful work."

Rossman walked over to a small table where there was a silver water pitcher and a set of crystal glasses embossed with the network's logo. He took a pill from a small vial in his pocket, poured some water, and swallowed the pill.

"My migraine's been acting up," he told Neale, who was thumbing through the final edition of the *Daily News*.

"There's nothing in any of the columns today," Neale observed. "We must be losing our touch."

"Listen Sid, we've got something to talk about," Rossman said grimly.

Neale put the paper back down. "What's happening? Is there a problem?"

"A big one. Unbelievable," Rossman said.

What the hell can it be, Neale thought. The last time it was Cornwall leaving. What else? A suicide? A drug arrest? Something must have happened over the weekend, something he hadn't heard about.

"One of our people in trouble?" he asked worriedly.

"It's the Cornwall problem. We can't go with Burton.

Malachek told me today that Burton's got a bad war record, something that happened in Vietnam."

"Vietnam?" Neale said anxiously. "Was he a deserter or something? Jesus, I don't believe it."

"No. He got scared out in the jungle someplace and didn't save some GI he could have rescued. He won a medal for saving somebody else but nobody knew he left this other guy to die."

"I guess things like that happened," Neale said. "But what's the problem? When the hell was Vietnam, fifteen, twenty years ago?"

"The problem is the GI was taken prisoner. He didn't die, like Burton thought. All this time he's been alive. And then he saw Burton's picture in the paper last week and he recognized him and he wrote a letter to Malachek."

Neale was dumbfounded. "Didn't the guy ever watch television, for Chrisake? Burton's been around."

"Apparently he's some kind of a bum. Not the kind who would be watching *Focus* or any of the news shows."

"How does he know it's Burton? Couldn't he be mistaken?"

"Burton admitted it to Malachek. It happened just like the guy said it did."

Neale slumped back on the couch, shaking his head in disbelief.

"Incredible. And this guy wants money, right?"

"Yeah, sure," Rossman said, starting to pace back and forth on the carpet.

"Has anybody spoken to him?"

"Malachek spoke to him on Friday for about two minutes. He says the guy is serious."

"What is he, a jailbird or something? What do we know about him?"

"Who the hell knows what we know about him?" Rossman answered sharply. "All we know is that a piece of shit out there has got some bad paper on the man we were going to have anchor our news, thanks to Malachek, and now Burton's out. It's some goddamn mess, Sid."

"I'll get his number from Malachek," Neale said. "I'll call him."

Rossman did not respond. He knew that, over the years, Sid had handled, quietly and discreetly, other problems that had been potentially harmful to the network. A drunk driving charge on one of the soap opera stars, a bad check that a general manager at one of the affiliates had passed, even a homosexual pandering charge against one of the game show emcees.

If Sid was going to handle this one, Rossman didn't want to know about it. It was better this way. Cleaner. Sid would know what to do.

"So what about Antin?" Neale asked. "You'll make a play for him, won't you?"

"I already did," Rossman said despondently. "I called Mickey Schirmer just before I asked you to come in. Schirmer's cut a new deal for Antin. He's staying where he is."

"I never did trust that SOB," Neale said. "He used us as leverage. The son of a bitch probably took them to the cleaners."

"Four years, no cut. But what can you do?" Rossman said wearily, as if he already had resigned himself to Schirmer's tactics. "These agents are all the same."

Neale got up from the couch and walked over to the window behind Rossman's desk and rested his hands on the windowsill. He peered down to the street below and, for a moment, indulged himself with the idea that somewhere down there he could find the next anchor. Some good-looking guy with a great voice. I'll make him a star, he thought.

But, instead, he turned to Rossman and said, "I don't have any ideas. Will Cornwall stick around until we get this settled?"

"Malachek doesn't think so. He's closer to Cornwall than I am. Anyhow, I don't feel like begging. He's already stuck it up our ass."

"So what does Malachek think? Has he got anybody?"

"He gave me three names from our own people. He says the best possibilities at the other networks are all locked up already."

"What about the locals, or overseas?"

"Too big a gamble," Rossman said.

"So who does he have?"

"Swanson, McVea from the weekend news, and Samantha Stuart, from *Focus*."

"Stuart?" Neale said, surprised. "She's good but I never thought of her as an anchor."

"She did *Sunrise* last year. I missed it, but I've seen her on *Focus*."

"Why in hell would Malachek suggest a woman to anchor the evening news?" Neale wondered aloud. "The other nets have never had a woman during the week, even as a vacation substitute, have they?"

"Not that I recall. It would have gotten some press, I'm sure. We would have heard about it."

"Yeah, lots of press," Neale agreed. Any woman anchoring the evening news would get big press. It figured. He thought about it, abstractly for a moment, and then, specifically, about Samantha Stuart.

There was a gleam of a possiblility there, something that needed exploring.

"Do you have any research on the Stuart woman?" he asked.

"C'mon, Sid," Rossman said, annoyed. "The clock is ticking on us. We can't consider putting a woman on there."

"It's an idea, Jerry," Neale said, trying to edge Rossman a little closer so that they both could at least examine the idea. "She's good-looking, sexy, smart, and she's a good reporter."

"And the White House knows her," Rossman said dryly, recalling the Willows episode.

"So what have you got to lose by testing her? How long does it take?"

"I don't know. Marty Merrett could give us a better answer. He's going to have to set up some test groups for anybody we come up with. We can't go with our guts on this one, not now. Probably we'd know some results in a week or two after he went into the field."

Rossman said it with no enthusiasm but the idea was taking hold in Neale. It was starting to excite him. He could see the potential in it if Stuart worked out.

"Jerry, this is not such a cockamamy idea, believe me," he said eagerly. "Supposing she tests out well and supposing you've already presold some of the affiliates on the possibility—just the possibility, mind you—of Stuart doing the evening news. You know, Hap Hawkins and a few of the big group owners. Can you imagine the payoff for us if she works out? My God, the whole country will be tuned in if we promote it right. And she's promotable, Jerry. Half the men out there probably want to fuck her every time she appears on camera."

He was talking more rapidly now, trying to catch up with the ideas running through his mind. The cover stories in the news magazines. The column interviews. The personal appearances at major affiliates. Jesus, it all could work!

"Malachek may have done you a big favor," Neale said excitedly. "This can make you look awfully good, particularly if she comes close to holding Cornwall's ratings."

Rossman was incredulous. Was Sid really serious, carrying on this way about the Stuart woman as if she were John Cornwall in skirts? What the hell was the matter with him?

"Sid," he said in an agitated voice. "There's no way the viewers are going to buy a woman anchor five nights a week, fifty-two weeks a year. They're just not going to accept it."

"Jerry, what have we got to lose?" Neale argued. "You said it yourself, the clock is ticking away. A couple of weeks from now, we've got the affiliates meeting. Right after that, the new season starts. You don't have too many options. Let's face it. We're in the same fix one of the other nets would be in if their anchor got run over by a truck this morning."

"Yeah, well, we did get run over by a truck, goddamn it," Rossman said glumly. "Stuart's an unknown, for Chrisake."

Neale ignored Rossman's comment. "If you lay the groundwork, and Stuart tests out well, we can have this thing rolling by the time we go to LA. Schumacher's people can get a new ad campaign going on a crash basis. The same with the promos. It's not impossible, Jerry. We can turn this whole thing around."

"It won't work," Rossman declared. "Trust me. I've been in the business a long time. A woman doesn't have the same authority as a man. That's just the way it is. You want to commit harikari? Go to Japan. But not on our network, for Chrisake."

"How do we know?" Neale asked. "There's plenty of women in news; they're all over every network. So we promote one, make her our number one anchor. Is it so fucking unheard of?"

He paused for a minute to let it sink in.

"What have we got to lose, Jerry?" he continued. "If she doesn't work out, it was a noble experiment. We can put that spin on it very easily. But if she makes it, and makes it big, she'll make everybody forget about John Cornwall or Robert Miniver. And you'll be the biggest pioneer in the business since Sarnoff. Christ, every feminist group in the country will be canonizing you."

Rossman played with the idea. Maybe Sid was right. Maybe it could work. Besides, what choice did he have? He had to try something.

"She may not be interested," he offered as a last defense against Neale's arguments "Malachek said he's never even spoken to her about anchoring."

"All it takes is money," Neale said, smiling.

Rossman laughed at Neale's use of his own favorite phrase.

"Yeah, sure, all it takes is money," he repeated. "But I don't want to take any chances even before we do any research. Stick around."

He gestured for Neale to sit on the couch again while he told his secretary to get him Hap Hawkins in Nebraska.

"You calling Hawkins?" Neale asked.

"You're damn right I am," Rossman said. "I want to see how this will play before we go any further."

"Hap, how are you?" he said as Hawkins came on the phone.

"Fine, fine, Jerry. It's good to hear from you," Hawkins answered.

"How's everything, Hap? Any problems?"

"We're doing fine, Jerry. We're practically sold out on local spots for the first quarter already and that's not even counting the Sunday morning paid religion."

"Hap, I wanted to speak to you about the Cornwall problem," Rossman said, lowering his voice.

"Do you have some news for me?" Hawkins asked anxiously. "I've got to tell you that a lot of the stations are getting very antsy, Jerry. This isn't like the network, to be taking this much time."

"These things take time, but we're coming to the decision point this week," Rossman said, trying to sound calm, reaching in his pocket for his pill container. "But I wanted to get your reaction because it obviously means a lot to us."

Neale looked at Rossman with admiration. He hasn't lost the touch, he thought.

"Is it going to be Antin? Did you get him?" Hawkins asked eagerly.

"No, he re-signed for a new deal," Rossman said. "He

wasn't available. Anyhow, he may not have been right. Our sales and research people all said we need somebody with solid news credentials anchoring the program."

"There's a lot of stations who feel that way," Hawkins reminded him.

"Are you familiar with Samantha Stuart's work, Hap?" Rossman asked.

"The good-looking blond? The one on *Focus on America?*"

"Yes. She filled in on *Sunrise* last year. Very strong on camera."

"Are you thinking of her? For the evening show?"

Rossman could not tell if Hawkins was stunned or intrigued.

"We're thinking very seriously about her. We think she may have tremendous potential. It would be a first in the industry, I realize, but we've never been afraid to be a leader."

"What about Burton or Swanson? Anything with them?"

"Burton didn't test well in the anchor role," Rossman said casually. "Swanson's still a possibility, although it obviously would hurt us in the morning if we moved him to the evening."

"You've got to do something, Jerry. By the end of the week at the latest. Can't you reach a decision by then? I'm getting calls all the time and I'm sure you are too. Frankly, I'm a little disappointed it's taken this long."

"We didn't want to rush into anything too quickly and regret it later on. It's been a hell of a problem but we think Samantha Stuart may be the one. All of us are really excited about her but I didn't want to let it out until we were sure in our own minds."

"Is there any research on her? I assume the demographics would be good."

"We're ordering a crash project this afternoon. It will take a couple of days at most. The demographics should be excellent. There's no question about it."

"It's an interesting idea, I'll say that," Hawkins observed. "How does she feel about it?"

"It won't be a problem," Rossman said confidently, relieved by Hawkins's response. He smiled broadly and gave Neale an "okay" sign with his thumb and forefinger. Neale smiled back.

"What about Malachek?" Hawkins asked.

"Carl wants her too."

"Well, he's a pro, all right."

"One of the best."

"Samantha Stuart," Hawkins said and Rossman could tell that Hawkins was picturing her in his mind. "It's an interesting idea, Jerry."

"We think so. There's a lot of upside to it."

There was a pause on the other end. Then Hawkins said, "I'd go for it. It's a gamble but, you know something? If she works out, she'll light up that screen like a million Roman candles. That gal's got one hell of a smile."

"I'm glad you feel that way," Rossman said, his face flushed with excitement. "I'll stay in very close touch, Hap, you can be sure of that and I'll let you know as soon as we know something. I think it's going to work out very well for everybody."

"Yes, please. Good talking to you, Jerry," Hawkins said, and hung up.

"He loves it!" Rossman said excitedly.

"Beautiful!" Neale exclaimed. "Can you imagine the sensation she's going to cause at the affiliates meeting if it works out? Half of the general managers won't even care that she's good. They'll be humping her in their minds."

Rossman felt euphoric. It was all going to work out. It all could be handled.

"See what you can find out about that guy who wrote to Malachek about Burton," he told Neale.

Then he went to the intercom on his desk and told his secretary, "See if you can get me Samantha Stuart."

Chapter 43

Samantha Stuart sat on the couch in her office and watched herself on a cassette playing through a television monitor in a corner of the office.

The cassette was one of ten tapes she had shot Monday afternoon in a two-hour interview with a young Hollywood actress who had recovered from cocaine addiction.

The interview, which was to be used as part of a segment on drug use in one of the first *Focus* programs of the new season, originally had been scheduled for the end of the week.

On Monday afternoon, however, Samantha had received a call from the actress's press agent.

"She has to go to the Coast early," the agent said. "They just asked her to do a charity luncheon at the Beverly Hills Hotel on Thursday and she wants to do it. It's the drug thing, you know, she's really into it. She may even do a book on it. Very brave kid. Can we possibly get together with her early this afternoon?"

"I'll see if there are any crews available and I'll get back to you," she told him.

Getting camera crews always was a problem. George Durgin dispensed them like a doctor's prescription. Two-a-day for the next two days. Then three-a-day for the next three days. Sometimes four-a-day if the program needed it.

Monday was a four-a-day prescription and there was a crew available.

She was glad. The need to quickly immerse herself in research about the actress would help her to stop thinking, at least for a little while, about what had happened to Art and his chances for the anchor job.

Ever since he had told her about Malachek's decision, she had been able to think of little else.

Even on Sunday, when they finally had gone out on the boat and spent the day sailing along the Cape Ann coastline, she had been unable to concentrate on what Art was saying.

It had been a magnificent day; brilliant sunshine, a cloudless sky, a strong breeze that was caught by the billowing mainsail, but her thoughts kept coming back to her belief that Art had been crushed by Malachek.

It was that fact she was unable to escape. It hovered there throughout the day, like one of the seagulls constantly trailing the boat.

Even on the five-hour drive back to New York City Sunday night, it had crowded, filled the sports car with an

overwhelming presence that no amount of innocuous conversation could get rid of.

They kept coming back to it—there was no way to avoid
it—Malachek, Ducoin, the Cornwall job; and when the long
trip was over and they were lying in bed in Art's apartment at
the end of the evening, he told her again how sorry he was
that everything had fallen apart.

"Maybe it just was never meant to be," he said.

"What?" she asked, suddenly fearful that he was talking
about them.

"The anchor job. Keeping the Ducoin incident buried.
Maybe I should have figured that he was alive all these years
and that I'd pay the penalty someday."

"It's late at night, darling," she said. "Don't torture
yourself all night with this."

"I won't," he said, even though she knew he didn't mean
it. He finally fell asleep at one-thirty in the morning but she
lay awake for half an hour more, unable to let go of all that
had happened.

On Monday, when she went to the Carlyle to interview
the young actress, she welcomed it as a respite from the
emotional roller coaster she had been riding the last few
days. But the interview did not go well.

She found herself asking perfunctory questions, failing to
follow up on half-assed answers, showing no interest in
finding out any details beyond the basic information in the
publicity handout.

The trouble was that her heart and mind were else-
where: sitting in the yellow canvas chair in the cottage at
Gloucester, sitting in the shadow of the rocks at the end of
Good Harbor Beach, swimming in the water, driving on the
Mass Pike and then the interstates to New York, lying in bed
in an apartment on West Ninety-second Street.

Her thoughts were interrupted by the phone ringing on
her desk.

She shut off the cassette machine. "Yes?" she said.

"This is Yvonne, Mr. Rossman's secretary. Mr. Rossman
is asking if you can have lunch with him in the private dining
room today," the secretary said.

"I'm sorry, I didn't quite understand you," Samantha
said, too stunned to think. Was this a joke?

"Mr. Rossman was asking if you could have lunch today.

Would twelve-thirty be all right?" the secretary said in a slightly annoyed voice.

"Yes, of course," Samantha replied.

Suddenly, for some inexplicable reason, Jerry Rossman was asking her to lunch. But why?

There was no explanation for it, and nobody to whom she could turn for an answer.

Art wasn't in his office and she had no idea where he was. Malachek was the only other person she could ask, but her instincts told her that Malachek would not know. If he did, she reasoned, he would have called her ahead of time.

Could Rossman want to talk to her about Art and Ducoin? But she and Art always had been discreet about their relationship and there was no way Rossman, or anyone else, could know that they were in love or that she knew what had happened.

There was also the dreadful possibility that Rossman was interested in her sexually and the luncheon invitation was a feeler, a test to see if she were approachable. Things like this happened, she knew, although she had never heard a whisper of scandal concerning Rossman. Besides, Rossman had to know that she wasn't the type.

She considered the idea that Rossman wanted to talk to her about anchoring *Sunrise* in the event Michael Swanson was picked to succeed Cornwall. But she'd never publicly pushed her ambition to anchor a show, the way some other correspondents had. She assumed the News Division and the network regarded her as a strong correspondent but not as someone who wanted to anchor.

Besides, if she were being considered for *Sunrise*, Malachek would have said something to her by now. It hadn't even been on the A-wire.

The only other possibility was that something had happened regarding Herman Willows. Maybe his wife was filing some kind of lawsuit, charging harrassment leading to his suicide, and Rossman wanted to talk to her about it. Maybe there would be a couple of attorneys from legal at the lunch.

But, again, why wouldn't Malachek have told her?

None of the explanations fit.

An hour later, as she rode the elevator to the twenty-fifth floor, she tried to remember the last time Rossman had even spoken to her.

It must have been two years ago, she decided, at a reception the News Division had given for some visiting executives from a Japanese television network.

Rossman had been present and there had been a small ceremony, exchanging gifts; Rossman giving the Japanese a silver casting of an American eagle, the Japanese presenting him with a hand-painted porcelain vase.

It all had been very polite and formal, she remembered, with the Japanese taking pictures of everyone and the News Division people standing around trying to look interested.

Afterward, Rossman had circulated among the crowd and had said to her, "Nice to see you here," as if she had been a guest from the outside. That had been it.

She had seen him a few times since then, at a distance; at other receptions or at luncheons where he had been the guest speaker, and she had been at the News Division's table, but there had not been an opportunity, or a reason, to speak to him.

She had, in fact, never even been in his office. As the elevator doors opened onto the twenty-fifth floor, she wondered, as a last, remote, possibility, if she were about to be the victim of some malicious practical joke.

It wasn't a joke. A smiling Rossman was waiting for her as she came into the dining room.

There was nobody else in the room and she quickly noticed that the table was set for only two people. *He can't be thinking of making a move*, she thought. *He can't be*.

"It's nice to see you, Samantha," Rossman said pleasantly, trying to remember when he had last seen her. "I'm glad you were able to make it."

"It was something of a surprise when your secretary called," she admitted, accepting his handshake. "I didn't know that correspondents were invited to lunch up here with you."

"Once in a while," he said casually. "John Cornwall and I have lunched here several times, maybe one or two others."

Who? she wondered.

"Would you like a drink?" he asked as a waiter appeared from the entrance to the kitchen.

"Just a glass of white wine please."

"Two glasses of white wine," Rossman told the waiter and he gestured to Samantha to take a seat at the table.

"How long have you been at the network now?" he asked as he sat down at the head of the table, flanking her.

"Four years," she answered.

"When did you start in the business?"

"Right out of college, UCLA. Then I spent almost seven years in the affiliates before the network offered me a job." Why is he asking me this, she thought.

I should have checked with Sid Neale to get a bio, Rossman thought. What is she, thirty-two, thirty-three?

"I'll try and end the suspense for you," Rossman said suddenly. "Have you ever thought about anchoring one of our shows?"

It's *Sunrise. They've decided on Swanson and they're considering me to replace him.*

"Yes, of course. I would like to anchor a show here. I did *Sunrise* a few times and I enjoyed it." She looked at the network president, trying to figure out what he wanted.

"I just haven't actually pursued the anchoring end of the business," she added.

"But you'd like to?" he asked cautiously.

The waiter then brought the wine. She felt herself clutching her glass too tightly. She was afraid it was going to break and the glass was going to shatter all over her, the tablecloth, everywhere. What is he leading up to? she thought.

"Yes, of course," she said again.

Rossman felt relieved. From now on, it could be handled.

"Samantha, I want you to know that we are very interested in having you anchor our evening news. We'd like you to replace John Cornwall, take over the show from him."

Oh my God, she thought. It's me! Me for Art! It was inconceivable.

"We've been doing a lot of thinking," he continued, studying her, trying to fathom her reaction, trying, at the same time not to be distracted by her gray-green eyes, "and we think that you are the best choice. We all have a lot of confidence in you."

The impact of what he was saying had a paralyzing effect on her. She was silent for a long moment.

"I don't know what to say, or to think," she confessed. "This is something I just wasn't prepared for. I don't know what to say, or do." She felt herself starting to stumble over her words and she quickly stopped talking, as if she were afraid that she was going to fall apart, right in front of him.

Rossman had not known what to expect but he could tell that he had unnerved her. He wanted her to calm down so that he could talk it through with her.

"As you can imagine, we considered a lot of possibilities. There's no question in my mind that you will do extremely well. I'm sure the affiliates will regard you as a strong and exciting choice."

It can't be happening like this, she thought. There must be more to it.

"What about Art Burton and Michael Swanson?" she asked, clearing her throat, which suddenly had gone dry. "I thought they were the leading candidates."

"The testing on Burton didn't come out too well," he replied smoothly.

She felt disgusted, sitting there and listening to him lie about Art. She wanted to tell him how she felt, but she said nothing.

"And Swanson?" she asked.

"We don't want to take him off *Sunrise*."

She did not know whether or not to believe him.

"There were some rumors going around the News Division that Mark Antin was being considered," she said.

"Antin didn't have strong enough news credentials. All of our people felt that a person with a legitimate news background, like you, was essential," he replied.

Rossman's reference to "news credentials" jolted her into realizing that Rossman had not yet mentioned Malachek. What had happened?

"Could you tell me how Carl Malachek feels about this? I would have figured he'd have talked to me about this, but he never said a word."

"I can tell you that Malachek was one of the people who recommended you," he said.

She was stunned. Could it be true?

Rossman looked directly at her but this time he was not distracted by her cat's eyes. "You must keep this confidential, Samantha, but Carl has decided to resign. It won't be announced for a little while but apparently it's something he's been thinking about for a long time."

She was shocked. "When?" she asked. "When is it going to happen?"

"Before the affiliates convention in LA, I'm sure. But he'll be winding down for the next several days and will not be involved in the anchor situation."

"Why would Malachek want to resign?" she asked with a puzzled expression that she hoped looked sincere. "Is it because Cornwall walked out?"

"Nothing to do with that," Rossman said quickly. "I think it's something very personal."

She was silent again and Rossman was grateful. Her questions were beginning to bother him although he understood where she was coming from. What the hell, she wanted to know. He could understand that. But how much does she need to know, for God's sake?

"Would you like to eat now?" he asked.

She didn't feel like eating. She could feel her stomach churning and she wanted to leave, to go somewhere and think.

It all was coming down on her again, just like it had when she had heard about Herman Willows's suicide on the eleven o'clock news. It was too much, too fast.

"I hope you'll understand," she said quietly, "but all of this has been overwhelming. I think I'd rather not eat, if you don't mind, and just go back to my office and settle down."

"I understand," he responded. "Please don't feel it's necessary to stay. We can talk about it later when you're over the initial surprise. I would like you to make up your mind in the next day or two. We need to do some focus group testing, just to validate our own instincts. I wouldn't worry about it if I were you, but we need to get it out of the way. Tell me, are you represented? Who's your agent?"

"I don't have one," she answered, realizing for the first time that she had not even thought about the money involved.

"I will let you know in a day or two," she said. "I just can't say yes or no right now."

"Of course," he said.

"I'll let you know very soon," she assured him, offering her hand.

"We'll be very generous on the salary. You don't have to worry about that," he remarked as he walked her to the door.

"I'm sure," she said numbly.

The elevator ride down to the seventh floor seemed interminably slow but she was grateful. For some inexplicable reason, nobody got on between twenty-five and seven and the privacy, in even that tiny frame of space and time, helped her adjust to the shock of Rossman's offer and its implications not only for her but also for Art.

She went into her office, closed the door, and absent-mindedly picked up the toy UCLA Bruin from her couch. She tried to remember who had given it to her but she couldn't. She had been a freshman and he had been a junior but that was all she could remember. It had been so long ago.

She rubbed the bear's fake fur against her face as if it were a magical lamp that, at her command, would endow her with all the strength she needed to cope with what was happening.

Oh God, it wasn't supposed to happen this way. Never. Never. Never.

She could feel herself starting to cry and she clutched the bear tightly, the way she had held Plato years ago. Then she put the tiny mascot down, wiped the tears from her eyes, and went over to the phone and called her sister.

She could not remember whether Helen had any Tuesday afternoon classes and she was happy when Helen answered the phone.

"Hellenic, it's me," she said, calling her sister by the nickname she had given her years ago.

"Samantha!" Helen answered, surprised. "Where are you? Gloucester? Newton?"

"No, here in New York. In my office."

"Is everything all right? Mom and Dad?"

"They're fine," she said. She paused. "I need to talk to you about something, Helly. It's important."

"I can tell that by the tone of your voice," her sister said.

"It's about Art and me," she said glumly. "I don't even know where to begin."

"It's not over, is it?"

"No, nothing like that. But have you been following the stories in the papers about John Cornwall and who's going to replace him on the evening news? There must have been something in the *Globe* about it."

"You know I'm not one of those cloistered academics who

won't even admit to owning a television set but I really haven't paid that much attention. Should I?"

"Well, there's a lot of interest. The main thing is—Art was going to take over from him. He was going to anchor the network news, every night."

"I'm impressed, seriously." She paused. "But you said was."

"Yes, it's a long story that has to do with the president of the News Division and something else but the long and the short of it is that Art was told Saturday morning that he's not going to get it."

"He must be terribly disappointed. And you too."

"That's the problem, Helly. I've been asked to replace him."

"Fantastic!" Helen exclaimed. "You should be thrilled, but I gather you're not."

"How can I be? To anchor the evening news now, after Art was treated the way he was, would be like rubbing his nose in dirt. It would be so damn cruel to him, Helen."

"Does he know yet, that you've been asked?"

"No, it just happened. I had lunch with the president of the network. He made me the offer."

"And when will you tell Art?"

"Soon. This afternoon. He needs to hear it from me first, not from the grapevine."

"And what will you tell him, Sam? Will you tell him you're taking the anchor position?"

"I don't know what I'm going to do," she admitted. "That's why I called you. I'm just so damn confused. I thought maybe you might have some good sisterly advice."

"I can't offer any help on this one, Samantha. I know how much Art means to you—I could see that just by looking at you two when you stopped by the house last October—but I have no idea what anchoring the news means to you. I know that professionally it's as prestigious as it gets. But it's a world I know nothing about.

"This is something you'll have to decide for yourself and then measure it against Art's feelings, whatever they may be, if you think one has to be weighed against the other."

Samantha sighed. "It all sounds so practical, doesn't it? Pure Aristotelian thinking."

Helen caught the dejected tone in her sister's voice.

"You should speak to Art first before you make up your mind," she advised her.

"Yes," Samantha agreed. "I was planning to do that anyhow. I wanted to get my head straight first. You helped."

"Do you remember that quotation from the 'Funeral Oration of Pericles' that's on the living room wall?" Helen asked. " 'We celebrate games and sacrifices all the year round.' "

"Of course," Samantha answered, picturing the hand-sewn Roman-style lettering embroidered onto the linen fabric in the black and silver frame.

"I tell my students that at the beginning of every term," Helen said. "Games and sacrifices. You just have to know which is which sometimes."

"I'll keep that in mind," Samantha said, laughing. "Thanks, Helly, for everything."

When she stepped out into the hallway, the door to Art's office was open and he was sitting at his desk, reading *The Washington Post*.

She walked in, closing the door behind her. Art put the paper down, noticing immediately how pale she looked.

"Are you feeling okay?" he asked.

"I'm fine," she said, but with no conviction, as she sat in a chair across from his desk.

"Are you sure?" he asked, concerned. "You look as if you've been through the wringer today."

"Maybe I have," she tossed off, instantly regretting the remark. But it was too late.

"What's wrong?" he asked anxiously.

"I don't know where to begin," she said helplessly, exhaling a deep sigh. He sat on the edge of the desk, facing her. "Try me," he said.

She told him about the lunch with Rossman and the offer to replace Cornwall. When she finished, she took his hands in hers. "I never dreamed it would turn out this way, Art. Me getting the job because you didn't. It seems so unfair."

He was stunned. It hadn't occurred to him that Samantha would be considered as a possibility for the evening news. All of their talk about anchoring had always been about him. Never her. Now she was getting it because he had lost it.

He wondered if she had been the choice all along—a secret weapon that Malachek and Rossman had been plan-

ning to unveil all this time, using him as a decoy. Had
Malachek's insistence on the clean slate for the anchorman
just been a lot of bullshit? Would he have thrown him out at
the end even if Ducoin had not appeared? God, could they
be that deceptive?

"Have you spoken to Malachek yet?" he asked. "What
does he say?"

"No," she answered. "Rossman said only that Malachek
had recommended me."

Could it be true? he asked himself.

"It's a hell of an opportunity for you, Samantha. You
should take it."

Her eyes were starting to well up. "I don't know what to
do," she said softly. "I want it, of course, just like I wanted it
for you. I always wanted to anchor but I never thought any
woman had a chance for the evening news. It was a dream I
abandoned a long time ago. All of my emotions, all my
dreams, my hopes, were with you. That's all I wanted—for
you to get it."

Her voice was starting to crack. "And now I'm being
offered the job that should have been yours. And I don't want
it this way. I don't know if I can handle it, Art. It's tearing me
up. Everything that's ever happened to me in this business
I've gotten on my own merits. But this is like getting your big
break because the leading actor died."

"Jesus, don't put it that way."

"It's true. I should be happy. It's the biggest chance of
my life but I don't feel good about it. I feel like you did last
week, that Malachek had picked you for the wrong reasons.
Well, I don't like what Malachek did to you in the end. And I
don't like Rossman. He makes me squirm."

"Don't feel that way," he pleaded with her. "You should
be thrilled by this."

"How can I be? How can I be thrilled that I'm being
picked for the biggest plum in television, as you once called it
yourself, only because they've ruled you out?"

"They didn't have to pick you," he pointed out. "They
could have gone to Swanson, McVea, even Antin."

"Rossman said the research people were opposed to
Antin."

"That still leaves the others. Don't tear yourself up over
this, Samantha. They're coming to you. They want you."

"He lied to me about you."

"Who? Rossman?"

"Yes. I asked him about you, why you weren't picked. He said you didn't test well."

"What could he say? You didn't expect him to tell the truth, did you? About me and Ducoin? He'd have no reason to tell you that. That's the one damn thing they don't want anybody to know, isn't it?"

A half-smile, tinged by a trace of bitterness, crossed his face.

"I know it hurts you darling," she said. "You can be honest with me. That's why I'm so confused and torn up about this."

"It doesn't hurt. Ducoin hurt and Malachek hurt but this doesn't hurt."

"Rossman said Malachek is resigning."

"Jesus," Art muttered. So Malachek had not been deceiving him. He really did believe in the purity of the anchorman. In a way, Art was relieved. It was what he had suspected in Malachek's office, that Malachek felt so strongly about his beliefs that he would quit rather than give them up.

"Take the anchor job," he told her again. "It only comes around once. Never mind about Rossman or Malachek or the rest of them. Just take the job and show them how damn good you are."

He leaned over and pulled her up from her chair. He held her by the shoulders and then he drew her closer to him and put his arms around her.

"Take it," he said. "For the both of us."

"And will you stay by me?"

"Of course I will. You didn't have to ask."

"And *Focus*? You'll keep doing it?"

"Yes. I'll blow their socks off I'll be so fucking good."

"Maybe things will turn out the way we wanted after all," she said, smiling wistfully. "It will be easier to make plans, to be together. I'd be here five nights a week, week after week."

"Yes," he answered, smiling at the irony of it all.

They finally had the chance to shape their lives, but it was because of her, not him.

"I was just thinking the same thing," he said.

She smiled and threw her arms around him and held

him in a tight embrace, so tight that she was afraid for a moment she was going to squeeze the breath out of him.

He welcomed her strong embrace. He had felt a sudden chill and now she made him feel warm.

"Hold me tighter," he whispered.

He said nothing but held on to her, stroking the back of her head with his hand, his eyes open, staring into space, staring at the closed door.

PART
FOUR

Chapter 44

Bobby Ducoin is getting hard, right in the middle of the Delta Air Lines waiting area at O'Hare Airport, thinking about Corinne Anne and what it's going to be like if he sees her again, wondering if she'll remember him right away, even after all this time, wondering what it's going to be like when he goes to the downtown in Fire Point and they see him, all changed like this.

Oh Lord, he's thinking, I knew you'd help me to go back some day, help me to try and see her again, probably just as beautiful as when she was strutting in front of the Three Cs band, with the sun shining on that golden face and those beautiful breasts bulging out of that glittery costume and those legs spread wide open like she's been waiting all this time for me to come inside her.

Only this time we won't have to do it on a blanket out in the pine woods with the ground shaking every time one of the big semis hauling lumber goes down the highway a mile away and with the pine needles turning brown like wet hay after a rain.

Oh no, we're going up to Memphis, or down to Jackson, maybe even to New Orleans, and get the best goddamn hotel room there is and we'll drink champagne and eat the biggest steaks and then we'll do it.

Oh my beautiful Corinne Anne, we'll fuck all night, like I never been away, like it all never happened to me, and then, when we wake up in the morning with the blankets all over the floor and nothing but you and me and the wet sheets on the bed, you'll say "Oh Bobby, it don't make no difference about your arm, you're the best that ever was."

457

Bobby Ducoin sees himself in the reflection of one of the big plate glass windows looking out over part of the tarmac at O'Hare, with the planes taxiing behind his reflection, like he was transparent, and he sees the new three hundred dollar suit and twenty dollar tie he's wearing and he knows his Daddy was right.

The good Lord helps those who help themselves.

Oh yeah, seeing that picture of Lieutenant Bertrand and writing those letters is what did it. He showed them, all right, Bertrand and that Malachek too, coming down on him like he didn't mean no more than a lump of dog shit, trying to scare him away with all that talk about lawyers and getting in trouble.

But none of their bullshit worked, did it? The only ones scared was them, sending out that sharp-suited guy with the contract and the money right away.

Hell, they want to pay him ten thousand dollars, he'll tell them whatever they want to know about fighting in Vietnam, even if they never make a damn program about the war. Only thing they don't want to know about is the Lieutenant, that's for sure. He understood that part real easy.

Shit, he wasn't born yesterday. It's like his Daddy told him once. It ain't what you plant, it's how the crops come up.

Bobby Ducoin has got some money now, more money than he's had since the War, since the time he got all that back pay from the Army, and it's all nice and legal.

He put the money in the bank right away, the teller looking at him like he was some kind of freak, and he thought about Fire Point. He had thought for a long time, long after his Mama and Daddy died, about going back just once, just to see what the house on Barnett Street looked like and to walk around the Courthouse Square with the statue of the Confederate soldier and to see the old men sitting there, seeing him, remembering the time they had the welcome home parade for him, right down Lamar Avenue.

And then, when he was lying on his bed at night at the Y, on the same day he had put the money in the bank over on Michigan Avenue, and thinking again about Corinne Anne and wondering if she was still around, he realized that he really could go back and everybody would say, Hey, look at that Bobby Ducoin! Ain't he something now!

Oh yeah, look at him walking through O'Hare Airport.

Just like everybody else going somewhere, flying some place, on this Labor Day weekend.

Nobody's paying him any attention, even with one sleeve of the new suit he bought at Marshall Field's sewed carefully to the side of his coat, but that doesn't matter now because Bobby Ducoin knows he's special.

The good Lord has paid him back for all those years in the prison camp. All those years out there shoveling shit for a living and now he's got enough money to last him a long time and he knows how to get more. Real easy.

And in a little while, he'll be on that plane to Jackson and if the Trailways is still running the afternoon bus that goes up along the Natchez Trace he'll be back in Fire Point before the sun goes down. Since it's a holiday, there might even be a barbecue or a big picnic out by the fairgrounds. Maybe the Three Cs Band will be practicing, like they used to, out by the football field and everybody will be coming out to watch them. Maybe even Corinne Anne.

He wonders if she will remember him.

Chapter 45

Jerry Rossman moved smoothly through the crowd that was beginning to mill around the Grand Ballroom of the Century Plaza Hotel in Los Angeles.

He moved easily, like a big fish gliding gracefully through the waters of a huge tank at an aquarium.

His leisurely walk matched the mood of the people in the ballroom—serene contentment—and, as he circled the room, slicing through a crowd of men and women pushing toward one of the room-length bars that had been set up on each side of the ballroom, he was happy that everything had worked out.

The affiliates could not be happier. They had been telling him so ever since the first day of the convention.

There was no question that the announcement that Samantha Stuart would anchor the evening news was generating enormous interest. The excitement about her had been building ever since he had announced, at the very first session, that she would replace John Cornwall.

Thank God he had been smart enough to get Hap Hawkins to go along with the idea before he had even approached Stuart. *Schmoozing* him had paid off big.

Hawkins had been lining up support for her ever since her name had been floated through the affiliate ranks. Now, as he searched out Hawkins, he congratulated himself for having brought Hawkins in from the start.

He found Hawkins standing with his wife near the buffet.

"Hell of a party, isn't it, Hap?" he said, grinning happily and leaning over to kiss Hawkins's wife on the cheek.

"Have you been enjoying it, Rosalie?" Rossman asked, not waiting for an answer from her husband.

She paused to swallow a little frankfurter and replied, "LA is one of my favorite places. I look forward to this so much every year. And it's so nice to see so many wives again. Everybody's had a wonderful time."

He smiled at her and turned to Hawkins and put his hand on Hawkins's arm.

"I can't tell you how much your support on Samantha Stuart has meant to us, Hap," Rossman said. "That resolution you sponsored this afternoon is something I'll personally treasure for a long time," he added, referring to a resolution from the Council of Affiliates commending the network for its "foresight and leadership" in choosing a woman to anchor the evening news.

"We all feel we're on the threshold of something big," Hawkins said. "There's a real spirit of enthusiasm here."

"Listen, Hap. I'm giving a little breakfast tomorrow morning for Samantha in our suite. I'd like you and Rosalie to be our guests. It'll give you a chance to get to know her a lot better."

"We'd love it," Hawkins responded. "Look forward to it," he added.

"Nine-thirty in my suite," Rossman reminded him. He nodded good-bye and wandered toward a group of general managers standing by a white-jacketed waiter who was holding a tray of canapés.

"Don't eat too much, men. Save some for dinner," he said jokingly as he approached them, thinking: where the hell is Barry Kovaks?

The final banquet was due to start in half an hour, when the cocktail hour ended, but he hadn't seen Kovaks anywhere. Not that anything could go wrong, God forbid, but, still, it would be nice to have Kovaks's assurance that everything was set for the entertainment following the meal.

So far, the convention had been perfect. The two days of business sessions over at the old theater on Sunset Boulevard had been a love feast and he didn't want anything to louse it up now.

John Cornwall's speech at yesterday's luncheon had been warm and gracious, just as he had figured it to be. Even that son of bitch Malachek had handled his resignation with just the right touch of regret. Not that he had a choice. Fuck him, Rossman thought, maybe he'll be happier teaching.

He glanced around the ballroom, the walls festooned with enormous caricatures of the network's stars and the ceiling speckled with hundreds of balloons in the network's brown and red colors. A huge curtain, with the network logo hanging in the center, was drawn in front of the stage at the front of the ballroom and, to the side of the stage, members of a band were beginning to straggle in.

Where the hell is Kovaks? To his relief, he saw Barry Kovaks standing across the room.

He signaled him to break off his conversation and motioned toward a corner near the stage where nobody was standing. It seemed to be the one empty space in the whole room.

"Jesus, Barry, I've been looking all over for you," he said in an agitated voice as Kovaks came over. "Where the hell have you been?"

"Is something wrong?" Kovaks asked nervously.

"No, I want to make sure that everything is okay for after the banquet. The lights, the band, everything."

"We had a rehearsal this afternoon. Even Winston went through his bit. It was great," Kovaks assured him. "They're going to eat it up."

"Listen, just a reminder. When I introduce Samantha, make goddamn sure the band doesn't play any music. No drum rolls or anything like it. She's not an entertainer. She's our meal ticket on the news. It has to be dignified. I don't want any bad press on her introduction."

"C'mon Jerry, relax," Kovaks said.

"Yeah, sure," Rossman said. Just let this evening be a success, he silently implored nobody in particular. So far, at least, Sid Neale's recommendations had worked out. Keeping Samantha Stuart and Jarvis Winston away from everybody; the owners, the general managers, their wives, the press, even the network people, had been a smart play. Everybody was pissing in their pants waiting to see both of them. Christ, it was going to be sensational!

"We figured your remarks at about five minutes. Is that about right?" Kovaks asked him.

"Yes, but figure in some applause for Cornwall. I'm going to give him another mention."

"Smart idea," Kovaks observed. "What about Malachek?"

"What about him?" Rossman snapped.

"I didn't know if you were planning to give him a kiss again," Kovaks said, oblivious to Rossman's reaction.

"No, I thought my remarks about him at the Cornwall luncheon yesterday were appropriate. I don't think he expects anything else."

"It'll be fine," Kovaks assured him. He pointed to the room where people were beginning to drift toward the candlelit tables and take their seats. "Happy people," he said.

"They should be," Rossman remarked. "We've had a hell of a run. Sold out up front on some of our new shows. If the news holds up, we're going to do just fine in the new season."

"We've got America's Favorites," Kovaks said. "Just like our promos say we do."

"How's Winston?" Rossman asked. "Nervous?"

"Nah, he'll be fine. He's a pro. He's got a very funny routine," Kovaks said. "I spoke to Samantha Stuart up in her room about an hour ago," he added. "She'll be backstage when the entertainment starts so nobody will see her until she's actually introduced."

"Good," Rossman said approvingly. He scanned the room, trying to find his wife in the crowd. "I'd better find Gloria," he said to Kovaks. "Talk to you later."

*   *   *

At exactly ten o'clock, the lights in the ballroom dimmed and the stage curtains parted to reveal a huge screen. As the ballroom went completely dark, a series of highlights from the network's top programs were shown on the screen. Each segment was greeted by enthusiastic applause from the audience. As the last segment, an excerpt from *The Jarvis Winston Hour*, was shown, the applause built to a loud crescendo.

The screen went black and a voice, seeming to come from nowhere intoned, "Ladies and Gentlemen . . . Jarvis Winston!"

A single spotlight focused on the far left corner of the stage and then Jarvis Winston stepped into the pool of light. The band began to play the theme song from Winston's program and the audience rose to its feet and cheered loudly.

Winston, holding his hands in front of him like a Buddhist monk, bowed his head to acknowledge the ovation.

I'm okay, he thought. I'm okay.

His left arm was in a sling and even though Barry Kovaks had advised him to use stage makeup to cover the purple markings on his face, he had decided to show his facial bruises. It was his first appearance in public since the beating and Mickey Schirmer had told him, "Milk it. Make them love you."

Mickey was right. As usual.

"A funny thing happened to me on the way to the convention," he began as the audience broke out in laughter.

"You know," he continued. "I always knew Jerry Rossman was a tough guy to negotiate a contract with, but this is ridiculous. And you should see my agent!"

This time, there were howls of laughter. Winston peered into the darkness, found the front row of tables and saw Rossman convulsed with laughter. Fuck you, he thought. I'm going to cost you plenty the next time around.

"You know, Rossman used to train kamikaze pilots," he said and, again, he could hear the laughter coming back at him. I'm on a roll, he told himself.

"He is the funniest man alive," Rosalie Hawkins told Rossman, wiping her eyes.

He's the luckiest son of a bitch alive, Rossman thought, but he nodded vigorously. "He's wonderful."

In the row of tables behind him, Carl Malachek squinted through his cigar smoke at Winston and thought, "We could have had your ass."

But, on the stage, Winston knew only that he was scoring big. He was back, doing the shtick, and it felt sensational. Maybe tonight, after the show, he could fuck that little makeup artist he had seen backstage. Why not? His luck was running good. He had won a bundle on the Rams' first exhibition game and if that wasn't a good sign, what the hell was? Not only that, but the cops still didn't have any idea why he had been beaten up. And, according to what Mickey had told him, the news people at the network must have dropped whatever investigation they were doing on gambling. Talk about a parlay! This was the Big Trifecta and little old Jerome was right at the cashier's window with the winning tickets.

"Hey, people," he said, glancing backstage where Barry Kovaks was giving him a wind-up sign. "I don't care what John Cornwall thinks. I liked the meal tonight."

A wave of laughter crashed against him and he suddenly raised his hand, as if he were giving a stop sign, to signify that he wanted silence.

"You know I've done a lot of kidding tonight," he said quietly, quickly changing the mood of the audience. "But now I want to get serious for just a minute. I've had a rough time in the last few weeks but there's one person whose support and friendship has helped me more than any doctors or nurses."

He could tell the audience believed him. They were lapping it up.

"I'm talking about a man who represents everything good in television," he continued, trying to sound as sincere as possible. "He's got taste, he's got class, he's got the best damn network in America! I'm talking about my boss and I want to bring him up here right now. Jerry Rossman!"

The band began to play "Hey Look Me Over" and the spotlight swung away from Winston and picked out Rossman at his table.

He got up, raising his hands over his head like a prize fighter and, as the spotlight bathed him in a white glow, he walked up the steps to the stage. The audience was on its feet again, cheering, and Rossman stood with his arm around Winston and acknowledged the applause.

Rossman gestured with his palms for the crowd to sit down.

He waited until there was silence. Finally, he said,

"Jarvis, what can I tell you except that, next time, use a stand-in for the fight scene."

The crowd erupted in laughter and Rossman was happy that he had said the line exactly as it had been given to him, earlier in the day, by a gag writer friend of Barry Kovaks.

"Seriously, Jarvis, all of us are delighted that you are back with us and we look forward to having you as part of the network family for many, many years."

There was sustained applause from the crowd and, as the band played the theme song from *The Jarvis Winston Hour*, Rossman threw his other arm around Winston and gave him a bear hug.

Carl Malachek looked at the scene on the stage and thought: you phony prick.

He felt like walking out of the room, now, and not giving a shit if everybody stared at him and wondered why he was leaving.

But he wanted to see what kind of a reception Samantha Stuart would get.

He had been genuinely surprised when Rossman told him that she had been chosen to replace John Cornwall. So had Cornwall.

"I'm finding it a little hard to accept, Carl," Cornwall had told him at the luncheon yesterday, "that I'm being succeeded by a woman whose biggest credentials are a great smile and a beautiful pair of eyes."

"She's a good reporter," Malachek had said in her defense. "She's credible."

"That's maybe why you would have picked her but don't tell me that's why Rossman picked her or why all those general managers out there have their tongues hanging out waiting to meet her."

"You win some and you lose some," Malachek had responded.

In fact, he had suggested her to Rossman as a possible replacement for Cornwall because she was a good reporter and had solid credentials, but it had been a throwaway idea. Intellectually, it was an interesting idea to have a woman anchor the evening news but he never expected Rossman to follow up on it.

Rossman, of course, was taking all the credit now for a bold move.

At first, it bothered him that Samantha Stuart never came to him, even as a courtesy, to speak to him about the job. But his resignation had been announced by then and, he knew, his opinions didn't carry weight anymore, even in Seven West.

He was a one-man government in exile, waiting for a successor to be named in order to have an orderly transition of power.

Still, he wondered why she had been so aloof to him in his final days.

It troubled him but it was too late to do anything about it.

Winston had left the stage and Rossman stood alone now in front of the huge curtain. The audience was silent, almost out of respect, waiting for him to speak.

"Friends and partners, because that's what we are," he began, "we've come to the end of another convention and I have only one last function to perform. But it's one of the most important I've ever had to do."

He waited to let his words sink in.

"Before I do," he continued, "I want to pay tribute once again to two people who have contributed so much to our success over the years. As you know, they both are leaving— one to teach, the other to write. But whatever they do, and wherever they go, they always will have a home here. They are two of the finest professionals I've ever had the pleasure to know and to work with. Please stand up, Carl Malachek and John Cornwall!"

The spotlight came on again and its broad beam swung around the room until it picked out Malachek and Cornwall. The two men, seated at tables near each other, rose to the ovation and waved awkwardly to the audience.

Malachek's eyes roamed around the ballroom. He was glad that he had told Mary Lou to stay home in Rye and not come out to the Coast this year for the convention.

She would not have liked any of it, particularly this. Had she been here, he knew, she would have gone right up to Rossman at the end of the evening and called him a hypocritical son of a bitch right to his face.

He was tempted to do it himself, later, but why cheapen himself?

He was going to go out clean, with the dean's job at a

J-school waiting for him in January and a good buy out on his contract already in the bank.

As soon as his successor was named, he could relax and not have to worry anymore about late-night phone calls or other networks getting exclusive stories or the White House climbing all over his back.

He told himself he would not miss it.

When the applause for Malachek and Cornwall subsided, Rossman paused for a moment, making sure that the audience knew that he had come to the most significant moment of the evening.

"As you all know," he said solemnly, "John Cornwall's departure presented us with a major problem because a John Cornwall just doesn't come along every day. But we also looked at John's leaving as an opportunity to reaffirm to our audiences, your audiences, our commitment to excellence. We wanted the best person we could find as a replacement for John Cornwall and we found that person, as I always knew we would, in our own network family.

"You all know Samantha Stuart's background. She's one of you. She came from the affiliates and she's been a local reporter and a network correspondent. The times she filled in on *Sunrise* were our first indication of her potential as anchor and I don't have to tell you that she's been one of the major reasons for the success of *Focus on America*, where she's been a featured correspondent for the past few years.

"And I can also tell you that when we went out into the field and did some sampling with test groups on Samantha as an anchor, the results were as we expected them to be. They were highly favorable with few negative reactions.

"We've picked her for anchor of the evening news not because she's a woman, but because she is the best. It is my great pleasure to introduce to you our new anchor of the evening news, Samantha Stuart!"

Samantha stepped out from behind the curtain and heard the cheering and the loud applause. The waves of applause seemed to career around the room, bouncing back at her from all sides, and her eyes began to moisten as she realized it was all for her.

She was dressed in a red silk crepe cocktail dress, and she was wearing only one piece of jewelry, a tiny, gold pin in the shape of a seagull, that Art had given her last night.

The audience was still applauding and now the spotlight that had earlier focused on Jarvis Winston was shining on her, bathing her in a strange glow, even though all the lights in the room were still on.

This isn't me, she thought. *This is happening to somebody else. I'm just playing a role.*

This can't be me, standing here in a spotlight, in a Valentino dress and a Cartier pin, and all those people out front applauding.

She wished the lights would dim, because the brightness was bothering her.

Art had told her, before she left her room, that he would come to the ballroom and stand in the back but she could not pick him out through the lights and the smoke.

Art darling, she silently told him, don't be hurt by all of this. This isn't me, I swear to you. You told me to take the anchor job because I deserved it, but so did you, dammit, and now look at me—lit up like a neon sign and being stared at as if I were some sort of a movie star goddess.

Art, she whispered to him in her mind, I wish I had stayed in Salinas and that you were there with me.

She peered out into the audience again and saw Jerry Rossman seated at a table right below the stage.

Oh God, she thought, I hope I can do this.

Her eyes darted around the audience and, when she sensed that the crowd was waiting for her to speak, she began softly.

"I realize," she said, "what a tremendous responsibility this is, and what an honor. I intend to live up to it in every way possible."

There was a long burst of applause and she waited until it subsided. At his table, Rossman gave a "thumbs up" sign to Hawkins. Hawkins returned the gesture.

"I hope to carry on in the tradition of Robert Miniver and John Cornwall and in the tradition of news excellence that has always been a hallmark of this network."

Again, she was interrupted by thunderous applause.

"I feel confident that I can handle the job," she continued. "All of my professional life, it seems, has been pointing to this, even if others may be more experienced. But I am still a reporter and, I hope, a damn good one."

She focused her eyes on an empty space on the wall at

the far end of the room. She knew what she was going to say next and she didn't want to look at Rossman, or anyone, when she said it. She wanted it to be just as she had rehearsed it in her room upstairs, staring at the bathroom wall.

"My goal," she said slowly, "is to anchor and report. I don't want to sit behind that desk week after week. I want to be able, once in a while, to report on stories that I have covered. Right now, for example, I'm working on a story about a gambling conspiracy that involves a major personality and I hope to be able to report that story on the evening news in the near future."

A low murmur of excitement rippled through the room, in admiration for what she was promising.

Carl Malachek listened and thought, where the hell did she get it from?

Then he realized that Burton must have told her the whole story. A wide grin creased his face and he looked over to Rossman's table. Rossman seemed to be transfixed, staring into space.

He got up from his chair and walked over to where Rossman was sitting. He leaned over, patted Rossman on the shoulder, and said into his ear, "You win some and you lose some, Jerry." Then he walked away.

Sid Neale whispered urgently to Rossman, "What the fuck did Malachek want? What's Stuart talking about?"

"Nothing," Rossman answered abruptly. He glared at Samantha as if expecting her to explain it to him, right from the stage. Son of a bitch, he thought. Why was she doing this? Malachek put her up to it, he figured, and there was nothing he could do about it. Well, Malachek would be gone. Tomorrow at the latest. And then he'd worry about that smart-ass twat up there on the stage even though she had him by the balls.

Backstage, Jarvis Winston hurriedly asked a stagehand where he could find the nearest phone. He needed to make an urgent call to New York.

Less than a minute had elapsed since Samantha had made her statement and, in that time, she had managed to spot Art, standing by a doorway at the rear of the room.

The tiniest of smiles, so small that it was imperceptible even to the people seated in the front row of tables, crossed her face.

From the back of the room, Art returned the smile.

Chapter 46

It was almost midnight when Samantha returned to her room. Art was waiting for her.

"I couldn't find you when it ended," he said, taking her in his arms and kissing her on the cheek. "How did you get out of there, I mean, after that?"

"I went backstage," she said, sinking into a chair and taking off her shoes. "I didn't feel like meeting anybody and answering a lot of questions."

"You really did it, didn't you?" he said, smiling proudly at her.

"Just like I told you," she answered cheerfully, rubbing her feet.

"They'll be calling here, I suppose. Rossman, maybe even Malachek," he predicted.

"No they won't," she said. "Sid Neale came backstage right after I finished."

"And?"

"I told him I had an upset stomach from all the excitement. I asked him to make my excuses to Rossman and the rest. I'm supposed to have breakfast with Rossman in the morning, he told me."

"Can you handle it?" he asked anxiously. "I think he can be pretty rough when he wants to."

She shrugged. "What can he do? Bawl me out? Say I'm ungrateful? Besides, supposedly he doesn't know anything. Right?"

He came over and sat on the edge of the chair so that he could put his arm around her.

"There's really not much he can do," he said with assurance. "You're the anchor. He's not going to can you."

"The Winston story should have been your story, Art,"

she said. "But you were right. Now that I'm anchoring the show, I have a better chance of getting it on than you ever would have had. I'm glad we decided to do it together."

He kissed her again and said, "I wonder how Rossman felt. And Malachek. And Winston for that matter."

"Who knows?" she said.

He was quiet for a minute. "What are you thinking?" she asked him.

He jerked his mind back from where it had wandered, to the clearing, in the tall grass. "I was wondering about Ducoin, if he'll try something again, if I can ever really be rid of him."

"Please, Art," she said. "Don't punish yourself anymore over this. It's over, no matter what he does. He's already hurt you enough."

He smiled at her even though he knew that her appointment to the anchor role could never compensate for what had happened to him. He had been so close . . . But she knew that too. She had told him so when she had decided to accept Rossman's offer.

"It won't make up for everything," she had said. "But it will help. The good guys will win."

It was Art who had suggested, later, that she disclose at her banquet appearance her interest in the Winston story.

"It will at least put Rossman on notice that you're not going to be a pushover," he had advised her. "I'll keep working on the story, and you put it on the air, if Rossman doesn't throw up too many roadblocks."

She had readily agreed. "We decided a long time ago that the story should be reported. Remember?" she had said, smiling.

She got up now from the chair and walked over to the door leading to the bedroom.

"Are you tired?" she asked.

"Yes," he answered. "You must be exhausted."

"Mmm," she responded.

He followed her into the bedroom and stood behind her and slowly unfastened the buttons at the back of her dress.

She turned to him. "Aren't you going to undress?"

"Yes," he said, smiling, as she was.

In a few minutes, they were in the bed, naked. She put her arms around his neck and said, "I love you, darling."

He drew her closer to him, as if he were trying to join

their bodies. It seemed as if he always had wanted her like this, as part of him. She was all that mattered, more than anything else.

"I think we should think about getting married," he said.

"I was thinking that too," she said, smiling at the ceiling.

"Let's think about it tomorrow," he said.

"Like Scarlett O'Hara?" she asked teasingly.

"No," he answered. "I really want to talk about it."

She laughed and reached for his hand under the sheets. He was quiet for a minute. "What are you thinking about?"

"Nothing," he said, even though he had been thinking about New Orleans and how much his life had changed since he'd left it.

It all seemed so long ago and now, lying next to Samantha, he thought: we should go there for our honeymoon.

I'll take her for a walk in the French Quarter, he thought, and we'll eat at Commander's and Antoines and I'll show her where I grew up, introduce her to Frankie Baglio. We'll go on a streetcar ride and one day we'll take one of those paddle wheel riverboats that go down the Mississippi, the ones with the calliope playing on the top deck.

"I'm going to turn off the light." He reached for the lamp on the nightstand by the bed and switched it off.

They lay in the darkness for a few moments and then he kissed her softly on the mouth. She opened her mouth to draw him inside her, to caress his tongue with hers.

When the long kiss ended, she murmured, "Do you see anything when we kiss?"

"Yes," he told her. "I see a rainbow. I see you."

"You told me that once. I like that."

"You are the rainbow," he repeated. "When I see you, I see rainbows. I love you, Samantha."

"I'm glad," she said, her eyes closing, her whole body relaxing, starting to fall asleep.

He lay awake, looking at her, and he saw a rainbow again. It was arcing over the Mississippi River, softly radiant in the morning light, its band of bright colors disappearing into the city, somewhere near where he used to live.

In the distance, he could hear a jazz band playing.

I'm happy, he thinks.

ABOUT THE AUTHOR

ED PLANER began his career in television in New Orleans in 1956, where he spent the next sixteen years. He joined NBC News in 1972, and since then has held a number of management positions in Chicago, New York, and London. He was appointed a vice president of NBC News in 1978, and in 1986 became Vice President for News, Europe, stationed in London. He is married and the father of three children. *Shattered Images* is his first novel.

DON'T MISS
THESE CURRENT
Bantam Bestsellers